Getting Back Our Stolen Bootstraps

The Third Paul Makinen Novel

David R Yale

A Healthy Relationship Press, LLC
New York

Second, Revised Printing, 2024

Getting Back Our Stolen Bootstraps: The Third Paul Makinen Novel
Second, Revised Printing, 2024
First published in 2022 as *The Real Paul Makinen? Part 3*

Copyright © 2022, 2024 by David R. Yale

For more about this author please visit https://davidryale.com/
This is a work of fiction. Names, characters, businesses, organizations, places, events, locales, politicians, officials, and incidents are either the products of the author's imagination or used in a fictitious manner. Character names are chosen at random. Any resemblance or similarity to actual people, living or dead, or actual events, is purely coincidental.

All rights reserved. No part of this publication may be reproduced, distributed, stored in a retrieval system, or transmitted in any form or by any means, including photocopying, recording, or other electronic or mechanical methods, without the prior express written permission of the publisher, except in the case of brief quotations embodied in critical reviews and certain other noncommercial uses permitted by copyright law. No part of this book may be used for the training of artificial systems, including systems based on artificial intelligence (AI), without the author's prior express written permission. This prohibition shall be in force even on platforms and systems which claim to have such rights based on an implied contract for hosting the book. Please do not participate in or encourage piracy of copyrighted materials in violation of the author's rights.

For more information, please see https://davidryale.com/
A Healthy Relationship Press, LLC, New York City, SAN 852-6958

Interior and Cover Design by IAPS.rocks
Psychotherapy Consultant: James Kousoulas, PhD
Finnish language consultants: Kati Laakso and Laura Koskela, The Finnish Cultural Institute in New York.

Taking Away the Tracks, a short story excerpted from Chapter 8 was reprinted in *Blue Collar Review*, Fall 2022.

I Have to Go Away, poetry excerpted from Chapter 15 was reprinted in *Which Side Are You On? Labor Day 2023 Poetry Anthology*, Moonstone Arts Center.

You Ain't Done Nothin' if You Ain't Been Called a Red, Lyrics by Eliot Kenin. Copyright © 1982 by Eliot Kenin, www.EliotKenin.Com. All rights reserved. Used by permission of Eliot Kenin.

eBook ISBN: 979-8-9863006-6-5
Paperback ISBN 979-8-9863006-5-8

FIC044000 FICTION / Women
FIC037000 FICTION / Political
FIC040000 FICTION / Alternative History

Union Organizing, Strikes, Blue Collar, Labor History, Protests, Income Inequality, Social Justice, Mental Health, Working Class

Library of Congress Control Number: 2023916575

DEDICATED TO:

Generation Z and the Millennials, with thanks for your talents, awareness, and activism. I know you're being screwed worse than anyone else by the Fat Cats. My fervent wish is that what you read here will inspire and help you in the struggle for economic, class, social, racial, gender, and climate justice.

TABLE OF CONTENTS

Welcome! vii
Chapter 1, Just Call Me Alice 1
Chapter 2, Gonna Study War No More! 17
Chapter 3, Locked Out! 34
Chapter 4, Secret of The Steel Wedding Band 50
Chapter 5, Do Valentines Have Hearts? 69
Chapter 6, Do Lions Have Teeth? 85
Chapter 7, Many Mickles Makes A Muckle 103
Chapter 8, Taking Away the Tracks 127
Chapter 9, Polychrome Woman Returns 147
Chapter 10, Stepping on the Gas Hard 169
Chapter 11, The Off Switch for Your Economy 180
Chapter 12, Finding the Purple Throne 197
Chapter 13, Mommy, Make Me Stop Dying 212
Chapter 14, Unblaming Myself 226
Chapter 15, Crossing Jordon's River 244
Chapter 16, The Forever Nines 267
Chapter 17, Turning Nightmares Inside Out 290

Chapter 18, Throwing Fat Cats Off-Balance … 314
Chapter 19, Rock and a Hard Place, Bam Boom! … 333
Chapter 20, Getting Back Our Stolen Bootstraps … 348
What Happens Next? … 373
A Note From the Author … 375
About the Author … 377
The Facts Behind the Fiction … 379
Acknowledgments … 380
Character List … 381

WELCOME!

Welcome to Shingle Creek, my friend! If you haven't yet read the first and second Paul Mäkinen books, *No Free Soup for Millionaires* and *They Break the Laws We Must Obey*, don't worry. This book, *Getting Back Our Stolen Bootstraps*, was written to stand alone. But I thought it would be helpful to have a quick summary of what happened in Shingle Creek right before this book starts.

In *Soup*, friends Paul Mäkinen and Karen Ahlberg have just begun leading the Shingle Creek Park Teen Council and its programs for kids. She has a crush on him. Although he's impressed by her smarts and sensibility, he's afraid he'll hurt her if they get romantically involved. As they work closely together, they both realize they have a kind of magic between them they've never felt with anyone else. But because of his personal problems, Paul's fear of having a romance with her intensifies, even as they grow closer, causing such violent physical pain, Paul imagines he has snakes biting his insides.

In *Obey*, Paul kisses Karen for the first time. They're sleeping together, but not having sex. She asks him to, but he says he can't and doesn't know why. When she tells him she loves him, he wants to respond but is afraid of his snakes, which also keep him from talking about his problem.

He builds a wall around himself so nobody will know he's a weakling fighting a losing battle. Karen finally confronts him about not letting her turn him on and not telling her she's beautiful and sexy. He says he can't. So she has an affair with Greg, a guy she met at the university. Paul is devastated. But he doesn't blame her. He talks with his therapist about what he has to do to win Karen back and starts taking steps to do that.

In *Soup*, Paul and Karen realize that something is making neighborhood adults grumpy and angry, but they don't know what it is. Working with two adult neighborhood leaders, they hold a soup 'n' sandwich community meeting where Paul asks, "What do you want to see happening here?"

They find out most Creekers feel demeaned at work. People are furious that though Gremling, the bug spray factory owner, got community development funds to stop fumes and smoke from poisoning their air, he pocketed them. They decide to sue Gremling as well as campaign for a raise in the minimum wage.

Gremling attends their first soup 'n' sandwich meeting and accuses the Creekers of being socialists. They ask if he paid for his soup, which is only free to neighborhood residents. They make him pay and escort him out of the meeting. Gremling sues them for slander.

Right before their second soup 'n' sandwich meeting they get anonymous death threats. A paid provocateur accuses them of running a kidnapping ring that sells stolen kids. Troublemakers try to disrupt their meeting.

Paul has nightmares that the provocateurs are going to kill him. Karen and Paul are terrified. But they realize they don't have a choice. They have to keep fighting for working people's rights.

In *Obey*, the Creekers get a positive article about their community in a national magazine. They start a daily newspaper and a radio station. Form alliances with other working-class communities. Win their lawsuit, which makes the bug spray factory owner return the stolen community development funds.

When the bosses force the railroad track maintainers' pay below minimum wage, the Creekers vote to support a strike. And they manage to get a charter for an industrial safety commission, which will permit them to legally remove unsafe factory equipment and railroad tracks.

All of which provokes the Fat Cat Bosses' fear and anger. The slander campaign against the Creekers gets more vicious. The county tries to raise Shingle Creek real estate taxes by 450%. Protesters at the second soup 'n' sandwich meeting shift from threats to violence, which shuts down the Creekers' gathering. Assault charges are filed against a Creeker who defended herself from a thug attack. And the police assassinate the superintendent of parks, a longtime Creekers' ally.

So that's what happened in my imaginary Shingle Creek right before *Getting Back Our Stolen Bootstraps* starts. Please join me as I spin more of the tale about teens in a blue-collar neighborhood continuing to lead the quest to build a community that works for "ordinary" people. It's a heartwarming story of kindness and the glorious potential of working people finding their power.

David R. Yale
New York, 2024

CHAPTER 1, JUST CALL ME ALICE

SATURDAY-TUESDAY, FEBRUARY 19-22, 1972

WE WERE HANDCUFFED AND CHAINED to our seats in the school busses, even the four- and five-year-old kids, all of us shivering without our coats. Subzero wind blowing through the open windows cut right through our clothes like freezing daggers. Kids sobbed. Even some of the men did. I closed my eyes, hoping to make the horror go away, but all I could see was Fred, my hero, my inspiration, lying on the floor in a pool of blood.

Outside, on the snowy sidewalk, a dozen cops stood, pointing at us and laughing. A lieutenant said, "We're going to let those hotheads cool off a bit more."

I sat tight against Karen, felt her shivering. She leaned her head on my shoulder, tried to take my hand, could only touch my fingertips.

Downtown, the cops herded more than 200 of us concertgoers into the county jail and jammed us into a holding cell so tightly, we could not sit or move. The cells next to us were empty. But at least it was warm. We stood there, handcuffed. Children were still crying. Finally, Paz, the conga drummer, started clanking his handcuffs against the cell's bars, pounding out a beat. Clank-clank-clank-clank. "Let's chant!" he bellowed. "We demand freedom!" Clank-clank-clank-clank.

Earl Smith, the prison guard, came running down the corridor, looked horrified when he saw us. "What the…? Who put all of you there, Paulie?"

"Earl! Earl!" I cried. "The cops killed Fred Corwin and busted us all. Just for listening to music."

"What? They killed Fred? Oh my gosh! I better tell the judge right this minute," Earl said. He took off running, came right back. "Paulie, Judge Woodruff wants to see you. I told him you'd know what's what."

"Karen must come with me!" I said.

"You bet!" Earl said. "Folks, please help me out. I don't know what's going on here anymore than you do, but we're going to get you relief fast!"

He opened the holding cell door. It was like undoing a human jigsaw puzzle, with people stepping into the corridor to let others move, then back into the cell. As we walked down the hallway, Earl said, "Those cops were supposed to take your handcuffs off and check you in with us. Judge Woodruff will be ticked. We have the keys for this type," he said, pointing to Karen's. Then tapping mine, "But not this one." He stopped, unlocked Karen's cuffs. "Wobble your hands, Karen. That gets the circulation going again."

In the courtroom, Todd from KPFP radio, Susie from *People's Free Press*, and the TV camerawoman, who all witnessed Fred's assassination but had managed to escape arrest, were talking with a court clerk. When Judge Woodruff saw us, he stood up and said, "Bring them right up here please, Mr. Smith. Why is Mr. Mäkinen still restrained?"

"Your Honor, we don't have keys to KS-40 type cuffs."

"I can open it," Karen said, reaching into her pocket.

"They weren't searched, Your Honor," Earl said. "Nobody even told us they were here. The police dumped them and ran. Never inventoried personal possessions."

"Paperwork?" the judge said. "Summonses?"

"No, Your Honor."

"This is highly irregular! No charges against them, but detained," the judge said. "Miss, please open Mr. Mäkinen's cuffs."

Karen diddled for a moment with her wrench, and the cuffs clicked open.

"Please don't tell me how you learned to do that, Miss. But please do tell me what happened," the judge said.

A wave of sobbing I had been trying to hold back overcame me. "A police lieutenant killed the Parks superintendent. He had his hands up."

CHAPTER 1, JUST CALL ME ALICE

"Fred? Killed? Why?" the judge said, clasped his hands together, bowed his head.

Karen and I held each other, crying as we told the judge everything.

"KTCA-TV filmed it all, Your Honor," Karen said.

Judge Woodruff shook his head. "They acted illegally? Enforced a non-existent regulation? Defied Judge Havemeyer's injunction? Covered their badge numbers? Didn't write summonses? I cannot believe this. How many arrested, Mr. Smith?"

Pull yahrself together, I thought. *Ya can cry more later.* I took a clean handkerchief from my back pocket, handed it to Karen, used my other to wipe my face.

"They're packed into holding cell C too tightly to count," Earl said.

"We tallied everyone inside the Portland Park building, Your Honor," Karen said. "About two hundred and sixty. Including children, young teens, and two reporters."

"Thank you, Miss…?"

"Karen Ahlberg, Assistant Director of Shingle Creek Park."

"We can't hold these people with no charges, no documentation," the judge said.

"Your Honor, there's a problem," Karen said. "The police didn't let us take our coats. It's five below with wind chill tonight."

"Does anyone have the keys to the Portland Park building?" the judge said.

"I think so," I said, and named them.

"One of our court clerks can drive them down to Portland Park to gather all the coats. But first, Mr. Smith, please bring everyone here so they can sit down. This courtroom will hold them all. Are there other guards to help you?"

"No, Your Honor. I'm on alone tonight."

The judge motioned to the two court clerks. "Miss Swanson, Mr. Juntenen, please help Mr. Smith."

"Of course, Your Honor," Miss Swanson said. "But with all due respect, shouldn't we gather evidence?"

"You're right, Miss Swanson."

"Your Honor," she said, "you and I can interview everyone while Mr. Juntenen goes for the coats. We can use our court reporter to take the statements."

"Your Honor, it would take fifty-two cars to get everyone back to Portland Park," Mr. Juntenen said.

"Portland Park has a phone calling tree, Yahr Honor," I said. "They can get volunteers."

"So does Shingle Creek," Karen said. "Us Creekers will be glad to help any way we can, Your Honor."

"I guess I've heard the wrong things about Shingle Creek and Portland," the judge said. "You don't seem like rowdies at all. Miss Ahlberg, will you please open all the KS-40 cuffs?"

"My pleasure, Your Honor."

When Earl, Miss Swanson, and Mr. Juntenen had brought everybody into the courtroom, Judge Woodruff stood up and raised both hands. The room quieted immediately. He apologized for the situation, explained exactly what the court would do to fix the problems created by the police.

When he finished speaking, Sarah Nesheim raised her hand. "May we applaud, Your Honor?"

"This is an unusual situation. Thank you, yes, you may."

A sound like the first pounding rain after a drought filled the room, fading away only gradually. We worked with the judge's staff, activated the calling trees, got volunteers to help with the statement-taking process, supervised sorting out the coats and getting them to the right people, and matched arriving cars with their passengers. When we were sure everybody had a coat and a ride, we reported back to Judge Woodruff.

"I am so impressed with your leadership, Mr. Mäkinen, Miss Ahlberg. I have never seen a situation like this in my eleven years on the bench, or a response like yours. There *will* be repercussions from the police actions tonight. Can I count on you to work with me to respond to them?"

"Yes, Your Honor," Karen said.

"Of course. Fred was our close friend," I said. "We take this very personally."

"I've known Fred since high school," Judge Woodruff said. "We didn't always see eye to eye, but we agreed to disagree." He shook his head. "I can't believe they did this to him. What a terrible thing. What a terrible loss." He was silent for a moment, brow furrowed, eyes closed. Finally, he said, "Do you need a ride home?"

"Thank you, Your Honor. We have one," I said.

In Merrill's car, Karen and I clung to each other in silence all the way to Portland Park. As we drove home in my car, she sat clamped against me, neither of us able to talk. We cried all night, pressed together as if we needed to combine ourselves to find the strength to endure Fred's death. The snakes inside me, set off by my fear whenever I got emotionally close to Karen, hissed and bit. I ignored them.

Fred's funeral was at the Episcopal church downtown early Monday morning. The huge nave was filled with hundreds of people. I had no idea how I managed to give a eulogy for Fred. Florie, his wife, had asked me to, so I forced myself even though tears streamed down my cheeks as I talked. I figured people would forgive my incoherence. Then Todd ran my speech on KPFP radio several times, and people said I did a great job.

When we went up to the coffin to say our last goodbyes, I bent down, kissed Fred's forehead. I was shaking so hard, I could not speak, feeling like the very atoms in my body were flying apart in three trillion different directions. My knees started to wobble. Someone embraced me from behind, walked me over to a bench, sat me down, put large, strong arms around me. I just closed my eyes, leaned against them, and sobbed.

Carleton's voice comforted me. "I know he was like a dad to you, Paulie. I know how much you're hurting. Just let yourself feel it right now. It's okay. I've got you, Paulie. I've got you." He held on to me, drove us to the cemetery, supported me through the burial, drove us home.

Karen and I fell fast asleep on the living room couch in Great-Grandma Clara's house, melded together again.

At one in the afternoon, Karen woke me. "Holy buckets, Paavali, we should go check in 'n' see what's going on 'n' I made us some lunch 'n' stuff."

It made me feel so good to hear her call me Paavali, my Finnish name. That is what I have called myself in my head since I was a little kid. She calls me Paavali as a love name. My affectionate name for her is Rennie. I have finally realized I do love her, but my serpents will not let me tell her. They are biting me hard inside right now just for thinking about it.

After we ate, we headed to our office. Everything outside was covered with snow, stained bright blue by dust from the neighborhood roofing factory. It was a hard slog through the deep snow with sorrow sitting so heavily on my shoulders.

At our community building, Betty Hall, our staff lawyer, Russ, watched us drag ourselves in. "Are you two okay?" He hugged us.

"We're having a hard time as far as that goes," Rennie said.

"Do you want to talk legal stuff, or should we wait for a better time?"

"Yikes, there probably will not be a better time for a good long while," I said. "We will catch hell worse if we do not plan how to deal with the murderers."

"Precisely. Let's go to the conference room. I'll get the quartet to join us." Russ picked up the phone.

A moment later, Ma, Irene, Mabel, and Evelyn sat down next to us. They had become really close since Ma turned to them for advice about her new job as Neighborhood Association administrator. *Gosh I am proud of Ma. She has come such a long way since she was the silent victim of her husband's violence.*

Sylvia and Jason, our law interns, put their case folders on the table, sat down. Susie and Todd arrived, talking a mile a minute. "You've got a big story for us?" Susie said.

"Does corn have kernels?" Russ said. "At least one."

Todd plugged the mic into his tape recorder. Susie grabbed her pad and pen.

Teen Council members Li'l Mikey, Billy, Ruka, Barb, and my stepsister, Linda, joined us, as well as several other people active in the Neighborhood Association.

Burt, the mill owner who supported us Creekers, came striding into the room, took the last seat at the table. "This is a rough time for all of us, but a little bit more good news should help us out. For the first time since World War II, women are working at General Grain! The first five female millhand trainees started Friday. They include Paulie's friends Lori and Lola, and what great questions they're asking! Me and my guys are impressed!"

"What're you paying them, Burt?" Susie said.

"Two an hour during training, two-fifty and benefits after that."

"That *is* good news," Mabel said. "Any of them Black?"

"Two in this first group."

"Honey, you made my day!" Mabel said.

"Russ, how are we going to fight back against the bosses for Fred's death, as far as that goes," Rennie said.

"Three ways," Russ said. "One: lawsuits. Two: coverage in the media about Fred. Three: run candidates for office in the June election. Just to update you first, we did file a suit for the Neighborhood Association against the City Assessor's Office, demanding a reduction in real estate taxes to cover our expenses for the Fourth Grade Freedom Academy we're running. Sylvia found a precedent for it, so we have a pretty good chance of winning."

"I hate to pile on more difficult news," Russ said, "but we have to start more lawsuits. Sylvia, please tell us about the City Buildings Department."

"Just call me Alice!" Sylvia said. "Because I definitely feel like I'm in Wonderland when I talk with *them*. They say there are no standards for large retail stores in brick buildings with compound arch construction, so the permits have to be denied. Even though we comply with every one of their standards for retail stores."

"Russ, do ya think that Communal Association memo from Fat Cat Archibald Hastings-Dankworth is behind this?" I said.

"Do roses have thorns?" Russ said. "Dankworth made it clear the bosses don't want working people starting their own businesses. Sylvia, what's your recommendation?"

"This is illegal restraint of trade. We've already asked for an injunction under Minnesota anti-trust law, but we haven't heard anything on it."

"What would an injunction do?" Ma said.

"Force the Buildings Department to issue permits," Sylvia said. "And keep them from stopping construction."

"Do we stop work until we have permits?" Evelyn said.

"No. Way!" Rennie said. "That's letting them win, yes it is."

"I think we need a phone survey on this one," Ma said, "especially if we're going to continue work without a permit. But let's take a vote to see where *we* stand." She looked around the room. "Alrighty! All hands on deck."

"Jason, tell us about the sealed lawsuits," Russ said.

"Just call me Alex," Jason said. "Because I'm in Wonderland too. We have filed five lawsuits that are not on the court's docket." He held up his hand, counted off on his fingers. "One, the Flynn and Korhonen suit against Mrs. Elak for maiming Bonnie and Ruthie's hands when she 'disciplined' them in her classroom."

Todd's face got red. He stamped his foot.

"Two, Paul's libel suit against Nancy and the *Gazette*. Three, the Teen Council and Neighborhood Association libel suit against the *Patriot* for the 'state-funded indoctrination center, stolen materials' slur. Four, Ma, Russ, Harry, Bebee, and Gloria's *Journal* libel suit for claiming they're communists. Five, Paul and Karen's libel suit of Pukari, Tewksbury, and the Hastings-Dankworths. That one would hold each of them liable for five million bucks for calling Karen a whore and Paul a pimp."

"Do we have receipts for the filing fees?" Sylvia said.

"Yes, we do," Jason said. "All the clerk would say is, 'Those cases are sealed.' I asked who sealed them, and the clerk said, 'That information is in the sealed files.' So I said, 'Well, how do I petition to unseal them?' She replied, 'Address your petition to the official and or officials who sealed them.' When I said, 'But that information is in the sealed files!' the clerk said, 'I already told you that,' and walked off."

"This is a big-ass problem!" Li'l Mikey said. "Who's in charge of the courts? Can't we sue them?"

"They will just seal it!" I said.

Todd jumped up, clapped his hands together. "Actually, the sealed court cases, the rail yard accidents, the libels against us by the big daily papers and that rightwing magazine, and Fred's murder are part of the same problem. The rule of law is under attack. The bosses are doing anything they want, anytime they want. We have to raise a ginormous, loud, commotion. KPFP is already working on it. Susie, can you still get something in today's *People's Free Press*?"

"Double check!" Susie said. "We left some space for last-minute news. Dad and my sister Shari are ready to roll the press soon as my team has the front- and back-page articles finished. We can do a doorbell distribution tonight."

"What's that?" Burt said.

CHAPTER 1, JUST CALL ME ALICE

"The delivery kids ring the doorbell, call out the headline when the door opens, hand the paper over, and say, 'Urgent! Please read it now!'"

"Let's support that with a phone calling tree and CB radio announcements," Billy said.

"You folks are incredible!" Burt said.

"Todd and I been talking with Harrison Barrow from the *Hennepin Afro-American,* Chester Moller of the *Minneapolis Labor News,* and Elżbieta Witkowski from KTCA-TV," Susie said. "We're all breaking Fred's assassination story tonight. Of course, the big dailies are ignoring it."

"Sounds like a good plan," Ma said. "Hit them with it all at once!"

"It is! It is!" Burt said. "But we need national and international coverage to put even more pressure on the bosses. Remember when you publicly fed Walt and Joyce in defiance of a court order? How did you get the Associated Press there?"

"I invited them," Susie said, slapping her palm to her forehead. "But since the *Journette* stopped covering us—"

"*Journette?*" Mabel said.

"The two big dailies, *Journal* and *Gazette*. I haven't called the news wires. Big mistake, huh?"

"Don't worry about it," Billy said. "It's easy to fix!"

"I just don't have the time anymore," Susie said.

Linda looked at Billy, eyebrows raised. He nodded. "We can do it. You told us how in leadership class," Linda said.

"I'll work with you on it," Irene said. "Just tell me what to do. All hands on deck? Yes! Let's do it!"

"Maybe we could get Lije and Águeda to write about us again," Ruka said. "Like they did in *LIFE* magazine. There's enough going on here for a dozen big articles."

"Great idea," Barb said. "I'll work with you."

"Anything else on the press for now?" Ma said. "No? So, tell me something. Who does the police chief answer to? And the courts? Who supervises them?"

"The courts are supervised by the county commissioners," Russ said. "Yeah, they're elected. Any of you remember voting for them?"

Everybody shrugged, shook heads.

"That's the problem," Russ said. "Nobody thinks they're important. Until they are! And the police chief? Well, he sort of reports to the Aldermen but not really. A little bird told me Dankworth hires, controls, and fires police chiefs."

"How does he do that?" Irene said. "Is that even legal?"

"He buys politicians," Burt said. "With campaign fund donations and gifts. He appoints non-elected officials and makes sure they can earn a lot of cash. But those politicians and officials have sold their souls to the devil, and what a demanding devil Mr. Dankworth is!"

"Alrighty, you know how they did sit-ins down at the University to protest the war?" Ma said. "Why can't we do that at the commissioner's and alderman's offices?"

"Ma, they will have the cops shoot us," I said. "Just like they did to Fred."

"Hang tight," Ma said. "Suppose we don't call them sit-ins. We go two or three at a time, and we schedule appointments. Lots of appointments. One after another. Keep calling until we get scheduled. Go there and give 'em hell. When are they up for reelection, Russ?"

"Primaries are in June," Russ said.

"We'll tell them we'll primary them if they don't make the courts and the police stop their shenanigans!" Ma said.

"Awesome! But who is gonna run against them?" Li'l Mikey said.

"How about Clarence for alderman? Ndidi for commissioner?" Ma said.

"Holy buckets, Ndidi's way too busy," Rennie said.

"Does it hurt to ask?" Ma said.

"Mom's busy, all right," Ruka said. "But this might appeal to her."

"Ma, that's an awesome idea," Li'l Mikey said.

"Which part, Mike?" Ma said.

"All of it!" Li'l Mikey said. "Now let's talk through the details."

Two hours later, we had a plan for our serial sit-in, another for recruiting candidates, a third for a press conference.

"Paulie, Karen, can you do proofreading for a couple of hours?" Susie said. "We need help to get the front and back page done by deadline!"

"Yes siree!" Rennie said.

We walked down the corridor. Susie took out her keys.

"Holy cowbops! The pressroom door is locked?" I said. "Why?"

"There are some people here taking sick and vacation days off to help us," Susie said. "Top secret. We don't want just anyone barging in and seeing them. If you know them, don't use their names or refer to their jobs, K?"

"Heavy duty. I totally hear ya," I said.

I had never seen the pressroom full of people before. AWOL reporters from the *Journette* worked side by side with journalism students, housewives, and teenagers, clacking away on all ten typewriters. Pete, and Susie's sister, Shari, were adjusting the press. In a corner, the insides of the paper were stacked in piles.

"Last time," Susie said, "we ran the whole paper at once and let the machine cut, fold, collate it all. This time, we waited on breaking news, so we have to hand-wrap the front and back page around the inside. Just let me bring some of the reporters up to speed based on our meeting. I'll be back to you in a flash."

I looked around again, recognized Tom Hayes and Georgia Giordano from the *Gazette,* Kirby Kenworthy from *TC-News Six*, and Minnie Olander from *Channel 8 Morning News.*

Would our Susie ever have learned so much so fast in that poor excuse of a high school? This is just breathtaking!

Within minutes, Susie dropped a couple of stories in front of us, said, "Please read for grammar, spelling, and factual correctness."

We read, caught errors, read again, then reread the same stories set in type.

"Ready for the darkroom!" Susie called out.

She, Georgia, and Pete ran for darkroom two, then emerged fifteen minutes later carrying two large, thin sheets of metal with pictures of the front and back pages burned into them.

Pete, Susie, and Shari clamped the metal plates onto the press, ran a few test copies. I grabbed one. At the top of the front page, it said, " 'Don't mourn! Organize!—Joe Hill.' *People's Free Press* founded 1971 by Bobby Lund, Charlie Ward, and Susie Hakkala."

"We're rolling!" Susie called out.

Minutes later, a volunteer I didn't know yet took a pile of printed pages, dropped them in smaller piles on the long, narrow collating tables.

Everyone who wasn't printing or cleaning up the darkroom rushed over, sat down, put papers together. Ambrose Anker and Susie's thirteen-year-old sister Janet loaded them on red pull wagons.

The phone rang. Susie picked up, listened, called out, "Portland Park is at the reception desk, needs 935 copies."

"We've got 'em!" Janet called out. She and Ambrose pulled two loaded wagons out the door.

"On the way!" Susie said into the phone. "Denise, please tell them to distribute as soon after six as possible."

By five thirty, all forty-two neighborhoods where we had kids signed up to deliver *People's Free Press* had gotten their copies.

In the Teen Council Meeting Hall, Ron Svoboda was explaining to the Shingle Creek carriers how to do a doorbell distribution. "Try it like this, kids. 'Extra! Extra! Beloved Park Superintendent Fred murdered by police. Cops lock up concertgoers, throw away key. Read about it now!' Try it, Sheila."

Sheila said it, but she was kinda soft and quiet.

"C'mon, Sheil!" Ellen Lund said. "I've heard you yell louder than that!"

"Yeah, like really be angry about what they did to our Fred!" Walt said.

Sheila thundered it out, looked pleased.

"Remember, kids, there's *nothing* about Fred in tonight's *Gazette*!" Ron said.

"Can I try again?" Sheila said. "Extra! Extra! Beloved Park Superintendent Fred murdered by police and the *Gazette* ain't tellin' ya. But *People's Press* is! Read it now!"

"That's great, Sheila!" Tommy Hillilä said.

Sheila was beaming.

At six, my family switched from channel to channel on the TV. There was nothing on the news about Fred. At five after, KPFP radio had a fifteen-minute breaking news special, including sound bites from Todd's tape. At 6:25, KTCA-TV had a twenty-minute special with Elżbieta Witkowski, the camerawoman, hosting. The film she showed of the police attack on us was terrifying. In her interview with Judge Woodruff, he very clearly said, "What the police did here was totally illegal."

At 6:45, Keanna announced, "KPFP, Twin Cities home of the Jill Frisk Quintet, presents Under Attack. The war against the working class in Shingle Creek."

Todd, who had interviewed a bunch of the gandy dancers, talked about their wage cut and the hazardous conditions in Camden Yard; the sudden, unexplained jump in property taxes; the sealed court cases; Fred's murder; the closing of our Red Crow store; and the continual lies about us in the mainstream press, explaining how they were all part of an organized offensive. The way he used short interviews, facts, and several voices besides his own made it fascinating, even though I already knew the whole story.

Early next morning, the twin couriers of evil were at it as usual. The *Patriot* screamed that I had admitted at a public meeting I planned to seize the parkland at Shingle Creek for a soviet-style collective farm run by slave labor. "Mäkinen and his minions are training nine-year-olds to be totally obedient workers at their so-called Freedom Academy. These poor kids have been seen shoveling snow on the hill in Shingle Creek Park at two in the morning, coatless, hatless, and crying while Mäkinen cracks a twelve-foot bullwhip."

A hill in Shingle Creek Park? Me with a whip? What will they make up next?

The *Journal* had a front-page editorial that attacked Judge Woodruff for dismissing charges against the "Conga Rioters," demanding Fred be tried for aiding and abetting "illegal" activity and the "rioters" be locked up for the next ten years. It mentioned a letter from Archibald Hastings-Dankworth and 229 unnamed "eminent civic leaders," demanding Judge Woodruff be indicted for "obstruction of justice." Nowhere did the *Journal* reveal Fred was murdered by the police.

In Russ's office, me, my sister Sandi, and Sylvia rehearsed for our forced testimony before the Minnesota Senate Civil Safety and Security Committee charging me with falsifying documents to get a draft deferment. We agreed on hand signals we could use if needed.

When we arrived in the senate's hearing room, I noticed an older woman sitting in the back row with a microphone almost buried in her shawl and wondered who she was.

A few moments later, Sylvia marched in, right up to Senator Johnson. "Oh, Senator!" she said, shaking his hand. "I've so wanted to meet you!"

She pulled an envelope out of her coat pocket with her other hand, dropped it on the dais in front of him, changed her voice. "You are served, sir!" She dropped his hand, turned, started walking away.

"What the hell is this?" Senator Johnson said.

"A complaint against you filed with Hennepin County Civil Court, Senator."

He took the papers out of the envelope, looked at them, shook his head. "What the hell does this have to do with me, little girl?"

"You don't know how to read, Senator? That's so sad!" She walked across the room, served the complaint on Senate President Larsen.

He threw the envelope at her and yelled, "You are engaged in activity forbidden in this building!"

"Under what statute, Senator?" She caught the envelope, threw it back toward him so it landed on the floor. He had to bend down to pick it up. "Cite the statute, please, Senator!" she said, walking away and out the door.

Senator Larsen, face bright red, stomped across the room and talked with Senator Johnson as they looked at the complaint. "Five million? Outrageous! How dare they?"

"We'll just refer this to counsel," Senator Larsen said. "They'll take care of it."

Both men left the room. Staff members scurried around. Half an hour later, the senators took their seats. Senator Johnson pounded a gavel. "I call to order this hearing of the Minnesota Senate Civil Safety and Security Committee, this twenty-second day of February in the year of our Lord 1972, at ten-oh-three in the morning, on the subject of Paul Mäkinen, residing at 4975 Knox Avenue North in Minneapolis. Mr. Mäkinen, do you swear to tell the truth, the whole truth, and northing but the truth, so help you God?"

"Yes. Do you, Senator?"

"I am not the subject of the inquest here!"

"Are ya sure of that, Senator?"

"Mr. Mäkinen, this is a serious inquiry into your criminal behavior. We want to know exactly how you created a forged identity for a non-existent brother so you would get a draft deferment."

"And the name of this alleged non-existent brother is, Senator?"

CHAPTER 1, JUST CALL ME ALICE

"Mark Mäkinen."

"Oh, him! Four years before I was born, I created a walking, talking human brother. And I didn't even use the dust of the ground! Just snapped my fingers, there he was. Then, I went back to being unborn for another four years."

"Mr. Mäkinen, I shall have to hold you in contempt if you don't answer my questions truthfully. We know you run a sophisticated forgery laboratory where you created fake photos of and documents for this supposed brother, down in the basement of the Shingle Creek Park warming room. We have witnesses to your felonious acts."

"Senator, may I remind ya that yah're under oath?" I said.

"I am not going to tolerate this."

I grinned. "Senator, the warming room at Shingle Creek Park is built on a cement slab. It does not now and never did have a basement."

"Mr. Mäkinen, how can you explain that the Ramsay County Vital Records Office has no record of a Mark Mäkinen?"

"Who does yahr research for ya, Senator? One of yahr staff members? They were too lazy to drive to Minneapolis where Mark *was* born? Here are raised-seal, notarized copies of Mark Mäkinen's birth and death certificates and a copy of my paid check for the record clerk's fee. I enter this as exhibit A."

"I have to say, Mr. Mäkinen, you are an expert forger."

Four senators stood up. One of them said, "Senator Johnson, your party controls the senate by one vote. That does not allow you to lie and waste taxpayer money on a phony hearing designed to harass Mr. Mäkinen."

Senator Johnson stood up, shouted, "Are you calling me a liar?"

I looked at Russ, pointed to myself.

Russ bumped his fists together twice.

"That's exactly what *I'm* calling ya," I said. "Under oath, and on the record."

"I call Sandi Mäkinen to testify," Senator Johnson said.

"Why are you trying to erase my brother Mark?" Sandi said, tears rolling down her cheeks. "Here is a photo of Mark's grave in Ft. Snelling National Cemetery and a copy of Mark's burial record certified by the cemetery and notarized."

"These *are* expertly done, but they are forgeries," Senator Johnson said. "They taught you well in Moscow, Mr. Mäkinen."

"I have never been to Moscow!" I said, not grinning this time.

"We have photos of you in Red Square, Mr. Mäkinen. Now, Miss Mäkinen, do you have any genuine documents that are not forgeries?"

Sandi presented certificates, photographs, news clippings, and copies of Mark's draft card, Service papers, and Social Security card. One by one, they were rejected as fakes.

"Senator Johnson! What will the senate do to rein in the Minneapolis Police Department?" I said. "And stop them from murdering public officials like Fred Corwin?"

"That's not the topic here!"

"I'm done hearing tall tales about yahr slanderous fantasy world, Senator," I said. "Time to talk about saving the democracy ya swore to protect in yahr oath of office." I pulled my clasped hands apart.

Russ nodded, tapped his forefingers together.

Senator Larsen, face looking like an angry beet, said, "Your forgeries will—"

"I will see ya in court, Senator. Good day." I stood up.

"I hold you in contempt of—" The senator's words faded as we left the room.

CHAPTER 2, GONNA STUDY WAR NO MORE!

TUESDAY-FRIDAY, FEBRUARY 22-25, 1972

IN OUR FREEDOM ACADEMY CLASSROOM, Bonnie, Mamie, Terri, Tess, and Kurt sat at a table with Joanna Pajari, our librarian, looking at a book called *Writer's Market* and a copy of Bonnie's *My Mommy Questions* poem, and her mom, Irene's, poetic answer.

"I get what a heading is," Bonnie said. "But what's a short biography?"

"Just thirty words or so," Joanna said.

"Just writing about all my sisters would take hundreds!" Bonnie said.

Joanna chuckled, put her arm around Bonnie's shoulders. "All they want to know is who you are and where you've published."

"Like, Bonnie Korhonen is in fourth grade?" Mamie said.

"But you have to tell them where, right?" Tess said.

"At Freedom Academy in Shingle Creek, Minnesota?" Bonnie said.

"That's perfect," Joanna said. "Now just say where you've been published."

"Everybody knows she was in *LIFE* magazine," Terri said. "Why even say it?"

"But not all the people reading *Journal of American Poetry* know it," Joanna said. "They might not read *LIFE*."

"So, how about, her poems have been in *Shingle Creek News* and *LIFE* magazine?" Kurt said.

"That works well," Joanna said. "How else can you say 'have been in?'"

"Were published in," Terri said.

"Appeared in," Tess said.

"How's this?" Bonnie said. "*LIFE* magazine and *Shingle Creek News* have published her poetry."

"All those work," Joanna said. "Put them together the way you want, Bonnie." She waited while Bonnie wrote.

"Good! But what have you left out?" Joanna said after Bonnie read it aloud.

All the kids looked puzzled, until Terri's face lit up. "Bonnie, what about Mommy? She wrote the second poem, right?"

Bonnie put her hands on her cheeks. "Sorry, Mommy!" she said. "Joanna, what do I say about who she is?"

"She's your mom," Tess said.

"She does stuff for the Shingle Creek Neighborhood Association," Terri said.

"Remember she told us about that, BonBon?" Mamie said.

They talked. Wrote. Rewrote. Until Joanna said, "This looks good! Now let's count the words."

"Thirty-seven," Bonnie said. "Am I okay?"

"Perfect!" Joanna said. She explained what else had to be in the letter, actually making a dull topic quite interesting just like Lucy, the Fourth Grade Freedom Academy teacher, does.

When Bonnie sealed the envelope, licked the stamp, and put it on the corner, I felt my mood lift. Our Bonnie was going to be published in the best poetry magazine in the USA! I was so happy for her.

I heard the phone in our office ring, sprinted to answer it.

"A lady named Nora O'Farrell would like to see you," Denise said. "Says she knows Todd. Says she has something you want. Send her in?"

Who is that? A minute later, the lady with the microphone buried in her shawl walked into our office. "Paul, I'm Liam's wife, Todd's great-aunt, and an activist in my own right. I am so pleased to finally meet you! Can we have some bread and jam?"

We shook hands, and I pulled my jammer from my pocket, switched it on. "Nora O'Farrell. This is a big-huge honor!"

"You, your sister, and the young woman who served the papers at the hearing put on a great show today. Those poor fools were so distracted, they didn't even see me, let alone try to stop me from recording. Todd's going to play the tape on KPFP this afternoon. I thought you could use a copy for your lawsuit. That was pure genius, serving your complaint right before the hearing!" She handed me a cassette tape. "It's a copy. You can keep it, use it in court." She pointed to a framed color photo of me, Sandi, and Mark. "That's your brother?"

"The day he came home to visit after basic training. Only time we ever saw him in uniform."

"You all have the same amazing yellow eyes! He looks like you both."

"Nope! That is actually a wax dummy from that famous museum in Europe, Madame Tussaud's. Senator Johnson told me so."

She laughed long and loud. "That's rich! You're going to win in court, you know."

"If they ever allow the case to be heard."

"Sooner or later they'll have to. But now, I have a favor to ask of you. Can I interview you for a KPFP special on how activists can create something from nothing, like you did here at Shingle Creek?"

"We made something from nothing?" I rubbed my chin, thought for a moment. "Yup! I guess we did. Sure, roll the tape!" I did not even know I had so many ideas until she got me talking by asking questions that really made me think.

More than an hour later, she said, "Great ideas, great material. Paul, we have enough for a lot more than that one show."

My phone rang. Daniel, one of our senior recreation staffers, sounded very upset. "We need you at the warming room right now!"

"On my way!" I said, excused myself, shook hands with Nora, gave the hearing tape to Russ on the way out, jogged across 49th Avenue, up Morgan, to the park. I saw the problem the moment I opened the warming room door. Two Communal Association agents sat on the cement bench. The nine- and eleven-year-old groups stood silent, staring at them.

"Can I help you?" I said to them.

"We just want to sit here and warm up."

"He doesn't mean warm up," nine-year-old Bobby Lund said. "He means spy. And say nasty things about the girls."

"Yah're not welcome here. Please leave now!" I held the door open for them, gestured toward it.

"They're making us feel unsafe," Tess said, "talking about how we're going to have nice boobies someday. Like the time Duane Pukari tried to kidnap our Peggy."

"And they made our Sheila cry," eleven-year-old Tommy Hillilä said. "Like Duane did to my sister Darlene."

"Ya have ta leave! Now!" I said.

The agents sat, stone-faced, unmoving. "This is a public place, sonny boy," one of them said to me.

"Daniel, Laura, Barb! Gather whatever you need for this afternoon's programs. We are going to Betty Hall."

The kids helped pack stuff up, got their coats. I locked the office and the gym room. Everyone but me and the agents left.

"We do not allow child molestation here. For the children's safety, I am officially closing this facility until further notice. Ya have ta leave. Now!"

"We're staying right here!" the brown-haired one said.

"Fine! I will just lock ya in. See ya later, grazies. *Much* later!"

"Grazies?" the black-haired agent said. "What does that mean?"

"Crazy men who sit in gray cars and harass hard-working people."

I took out my keys, walked toward the door. They got up, grumbling, and walked outside. I locked the door, started walking back toward Betty Hall. They followed me. At the entrance to Betty Hall, I said, "Stop! Right there! *This* is *not* a public place. Yah're not allowed in there."

They followed me inside.

I jogged to our office, picked up the CB radio mic, paged our community police lieutenant, Gordy Walden, went back to the Teen Council Meeting Hall, saw the bunch of silent, angry kids staring at the grazies again.

"Hang tight, kids! We are gonna handle this in a heartbeat."

"I still say that little cutie has nice tits budding out," the black-haired grazy said, pointing at Sheila.

"Bastard!" Sheila yelled and started crying. "Just like my father."

Barb ran to Sheila, held her, talked to her.

Greta, Becky, Ellen, and Walt formed a circle around Sheila and Barb. Tommy Hillilä strode right up to Black-Hair, yelled, "Stop your nastiness," and kicked his shins hard.

"I'm going to kill that little shit!" Black-Hair yelled, clutching his legs.

A double circle of kids surrounded Tommy.

"You touch that kid, or any kid, I'll put your head up your ass!" Laura said.

"She's a karate black belt," Bobby Lund said. "Better not mess with her!"

"Put a lid on it, Rex!" Brown-Hair yelled. "Or else."

We heard a siren outside, brakes screeching, a car door slam. Lieutenant Gordy strode into the room, right up to the grazies. "Gentlemen, you have been asked to leave. This is private property."

The grazies pulled out wallets, showed badges.

"Don't bother me with those counterfeits," Gordy said. "You have no legal authority of any kind. You are not cops."

"We're deputies and—"

"Deputies, my foot! You have ten seconds to leave, or I'll arrest you for trespassing."

"And child molestation!" Laura yelled.

"Just try it!" the brown-haired grazy said.

"Daniel, Laura! Tough guy here needs some love," Gordy said.

They put Brown-Hair in a tight bear hug. Laura stood on his shoes with her Doc Parton boots clamping them to the floor.

"You're never going to get away with this!" Brown-Hair yelled. "We'll have you fired!" He tried to break free, could not even move his legs.

Black-Hair lunged at Gordy, who sidestepped, grabbed his arm, twisted, turned, and sent him flying. The kids gasped as Gordy sat on the guy, snapped handcuffs on, then cuffed Brown-Hair. The room filled with cheers and applause, then a chant, "Bad dude, Gordy! Bad dude, Laura! Bad dude, Paulie! Bad dude Daniel!" and applause again.

Gordy, Laura, and I walked the grazies to the squad car. We eased them into the back seat, closed the doors. Gordy drove off.

Back in the Teen Council Meeting Hall, the kids were talking a mile a minute. Laura, Daniel, and I answered dozens of their questions.

John Bruno, a tall, tough kid Walt had finally persuaded to join the Elevens two weeks ago, listened intently but said nothing until the very end. "If anyone makes our Sheila—or anyone else—feel bad like that again, I'm gonna show them some bear hug love until they apologize. Then, I'll tell them why it's not right and they better not do that again."

Laura shook hands with him. "Well said, John. I'm really glad you're with us!"

Afterward, Laura told me John had been almost totally silent since he started coming to the Elevens and had never talked with her, just listened. "He took everything in," she said. "Gol! What an amazing kid!"

Wednesday morning at 8:30, Rennie met me at Club Nicollet for our press conference about Fred and the attack on Shingle Creek. "Holy buckets, Paulie, I should've been there with you yesterday at the senate, but I had some exams, 'n' Greg was jealous 'cause I haven't been spending as much time with him as usual 'n' I was so tense I just needed to be with him for the night, but this morning when I told him I wouldn't see him for a few days, he was sulking 'n' that's his problem but it makes me crazy, yes it does." She leaned her shoulder against mine.

I took her hand. "I wish it was not so complicated for ya. For me. For the two of us. I am not jealous, but I sure missed ya. I have so much to tell ya about yesterday!" I talked almost as fast as Bonnie thinks until Arden Winchester opened the press conference.

"Good morning. This is the first time Club Nicollet has hosted a press conference. But what happened in the last few weeks here in Minneapolis is such a danger to American democracy, I felt we had to do this. Please open your ears, eyes, and mind. Now let me present our hosts, Teen Councilwoman Belinda M. Frisk and Teen Councilman William R. Anderson from Shingle Creek."

Belinda? Since when?

Billy and Linda started with the facts. The history of police harassing conga players and listeners at Portland Park. Judge Havemeyer's injunction forbidding the police persecution. Judge Jeppesen's ruling that dancing was not illegal in Minneapolis parks and issuing tickets for it was malpractice. The beating and arrest of Judge Haddad's court officer, who was investigating police malpractice at Portland Park. And the court documents about all of this in the press information packet.

"All this was bad enough," Billy said. "But even after Judge Havemeyer's injunction, the police raided and shut down a Park Board sponsored conga concert at Portland Park."

"The police lieutenant claimed it was an illegal gathering," Linda said. "But it broke no laws, violated no rules or regulations."

CHAPTER 2, GONNA STUDY WAR NO MORE!

"KTCA-TV reporter Elżbieta Witkowski was there with her camera," Billy said. "She actually recorded the assassination of our Parks superintendent, Fred Corwin."

"KPFP radio reporter Todd Flynn recorded the audio," Linda said.

"You have both the audio and the film in the packet we gave you," Billy said. "Elżbieta, would you tell us what happened?"

"I had a feeling something bad was about to occur. So I stood on a chair to get a good view. Let's roll my film first, then Todd Flynn's tape."

Rennie wrapped her arm around mine, took my hand, leaned against me. By the end of the tape, we were both sobbing. Reporters took photos of us.

"Miss Witkowski, how did you keep the police from grabbing your camera, taking your film?" an Associated Press reporter asked.

"I scooted right out the door and ran like a bat out of hell through deep snow, saw Todd Flynn from KPFP and Susie Hakkala from *People's Free Press* following me, yelled, 'Come on, jump in my van. Let's get the hell out of here.'"

"Mr. Flynn, how did you get Judge Woodruff to make such a strong statement?" the *Wall Street Journal* reporter said.

"The judge was very angry about the police behavior that had just flooded his courtroom with handcuffed concert-goers, including little kids, none of them with arrest papers. He was livid that Superintendent Corwin had been killed. I had already turned on my recorder when he called out to me. You heard him beg me to record him. I know it's highly unusual for a judge to make a statement like that, so I called him the next day, offered to edit his statement out of my tape. He said 'No! I stand by what I said.'"

"Councilman Anderson, Councilwoman Frisk," a reporter from the *New York Times* said, "did the *Minneapolis Gazette* and *Journal* know about the brewing problems with the police?"

"Yes, our press coordinator, Councilwoman Susie Hakkala, called them *and* hand delivered news releases to their office."

Perrine Fournier from Agency France-Presse asked what other issues the Shingle Creek community was facing.

"Paul Mäkinen, chair of the Teen Council, can best answer that," Linda said.

23

I went up to the dais, took a deep breath, talked about the war on working people in Shingle Creek and Portland Park. Suddenly, there were a dozen mics in front of me. As I talked, Rennie, Billy, Linda, and Todd kept nodding. When I was finished, Perrine Fournier asked if she could visit Shingle Creek. I gave her my card, invited all the reporters to see us at the park and also to cover the combined funeral for the six boys killed in 'Nam.

"Mr. Mäkinen," the United Press International reporter said, "in your support packet, you have a copy of a confidential memo from Archibald Hastings-Dankworth and Clyde Gremling to Police Chief Jensen and other parties. How did you get it?"

I rubbed my chin. "Well, I have ta say, we have confidential sources just like journalists do."

"How do you know it's a legitimate copy of an actual memo?"

"Every time we get a copy of a Communal Association memo or letter, whatever is mentioned happens pretty quickly afterward."

"So you're saying that Mr. Hastings-Dankworth and Mr. Gremling ordered the police chief to raid the conga concert and shoot Mr. Corwin?"

"Do lions have bloody fangs and claws after a kill, sir?"

"So you're saying that memo was a direct order?"

"I am saying exactly what I said. No more, no less."

"How much do you pay your sources, Mr. Mäkinen?"

"Not a cent, sir! They send me things anonymously. I have not met them. Besides, paying sources is flat-out unethical. Probably illegal. We believe in the rule of law."

"Okay, Gilbert, my turn now," the *Washington Post* reporter said to the United Press guy.

I stepped down from the dais, sat next to Rennie again.

"Mr. Mäkinen, Miss Ahlberg, how did Fred Corwin's death impact you?"

Rennie began crying again. "Fred Corwin was our dear friend, our inspiration."

Tears rolled down my cheeks. "How do I even explain? He helped me every step of the way, like…like…the father I never had. I do not know what I will do without him. Ya just cannot believe cops would kill a man like Fred."

"Not here, in America," Rennie shook her head. "No, not here."

On the drive back to Shingle Creek, the four of us were quiet. The air felt thick with grief. Finally, I said, "Can we change the channel? I know I could use a few moments of joy, because we are headed into a big-huge sea of sorrow at the funeral. That okay with ya?"

"Fine with me," Linda said.

"Holy buckets, yes! But how, Paulie-Paul?"

"Well, Linda and Billy, ya sure as heck did a tip-top job putting together the press conference in record time."

"No big deal," Billy said.

"Big-time big deal 'n' you got fourteen reporters there from big publications 'n' wait until the Communal Association sees that, 'n' besides, it will really help us get court cases unsealed, yes siree!"

"But if we did such a great job," Billy said, "why did we have to ask Paul to answer the big question?"

"Because ya knew what ya needed help with. But if it were not for the two of ya, there would have been no question for me to answer. And that information packet ya gave out was true genius in bloom! If the press writes about those issues, can the courts ignore them? Wanna answer that question, Belinda M?"

Rennie grinned. "Since when, Belinda, do you have a far-out formal name that you've kept hush-hush forever, as far as that goes?"

Billy chuckled. Linda turned beet red.

"May I remind ya, Ms. Belinda M. Frisk, yah're under oath?"

"Well, it's not fair! Billy has William and a middle initial, so he has his bases covered. Why can't I?"

"All right then, I think it's really cute 'n' stuff, but can we call you Belinda to be formal 'n' what does the M stand for?"

"Um, Marianne, but I never go by that. Belinda M. is my professional name, so please don't call me that in day-to-day talk."

"I hear ya. I sure as heck will not until the next time I have ta introduce ya at a press conference. Except for this. Three cheers for a job well done, William R. Anderson and Belinda M. Frisk!"

Rennie turned on the radio to WCCO, and Apollo 100 filled the car with the sound of their hit, "Joy."

"Can ya believe that?" I said. "They knew we needed some."

"I think it's a sign and a signal we're groovin' up for better times," Linda said.

The four of us sang along to one hit song after another all the way back to Jericho Church in Shingle Creek.

"I feel so much more ready for this now," Billy said.

Inside, at the front of the church, six families were gathered around the coffins of their beloved boys, trying desperately to get some comfort by talking to them.

Pastor Broadwater stepped up to me, gave me a Carleton-style hug. "I had some volunteers clear snow off the lawn, set up speakers outside, case we get an overflow crowd. Daniel's bringing chairs from the park. The small trash can you asked for is next to the microphone."

Perrine Fournier from Agency France-Presse arrived in a taxi, and the Associated Press reporter drove up soon after. Lucy and Laura came walking along the street with The Nines. Daniel pulled in, the trunk and back of his car full of folding chairs from the warming room. The Nines carried chairs, set them up, singing as they worked. Both journalists took photos. While I planned our speech with Rennie, the wind died down, the sun liberated itself from behind a cloud. Daniel came back with another carload of chairs. The Nines sang again, went inside, one by one hugged Jeffie, who had just lost his big brother Roy, then sat in their reserved row.

Inside, the church was full. Through the open doors, we could see people sitting outside, others standing behind them.

Rennie and I went up to the stage with Jeffie. Tears streamed down his cheeks.

The room went silent.

Jeffie held my hand tighter than a lock wrench. "My brother Roy, this is my last chance to talk with you. You always believed in me when I needed you most. Even when my teachers called me dumb, you didn't. You talked to me, helped me do things that made me feel smart. Like the dollhouse you showed me how to make Cousin Bethie for her fourth birthday. I wanted real shingles on it, so you got scraps from the roofing factory, showed me how to cut them, glue them on. And told me dumb people can't do that, so I was *not* dumb. When I had trouble in school, you blamed the teachers. And you were right, Roy. When I got glasses, I *could* read books just like you said. The school wouldn't listen to you, Roy. But me, I'll remember every word you said. Forever."

Jeanette came up onto the stage, hugged Jeffie. "The Nines love you, Jeffie." She led him, still crying silently, to his seat, sat next to him, held him.

"Roy Gulbrandsen, Dennis Brekke, Timothy Clausen, you are *our* boys," Rennie said. "They have taken you from us. We will not forget."

"Kenneth Walsh, Douglas Viklund, Terence Berg, you too are *our* boys," I said. "We will never forget who ya were, what ya did."

"Timothy, we remember when Monya Pedersen's cat climbed that icy tree and couldn't get down," Rennie said. "We never could figure out how you scooted up like you had suction cups for feet and brought Tiger to safety."

"Terence," I said, "we remember how ya used to go up the Creekside Trail and play yahr harmonica in private. We never told ya that a bunch of us would sneak up right close to ya, sit there and listen. Those were good times, Terrence. We will miss ya!"

"Dennis, you weren't much older than us," Rennie said. "But you taught many of us how to ice skate when we were kids, 'n' you were so patient, especially when I kept falling 'n' crying 'n' we wish you were here to teach our younger brothers and sisters."

Rennie and I shared more memories about each guy. Then, she said, "Paulie, they're murdering working people, strikers, protesters."

"They have done it again and again for years," I said. "In 1932, the government promised unemployed veterans bonuses. 'Sure, ya can have them, but ya have ta wait thirteen years. What? Yah're hungry now? Too bad. Ya cannot camp out here in Washington. Go home!' The vets would not leave, so the army shot at them and killed William Hushka and Eric Carlson."

"Say their names," Rennie said. "William Hushka, Eric Carlson."

The crowd chanted their names.

"In 1934," Rennie said, "the Teamsters Union fought a long, bitter strike. Minneapolis cops fired on the picketers. Henry Ness and Jack Belor died."

"Say their names," I said.

The crowd chanted their names.

"In 1969," I said. "Darlene Hillilä, just fifteen years old. Viewed as a toy, a plaything, by a bossman's wealthy nephew. Forcibly drugged, raped, and made pregnant. Took her own life."

"Say her name!" Rennie said.

The crowd chanted.

"In 1970," Rennie said, "Alison Krause, Jeffrey Miller, Sandra Scheuer, William Schroeder demonstrated for peace at Kent State University in Ohio. Shot dead by the National Guard."

"Say their names," I said.

The crowd chanted.

"In 1972," I said. "Roy Gulbrandsen, Dennis Brekke, Timothy Clausen, Kevin Walsh, Douglas Viklund, Terrence Berg, forced into the army to kill and be killed in 'Nam."

"Say their names," Rennie said.

The crowd chanted.

"Why? Why?" I said. "Why do we send our boys around the world to kill people? Just to make big profits for the war machine? Are we going to finally say, no! No more?"

"Say it loud!" Rennie said.

"No! No more! No! No more!" the crowd chanted.

"Now, finally we are saying no! No more!" I said. I took a card from my shirt pocket. "This is my draft card. Yes, I do have a sole surviving son's deferment. But I do not want a symbol of the war machine in my pocket anymore."

Two reporters ran up to the front, cameras aimed at me.

I tore the card into bits, dropped them into the little trash can. "This is an official notice to my draft board. I am laying down my weapons. Gonna study war no more!"

From the choir platform, Charlie, Louie, Daniel, Ruka, Bobby, and Diane sang out, "I'm gonna lay down my sword and shield, down by the riverside, down by the riverside, I ain't gonna study war no more."

The pianist joined in. Soon everyone inside and out was singing.

Coffins were carried out to hearses. Banners that said, "Stop the War—Bring Our Boys Home," were attached to cars. A long drive down to Fort Snelling National Cemetery where the six boys, childhood friends, were buried next to each other. Jeanette held a No More War! sign with one hand, Jeffie's hand with the other.

Afterward, half the caravan headed to the Brooklyn Center Draft Board. Rennie, Ma, Clara, Linda, Billy, and I went to Northeast with the other half. When we arrived at the Pulaski Park Draft Board with almost two hundred Creekers, Sherry, the thirteen-year-old who had organized the demonstration, had more than a hundred middle school friends picketing and singing, "And into plowshares beat their swords, nations shall learn war no more."

Soon, a parade of high schoolers appeared on the street, hundreds and hundreds of them. The crowd filled the entire avenue in front of the draft board building, forcing cars to take a detour. Standing on a wood box, holding a battery-powered megaphone, Sherry organized people to go inside the office three at a time to demand the draft board close down right now. The presidents of the middle and high school student organizations gave speeches.

Holding Jeffie's hand, Lucy whispered in Sherry's ear a moment. Sherry nodded. She and Lucy helped Jeffie climb onto the wooden box.

"My brother Roy, we just got back from his funeral. Killed in 'Nam. No more war! Say his name. Roy Gulbrandsen."

"Roy Gulbrandsen," the crowd chanted. "No more war! No more war!"

Susie, Todd, Elżbieta, Harrison, Chester, and the Associated Press reporter took photos and interviewed Jeffie, Sherry, and her friends. The *Journette* was nowhere to be found.

"We're going to be here every Wednesday at lunchtime," Sherry said to the crowd. "Why?"

The crowd chanted, "No more war! No more killing! Remember Roy!"

"Now, let's us all go back to school," Sherry said, "tell the teachers what we learned here!"

Back at Shingle Creek, Rennie and I stopped in at Russ's office.

"Meet Roland Kraus, our new intern. Tell them about court today, Rollie."

Rollie clasped his hands over his head. "Judge Havemeyer ordered the Building Department to issue permits for the Worker's Market. He made it clear he didn't like what we're doing. But he said Buildings acted illegally and he would not tolerate that."

"All. Right. Then!" Rennie said and did her little step dance. "Did you let Ronan and the stores committee know 'n' stuff?"

"Do trains have wheels?" Russ said.

"Strange guy, that judge," Rollie said.

"Takes all kinds, Rollie," Russ said. "Our job is to make him our friend, even if he's a frosty one."

"Guess there's a lot more I have to learn about the lawyering business."

"Ya came to the right place!" I said. "We will be in our office working on payroll if ya need us."

In the Freedom Academy classroom, Lucy was talking long division. Kids were standing, dancing, pacing, doodling, even tearing paper into little pieces. Jeanette was sitting tight against Jeffie, her arm around him, his head leaning on her shoulder.

"What's 96 divided by 24?" Lucy said.

"Four!" Jeffie immediately called out.

"How did you get the answer so quickly?" Lucy said.

"I knew four times 25 is 100, so four times 24 is 96, four less. Since division is the reverse of multiplying, 96 divided by 24 is four."

"Excellent, Jeffie!"

"But you make it so simple, Lucy," Jeffie said.

"It *is* simple *if* you're smart enough to see that," Lucy said. "And all of you are!"

"Lucy, there's something I don't get," Kurt said. "How come you let us doodle and dance in class? Mrs. Elak used to make us sit with our hands folded. She caught you doodling, she whacked you."

"Everyone? Which way do you like better?" Lucy said.

"Yours!" a chorus of kids said.

"Why?"

"It just makes it easier to concentrate," Terri said.

"I don't get all tense and nervous," Bobby said.

"Well, that's why," Lucy said. "Scientists studied how children learn. You know what they found? Many kids learn faster and better when they're not sitting stock still. Now, let's go to the five-times table. What's sixty divided by twelve?"

"Five!" a bunch of voices called out.

"Let's practice rhyming fives—"

"You children are all truants," a loud, harsh voice yelled from the back of the room. "This is not a real school!"

Kids turned around, saw Mrs. Elak, screamed.

"You have ten seconds to stand up, get your coats, and come with me back to the real school. If you do not, you will be arrested and sent to prison school."

Daniel ran to Bonnie and Ruthie, stood in front of them. Mrs. Elak strode toward Lucy, then suddenly darted at Jeffie, grabbed his ear, and dragged him toward the door. Jeffie screamed in pain. Jeanette jumped up, kicked Mrs. Elak's shins. Lucy sprang across the room like a lioness, landed a roundhouse punch in Mrs. Elak's gut. Mrs. Elak howled, stumbled, let go of Jeffie and tried to grab him again. Lucy hit Mrs. Elak twice more, knocking her to the floor.

"Belle, don't make me really hurt you," Lucy thundered. "Stay right where you are and be quiet. Laura, please check Jeffie's ear. Daniel, please call Lieutenant Gordy. Paulie, can you please call Russ? Jeanette, please hug Jeffie. Karen, please get the first aid kit."

"You're going to pay for this, Lucille Dahl, you communist pig," Mrs. Elak said. "You're going back on the blacklist where you belong."

"Lieutenant Gordy is on the way," Daniel said.

Still sitting on Mrs. Elak, Lucy said, "And now, kids, let's show Mehitabel Elak she can't disrupt our class. Where were we?"

"Rhyming fives," Mamie said. "Five, ten, fifteen, twenty, get that far, and you've got plenty!"

"Good work, Ms. Anderson," Lucy said.

Bobby called out. "I found a rhyme for forty in the rhyming dictionary, Lucy."

"Chant it loud and clear, Mr. Lund!"

"Twenty-five, thirty, thirty-five, forty, touching a frog won't make you warty!"

"Great, Mr. Lund! Who can do the next one?"

"Forty-five, fifty, fifty-five, sixty," Tess sang. "My ma calls me a little pixie."

"Fantastic, Ms. Iversen! Next?"

"Sixty-five, seventy, seventy-five, eighty," Bonnie sang. "I prefer a classroom where I don't have to be afraid-y!"

"Perfect, Ms. Korhonen! Next?"

"Me!" Jeffie said, looking up from the rhyming dictionary, Jeanette's arm around his shoulders. "Eighty-five, ninety, ninety-five, a hundred, when they hired Mrs. Elak, they really blundered!"

We laughed long and hard the way people do when they need to release a lot of anger and anxiety.

Gordy entered the room looking puzzled. When he saw Lucy sitting on Mrs. Elak on the floor, his eyebrows jumped way up, eyes got wide. He turned on his tape recorder, took witness statements from everyone, kids and adults. Shot photos. Looked at Jeffie's ear, took a photo of the cut in his earlobe from Mrs. Elak's fingernail.

"We want to press charges," Lucy said. "Assault and battery, trespassing, child abuse, attempted kidnapping."

"What about me?" Mrs. Elak said, struggling to her feet. "Lucille Dahl attacked and knocked me down. That savage has no respect for her elders."

"Please add slander to the charges," Lucy said.

"Mrs. Elak!" Gordy said. "*You* are under arrest. You have the right to remain silent and it would be a good idea if you do. For your own sake."

After Gordy cuffed Mrs. Elak and marched her out of the room, Jeffie said, "Lucy, how come you called all us kids Mr. and Ms. when Mrs. Elak was here."

"I wanted to show her how much I respect all of you. But you know, it's more than just respect. I love every one of you kids. Remember we studied how bears and lions protect their cubs? Someone tries to harm my cubs, I'm going to fight them!"

"We're your kids?" Charlie said.

"That's exactly how I feel," Lucy said. "All kids are my kids, but especially you."

Rennie and I went into our office, worked on payroll, with one of Jill's tapes playing softly on the boombox.

She sighed. "No halfway about it. This has been an intense day, big-time."

We had almost finished the paperwork when the phone rang. Mollie Whupple, Fred's secretary, said, "I have to warn you, they're on the warpath down here. Your budget's been slashed and your new building canceled. They're going to fire me, probably this afternoon. Here's my home phone number. Call me if you need to. Gotta go!"

"Dang, Rennie! How did ya know we were not even at the halfway mark?"

"Holy buckets, I wish I hadn't said that 'n' I brought us bad luck, but let's just finish payroll 'cause I don't know about you, but I need to think about it all, yes I do."

The phone rang again. "Oh, shit! Here it comes," Rennie said.

I put the call on speaker. "Mr. Mäkinen, Judge Woodruff here. I spoke with reporters from the *Journal* and the *Gazette* at length on Tuesday. The papers are ignoring me and still haven't mentioned Fred Corwin's death. I'm concerned—"

"This calls for an in-person visit, Yahr Honor. I will explain why when we meet."

"Can you come see me now?"

"We will be there in thirty minutes, Yahr Honor."

"Please hurry. I'm wearing a groove in the floor, pacing back and forth."

"On the way, Yahr Honor."

"Paulie-Paul, who besides me?"

"Billy or Linda."

"Easier to get Linda, yes it is, 'cause we can get Ma to bust her out of school. Grab one of the press packets from this morning 'n' let's go!"

CHAPTER 3, LOCKED OUT!

TUESDAY-WEDNESDAY, FEBRUARY 22-23, 1972

I drove downtown on North 2nd Street. No traffic. No signals. We really flew.

"Holy buckets, 'n' I can really hear that special sound your car makes, yes siree!" Rennie said.

"That is why I call it the mahrove-rove car," I said. "It likes this street, and it likes to go fast, so the sound is louder, like a purring cat."

Twenty-two minutes later, we were in Judge Woodruff's chambers. The three of us pulled out our jammers, turned them on, explained them to the judge.

"It's not just about me," the judge said. "I am worried about this threat to our democracy. You really think it's coming from the Communal Association?"

"We *know* it is, Yahr Honor. Here's proof." We showed him the copies of Communal Association memos and letters we had received. Issues of the *Minnesota Patriot*. Explained how many of their threats had come true very quickly.

"This is even more serious than I thought," the judge said.

"You're right to worry, Your Honor," Linda said. "And the press is key."

"How can I make them listen?"

"Expand your horizons, Your Honor," Rennie said. "Go beyond the *Journette* 'n' stuff. Teen Councilwoman Linda Frisk here"—Rennie patted her shoulder—"and her friend Councilman Billy Anderson held a press conference this morning 'n' it focused on Fred Corwin's murder but also talked about the courts."

Linda rattled off the list of attendees.

"You got Associated Press, *The New York Times, Wall Street Journal*? How?" Judge Woodruff said.

"Here's the invitation and a press packet we prepared for this morning, Your Honor," Rennie said.

The judge looked it over. "Councilwoman Frisk, could you and Councilman Anderson hold a press conference for this court? Could you both miss school to do it?"

"We sure could, Your Honor. Neither of us do our real learning at school. We're there for other reasons."

"When could we hold it?"

"Your Honor, Friday morning would be a very heavy lift. Monday morning is much better."

"How many hours would it take for you to do this?" the judge said. "The court would have to pay you for your time."

"That would be nice, Your Honor, but it's not necessary," Linda said.

"What's the next step?" the judge said.

"We set up a planning meeting for tomorrow," Linda said, "with me, Councilman Anderson, Councilwoman Hakkala, Councilwoman Ahlberg, and Council President Mäkinen. That way you would have all of our expertise."

"May I also suggest, Yahr Honor, that ya talk with Judges Haddad and Jeppesen."

"I don't always see eye to eye with them."

"Understood. But for things yahr eyes align on, Yahr Honor, it could be to yahr advantage to work together. With what has happened recently, I am guessing ya could find common ground. Three judges would make a bigger impact on the press."

"Hmmm. You're making me think, Councilman Mäkinen. I will consider it. But the planning meeting. Could we set it for nine o'clock? I can come up to your office. I'd like to see what you're doing up there."

"We will be pleased to give ya a tour, Yahr Honor, from our clinic to our pressroom, recreation center, and under-construction supermarket. Do ya like snowshoeing?"

"Hmm! That's one of my favorite things. I just don't get to do it much anymore now that I'm a judge. Why?"

"We have a lovely trail along Shingle Creek, and snowshoes in all sizes."

"I'll take you up on that! I'm looking forward to this," the judge said, grinning.

When we got in the mahrove-rove car, Linda said, "I never could have imagined this! Wait 'til we tell Billy, Susie, and Ma."

"That man is going to become an activist judge just like Judge Haddad, yes he is," Rennie said. " 'Cause his heart's in the right place 'n' most judges won't give women a chance to be clerks."

"Aren't judges supposed to be impartial?" Linda said.

"Yup, but none of them actually are," I said. "Because they are all human. Usually, they are biased against working people and Black folks and in favor of the bosses but still claim they are impartial."

At North 2nd Street and 23rd Avenue, we passed a parked, dark gray Ford that looked just like the Communal Association grazy-mobile. In my rearview mirror, I saw it pull into traffic, said, "We are being followed. Grazies."

I turned left on 26th Avenue, right on North Fourth, left on 29th, right on Lyndale. The car followed us. At Lowery Avenue, I made a sudden left and then a quick right into an alley. They were close behind us. I got on the CB, paged Gordy, drove up the alley, turned right, then left. Used our secret CB code words to let Gordy know where we were. On Lyndale and 39th, in the rearview mirror I saw Gordy pull them over. A quick U-turn, we parked across the street from them, got out, crossed the street.

Gordy stood outside their car, tape recorder running. They were different grazies than before.

"Why did you stop us, Officer?" the grazy with the blue scarf growled.

"You're scaring people by following them."

"We are on public streets. You have a problem with that?" Blue Scarf said.

CHAPTER 3, LOCKED OUT!

"Don't blow our cover," the brown-scarfed grazy said, spitting out his words. "We're law officers too."

"Show me your ID," Gordy said.

They flashed the same phony police badges and ID cards.

"You're not cops!" Gordy said. "Why were you following these people?"

"We were not following anybody," Blue Scarf said.

Gordy pointed at him. "You always turn up alleys?"

"We have every right to drive where we want," Brown Scarf said.

"What's that on the back seat?" Gordy said.

"Personal property," Blue Scarf said.

I looked through their window. "That is a snooper," I said. "They were listening to our conversation."

"No, we weren't. All we got was static," Brown Scarf said.

"So you're admitting you *tried* to listen to their conversation."

Brown Scarf winced. "That's not what I said."

"You're under arrest for impersonating police," Gordy said.

"We were doing no such thing," Blue Scarf said.

"Tell it to the judge," Gordy said. "This is getting old very quickly." He cuffed the grazies, got them in the squad car's back seat, closed the doors. "I've been getting complaints from the neighborhood about those grazies all afternoon. They're going house to house, trying to scare and bribe people into answering questions."

Back at our office, Kurt, Greta, and their friends were waiting for us. "The grazies came to our house," Kurt said.

"I told them our parents weren't home," Greta said. "The grazy with a blue scarf said to tell Dad he could make an easy two hundred bucks just talking about the gandy dancers' union."

"I told him to go bite himself," Kurt said. "He tried to force his way in. It took me, Walt, and Greta to push him out and close the door."

"So Kurt and Walt called me and Charlie," Bobby said. "And we called Jeffie and Becky, and I told my sister Ellen."

"We had a meeting," Walt said. "How to stop grazies from bothering people."

"How?" I said.

Walt held up his forefinger. "First, we found Mr. Grünwald delivering mail. Asked him if he needed street signs to do his job. 'Nah,' he said. 'I have it all memorized. Don't even look at house numbers anymore either.'"

"Well, my sister Peggy can climb right up a pole," Greta said. "And she's good with tools."

"So our block and the next one up," Ellen said, "we helped Peggy take down all the street signs and wrapped them up really carefully."

"And hid them under a pile of bricks," Charlie said, "in Bobby's backyard."

"Tomorrow, we're going door to door," Jeffie said. "Asking people if we can rearrange their house numbers. So like mine, 4938 Newton Avenue will become 3498. The next house, 4936 will become 9643."

"That was Jeffie's idea," Kurt said. "Lucy's wrong about him. He's not smart. He's a genius!"

"If you don't know our neighborhood, you won't be able to find anyone," Peggy said, chuckling. "It'll make the grazies go nuts! We'll get more kids to help us do every block soon. Bev Hakkala and Vanessa Korhonen can climb poles too. The three of us do it just for fun 'cause Mrs. Elak said girls can't do that!"

"And after we win," Tess said, "we just put the street signs back up and change the house numbers back."

"Gosh, I just love all you kids!" I said.

"So do I, to the max, 'n' when I have kids, I hope they're just like all of you."

"So, Karen, you'll name your boys Kurwaltbob and Charljeff and your girls Peggret and Becklen?" Jeffie said.

Denise came running into our office, sobbing so hard her entire body shook. "Karen! Karen! Daddy. Accident. Hospital."

Tears filled Rennie's eyes and quickly overflowed. She grabbed Denise, held her. "When? Denise, when?"

"Two hours ago. Jack Langacker just called. What'll we do?"

"We flat out have ta see him," I said. "Now!"

"C'mon, Paavali, let's go!"

The fifteen-minute drive to the hospital seemed to take a month or two.

CHAPTER 3, LOCKED OUT!

At the nurse's station on the ninth floor, the charge nurse told us Frank Ahlberg had broken legs, did not want company, and was mad angry. "A lot of men get that way when they're scared and in pain," she said. "Visit him anyway. It's good for him, even if he doesn't know it."

"Holy buckets, is he crippled forever?"

"No, but it'll take a while to recover."

We gasped when we saw him. Both legs in casts, held high in the air by ropes and pulleys, the bottoms of his feet pointing toward the ceiling.

"Daddy!" Denise and Rennie wailed.

"What the hell do *you* want?"

"Daddy, we love you," Denise cried.

"Both of us, 'n' we'll do anything to help you get better, yes we will."

"The bastards! I told them there was a bad spot on track fifteen. They killed me! I'll never be able to work again. Just go away. Let me die in peace."

"Daddy! You're not dying, no you're not, even if it feels that way 'n' the whole community stands behind you 'n' we'll get our Industrial Safety Commission to condemn that track 'n' we're helping organize a rail workers' strike, yes we are!"

"What the hell do you know about railroads?" Frank said.

"A lot 'cause *you* taught me 'n' I know how to figure stuff out 'cause I got my smarts from *you*, Dad."

"What the hell is an Industrial Safety Committee?"

Rennie and I explained how we set it up and what it was going to do.

Frank looked at us, said nothing, seemed to be thinking. "Whose idea was that?"

"Clarence's," I said. "But Karen spoke up at meetings and supported him. Track fifteen, huh? Frank? Was the accident just past the rebar factory?"

"Yeah."

"Was yahr switch engine moving?"

"No. So I did *not* cause that accident. No way."

"Ya sure did not. It was a standing derailment."

"How do you know all that?"

"I was there when Clarence found the track dip. Foreman would not let the crew fix it. Clarence, Obie, and Jack tried to call a safety strike. Outvoted. But that is changing fast. The guys are getting ready."

He pointed at me. "What's your name, kid?"

"Paul Mäkinen, Shingle Creek Park Director, chair of the Shingle Creek Teen Council, Shingle Creek Industrial Safety Commissioner, Member of the Hennepin County Court's Troubled Youth Advisory Board."

Frank's lips formed a perfect circle. "Big shot like you supporting union organizing? Why?"

"I once worked a non-union job at a factory. It was hell. Nobody should have ta work that way."

Frank pointed to Rennie. "Is he your boyfriend?"

"We work together and we're close friends, as far as that goes."

"Well, he seems like his head is screwed on right."

Rennie took her dad's hand. "Please bring the old daddy back! Please!"

Frank was silent. But his whole face was moving.

"Daddy, you're going to get better 'n' the pain meds will start working 'n' this is *not* the end of you, 'n' please keep telling yourself that 'cause positive thoughts are powerful medicine, yes siree!"

"She's right on target, Dad!" Denise said. "You gotta listen to her."

"How do *you* know?" Frank said.

"I got my smarts same place she got hers, Dad! And I want the old daddy back too!"

When we got in the car, Rennie started sobbing. "He said good stuff about you, Paulie, but nothing about me 'n' that hurts big-time."

"Rennie! He was not negative toward ya. First time in how long? Give him time."

I was amazed when Denise hugged and comforted Rennie. "You said all the right things, Ka Ka. Paulie's right. They'll sink in."

That night, the entire Teen Council went to a concert in our meeting hall. Diane Ward and Lucy Dahl organized it, got Nora O'Farrell to join them. They taught us old union and protest songs, going way back to the 1890s. Todd recorded it for KPFP. Linda and Billy wrote down the lyrics, so we could publish them in a pamphlet. Profits would go to our strike fund. I brought my boom box, recorded it for Frank.

CHAPTER 3, LOCKED OUT!

"That'll help cheer him up, and it sure was nice of them to dedicate that 'Drill, Ye Tarriers, Drill' song to Dad, 'cause he'll get a laugh from the part where Jim Goff gets blown into the sky 'n' the bossman docks his paycheck for the time Jim was in the air."

As we walked home after the concert, Rennie, still holding onto me tighter than ever, said, "I was going to sleep in my room tonight, but I know I will have nightmares about Dad's accident, 'n' I know it's not fair to you, 'cause I'm still involved with Greg, but can I please sleep downstairs with you, Paavali? I'm so confused, but I just want to be near you."

"I need ya as much as ya need me, Rennie. I am having awful dreams about Fred's murder. I do not have anyone else who fully understands that besides you."

"Me either," Rennie said.

"Not Greg?"

"Not Greg! Can I ever get everything I need from one person?"

"Wish I knew, Rennie. Wish I knew!"

Very early the next morning, I cooked a quick breakfast, read the usual drivel in *Minnesota Patriot* about how, "Kids ran out from the so-called Fourth Grade Freedom Academy yesterday, all the way to the real school, where they begged Mrs. Elak to be their teacher again. But Paul Mäkinen and an armed guard rounded up the crying kids, herded them back to the decrepit old dump they call a school, and severely beat the children one by one, then got into a fist fight with Mr. Sorensen, father of the little girl Mäkinen whipped most severely."

I know every single family in this neighborhood. There is no Sorensen. Oh, well, this will be an interesting one in court when they cannot prove their lies.

In Judith's office just after sunrise, I told her Rennie was calling me Paavali a lot, that she seemed upset with Greg, how she clung to me when she had bad dreams during the night. "Judith, is she in conflict just like me?"

"Yes, in conflict. No, not just like you, Paul."

"Why is hers different?"

"You're conflicted with yourself, not her. She's not conflicted with herself. It's with you. What does Greg do for her that you don't?"

"That is simple. He has sex with her. And he takes her on dates."

"What do you do for her that Greg doesn't or can't?"

"Understand her on a deep level. Care about her in a way Greg never could."

"How do you know that?"

"She told me. That is why she loves me, but she does not love him."

"Do you love her?"

I slumped way down in my chair. "My snakes will not let me."

"If your snakes suddenly vanished?"

"Shit! I should not have even thought that." Sweat started rolling down my face. I doubled over in pain.

"You couldn't say it, Paul, but your head actually nodded yes. You *can* work around your snakes. Now tell me, what is Karen's conflict?"

"She wants a romance with me, and I cannot do that."

"What part of a romantic relationship can you start doing right now?"

"Nothin'."

"Somethin'. Take her on dates. Start horning in on Greg's turf."

"I cannot do that! My serpents!"

"Wasn't the union song concert last night like a date?"

"A little bit. But it was really for work."

"What kind of date does Rennie like most?"

"Dancing. She told me that."

"Is there a dance venue you need to know about for outreach work?"

"But my snakes!"

"Lie to your snakes. Tell them it's not a date! Tell them you're going to check out whether it would be a good place to recruit staff for Workers' Market."

"Er...we do need to start doing that."

"Next appointment, I want to know exactly when you and Rennie are going dancing. Promise?"

"Promise!"

"To me? Or to yourself?"

"Both. But mainly to myself."

When Rennie came to our office at 8:15 to plan our meeting with Judge Woodruff, I flat out asked her, "Could we go out dancing Friday night?" Which, of course, super-activated my serpents.

CHAPTER 3, LOCKED OUT!

Her face lit up…and then crumpled. "I promised Greg I'd see him then 'n' he called just before I left the house 'n' said he misses me, 'n' Paulie-Paul, you know why I need him so much, yes you do."

I could hear Judith's voice inside my head screaming, *"Ask her for Saturday. Or Sunday. Don't give up so easily, Paul!"*

"Gee," I said, trying to keep my feelings off my face. "Maybe another time." My snakes calmed as if I had sung them a lullaby.

"How about Saturday, as far as that goes, or Sunday?"

"I will have ta let ya know."

"Oh, Paulie, I hate when you get like that."

Yup. And so do I. But I cannot help it. The pain those reptiles cause is terrifying.

I compressed my feelings into another poison pellet, swallowed hard, tried to focus on our meeting with the judge. But a voice inside my head kept yelling, *Damn it, Paavali, yah're the Shingle Creek Park Director, chair of the Shingle Creek Teen Council, Shingle Creek Industrial Safety Commissioner, Member of the Hennepin County Court's Troubled Youth Advisory Board, and a really nice guy. Why is it ya do not deserve Rennie?* I looked at my right shoulder again and again. A four-inch-tall animated statue of my mother was standing there, laughing at me.

When Judge Woodruff arrived, we had coffee ready, Roger's Chocolate Coffee-n-Cake treats and Mabel's chess pie. As I told the judge how Roger transformed from an angry teenager who had threatened to kill my stepsister, Jill, into a kind and much-loved young man, I began to relax. My mother's statue shrank, quieted down.

Judge Woodruff nodded his head. "I must say, I did not understand how Judge Haddad sentenced Roger Tornquist to Maple Grove Therapeutic Center. But it's starting to make sense. What is he doing now?"

"I have ta tell ya, besides school and volunteer work at the park, he is Assistant Baker at *Pie Golly!* here in Shingle Creek." I pointed to the chess pie. "That is where this creamy lemon-laced delight comes from. They deliver homemade pies all over the Far North Side. We got them started with a hundred bucks out of our pockets and a donated old car. They count on Roger."

The judge was impressed with how we planned his press conference, with his tour of Betty Hall, Workers' Market, the warming room, and positively gleeful while snowshoeing on the Creekside Trail. "This has been highly productive, great fun, and a huge eye-opener," he said just before he left. "You've given me a *lot* to think about. Please put me on the invite list for the Workers' Market opening ceremony."

"Judge Woodruff, would ya be willing to speak?"

"You bet I would!" he said. "I am just so impressed that you're cutting ice from the lake and building your own ice boxes!"

Back at our office, Rennie looked at me. "Oh, Paavali, I just wish…"

"Sorry, Rennie. I just get so scared sometimes, I do not think right. Can we go dancing Saturday night?"

"Yes! Yes!" She grabbed me, whirled me, kissed my face six times.

Inside, I was punching several dozen snakes in the head. They still hurt me but not as bad as usual.

For the rest of the morning and right through lunchtime, Rennie and I handled a blizzard of paperwork. At one in the afternoon, we headed over to the warming room to set up the kid's skating contests.

My key would not go into the lock.

Rennie tried hers, cursed, looked closely at the door. "Holy buckets, Paavali, this lock has been changed, as far as that goes. Let's try the door on the other side."

We walked around the building. The framed photos of Jill and Joe, who started the Teen Council, were on top of piles of our stuff? In the garbage cans? We pulled out the photos, craft materials, our hand-made red pillows for the picnic table benches, and a whole bunch of equipment.

"What the hell is going on here?" I said.

Rennie checked the other door. "They changed this one too, yes they did." She banged on it. "Come help me, Paulie."

I stood beside her. "Help how?"

"Just be next to me." She pulled out her tools, opened the lock.

Inside, there was an open can of paint. The lower left corner of our mural had been blacked out. The office door opened. Someone stepped out.

Richard Prichard? Huh?

He mumbled, "I could've sworn I locked the doors."

"Just what do ya think yah're doing here, Richard? Got run out of Portland Park?"

CHAPTER 3, LOCKED OUT!

He took his glasses from his jacket pocket, put them on. "Oh, it's little Paulie and his miniature Paulette. Didn't anybody tell you? You've been fired. You're not qualified for this job. This facility is closed until I can clean out all the garbage and hire a proper staff. Time for you two to leave."

"Richard Prichard, huh? Anyone ever call ya Dick Prick?"

His face turned the color of a very hot pepper. Fists up, he took a boxer's stance.

I stepped toward him, ready to flip him if he tried to land a blow. "Better listen to me very carefully, Mr. Prick. Yah're gonna have ta deal with a bunch of very angry Creekers for defacing our mural."

Rennie moved in on him. "Put another drop of paint on it, and I'll cripple you for life, *Dick!* Got that?"

I took another step toward him. "Ya had best be gone before everyone arrives."

"You can't talk to me like that." He stepped toward Rennie.

"We can 'n' we did 'n' despite my small size, I am perfectly capable of seriously hurting you, yes siree!"

Harry came marching through the door. "What on earth is going on here? I just got back from my doctor visit. Someone changed the lock on my workroom." He looked at Dick Prick, wrinkled his nose. "Who are you?"

"The new director here. *My* maintenance man is on the way. I need someone competent to fix this dump up."

Harry laughed. "I see you're expert at winning friends and influencing people."

Karen went into the office, turned on the CB radio. "This is FastTalk. Mayday! 10-33! Forced out of HotBase by new bossman. Paul and me fired. We need you at HotBase now! Pass it on. Tell everyone. Telephone tree! Activate! Activate! Copy?"

A chorus of voices said, "Copy!"

Dick Prick stalked into the office.

"You touch Karen, and I'll kill you dead!" Harry growled.

"Thanks, Harry, but I'd rather take care of him myself." Her voice shifted gears. "Go ahead, Dick Prick. Just try putting a hand on me! I am so ready." She sounded ten feet tall.

"I can't let you stir up trouble," Dick Prick yelled. "Away from that microphone!"

"Dick! Yah're gonna hurt yahrself again!"

He grabbed Rennie's arm. She did what looked like a dance step, and suddenly, Dick Prick was on the floor, his face pale as fresh snow in a wealthy neighborhood. He lay there, curled into a ball.

Harry called downtown. They told him he and everyone else here had, indeed, been fired. Lucy, Daniel, and Laura came marching up the footpath, leading The Nines. Soon, the warming room and gym room were full of angry adults and kids.

"Good thing we have this CB radio," Daniel said, "so we can get folks uprised."

I stood on a chair, told everyone what happened. "Are we ready to move Mr. Prick out of here?"

"We are ready!" people chanted.

"Up on yahr feet, Dick Prick! Come on, move! They are waiting for ya."

He lurched to his feet, tottered into the warming room.

"Do you think his last name might really be Kedd?" Bucky said.

"Yeah! Dick Kedd!" Irene Korhonen said, laughing, which set off the rest of us.

Peri Korhonen blushed, put her hands on her cheeks, said, "Mah-mie!"

"Buddies! Moving circle!" Rennie said.

Still laughing, we surrounded the renamed Richard Prichard, walked him out the door, up the path, to his car. With every step, he gained more strength and venom. He turned, spat on the ground. "Think you're such big shots? Park Superintendent Hastings-Dankworth cut off Shingle Creek's payroll. You'll all be out on your asses in no time. But *I'll* be back!"

Stinkworth? Holy cowbops! How are we gonna deal with him?

"We won't be so gentle next time, *Dick Kedd!*" Irene said.

When Dick Prick's car turned the corner and disappeared, Rennie called out, "All right then, everyone, back to the warming room 'cause we have work to do!"

People followed us back, chanting, "Karen! Paulie! Harry!"

Rennie stood on a chair, said, "What do we have to do right this moment?"

CHAPTER 3, LOCKED OUT!

"Call Russ!" Billy said.

"And KPFP and Susie, so they can tell the whole city what's happening here," Bonnie said.

"I'll do that," Barb said and sprinted into the office.

"Harry's got to call his union," Norma Lund said. "And *we* need to call an emergency meeting!"

"We better guard this warming room round-the-clock," Earl Smith said.

"And continue all our park programs no matter what," Betty said.

"But we have to put everything back in its right place," Mabel said. "Dick Kedd really messed things up."

The phone rang. Jeffie answered it, called out, "Diane, for you!"

"I'll take photos of the mural," Laura said, "write a story for *American Muralist*. And figure out how to repaint that corner."

"Just spoke with Pastor Broadwater," Diane said. "He says if the schools won't let us meet there, we can use the church any time we need to."

"That's mighty kind of him!" Bucky said. "But let's not give up on the schools yet. The church is a little too small for us."

Susie came running in the door, Russ jogging behind her. "We're holding the press for a front-page extra." She opened her notepad, started interviewing people.

"Every job on the Park Board payroll is civil service," Russ said. "They can't just fire people without warnings, written reprimands, and hearings."

"So do we sue them?" Daniel said.

"Not yet. We try for an injunction forbidding the Park Board from firing any of you. Much quicker. If we can't get an injunction, then we sue."

Ma came out of the office, shaking her head. "Both the junior high and elementary principals said the Teen Council and Shingle Creek Neighborhood Association are banned from school property as subversive organizations. We can't have meetings, senior swimming, open gym, or team practice anymore. Starting yesterday."

"Guess we'll need two injunctions," Russ said.

"Should we be putting pressure on the Park Board and Civil Service commissioners?" Rennie said.

"Do devils have horns?" Russ said.

"How do you put pressure on people like that?" Peggy Björk said.

"Call them, write them letters, maybe even picket their offices," Russ said.

"Can a kid like me do that?" Peggy said.

"And me?" Kurt said.

"I can teach my class how tomorrow," Lucy said.

"What about us adults?" Evelyn said.

"What about me?" Peggy said.

"How about I teach all the kids how in the classroom, after the ice-skating contest," Lucy said. "And the adults tonight."

"Mommie, can Lucy eat dinner at our house in between? Please!" Bonnie said.

"We'd be honored to have you, Lucy," Irene said. "Sampa's working the night shift, so we have a seat free at the table."

"Thank you. Glad to join you," Lucy said.

"I have the best mommy," Bonnie said.

Jeffie came in the door, grinning. "Look at this! Are these the old locks? Found them by the creek."

"Sure are," Harry said. He put his key into one, turned it. "Still working. I'll clean them up and put them back in."

"Jeffie! Jeffie!" we all chanted.

Nora arrived, turned on her tape recorder.

Tommy Hillilä came running into the room, asked Laura to cup her hands, took a small sack from his pocket, poured a bunch of pennies, nickels, and dimes onto her palms. Susie shot a couple of photos.

"I broke my piggy bank open 'cause you got fired," Tommy said. "So you can have some food money. Laura, don't go away. Please don't!"

"Aw, Tommy, gol! That is so nice of you. Don't worry, hon! I'm not going anywhere. None of us are." She sat down, opened her arms.

He sat on her lap, leaned against her, talking away while Nora interviewed him.

CHAPTER 3, LOCKED OUT!

Burt opened the door, came striding in. "Bebee Blecher called, told me what's going on. I want to help you knock the Communal Association on its butt. Paulie, Karen, can we go over your payroll figures?"

We gave him the breakdown.

"I would be so very pleased to pick up the entire payroll until the Park Board rehires everyone. There are two conditions, though. First, you need to get approval at a community meeting."

"No problem," I said.

"Second, even if everyone gets back pay when they're rehired, you're not allowed to pay me back."

"Don't have a cow, man, but that doesn't seem fair to you, no siree!"

"What's fair and what isn't changes dramatically when you have millions of bucks in the bank. It is totally fair from my point of view."

"Hot dog! How about a compromise?" I said. "Any back pay people get is donated to the strike fund."

"That works for me. You know, I really like it here!"

Karen talked with Daniel and Laura, then stood on a chair again. "Okay, kids, our ice-skating contests are a little behind schedule today 'n' stuff, but we'll be starting in half an hour, yes we will." She jumped down, took my hand. "C'mon, Paulie-Paul, we better go to our office 'n' plan the railroad workers' strike meeting."

She came up with a brilliant way to present the information but was not sure it would work. We discussed each idea, each part, and how to make it even better.

"Yah're right on target, Rennie! Yah're the one who should chair the meeting." I hugged her. "I just love how smart ya are!"

"I wouldn't be without you, Paavali 'n' there's no halfway about it."

CHAPTER 4, SECRET OF THE STEEL WEDDING BAND

WEDNESDAY-FRIDAY, FEBRUARY 23-25, 1972

At 4:30, two hundred and twelve men and three women from Camden, City Line, and Northeast Lowry Yards filled Jericho Baptist church.

Clara knew they would be hungry at the end of their workday, so she and Burt had made a huge batch of *tomatsoppa* that morning. Kurt and Tess volunteered to serve it.

Todd turned on his tape recorder. Susie came running in, opened her notepad.

Rennie started the meeting. "Holy buckets, it's far out to see so many of you here. You may be wondering, why is a teenage *girl* talking at us? Well, my dad is a railroad man, 'n' I'm a North-Northeast Minneapolis Industrial Safety Commissioner 'n' I can vote to shut down unsafe track 'n' order it removed."

Gandy dancer Elmer McGill stood up, pointed at Rennie. "You and what army?"

"Police Lieutenant Gordon Walden and his six officers work for the Commission now, as far as that goes, 'n' any of you brave enough to help enforce the law of this land, because it *is* on our side, you know, are welcome to help out."

The room was quiet.

CHAPTER 4, SECRET OF THE STEEL WEDDING BAND

"For those of you who don't know my dad, he broke both legs yesterday afternoon because the bosses wouldn't fix a bad rail dip. His engine just fell over, like it died. It could've killed him, or anyone working near it, yes siree.

"Now I want to introduce some of our other Safety Commissioners. Clarence Björk from Camden Yard, Marek Witkowski from Northeast Lowry Yard, and our lawyer, Russ Linwood-Flink. They'll explain what we can do about our safety problems."

"Yeah, yeah. We just have to fix our dangerous work habits and be more careful!" a gandy dancer from City Line Yard, wearing a red cap, said.

"How could Frank Ahlberg have been more careful?" Clarence said. "Our crew reported that dip. We told Frank about it. So he slowed from five miles an hour to a halt. A minute and ten seconds *later*, the track buckled under his engine, threw it sideways."

"He shouldn't have gone so fast," Red Cap said.

"He. Was. Not. Moving!" Clarence said. "Now please let's stay focused. This Industrial Safety Commission can help us. If we let it."

The moment we had explained the Commission and Arnray, Elmer McGill said, "What you're saying is we should strike. You're just giving it a fancy name. You know our union has a no-strike clause in—"

"So we should just let them keep maiming and killing us, Elmer?" Clarence said.

"No strike fund, no strike," Elmer said.

"No strike *vote*, no strike," Clarence said, "and you voted no when I called for a strike 'cause the foreman wouldn't let us fix the track dip that got Frankie hurt yesterday."

I strode to the front of the room. "I have ta tell ya, we *do* have a strike fund. Shingle Creek community has raised forty-eight hundred and twelve bucks so far. We voted to help ya out with picketing and—"

"We don't have any other unions supporting us," a young guy with a green sweater said. "That's plain scary."

"Stop being so damned scared!" a tall, older woman said. "We haven't done the work yet, reaching out to other unions. Did you read today's *People's Free Press*? Page three, there are folks gearing up to strike for a two-fifty minimum. Nurses, office clerks, reporters, all looking to work with other unions like ours."

"What does a woman know about railroads or unions?" Green Cap said.

Marek stood up, pointed at Green Cap. "My Aunt Magdalena's been a car inspector and union gal since way before you were born. You'd best listen to her. Very few men know near as much as she does."

"Clerks? Nurses?" Elmer wrinkled his nose. "They're not workers!"

"They sure as shit ain't *bosses*, Elmer!" Obie said. "There's more kinds of workin' folks in these modern times."

"Yeah, sure, whatever," Elmer said. "But I can tell you this." He pointed at Russ. "Don't trust these lawyers. Fancy pants here will get rich off this. We'll get nothing."

Russ stood up. He was wearing his usual work shirt and jeans. "How much you think I make, Mr. McGill?"

"Fifty, sixty thousand."

"Yeah, in your dreams. No secrets. It's $7,139 a year."

"I don't believe you."

Russ shrugged his shoulders. "Ask Paul. Or go downtown. Check my pay card. I'm a city employee."

"Why're you doing this if it ain't for the money?"

"Revenge, man! Pure one hundred percent revenge."

"On us? Why?"

"My dad…" He stifled a sob, raised his hand, pulled off the steel wedding band, held it up above his head. "This ring! I made it myself. From my dad's remains."

"What're you talking about?" Elmer growled.

"Dad was killed at KHA Specialty Steel. Crushed and burned to death under 328 tons of white-hot molten steel. Couldn't even say goodbye to him. They gave us a lump of steel to put in the casket. I was ten." His face crumpled. His eyes filled with tears.

"Those bastards knew the ladle was opening too soon. Now I'm getting even. Every way I can." He pulled out his handkerchief, wiped his face. Stood there, breathing hard. The room was soundless. "You get where I'm coming from?"

"Yes, sir, Mr.—"

CHAPTER 4, SECRET OF THE STEEL WEDDING BAND

"Just call me Russ. Karen, please continue."

"Here's the skinny. Our community voted to picket with you railroad guys if there's a strike."

"And us nine-year-olds voted to picket with you too," Kurt shouted from the side of the room. "We have loud voices, and all thirty-eight of us know how to chant strike slogans!"

"Us girls too!" Tess roared.

Rennie grinned. "Tess and Kurt come from railroad worker's families. So can we vote on whether we would accept help on picket lines from the Shingle Creek community 'n' stuff? In case we do strike? This is *not* a strike vote. All in favor?"

There were 177 *yes* votes, 38 *nos*.

"Holy buckets! How many people in favor of asking the Safety Commission to condemn unsafe track in the two rail yards in North and Northeast, to the max?"

The vote was 179 for, 36 against.

"Do you want Arnray Rail Safety to hire you for $2.50 an hour 'n' benefits, 'n' negotiate a contract with the *railroad* that you would approve in advance?"

That tally was closer, with only 121 in favor. But it did pass.

"Now here's the real deal, yes it is! All in favor of a strike?" Rennie said.

The vote was still against striking, 134 to 81.

"Deal!" Rennie said. "Here's what we'll do now based on your votes, you're darn tootin' we will. First, we'll let the Shingle Creek community know you'll accept their help on the picket line when we come to that. Second, we'll call a meeting of the Safety Commission and start condemning unsafe track. Next, Kurt and Tess, please give everyone a copy of the proposed Arnray Rail Safety contract. Bring it home 'n' take a pen to it! Mark it up. Ask for changes. Make suggestions. Bring it to the next meeting so we can discuss it and make the changes you want. It has to be *your* contract, not ours, yes siree, Bob!"

"Is that it, Karen?" Clarence said.

"Just one more thing. My dad needs you to visit him. Room 1107 at the hospital over in Robbinsdale. Will you do that? If yes, please stand up."

Almost everyone got to their feet.

"Thanks, friends," Rennie said. "Workers at Northeast Lowry, tell Commissioner Marek about safety problems. Camden Yard workers, talk with Clarence or Obie. Workers at City Line Yard. You don't have a commission for your area yet, so you have some more work to do. Talk with Nelson about it. Will all of you do that?"

A resounding chorus of yesses filled the room.

"Holy buckets! Thank you, everyone, you did a great job today, yes you did, 'n' now go home, have the rest of your dinner, and enjoy your evening!" Rennie waved. "Until next time!"

When most of the people had left, Rennie grabbed my arm. "Did I do okay, Paavali?"

"That was brilliant, just like I knew it would be. As Jill would say, yah're five ways flippin' amazing!"

Nelson Nesheim shook Rennie's hand. "You managed to turn a failure into a success. Astounding, Karen!"

"Yes, you moved them much closer to striking," Clarence said. "Can you teach me how to talk like that?"

"We sure can, to the max. You *have* the brains for it!"

Kurt and Tess, holding hands, walked slowly to the front of the room, shoulders drooping, carefully studying the floor. "There's no strike, Dad?" Kurt said. "That makes Tessie so sad. Me too."

Clarence kneeled down, hugged them. "More guys voted yes tonight than ever before. I know it's hard to wait. But it's coming."

"You better let me talk to them next time!" Tess said, and stamped her foot.

"I will, Tessie. I promise!" Clarence said. "Next time *will* be the right time."

Todd gave us the thumbs-up. "Paul, Karen, we need to have a little bread, jam, and tea party up on the Creekside Trail."

With jammers on, we walked to the creek. It was iced over but still running underneath.

"Can you two write me a memo?" Todd said. "Telling me the no-strike vote dooms any hope for replacing the company unions at Minnesota Consolidated? Then we'll anonymously mail it to the Communal Association."

CHAPTER 4, SECRET OF THE STEEL WEDDING BAND

"We should explain why we think that 'n' stuff, in detail, as far as that goes."

"Holy cowbops! What a mega-magnificent idea. If we explain why the guys will not strike, it will help us understand what we still have ta do to convince them. But it would behoove us to show it to Russ before we send it, right?"

"I knew there was a good reason to ask you about it!" Todd said. "Behoove, huh? What exactly does that mean?"

"Be a damned good idea, almost a duty, yes it does! It was Paulie's word of the day a few months ago."

"What do ya think, Todd? Will the guys have the guts?"

"Hell yeah! They voted for most of the ingredients of a strike today. They're close as heat to fire. Asking them to visit your dad, I know why you did it, but when they see him in casts, legs in the air, they're going to get angry. Very angry. Smart move, Karen!"

"I never thought of it that way, no siree!"

"My next move," Todd said, "is making a copy of the meeting tape for your dad. Then I'll visit him, play it for him, interview him. And convince him *he* can help get the guys on board since a bunch of them will be going to see him. Whaddaya think?"

"Holy buckets!" Rennie patted Todd's shoulder. "You'll make him a union organizer once again, 'n' that will be the best medicine for him, to the max. You're the real deal, Todd Flynn!"

"Takes one to know one," Todd said.

Friday morning, Rennie woke up before me, had a big-huge breakfast ready when I came into the kitchen at seven. The *People's Free Press* headline was, "Rail Yard Crews Furious After Derailment Breaks Worker's Legs." Set out next to it, the *Journal* had a front-page editorial praising the Park Board for appointing Stinkworth as superintendent and calling on him to clean out the Shingle Creek communists.

"They never even mentioned Fred, no they didn't."

"It's like they're just erasing him," Clara said.

"They're afraid there'll be hell to pay," Ma said, "so they try to make it go away."

The phone rang, and Linda called from the living room, "Paulie, Karen, for you!"

We put our heads together, phone receiver in between.

"Chief Jensen ordered me to a meeting downtown this morning," Gordy said. "I told him I don't answer to him anymore. He said he's on his way up here at nine to fire me. I need a whole bunch of folks in the Council Meeting Hall, especially Safety Commissioners, for backup."

"You bet, Gordy! How about reporters?" I said.

"Terrific idea!"

We split up the call list. Clara made calls from home, Linda from the warming room, Ma, Rennie, and me from the three phone lines at Betty Hall.

When Chief Jensen arrived, Gordy sat at the dais with one of his officers and three Teen Councilors, me, Rennie, Ma, and the eight Safety Commissioners needed for a quorum. The room was packed with Neighborhood Association leaders and members, the rest of the Teen Council, eight reporters.

We left only one seat free, in the back row, between three of Gordy's cops.

"Please have a chair, Chief Jensen," I said, "so we can get started."

"I ordered you to a private meeting with me, Walden!" the chief said. He pointed to me, Rennie, and the Teen Councilors next to us. "Who are these kids?"

We introduced ourselves.

"I order all of you to leave now except Lieutenant Walden!"

A reporter stood up. "Jerome Accardo, Associated Press reporter here. Under what statute, Chief Jensen, do you have authority to demand we leave?"

"Title 10, Chapter 203, Section 2."

Russ laughed. "Chief Jensen, do you not know or not care that the law you cited defines what types of protein a grocery store sells? Do you see a grocery store here?"

"With all due respect, Chief Jensen," Gordy said, "I and my six officers do not report to you anymore."

"*All* police officers working within the boundaries of Minneapolis report to me," the chief said. "Is that clear?"

"It is perfectly clear ya *think* that," I said. "But it seems yah're not familiar with commission law. So our lawyer will explain it to ya."

CHAPTER 4, SECRET OF THE STEEL WEDDING BAND

Before Russ could finish, Chief Jensen interrupted. "I am paying your salary, Walden! You answer to me! Turn in your gun and badge this instant!"

Gordy pointed at him. "Chief Jensen! My men and I turned in our uniforms, badges, guns, ID cards, and equipment to the Minneapolis Police Department on January 31, 1972 before we reported to the North-Northeast Minneapolis Industrial Safety Commission. Were you not paying attention? Do you see Minneapolis Police Department anywhere on our uniforms?"

The chief did not answer.

"Chief Jensen, do you have anything else to say, as far as that goes?" Rennie said.

"There will be consequences," the chief said as he stood up.

"Under what statute, Chief?" the United Press reporter said.

"Why don't you ask Fred Corwin," the chief said.

People booed. Russ raised his hands high in the air. The booing stopped.

"Chief Jensen, was that a threat?" Russ said.

"No, just a question."

Gordy pointed to his officers. They stood up. "We'll help you find your way out, Chief," Officer James said.

"This is quite a story!" Perrine Fournier said when the chief left. She went over to Todd, pointed to his tape recorder. "Any way I can get a copy?"

"Give me about ten minutes," Todd said. "Where are you headed next?"

"Downtown with Jerry Accardo to interview the mayor about this," Perrine said.

"Can I go with? I want to hear what Mayor Back-to-My-Duties says."

"Sure!" Jerry said. "Can I get a tape?"

"You bet! I'll copy it on the way there."

When the reporters left, Russ said to us, "That was clearly a threat. We need to get an injunction *and* pressure the county attorney to bring charges. But let me tell you, having the press here keeps the chief from making good on his threat. A little bird told me he's in a bit of trouble after the national and overseas coverage of Fred's murder. Could even unhorse him."

Rennie and I went back to our office, were stunned to see Joanna Pajari standing, clutching a red loose-leaf book, shaking, sobbing out, "They fired me. Just now."

Rennie and I gave her a two-way hug. "Holy buckets, sit down, Joanna. Tell us!"

"They said I used communist propaganda to turn all you folks into rebels."

"What the heck? Who said that about ya?"

"Mr. Killeen, the Chem teacher who hated Jill. Mrs. Elak. Some guy I never heard of named Virgil Vihainen."

"Vihainen?" I said. "He gets cash money from the Communal Association to lie about people. He is not even from around here."

"I can't imagine never being a librarian again. What'll I do?"

Rennie's eyebrows shot upward. "Burt?"

I nodded. "Suppose we could get yahr salary paid. Could ya still use the library to get information for us?"

"It would be harder, but I could. We'd have to pay for copying."

"Did ya get any warnings? Poor evaluations?"

"No. Way. My evaluations are all excellent."

"Holy cowbops! That is totally a violation of civil service rules," I said.

"What can I do about it?"

"Give me five minutes on the phone," Rennie said.

Burt immediately agreed to pay Joanna's salary. We agreed on a plan. She would do the research we needed, work with the *People's Free Press*, and organize our papers, tapes, and photos so they would be all set for the Working Class Museum someday. Her office would be next to ours in Betty Hall.

"Now we have that settled, 'n' what's the skinny 'n' stuff on that red loose-leaf?"

"I was just about to come here and show you this. Coverage from the Vietnam Six funeral." She turned the pages. "It got ink in USA, Europe, Vietnam, Japan. Look at this photo of Jeanette holding Jeffie, saying, 'I'm

CHAPTER 4, SECRET OF THE STEEL WEDDING BAND

crying for Jeffie *and* for me, 'cause I loved his brother Roy too.' Ran in thirteen big papers and lots of smaller ones."

"Mourned worldwide, but ignored by the *Journette*," I said.

Joanna closed the book, went into the classroom to show it to The Nines.

"Okay, Paavali! We finally have time to work on your speech for tonight."

The phone rang. "Drummond Duncan, president of The Foundation for Trade Unions is here for his appointment," Denise said.

"He does not have an appointment, and I do not know him."

"He insists he made one last week."

"No way. Karen and I are busy."

"He says he needs to see you alone, today. He came all the way from Chicago."

"I can see him Monday at 9:30 p.m."

"I'll see Mr. Mäkinen for my appointment now!" someone shouted.

Rennie turned the boombox on record, hid it, climbed under her desk, pulled her coat over herself.

"Sorry, Paul," Denise said on the phone. "I couldn't stop him."

A loud knock. The door opened. "Mr. Mäkinen, I have the right room, I trust. Your secretary has horribly bad manners."

"My friend Denise was doing her job. What do you want, Drummond."

He stepped into our office, looked around, closed the door, sat down. "We were sorry to hear you got laid off, Mr. Mäkinen. That must be a big concern."

"Ya heard wrong, Drummond. I am here working, not twiddling my thumbs."

"The Park Board cut off your salary. Now how would you—"

"Ya may learn as ya get older, Drummond, all is not what it seems. I have nothing to talk to ya about, so please leave."

"We've heard a lot about you, Mr. Mäkinen. You're our top candidate for Senior Union Organizer at the Foundation. Salary is fifteen thousand a year."

I sat and stared at him. Even I could see he was wearing a cheap suit. *Foundation president? My foot.*

"There's a two thousand dollar signing bonus. Sign today, and I'll hand you a check."

I sat there silent, unmoving.

"We offer a six-hour workday, four days a week."

"For the workers ya organize?"

"No, no! Only for headquarters staff. What we offer workers is an end to corrupt unions."

"Exactly how do ya do that?"

"We install full-time, professional union management. Personnel love it because they don't have to manage their union affairs after work. So there's no more problems, corruption, and needless strikes. Bosses don't mind paying for a benefit like that."

"Your union contracts? They all have no-strike clauses?"

"Why yes, of course. In this day and age, strikes are no longer needed. As Senior Organizer for us, you can help thousands of working men avoid picket line sorrows."

"Was it yahr foundation that organized the Minnesota Consolidated Construction Services Union at Camden Yard?"

His eyes blinked fast. "No, of course not." His voice had gotten higher. His left hand did a tap dance on Rennie's desk.

"So yah're a union buster, huh? I know what yah're up to." With a lightning quick move, I opened his briefcase. Sure enough, there was a recorder. I turned it off. "So that is yahr game, eh? Tape someone going for the bait, use the recording to kill their reputation, then laugh in their face when they think ya made a serious job offer."

He turned the recorder back on. "I'm so pleased you're accepting employment with us, Mr. Mäkinen. This will be a huge turning point in your life." He pulled a white envelope from his jacket pocket. "Just hand me that signed contract and here's your bonus check."

I pulled the cassette from his machine, threw it on the floor, stomped on it, which made a very satisfying crackling sound. "Get the hell out of our office, scab! Karen, help me show this idiot the door."

She emerged from under her desk with such ferocity, Drummond walked backward fast, open briefcase in one hand, white envelope in the other. "Come here again, I'll use you for a punching bag, yes I will. Get out and stay out!"

CHAPTER 4, SECRET OF THE STEEL WEDDING BAND

Drummond tried to run ahead of us, but we jogged just behind him. He jumped in a beat-up 1961 Corvette with Minnesota plates, a bashed-in right door, and a half-empty liquor bottle on the passenger seat, drove off slowly, the car coughing and backfiring.

"What a waste of time 'n' stuff, but we can carry on now 'n' you sure enough figured him out really quick."

"Rennie, how did ya know to turn on the recorder and hide?"

"No halfway about it, something was off about how that man talked to Denise."

Joanna came out of Betty Hall smiling, headed toward her car.

"Do ya know anything, offhand, about The Foundation for Trade Unions?" I said.

She grimaced. "It's a front group for the Communal Association. The real unions at Camden Yard? It broke them. Clarence, Jack, and Obie can tell you a lot more."

Back in the office, we got my speech finished, polished, practiced. We were just ready to take a coffee break when the phone rang.

"Can I pop in to see you?" Gordy said.

"Sure! Bring cookies!" I laughed.

Ten minutes later, Gordy opened the door, box of cookies in hand. "Hungry teens must always get cookies when needed. Title 10, Chapter 203, Section 2!"

We had a nice laugh while I poured coffee. He set the cookies on a paper plate.

"We've got a new grazy problem," he said. "Three cars, all FBI. Better trained. Packing pistols. Harder to deal with than the Communal Association jerks. But you know what the kids did this afternoon? Took down all the street signs, scrambled most house numbers. It's making the grazies nuts! My daughter helped. I'm so proud of her!"

"Are people having cows about the grazies 'n' stuff?"

"Enough for a whole darned dairy farm! Grazies are ringing doorbells, asking where so-and-so's house is, making threats when residents won't tell."

I could not help grinning. "But now we will know when the grazies are interested in someone, so we can warn them, snap! Like that!"

"Good point, Paulie. Now, for tonight, I'm concerned we can't keep grazies from parking on the street in front of the church. With an overflow crowd and loudspeakers outside, they're going to hear everything we say."

"Do we have anything to hide, as far as that goes?"

"No, but I still don't like it. They intimidate folks."

"Don't have a cow, man! They show up anywhere near the church, 'n' bingo, we kuln them, loud and clear, to the max."

"And we gear everyone up to take flashbulb photos. Ya good with that?"

"Here's the plan. We get Betty and Bucky's tow truck there 'cause grazies might park in the church no parking zone or even on the church lawn 'n' stuff."

"I like our program," Gordy said. "Flashbulb and kulning psychological warfare!"

That evening, Laura and the Elevens cleared snow off the church lawn. The Nines and Daniel delivered and set up chairs. Linda, Billy, and Pastor Broadwater hooked up loudspeakers outside. Gordy had two squad cars parked across the street and three officers standing on the lawn.

Three grazy cars pulled up, parked right in front of the church entrance. Officer Anderson pointed to the no parking sign, pulled out his ticket book.

A grazy jumped out of his car, flashed a badge. "You can't ticket us. We're FBI."

"We can. We will. And"—he pointed up the block to the tow truck—"we tow."

Dozens of Creekers turned on their jammers. A squad of thirty-four women and girls surrounded the grazy cars, kulning so loud it made my teeth vibrate. Kids with flash cameras shot close-up photos of grazies. The tow truck drove up, lowered its hook. The three grazy cars drove away.

Gordy pinned deputy badges on Earl, Clarence, Ruka, Dozer.

We had a hundred and twenty-six more Shingle Creek folks than usual and dozens of visitors from other neighborhoods. People sat inside and out, and stood behind the chairs on the lawn, all the way down to the sidewalk, across the street, and onto the opposite sidewalk.

The grazies came back on foot, pistols holstered on their hips, wires running from knapsacks on their backs to lapel mics. People turned their

CHAPTER 4, SECRET OF THE STEEL WEDDING BAND

jammers back on. Women surrounded grazies, kulned again. Flashbulbs lit up the night. The grazies marched away.

Inside, I shook hands with Perrine Fournier of Agency France-Presse and Jerry Accardo of Associated Press, nodded to Elżbieta Witkowski, Todd, and Susie, and started the meeting. There was an explosion of fury. Rage about our Vietnam Six, Fred's murder, Frank's accident. Anger about the sealed court cases. Outrage that gandy dancers did not earn minimum wage anymore. Indignation that all our park staff had been fired. Ferocious opposition to armed grazies. One irate speaker followed another.

After half an hour, I said, "Are we going to stand for this?"

"No!" a bunch of people chanted.

I put my hand out behind my ear. "I could not hear ya! Are we?"

"No! No! No!" the crowd chanted. Those inside the church stamped their feet. People outside clapped their hands in time to the loud stamping.

I raised both hands, palms out.

The room quieted.

"So what are we gonna actually *do* about it? Can we get proposals?"

"We need our own very big inside space!" Carleton said. "Four, five hundred seats. Even if we just clear out an unused part of Betty Hall, even if we just use planks set on cinder blocks for benches. We need space inside, away from grazies, no wind, no snow. Long run, we can build something beautiful, but we need this now! Can we vote?"

There were hundreds and hundreds of *yes* votes, dozens of volunteers.

"We must continue all the programs in the park," Norma Lund said. "Burt Loftus is willing to pick up the payroll, and we thank him. But he needs to know, are we all in favor of this? Raise your hands!"

A sea of hands shot upward.

"We need decent pay!" Clarence said. "We need your support for a two-and-a-half buck minimum wage. All in fav—"

"Hold on a moment, Clarence!" Ronan jumped to his feet.

"Ronan? You're opposed?"

"Not opposed at all, but the last two years, inflation ate more than ten percent of our paychecks. That keeps up, and soon two-fifty won't be a living wage anymore. I'll bet Carleton has an answer because I sure don't."

Carleton came up to the mic, one eye closed, face tight, chin on his palm. But suddenly, he clapped his hands. His face relaxed, both eyes were open. "I've got it. We demand it be tied to inflation. Here's what I mean. If inflation is four-point-three percent like it was last year, then this year, minimum wage becomes two-sixty-one, or four-point-three percent more."

"Wait! Wait!" Bonnie hollered and came running up to the mic. "That means we working families never get ahead. Why can't we figure in an automatic actual raise? If inflation goes up four percent, wages go up five!"

"Bonnie, honey, *that* is brilliant!" her dad said. "How did you ever think of it?"

"It's just common sense after what Lucy taught us about strikes."

"Bonnie! Lucy!" the room chanted.

"The government keeps track of labor productivity increases," Joshua Williams said. "I use that index at work. Our new minimum wage must be tied to that too."

"So we finally get rewarded for our hard work," Blanche Drass said.

Carleton leaned down, whispered in Bonnie's ear. She grinned, climbed onstage, took the mic again. "All in favor?"

While we waited for the tally from the people outside, the crowd chanted, "Bonnie, Lucy, Joshua, Carleton!"

With the votes counted, Carleton tapped Bonnie's shoulder and she called out, "All hands on deck! Because all of us worked together!"

"We are doing a dynamite job!" I said. "But, friends, we almost blew right past some big-huge issues. So, can we slow down a bit? Can we discuss stuff in detail, get everyone's point of view so we do not miss anything important? Ya good with that?"

"Paulie! Paulie!" the crowd chanted.

We discussed the challenges facing us, got people's opinions, hopes, and fears out and on the table, then came to agreements. The amount of energy filling the church and rolling in from the folks outside could have lit up the whole Twin Cities for a week.

I saw Georgia Giordano come into the church looking upset, talk to Susie a moment, then come right up to me. "Can I please tell everyone some news, Paul?"

I motioned her up to the stage, handed her the mic.

CHAPTER 4, SECRET OF THE STEEL WEDDING BAND

"The *Gazette* and *Journal* just locked out all us journalists and the printing press operators because our unions tried to negotiate better contracts. We need your support!"

Earl Smith jumped to his feet and yelled so loud, they could hear him outside without the microphone. "I object! Why should we support *them*? They've been writing lies about us for months now."

"You're right, Earl, we have," Georgia said. "But we fought with our bosses about it the whole time. Now, one of our demands is to be allowed to write the truth about *this* community. It's not negotiable."

"How do we know you're really going to do that?" Earl said.

"Earl? What do you think of the *People's Free Press* articles by Dakota Persiani?" Georgia said.

"They are what you *Journette* reporters should have been writing all along."

Susie took the mic. "Believe it or not, Georgia *is* Dakota Persiani. She's been helping us as a secret volunteer, using that pen name. And she's not the only one!"

Burt sprinted to the mic. "Let's think strategy. A strike at the *Journette* helps our *People's Free Press* succeed. Let's break the bosses' news monopoly in Minneapolis!"

"This is a surprise!" Earl said. "Apologies, Georgia, I take back my objection."

"Georgia! Dakota!" people chanted.

"Can we get help on the picket line tonight?" Georgia said. "We want to be there twenty-four seven to stop deliveries of paper and ink so they can't use their scabs."

Nora stood up. "Georgia, my husband and I know a bunch of Teamsters Union members. Come, talk with me."

Susie moved that we support the journalists by joining their picket line. It was all hands on deck. Dozens of people volunteered. Almost two hundred people pledged to cancel their *Journette* subscriptions.

Sarah Nesheim from Portland and Vincent Wójcik from Northeast Lowry Park asked us to help organize a People's Union, to coordinate activities citywide.

"This is exploding like an angry volcano!" Vincent said. "We need to work together, move fast."

"It's bigger than me, larger than you!" Sarah said. "Because it's all of us!"

We passed a motion to support the People's Union, got volunteers, set up a committee.

Ma stepped up to the mic. "Lots of people asked for Paulie to do a give 'em hell speech tonight. Before he does, he asked me to tell you that our Karen helped him write it. So, moving right along…here, with Karen's help, is our Paulie!"

"Paulie! Karen!" people chanted.

I took my hand off my chin, stood up straight. "What Sarah said before is sure as heck right. It *is* bigger than me, larger than you. That is why it often looks overwhelming. It seems like every day we are faced with new problems and new demands on our time. Build a clinic! Start a school! Open a supermarket! Launch a newspaper. And now, make an auditorium out of nothing? Raise a strike fund from empty pockets? Somehow find time to join picket lines?

"The Fat Cats think they can wear us down and out. They know—oh, they are positive—they will win their war against us. They think it is only right, fair, and ordained by God that they control our world with an iron hand and keep that control by shooting us when they think we are out of line. Remember Fred! Say his name!"

"Fred, Fred," the group repeated.

"But we have this to say to the Minneapolis Fat Cats. For years, for centuries, in yahr Declaration of Independence, in yahr Constitution, in yahr political speeches, ya promised that we are all created equal, that we have the democratic right to express our points of view and to protest, that we are entitled to life, liberty, the pursuit of happiness. It is not easy to pursue happiness, in the cold grip of winter, when ya turned us out from our own schools, paid for with our hard-earned tax dollars, and declared, thou shalt not meet. But we *do* meet! And we will not give up our right to contentment!

"It is not easy to pursue happiness when ya sent an armed force of grazies to our neighborhood and declared, thou shalt not feel safe and secure. But we are creating our *own* safety and security here. And we will not give up our right to joy of life!

CHAPTER 4, SECRET OF THE STEEL WEDDING BAND

"It is not easy to pursue happiness when, in defiance of the law of our land, ya declared to the gandy dancers, thou shalt not earn the minimum wage by the sweat of yahr brow because yah're not worthy. But we know we *are* worthy, every one of us. And we will not give up our right to good spirits.

"It is not even possible to pursue happiness when ya pluck six of our finest young men and ship them off to die in a war nobody wants, fought solely so the defense contractors can make big profits. But we will *not* let that happen again. And we will not give up our right to satisfaction. We will *not* give up! Ya have *not* worn us down. Ya never can! Ya never will!

"So, Fat Cats, beware! We are putting ya on notice. Ya pushed us past the point of no return. We are coming to claim the promise *you* made to us. Life! Liberty! And, forget the pursuit of! We demand actual happiness! At home. And at work. We will fight for it in the courts. At the election box. On the picket line. On the airwaves. In our newspaper. And in the marketplace. We are going to win. There are more of us than there are of you. We believe in democracy, the rule of law and the majority. And we are going to use every legal tool to get what ya promised us. Fat Cats, the payment on yahr promise is overdue!"

Diane's powerful voice boomed through the church. Charlie joined her on the piano. We all sang together.

> We shall not, we shall not be moved!
>
> We shall not, we shall not be moved!
>
> Just like a tree that's standing by the water,
>
> We shall not be moved!
>
> We're Black and White together,
>
> We shall not be moved!
>
> We're Black and White together,
>
> We shall not be moved!
>
> Just like a tree that's standing by the water,
>
> We shall not be moved!"
>
> In our pursuit of happiness,

We shall not be moved!

In our pursuit of happiness,

We shall not be moved!

Just like a tree that's standing by the water,

We shall not be moved!

After the music and singing, foot-stomping and hand-clapping, with an electric energy still filling the church and the air outside, people stayed and talked much longer than usual, not wanting to let go of the power of bigger than me, larger than you.

I still felt that strength as I walked home holding hands with Rennie, talking with Clara, Ma, Linda, and Billy.

But then we turned the corner onto Knox Avenue. Greg was in the black car, parked in our driveway. Waiting for Rennie.

CHAPTER 5, DO VALENTINES HAVE HEARTS?

SATURDAY-SUNDAY, FEBRUARY 26-27, 1972

SATURDAY MORNING DID NOT FEEL like winter. A warm sun in a sky the color of Rennie's eyes when she is happy began melting the azure snow. Little bluish trickles ran across the sidewalk. Forty degrees actually felt tropical. The power of bigger than me, larger than you lifted me again. Last week seemed like a distant nightmare.

The black '52 Dodge dropped Rennie off and left immediately. Greg did not even kiss her goodbye? I hugged her, waltzed her around, singing, "We are goin' dancing tonight!" She sang my silly little song with me. It sorta felt like we melted into each other, bopping together almost perfectly. Only my snakes were in the way.

"Paavali, let's go inside for a bit 'cause wait 'til I show you this 'n' I bet it's going to help Russ sue the heck out of the *Patriot*, yes siree!"

I poured her coffee, added milk and sugar just the way she likes. On the kitchen table, she spread yesterday's *Minnesota Daily*, pointed. Right there on the front page was an article about the guy who groped her because the *Patriot* labeled her a whore.

An editorial inside called for the U to expel gropers. "This is a straightforward case of slander and sexual assault with eight eyewitnesses, both male and female. The university must send a loud and clear message to men. Keep your hands to yourself! There are no exceptions for football players. And an unsupported slur in an anonymous, sensationalist newsletter does *not* give you permission to assault the woman libeled. There is *never* an excuse for assault. Mr. Knight, who downplays but does not deny that he attacked Ms. Ahlberg, needs to learn beyond any doubt that sexual assault will not be tolerated at the U. He must be expelled. Period!"

I rubbed my chin. "That is definitely a dynamite editorial, but how will it help us sue the *Patriot*?"

"Holy buckets, it helps establish I was attacked because the *Patriot* smeared me."

It felt like a big-huge light bulb went on over my head. "Now I get it. Yah're gonna teach those dinks a lesson they will never forget!"

We headed for Carleton and Diane's house for breakfast, shocked to see the slowly melting snow had already turned the creek blue.

Rennie held my hand, gently swinging it back and forth as we walked. "This is such a big deal for our community 'n' stuff with Carleton hiring two full-time accountants for the General Grain account, yes siree! I love that we have a growing accounting firm here because it's a good thing for all of us, 'n' Ronan Flynn's getting a nice raise over what he made at Red Crow, 'n' Carleton's making sure Ronan has time to help with the Workers' Market committee, 'n' Louise Rivers will be able to help the Teen Council."

Even though it was a breakfast celebration for Carleton's new staffers, everyone was dressed in work clothes, even Burt. We drank a champagne toast to Ronan and Louise. Carleton and Diane piled our plates high and told us to eat hardy so we would have plenty of energy to get the ceiling installed at Workers' Market, which is where twelve of us, full of good food and good cheer, headed next.

The iron workers had finished installing a framework of steel beams overhead in Bucky Hall, so the market could have a lower, fourteen-foot ceiling and be easier to heat. They made it strong enough for a second floor above, which someday would be filled with small stores and businesses. Even though Workers' Market would be quite large, it filled only a small part of Bucky Hall, which extended from 49th Avenue down to 47th and from Knox to Thomas Avenues.

Harry signed us in, issued us hard hats, breathing masks, and gloves, made sure they fit properly, assigned us to work crews. The heating ducts, wiring, and light fixtures were already installed. Rennie and I measured and cut ceiling tiles while two other crews fitted them in, another put light

CHAPTER 5, DO VALENTINES HAVE HEARTS?

bulbs in. By lunchtime, half the store was brightly lit. Ceiling, shelves, and floor tiles in place, it looked almost ready to be stocked.

After a quick lunch, my family headed downtown for picket duty at the *Journette* building. There were only three picketers in front.

Rennie squeezed my hand. "This doesn't look good, as far as it goes."

"Dang! What a big-huge disappointment."

But the picketers were cheerful. "Out back is where it's happening, on Eleventh Avenue where the loading docks are," a tall woman said. "Many more of us back there. Could you head around the block because that's where we really need you."

The moment we turned the corner, we saw almost two dozen journalists and press operators. Georgia was talking with reporters from half a dozen news outlets, from *United Press International* to the *New York Times*. The picketers formed a line that blocked off the loading docks from the street, carrying signs that read, "Two-Fifty Minimum," "Locked Out!" "Scabs Go Home!" and "Let Reporters Write the Truth!"

Tom Hayes called out, "What do we want?"

The picketers answered, "To write the truth!"

"When do we want it?"

"Now!"

Then he started singing, "We Shall Overcome," and the picketers joined him.

Georgia hugged Rennie and me. "Tom and I learned how to be organizers by covering Shingle Creek. You taught us so much! Thanks for being here. I can't tell you what this means to us!"

We joined the line, sang, walked, chanted. Clarence and his family came down the block, picked up signs, walked with us. Then Blanche and Eugene Drass, Obie's family, Li'l Mikey's family, Willi Korhonen and four of his grandchildren. A semitruck turned the corner, stopped right near us.

"North Country Paper Company," Georgia said. "Here it comes, folks. Who's going with me?"

She got two volunteers, turned to us. "Karen, Paul, would you come too?"

We went to the truck. I noticed a small red heart painted on the door, thought that was weird. The driver looked down, held his head in his hands. When he looked up, we waved. Georgia motioned to him to roll down his window.

"Hi, I'm Georgia, a locked-out union reporter. How long were you on the road?"

"Twelve and a half hours." He shook his head.

"So we'd better help you out," Georgia said. "You need to eat and rest. And call your boss before you return your load, right?"

"Boss is gonna be mad as hell."

"What did you say your name was?" Georgia said.

"Cecil. Cecil Nilsen."

"So, Cecil, are you a union guy?"

"Been a member thirty-two years. Boss didn't tell me you're locked out."

"My two uncles are teamsters. You ever cross a picket line, Cecil?"

"My daddy would rise up from his grave and whup my butt if I did. But what do I do with my load while I rest? Can't leave it unsecured."

"How about two of us take you to dinner at a truck stop ten minutes away? They have decent sleeping rooms and secured truck parking too. Dinner's on us."

"You got class, Georgia. It's a deal!"

"We won't keep a hungry guy waiting more than five minutes. You'll follow a green Ford Falcon."

The five of us went back to the picket line, told them what happened. "Cecil! Cecil! Hooray!" the picketers cheered.

Cecil tooted the truck's air horn.

"How did ya think of that plan so fast?" I said.

"Spent four hours yesterday talking it through," Georgia said. "Well worth it!"

We picked up our signs, marched again. Cecil's truck followed Georgia's green car down the street and around the corner.

"Paavali, we need a plan like that 'n' especially if scab gandy dancers show up, so we get them working for us, not against us 'n' stuff, but I don't know how to do that so let's start thinking."

I kissed her cheek. "Yah're sure as heck right. And sure as heck smart! Marek told me about a yummy Lebanese restaurant right near the dance in Northeast. Just a couple of bucks for a meal. Wanna try it?"

CHAPTER 5, DO VALENTINES HAVE HEARTS?

My snakes went nuts. I punched them in the head. They did not bite as hard.

"Oh, yes siree! That would be far out, no halfway about it."

"Will ya wear yahr black dress?"

"Oh, will I ever!" She took my arm, wrapped hers around it.

At sunset, the ink delivery truck came rumbling down the street. The driver hopped out, flashed the V sign for Victory, asked what was going on. Tom Hayes talked with him. The guy accepted dinner.

"Listen up!" the driver called out to the crowd. "My boss will try to redeliver, maybe late at night. Your boss might get the cops here. And use a scab driver and thugs to force their way in. That's how it went down in Chicago. Keep your picket line strong! Don't let 'em catch you sleeping on the job!"

The truck rolled away, following Tom's blue Chevy.

"They don't have ink or newsprint enough to put out the full Sunday paper!" a press operator called out to the crowd. "And nothing for Monday. We did it! Now we have to keep it done!"

The picketers whooped and hollered, then sang and chanted even louder.

When my family got home, we activated six neighborhood calling trees, asking for volunteer picketers overnight. Then I put on my jacket, white shirt, tie. Rennie slipped on that magic dress and went from beautiful to stunning. My serpents woke up.

"Now you two go out and have fun!" Great-Grandma Clara said. "Don't even think about strikes and lawsuits tonight. There'll be plenty of time for that later."

When we entered the restaurant, Judge Haddad? Was sitting with two little girls and a man? She saw us, smiled, stood up. "Karen! Paul! What an honor to have you here. This is my husband, Farez."

He stood, shook hands.

"And my daughters, Sareena and Leyla. Welcome to my uncle and aunt's *aytri*, you would call it eatery in English. Do you know what to order?"

"Just a simple meal," I said. "But we do not know the names of Lebanese foods."

"May I order for you?"

"That would be ultra, yes it would!" Rennie said.

"We must get you a table. I will come by to chat later. Abila!" She called out.

A waitress came over to us. "This is my cousin Abila," Judge Haddad said, then spoke to her in Arabic.

Abila took our coats, seated us. Within minutes, she set some small bowls on the table. "This salad is *fattoush*, with crispy fried pita chips. The special flavor comes from sumac spice and fresh mint leaves." She pointed. "Spread this baba ganoush made from eggplant and sesame seeds on this fresh pita. Here is *tabouli*, cracked toasted wheat, garlic, more tomato and cucumber. These *warak enab* are grape leaves stuffed with spicy rice and chopped lamb, drizzled with lemon juice. These are just starters. I'll be back!"

We took tentative tastes. "Ya know, with all the new foods I have eaten recently, I thought I had tried every flavor in the world. But these are a whole new kind of yummy!"

"Holy buckets, I can't believe how good they taste 'n' they're light but really satisfying. What's your favorite, 'n' mine's the grape leaves, yes siree!"

"I have ta tell ya, it is the way the mint and sumac flavor the *fattoush*. I like the soft veggies and crunchy pita chips too. By the way, I have been thinking. We cannot just hire outsiders who are used to working for a bossman."

Rennie nodded, tapped the top of her head. "You mean we have to help them understand we're all working for our community 'n' what that signifies 'n' stuff? Otherwise, they'll be colliding with us all the time. And each other."

"Yup, how do we actually do that?"

"Bingo!" She stopped tapping. "Somewhat like how we teach leadership."

"So we use our leadership class as a starting point?"

"Yes siree, and figure out what needs to be added or taken away."

"How *will* we make our businesses big-huge different, aside from owning them?"

" 'Cause all our employees get the same wage, yes they do."

CHAPTER 5, DO VALENTINES HAVE HEARTS?

"But we do not do that now, Rennie. Russ gets more than Laura and Daniel. Judith gets even more."

"So maybe we have to pay more to college grads, as far as that goes."

"But what about a woman like Blanche? No college, but years of experience and on-the-job training, brings her own tools to work. Should she get less cash money than Judith? And what about union wages? They are all sorta different."

"Holy buckets, should Pete, with a large family to feed, get more than Russ, with no kids and a working wife, as far as that goes?"

"And what about this? Do we want our businesses to wham our community with stinks and fumes? Or flat out poison our streams, like the bug spray factory?"

Rennie looked upset. "Why didn't I think of all this before 'n' stuff?"

"None of us did. Ya know why? We did not have ta. But we do now!"

"We've got a lotta stuff to talk out, all of us, yes we do!"

Abila set three large bowls on our table. "Excuse me for interrupting your thoughtful conversation, but I brought you food for thought."

"Gosh, we can use plenty of that, so thank you," I said.

She pointed to a pile of grilled chicken chunks on skewers. "This *shish tawook* is soaked in yogurt, lemon juice, garlic, ginger, paprika, and tomato paste. And pardon us for serving you cheap peasant food, but this *mujadara* is so good! It's just lentils, rice, and golden-brown fried onions seasoned with cumin spice, mint, and cucumber yogurt sauce. During the thirties, when money was scarcer than purple eggs, my grandma fed an army of hungry relatives and friends with this one."

"That could come in handy when our railroad guys join the *Journette* reporters on the picket line and cash money is in short supply. Thanks, Abila! Is it hard to make?"

"The big job is chopping all those onions. Otherwise, it's just boiled rice, lentils, and spice. Easy as pie. Well, actually, pie is a lot harder!"

We spooned some *mujadara* onto our plates, sampled it.

"Whoa! That tastes glorious and ver-ry expensive, to the max!"

"Imagine bringing a huge pot of this to the picket line? Sure as heck would lift yahr spirits and warm yahr innards on a cold, windy day."

"The *shish tawook* is another surprise batch of flavors, 'n' we should probably invite people interested in jobs at Workers' Market to an orientation meeting, so they know what they're getting themselves into ahead of time 'n' then only hire and train people who are really interested in what we're doing, as far as that goes."

"Hot dog! How about a dinner meeting with *mujadara*, all ya can eat!"

We chatted and ate, laughed and joked, and as usual with Rennie, discussed a whole lot of interesting and important ideas. I wished I was not distracted by having to whack my serpents every time they bit or hissed, but at least I could control them a little bit so I could enjoy Rennie's company more than usual.

When our plates were empty, Abila brought dessert. "This is *jazarieh*, caramelized pumpkin bites with pine nuts and cardamom spice. These small squares are *nammoura*, semolina wheat cakes drowned in sugar, rose water, and mahlab spice. And these little *ma'amoul* semolina cookies, stuffed with dates or pistachios and sugar, are much richer than they look! Would you like cardamom coffee or sweet and sour apple tea?"

"Coffee, please," I said.

"Paavali, if I have the tea, can I taste your coffee?"

"Do valentines have hearts?"

"So it's tea for me and a coffee taste or two!"

Judge Haddad came to our table. "May I join you?"

"Of course, Yahr Honor!"

"Here in our family's *aytri*, we can be informal. So please call me Badah, and may I call you Karen and Paul?"

"Sure enough 'n' that would be an honor, right, Paulie-Paul?"

"A big-huge one!"

"I have been reading *People's Free Press* and listening to KPFP," Badah said. "I am just so impressed with what your community is working toward. How are you managing to get all that done? What secret did you use to persuade Judge Woodruff to ask me and Judge Jeppesen to work with him on the press conference?"

"We suggested he find common ground with ya because that would make all of ya stronger. Just sorta planted the seed and let it grow on its own."

When we told Badah we were going dancing at Lowry Park, she asked why there.

"We've been helping them organize, so we feel at home there, yes siree, 'n' they have a good deejay 'n' we love to dance 'n' Shingle Creek doesn't have a dance space, especially now that the schools won't let us use their gyms anymore 'cause they say we're communists, which is news to us."

"Also, we need to hire employees for our new Workers' Market. We know there are unemployed youth there who could use solid union jobs."

"Why not recruit from Shingle Creek?" Badah said.

"Nobody else is available 'cause we put them all to work, 'n' even people with full-time jobs are working on their time off as volunteers 'n' stuff."

"So you created jobs for everyone in Shingle Creek who needs them? And now you're creating jobs for other neighborhoods?"

"Holy cowbops! I sure as heck never thought about it that way."

"Me either, but when you say it like that, I realize it's way more impressive than I ever thought, to the max."

We talked and talked through three cups of coffee and tea and seconds of dessert, about our hopes and dreams and her family's history in Minneapolis. When it was time to leave, she said we were absolutely fascinating and refused to let us pay for our dinner. Abila brought our coats and handed us a package.

"For my favorite hungry teenagers," Badah said. "A little snack for after your dance. See you Monday morning at Club Nicollet!"

As Rennie and I skipped to the car holding hands, I sang, "She gave us wings, now we can fly, cannot stop doin' it even if we try, we are way up there on cloud nine, feeling so good, feeling so fine!" And she sang with me.

The dance floor at Lowry Park Recreation Center was crowded with older teens and young adults bopping to music from a deejay. A lot of people knew Rennie from her organizing visits up there, and some knew me from *Shingle Creek Sagas*.

The deejay put on a slow dance. I held Rennie close. My snakes hissed and bit. I punched their heads, which subdued them a little. But they still managed to divide my attention. And I did not get an erection despite how gorgeous she looked. The little statue of my mother was on my shoulder laughing at me. I knocked it off, heard it hit the floor and bounce.

At least I am out dancing with Rennie. And enjoying myself. Watch yahr asses, snakes! I am comin' for ya, one step at a time!

Next dance was "I'm Lost, I'm Lost." I started singing along. She did too.

"Paavali, how do you know this one?"

"From Boogie Barn. I went there to try to find myself but just felt more lost."

"Without me?"

I pursed my lips, nodded. "Lost without you."

"Dance me, Paavali, up, over, and around!"

I swirled and dipped her, lifted her over my head, stepped left, stepped right, set her down, twirled her around, invented three new moves. Her cheeks, usually rosy, were positively glowing, her grin so wide it must have been tickling her earlobes.

A circle formed around us, watching, clapping their hands. As the song faded out, the deejay said, "It's that dancing duo from Shingle Creek, Karen and Paul, just in from an afternoon on the *Journette* picket line! Let's give them another fast dance folks, see what moves they'll come up with next!"

"That must've been Marek told him to say that, yes siree, Bob!"

Next song started, I picked up on the beat, did a step dance all around Rennie, then a whole new routine. I still do not know how I invented so many moves, but the crowd was cheering, Rennie was beaming, my mind was in high gear, and I was having a great time, snakes or no.

At the end of the song, the deejay said, "Support the *Journette* strikers. Cancel your subs! Better news and more coupons in *People's Free Press*!"

Dancing fast or slow, fancy or plain, it just feels so good to be with Rennie. I must solve my problem somehow or other. I deserve her, snakes! No matter what ya say. More than Greg does, because I am better for her. She told me so. I have ta talk with her tonight. I just have ta!

After the dance, the moment we got down to my room, Rennie said, "Hold me, Paavali! Kiss me!" So I did. Arms around me, still kissing me, she led me to our bed, step by step, eased me down on top of her. Even though the pain from my snakes was severe, despite my slamming them in the head, I loved kissing her.

When I licked her face, I tasted her tears.

CHAPTER 5, DO VALENTINES HAVE HEARTS?

"I love you Paavali. I love you so much."

I could not tell her I loved her too. But I held her tight, even in my sleep.

Sunday morning, there was no *Journal* on the doorstep, just the *People's Free Press* and a note from Sheila saying the truck did not bring *Journals* to her today. Then we got a call from Georgia. With help from dozens of people from all over Minneapolis overnight, the picketers kept delivery trucks from picking up newspapers. A few scabs crossed the line to walk small bundles of papers to their cars, but it was hundreds of copies, not tens of thousands.

Georgia also told us Cecil delivered the load of paper to an independent warehouse on North 2nd Street and suggested we offer to buy it all at a discount from North Country Paper Company.

Burt arrived for breakfast at 7:30, kissed Clara, spread the *Journal* on the kitchen table. Only one section, just eighteen pages, more than half of it ads, no local news. The news articles were rewrites of wire service stories, full of typos. *People's Free Press* had thirty-six pages in two sections. Burt said, "I had to drive all over downtown to find a copy, but witness the dying corpse of the *Journal*! Now is the time to go head-to-head, push hard, and try to put the *Journal* and *Gazette* out of business!" He banged his fist on the table.

"Is that fair?" Linda said.

"Holy buckets, Linda, that's what the bosses did with newspapers, mills, banks, railroads, you name it," Rennie said. "Ask the *Journette* what happened to the *Minnesota Telegram*. Or the *Minneapolis World*. So if they can do it, why can't we 'n' don't they say competition is a good thing? So, Burt, what's your plan 'n' stuff?"

Burt smiled. "One, pay for wire services so we can cover national and world news. Two, hire locked-out journalists at two-fifty an hour. Three, find a couple more ad sales people and go after every company that advertised in the *Journette*. And those that didn't too. Four, try to recruit the *Journette's* delivery kids by offering them more money. That means raising the pay for kids we already have signed on. Yes, I know, how will we pay for it? I made some phone calls. I have eight small businesses and three large ones who have pledged a quarter-of-a-million bucks total to make it happen."

"Nice going! But is that enough to pull this off?" Ma said.

"No," Burt said. "I'll pick up the rest. Assuming the Teen Council and Neighborhood Association approve."

Clara hugged Burt, kissed his cheek. "Burtie, you sure you have enough cash to do this, sweetie?"

Burt blushed. "I saw this coming. Went over it with Carleton. It is not a problem for me. I'll still be filthy rich, which is a situation harder to get out of than I ever imagined. The damned interest income alone is still four hundred thousand a year. Besides, it's *not* my money. It came from the sweat and toil of my father's workers and ought to be returned to its rightful owners."

The phone rang. Todd Flynn wanted to know why there was no Sunday *Journal*. Susie called with the same question. When I said we had a copy, they came by to see it.

"Did you know there's a grazy car parked outside?" Todd said.

"We have our jammers on, yes we do," Rennie said.

We briefed Todd and Susie on the picket line but asked them not to cover Burt's proposal until we were ready to announce it.

"What about Georgia?" Susie said. "Can we hire her yet?"

"But she should be on the picket line," Rennie said.

"Why don't you hire her and make that her beat for now?" Todd said.

"That is brilliant!" Burt said.

"But I need her here, working with me," Susie said.

"Can she do both?" I said.

"Let's ask her," Clara said. "Yah?"

"Okay, we will get going on that," I said.

"Can I move to another topic?" Todd said.

"Sure. What's up?" Linda said.

He turned on his tape recorder, opened his briefcase, took out a gizmo with an antenna, meters, a speaker. "Everybody, turn off your jammers and talk about the weather. When I wave my hand, turn your jammers back on. I'm aiming this at the grazy car. Listen!"

"Finally, we can hear them talking," a grazy voice said. "What? About the damned weather? Must be a hidden meaning there, but I don't see it."

Todd waved his hand.

"Shit! There's that static again. What're we going to say in our report?"

CHAPTER 5, DO VALENTINES HAVE HEARTS?

"We'll just use some stuff from the *Minnesota Patriot* and claim those red creek rats are saying it. Nobody will know."

Todd turned his recorder off. "I got their license plate number on the way in."

"Holy moly! How do we keep them from doing that?" Ma said.

"We'll play the tape on KPFP tonight," Todd said. "Suze, can you do a story?"

"Check! Bases covered," Susie said.

"Can we make those grazies leave?" Clara said. "They give me the willies."

We went outside, cameras ready, surrounded the car, took the grazies' pictures. Ma, Clara, Susie, Linda, and Rennie kulned, "Tomorrow's predicted storm is here today! Prudent travelers must now be on their way!"

The grazies covered their ears, started their car. We jumped to the sidewalk when they gunned the engine, tires screeching as they raced away. We stood there, laughing our heads off.

The yellow Chevelle turned the corner, parked. Duane Pukari jumped out, went house to house putting a copy of *Minnesota Patriot* in each mail slot.

"Let's get photos of him doing that," Todd said. "It's illegal. We'll get the Post Office to nail *Minnesota Patriot* with a huge postage bill!"

Each of us walked toward a different house. He did not notice Susie, Todd, Linda, and Ma taking photos.

But he saw me and Rennie. "Why the hell you taking photos, bitch?"

Todd ran over, tape recorder on.

"We know what you did, Duane!" Rennie said. "No. Not this. Something much worse. Better get your affairs in order!"

"I'm gonna put your legs around your head," Duane said. "Give me that camera!"

Rennie put it in her pocket.

"Little Duane is about to get himself hurt again!" I said.

Duane grabbed Rennie's left arm. She hit him so hard, the buttons popped off his coat. He landed on his back in a blue snow bank, out cold. We stood there with him, making sure he came to. His eyes fluttered open, he stood up, cursed, tottered back to his car, and drove off.

"Let's get statements from people who got the *Minnesota Patriot* in their mail slot today," Todd said. "It's going to cost the *Patriot* big-time."

"Whoa, look at this!" Rennie said, pointing to the ground. "The buttons from Duane's coat! Anyone want a souvenir?"

"Me!" I said. "For the Working People's Museum. To go with our photos."

"You got 'em," Todd said as he took the *Patriot* from our mailbox, opened it, laughed.

"What's so funny?" Susie said.

He was guffawing too hard to talk, just pointed to the headline. "Paul Mäkinen and Karen Ahlberg admit in Confidential Memo: Camden Yard Gandy Dancers Will Never Strike."

Rennie and I busted out laughing.

"C'mon! Bring me up to speed," Susie said.

"We sent the Communal Association that memo as an anonymous friend," Rennie said. "To throw them off."

We had already lost our heads laughing, so this time we laughed our asses off.

"Two laughing fits in less than fifteen minutes! I haven't had so much fun in a long time," Burt said. "Shall we go meet with the auditorium planning crew?"

We walked to Betty & Bucky's Repair Shop, sat down in their meeting room with Blanche, Harry, Dozer, Laura, Betty, Bucky, and a man I did not know.

Burt shook hands with him. "Clifford Ruona, an architect, volunteered to help us figure out an overall plan for the auditorium. He will save us a lot of time and energy."

"Before anyone says anything, I want to thank Blanche for volunteering to be the auditorium forewoman," Harry said. "We are in the best hands possible!"

We gave her a round of applause.

Clifford stood up. "Blanche and I looked at the space yesterday. First off, it's beautiful! You will have an amazing auditorium. Build it at the south end of Betty Hall, away from your clinic and offices, to leave them room for growth. Also, those huge doorways where the steam engines used to drive into the building? You can turn them into a dramatic entryway to

CHAPTER 5, DO VALENTINES HAVE HEARTS?

your lobby, looking better than any Broadway theater." He showed us a quick sketch.

"That looks great!" Harry said.

"Next, how about a stage surrounded with, say, five rows of seats on three sides, total five hundred and ten seats. Is that enough?"

"Based on our last two meetings, no siree 'n' I think we need seven hundred," Rennie said.

"We can leave space for more plank-and-cement block benches if you need them later," Cliff said. He made a diagram on the chalk board. "There's enough room to build the temporary hall here"—he pointed—"and the auditorium next to it later. That way you can continue to meet while the auditorium is being built."

"Gol! Makes sense to me," Laura said.

"So we end up some day," Blanche said, "with the auditorium all the way at the south end and all the unused space in between for future community offices? Will they ever fill that space?"

"*People's Free Press* is about to grow big-huge," I said. "And we need space for the Working Class Museum. So the question may be do we actually have *enough* space?"

"You are such an optimist, Paulie!" Dozer said. "Thank goodness."

We went back and forth with Cliff for more than an hour. He showed us how to make the temporary meeting hall comply with building codes. How to install the furnace. Where to bring in the gas main and electric service so everything would work for the temporary meeting hall and then the auditorium later. And how to cut emergency exits into the brick walls without weakening them. From there, we worked out a detailed plan, from clearing out the space to fastening the bench planks to cement blocks.

"I think we're ready to roll," Blanche said. "We have 'bout forty-five minutes before volunteers start arriving."

"Did the floodlights, forklifts, pallets, tools, and portable toilets I rented arrive yesterday?" Burt said.

"All here," Blanche said.

"Should we go set them up?" Harry said. "All in favor?"

We marched to Betty Hall, opened the door to the unused part. I had not realized we had such a big-huge stock of lumber, cement blocks, bricks, steel beams, hardware.

"Let's map out the meeting hall area," Clifford said.

We measured, sprayed lines on the floor with bright orange paint. MH for meeting hall and ST for storage.

"Now we know exactly where we need to clear and where to stack stuff," Blanche said. "Who can make ten sawhorses for workstations?"

Rennie and I raised our hands.

"Paul, Karen, you're on!"

"Who can cut eight-foot lengths of two-by-six planks to put on top of the sawhorses? We need five tops, three feet wide. Laura, Dozer, you got it! Who can plan how to stack stuff now in the storage area to make empty space for the stuff we're moving from the meeting hall space? Betty, Bucky, it's yours!"

Within minutes, Blanche had us all working. She darted from place to place, making and taking suggestions, answering questions, helping out.

A couple of dozen volunteers arrived. Blanche got them all going. The room hummed with power tools and forklifts. By late afternoon, we had cleared half of the meeting hall space. Crews were cutting planks, making benches, building the stage.

Hot dog! We are actually getting this done!

At six o'clock, Blanche blew a whistle, and we all stopped working. She called out, "We got two day's work done today. Thanks, everyone. You done good! Go home and enjoy your dinner."

Clarence came over to us. "Welcome to the Ray Iversen Concert Hall!" He closed his eyes. "Can you see it?"

"You bet!" I said.

"Yes siree!" Rennie said.

"We have ta vote on it," I said. "But I sure as heck think that name will stick!"

CHAPTER 6, DO LIONS HAVE TEETH?

MONDAY, FEBRUARY 28, 1972

MONDAY MORNING WAS UNSEASONABLY WARM again, and the blue snow kept melting. There was no *Journal* delivered. But *People's Free Press* had a front-page photo of Cecil's truck stopped on Eleventh Avenue, with the picketers in the foreground. Next to it was a photo of the grazies with the headline, "FBI Agents Admit Reporting Phony Shingle Creek Info."

Linda, Billy, Susie, and I headed to Club Nicollet for the judges' press conference. Judge Woodruff, face tight, was pacing in circles in front of the stage. He relaxed when he saw us.

All three judges spoke. More reporters from more newspapers and wire services asked more questions than usual. For the first time ever, we had reporters from the Duluth, St. Paul, Chicago, and Milwaukee dailies.

Susie asked the judges several questions. When the press conference was over, four reporters who had heard about *People's Free Press* wanted to interview her. She explained she had a breaking story to cover in federal court so she set up a group interview with them in the Teen Council conference room for late afternoon.

We met Jack and Obie in front of the federal courthouse. Clarence was already inside, with Kurt holding his hand, Tess and her mom next to them. Russ came a moment later with Lois Gustaffson and Brucie.

The jury entered, sat down.

"Please rise for Judge Niemi!" the court officer called out.

The judge called the court to order. Russ summarized our case.

The railroad's attorney said, "There is no case. Ray Iversen and Arne Gustaffson agreed, in writing, that they worked for Minnesota Consolidated Construction Services, which is not a railroad and therefore they are not covered by the *Federal* Employers' Liability Act. I petition this court to dismiss this frivolity and award my client damages in the amount of fifty-thousand dollars to—"

Judge Niemi banged his gavel. "Counselor! This court has already established that these men were doing railroad work and that your client must follow the law as it was written, not as they wished it was. The sole purpose of this trial is to examine the details of what happened to determine if the Arne Gustaffson and Raymond Iversen families are due benefits and if so how much. Is that clear?"

"Your Honor, you must recuse yourself from this case," the railroad's lawyer said. "It is impossible for you to be impartial."

"And why might that be, Counselor?" the judge said.

"Your grandfather, Tuovikka Niemi, was killed in a rail yard accident and—"

Judge Niemi banged his gavel. "May I remind you, Counselor, the decision to hold your client culpable was made by the jury, not me, and any benefits due will be determined by the jury, not me. Furthermore, the allegation that Mr. Gustaffson and Mr. Iversen agreed that they were employees of Minnesota Consolidated Construction Services was already proven false in this court. You are painfully close to being held in contempt. Please call your first witness, Mr. Linwood-Flink."

"I call Clarence Björk."

Clarence sat down in the witness chair.

"Mr. Björk, what were you doing when Mr. Iversen was killed?"

"Repairing track six in Camden Yard."

"Where was Mr. Iversen?"

"Ray was putting in a missing fish bolt on track eight."

"Mr. Iversen was working alone?"

"Yes, sir."

"Was that a violation of railroad safety rules?"

"Yes, sir!"

"Why didn't you try to stop it?"

CHAPTER 6, DO LIONS HAVE TEETH?

"We objected, but the foreman said, 'Do it now or you're—'"

"Objection!" the railroad's lawyer shouted.

"Objection overruled," Judge Niemi said.

"Fired!" Clarence said. "Foreman threatened to fire Ray and us."

"But aren't you allowed to walk off the job when there's a safety violation?"

"No, sir. The union's contract has a no-strike clause."

"Your union?"

"No, sir! The union we had to join when the construction company hired us."

"What kind of land was Camden Yard built on?" Russ said.

"Objection!"

"Overruled!"

"Swamp land. The tracks are always settling."

"Gradually?" Russ said.

"Sometimes. And sometimes suddenly."

"How do you keep the tracks stable?"

"Lots of new ballast rock, all the time."

"Objection! There is a limit to how much ballast tracks need, and—"

"Overruled."

"Did the crew you work on repair track eleven?"

"Yes, sir, a few months before."

"Did you bring it up to the railroad's standards?"

"No, sir. We were short two carloads of ballast."

"According to who, Mr. Björk?"

"A *Railway Maintenance Journal* article, 'Ballast Standards for Swamp Land.'"

"Where did you get that article?"

"Railroad gave it to us when they trained us."

"Did you use any parts to fix that track?"

"Yes, sir. Used ones from an abandoned railroad in Mankato. Parts were in awful shape. We knew something bad would happen. Foreman, Yard Boss, wouldn't listen."

"What was next to track eight where Mr. Iversen was working?" Russ said.

"Track nine was empty. So was ten. Track eleven had eighteen hopper cars loaded with grain, just sitting there."

"What happened next, Mr. Björk?"

"Those hoppers were standing stock still but track eleven just gave way. The hoppers tilted, derailed, jutted out into track ten's right of way."

"Then what happened?" Russ said.

"Four tankers of corn syrup came rolling fast down track ten."

"Is that normal for a rail yard?" Russ said.

"Yes, sir. It's how we sort railcars into trains. The yard is flat. You need a certain amount of speed to get the cars fully onto the sorting tracks."

"And then?" Russ said.

Clarence sat up really straight. "Tankers hit the derailed hoppers." His voice broke. "Landed on tracks nine and eight. Ray never saw what hit him." Tears ran down Clarence's face.

A piercing wail filled the court room.

"I apologize, Your Honor," Russ said. "That's Ray Iversen's nine-year-old daughter crying."

Judge Niemi banged the gavel. His face was tight. "Ten-minute recess. Miss Iversen, please approach the bench."

Tess came forward, clinging to her mother's arm.

"I know this is hard for you, Miss Iversen. Please be strong. We're here to get at the truth. You are part of that. Okay?"

"Yes, sir, Your Honor."

When the court reconvened, the judge said. "Does the defendant's attorney wish to cross-examine?"

"Yes, Your Honor. Mr. Björk, you weren't smart enough or skilled enough to get more than an unskilled, minimum wage job?"

Clarence laughed. "Could *you* line up track to a half-inch tolerance with proper cant, warp, and gradient using hand tools? In snow, wind, rain, cold?" He paused. "No? Then don't call me unskilled. When I started this job, before the railroad busted our real union, I was well paid. And by the way, I enjoy this work and it hurts my pride when the foreman won't let me do it right. Sir!"

The way Clarence said "Sir!" made it sound like a curse.

CHAPTER 6, DO LIONS HAVE TEETH?

The railroad's attorney looked angrier. "It was a cold, windy day when Mr. Iversen died. Mr. Björk, how much booze did you and Mr. Iversen drink to keep warm?"

"May be difficult for a suit like you to imagine, but the hard work we do heats us up. Sometimes, even on a cold day, we have to take off our jackets to keep from getting overheated. We never drink on a workday. If someone did, it would put all of us in danger. We would make them go home. Sir!"

The attorney went on and on, trying to make Clarence and Ray look bad. Clarence kept turning the tables on him. Russ had coached him well.

Russ called Jack Langacker next, had him explain what happened when Arne died. He had Tess describe how her father's death devastated her family. The railroad's lawyer made her cry again, telling lies about her dad and making her deny them. Then Russ called Brucie to testify. Lois sat beside her son, holding his hand.

"Objection! The child's mother is coaching him," the railroad's lawyer said.

"Overruled! She didn't say a word, Counselor."

Russ put his hand on Brucie's shoulder. "How old are you, Bruce?"

"I'm six now."

"Do you miss your dad?"

"I hear him calling me sometimes, when the wind is strong. From up in heaven. 'Brucie, Brucie, here I am. Come find me!'"

"What do you do then?"

"I skate fast back and forth across the ice, looking everywhere for him. But I can never find him."

"Do you get cold?"

"So cold my feet hurt. But I have to find him! I want my daddy!" Brucie was sobbing, shaking. Lois picked him up, held him, cried with him.

"Ten-minute adjournment," Judge Niemi said. He headed to his chambers, dabbing at his face with a handkerchief.

After the break, the railroad's lawyer said, "I want to cross-examine the kid."

There was a gasp in the courtroom.

"You. Are. Over. Ruled!" the judge thundered. "It would serve no judicial purpose whatsoever." He gave the jury instructions and asked if they had any questions.

"It seems pretty straightforward to me," the jury forewoman said.

The lawyer for the railroad stalked out of the courtroom.

Judge Niemi walked over to Brucie, knelt in front of him. "You are very brave, Mr. Gustaffson. What you said was important. Thank you."

Brucie stopped crying. Tried to smile.

On the way back to Shingle Creek, we stopped at the Park Board office. Lucy, The Nines, and a bunch of Nines parents were picketing to demand Shingle Creek staff be rehired. A crowd of reporters were there. Lucy had helped the kids write statements. Bonnie, Bobby, Terri, and Charlie read theirs. Reporters took notes, shot photos.

Back at the office, Pam Hakkala came running right up to us. "Suze, Paulie, Linda, Billy, help! The phone won't stop ringing. Me and the volunteers are taking orders for ads as fast as we can type. Full-pagers! Everyone wants to be in! They're saying coupon redemption from our paper is three times normal. Our ad revenue is way ahead of what we expected, so the foundation money will last longer. We need to plan. Carleton, Burt, and Betty are on the way. Ma ordered sandwiches for everyone from Camden Superette. Carleton's bringing dessert."

"How much newsprint do we have?" I said.

"Not enough," Susie said.

"I think we can buy that truckload the picketers turned away from the *Journette*," I said. "Ya good with that?"

"Let's check with Dad," Susie said.

Pete okayed it, so I ran down to the auditorium worksite, asked Blanche if they could clear an area near the doors for paper storage. Worked out with her how to do it. Ran back upstairs. Burt had arrived, said he would order it. We went into my office, phoned, and Burt bargained them down to twenty-five percent off the wholesale price, arranged to wire the money to North Country Paper Company's Bank.

In the conference room, everyone was talking at once. I held up both hands. "Friends, we got the paper coming today. What about ink?"

"That's easier to get," Pete said. "We have enough for a couple days, but we'll need a ton of it. Better start planning now."

CHAPTER 6, DO LIONS HAVE TEETH?

We set up a planning system for the number of ad and editorial pages we could have in each issue. Another for forecasting paper and ink needs. A third for setting up accounts for advertisers. Decided to hire Georgia and Tom as co-managing editors with Susie. The three of them would hire *Journette* reporters.

Two hours later when Susie saw everything was under control, she dashed into the pressroom, banged out stories on today's court hearing and the Park Board picket line, and finished just in time for her group press interview.

As I walked back to my office, Ma said to me, "Paulie, the owner of Camden Superette is furious. He thinks our Workers' Market will put him out of business. Can you talk with him?"

"I sure as heck can. Maybe we can offer him a free ad in *People's Free Press*. Am I on the right track?"

"You're on the beam. He *should* be our friend."

I stopped in Joanna's office, gave her the buttons from Duane Pukari's coat to archive for the museum and the attendee list from the judges' press conference. "Can ya have a press clippings binder ready Thursday, even if we have ta add to it later?"

"How many copies?"

"One for our library, three for the judges?"

"No problem, Paulie!"

At the back of the Teen Council Meeting Hall, a cluster of giggling Nines girls huddled in a circle, bent forward, cheek-to-cheek, whispering.

"Jeffie's so-oh cute in those glasses!" Bonnie said.

"We should keep telling him. All of us!" Terri said.

"Especially now, 'cause he's still hurting real bad about his big brother dying," Jeanette said.

"Let's do a be-nice gang up on him," Mamie said. " 'Cause he's so-o cool!"

"What's that?" Terri said.

"We all say and do extra-nice things for him," Bonnie said. "One thing after another. We did that to Walt when his parents were bad to him."

"Did you do that to me?" Terri said.

"Yep, when you came to live with my family, all of us sisters did," Bonnie said.

"And we did it to you at school too," Tess said. "But right now, Jeffie needs us."

"It really does feel wonderful when your friends do that," Terri said.

"That's what true, real friendship forever *is*," Mamie said.

"It's 'Love thy neighbor!' in real life," Ruthie said. "Girls *and* boys!"

"I'm gonna kiss Jeffie. On the cheek," Jeanette said. "I have a crush on him."

"We all do," Ruthie said. "But not as much as you!" She looked up, saw me. "Oh-oh, Paulie heard us."

They started giggling again.

"I will keep yahr secret," I said. *Nine-year-olds. Invented to make adults joyful.*

Each carrying a box, Daniel, Kurt, and Charlie came into the room, set them down on the table next to the girls. "We got them!" Daniel said. "Your permanent records from the school. Tomorrow, we can tear up all of Mrs. Elak's nasty comments." He took off his coat. "Did you hear about the writer who combined calligraphy with choreography and made the words dance on the page?" The kids laughed. "Don't worry, Paulie, I taught all the kids those words when we studied the -graphy word root."

I put my arm around his shoulders. "Dang! It is nice to have ya as a friend."

"Oh, man! You're something else, Paulie. Like Keanna says, *you dance people to a better place!*"

Back in my office, I called Carleton for advice about Camden Superette, then drove over there. Archie Pfeiffer, the owner was fighting mad.

"You're going to put me out of business with your so-called Workers' Market. Forty years of sweat and toil you're flushing down the drain. What the heck am I supposed to do?"

"Archie, man, we do not want to lose Camden Superette. I love yahr sandwiches, had two for lunch. I have no idea what spices ya put in that tuna salad, but there is nothing like it anywhere else. That is why we decided not to sell sandwiches at Workers' Market. But we want to go further than that. Ya familiar with *People's Free Press*?"

"Pretty good newspaper. Why?"

CHAPTER 6, DO LIONS HAVE TEETH?

"We want to offer ya a free, full-page ad, three days in a row, the week we open Workers' Market."

"That's *your* newspaper?"

"It belongs to the Shingle Creek community. *You* belong to the Shingle Creek community too. We are trying to make us *all* stronger and *People's Free Press* is a tool for doing that."

"What's the catch? I have to buy more ads to get the free one?"

"No dice. All ya have ta do is run at least one coupon in each ad. Could be cents-off, could be buy one, get one free, could be on sandwiches, or anything else."

"Why do I have to do that?"

"So ya can measure how much money the ads made for ya."

"That's a really clever idea!"

"Archie, who do ya buy yahr groceries from?"

"Dowling Wholesale Grocers over on North 2nd Street."

"Suppose ya could get yahr groceries at almost the same price we do."

"Not possible. I don't buy big quantities."

"Well, what if we bought for ya and added a small markup to cover our costs."

"I'd have to see figures, but why would you do that?"

"If we buy for a bunch of corner stores, we can order larger quantities, get better discounts. *You* could cut yahr prices but make more profit. So could we. If yah're interested, we can get ya facts and figures."

"Probably am. I have to think on it. All of it."

I handed him my card. "Call me if ya have questions. We can help each other!" I put three packages of cookies on the counter. "Meanwhile, I need to buy these cookies for my next meeting."

As I was driving on 49th Avenue, I saw Rennie walking from the bus stop, beeped my horn, pulled over. She hopped in. I felt a wave of joy go from my nose to my toes and started talking a hundred miles an hour about everything that just happened.

"Wow, Paavali! What an afternoon. Things are really going fast, yes siree."

When we walked into the clinic reception area, Denise said, "Blanche needs you in the auditorium, like now!"

There was a semitruck backed up at one of the big, arched doorways. Cecil stood against it, smoking a cigarette.

"I have paper here for you. Congratulations! Can I see that newspaper of yours?"

"You bet! But first things first. Do ya need the restroom? Are ya hungry?"

"Yes, on both, but who's going to unload?"

"We can," Blanche said. "We have forklifts."

"C'mon, follow us," I said.

We took him to the Teen Council offices, pointed him to the restroom. I got the last two sandwiches left over from lunch out of the refrigerator, added cookies, poured a cup of coffee. He read the *People's Free Press* while he ate.

"You know, this is a really great newspaper! I do a regular delivery run for the boss three days a week, bringing food and supplies to restaurants and diners along US 10 from Becker to Detroit Lakes. Could I distribute papers for you up there?"

"Sure, Cecil, we can work something out. We will bring it up at tonight's meeting. Can we get yahr phone number?"

He handed me an ace of hearts. "Turn it over."

It had his name, address, and phone number on the back.

"My son had these printed for me. I love them, but I don't play cards myself. You know, the story you got from that eighty-three-year-old guy about the 1913 ore dock strike up in Duluth? That's great stuff."

"We collected dozens of stories like that from all over Minnesota, 'n' we're still going out and getting more so we can run them in the *Free Press* twice a week."

The phone rang. "Truck's unloaded," Blanche said.

"That's great," Cecil said. "Have to go pick up my load for tomorrow's run for the Route 10 diners. I'll hit the road at six in the a.m. Thanks for unloading me. Now I'll make it home in time for my daughter's twenty-sixth birthday party for sure."

"All right then, here's a batch of today's *People's Free Press*, 'n' you can give them out to your diner owners, yes siree. We'll get back to you on what we can do as a regular thing, as far as that goes."

We walked him through the maze of Betty Hall to his truck, watched him back out and turn, looked at each other.

"Gee! Betty Hall is definitely the wrong place for the pressroom," I said.

"Holy buckets, with the parking lot full of cars for a meeting, there'd be no space for a truck to maneuver in and out, for sure."

"Aha! Getting those rolls of paper over to the pressroom is sorta a tall order too. We gotta do that late at night. They have ta be carted right by the clinic. We shoulda put the pressroom in Olson Hall where we plan to have industries. Dang!" I punched my palm with my fist.

She grabbed me, held me close. "Are you blaming yourself, as far as that goes?"

"I shoulda known better and—"

She squeezed me tighter. "Paavali! We didn't know *People's Free Press* would go big-time so fast, 'n' if this is the worst mistake we make, we shouldn't be putting ourselves down, no halfway about it. We'll make it work for now, but plan ahead to the max, 'n' anyway, our pressroom isn't big enough for what's about to happen either."

"Ya think we are gonna need all five presses in one room? And more darkrooms and typewriters, to be in tip-top shape?"

Rennie smiled. "Before we go aggravating ourselves, let's ask Susie and Georgia what the *Journette* does 'n' stuff, because it probably does that part right 'n' if it doesn't, they'll know what mistakes we should avoid, 'n' so will the pressmen, 'n' we can talk with them next time we're picketing. We can ask Clifford the architect to help us too."

"Phew! Yah're right. How about we change the channel and get ourselves to the Safety Commission meeting?"

She clasped her hands together, raised them high and said, "All hands on deck!"

Rennie, Russ, and I went out to the parking lot. Officer James and Officer Anderson were standing by their squad car.

"Lieutenant said there could be trouble for the Commission at the yard," Officer James said. "Can you brief us further?"

Russ took a wood post with a red "Condemned" sign on it from his car. "We'll order Yard Boss to take eighteen unsafe stretches of track out of service. We'll post these signs. Pretty straightforward, but Yard Boss won't be happy."

"Do you have an official Commission Order?" Officer Anderson said.

"Do lions have teeth?" Russ pulled a white envelope from his pocket.

Officer Anderson laughed, read the order, handed it back to Russ. "Between you and me, my uncle's a gandy dancer over in St. Paul. This is pretty awesome! We'll follow you over to the yard."

A blue '62 Chevy bounced into the parking lot. Tom Hayes jumped out. "Susie called me, said there's a big story breaking at Camden Yard. Am I too late?"

"C'mon with us, Tom," I said. "We will brief ya on the way."

We jumped in my car, drove into Camden Yard, parked beside the old boxcar that served as a crew shack. Clarence, Obie, Jack, and four commissioners from Northeast sat on a bench, waiting for us.

"Great! We have a quorum," Clarence said. "I call this meeting to order. Russ, you have the Commission Order, plus all copies filed properly?"

"Do beavers build dams?"

"First item of business," Obie said, "We serve Yard Boss with our order."

"We're coming with you," Officer James said.

"Karen! Will you be spokesperson?" Clarence said. "That'll really throw Yard Boss off! I'll clue you in on what you have to say."

He and Rennie talked for a minute.

"Got it!" Rennie said. "And I won't say yes siree or all right then!"

We marched over to the yard office, opened the door, stepped inside. I turned my tape recorder on. Russ got his camera out.

"What the hell is this?" Yard Boss said.

"North-Northeast Minneapolis Industrial Safety Commission," Rennie said with her ten-foot-tall voice. "Our commissioners have found eighteen stretches of track, including two switches, that do not meet railroad or federal safety standards. We hereby order you to take them out of service until they are brought back into compliance. There is a fine of—"

"Hank! Call the cops!" Yard Boss yelled to his assistant.

Officers James and Anderson stepped forward from behind the group. "We *are* the cops! You had best listen to what Commissioner Ahlberg tells

CHAPTER 6, DO LIONS HAVE TEETH?

you. The Commission is chartered by the State of Minnesota and has legal authority to close you down."

Russ handed Yard Boss the green copy of the Commission Order.

"Lies!" Yard Boss yelled. "The dip in track fifteen was fixed after the unfortunate accident and—"

"You shorted us a carload of gravel on it. You wouldn't let us replace rotten ties," Clarence said. "You knew that cant, warp, and gradient were out-of—"

"What's the big deal?" Yard Boss said. "I reduced speed limits."

"That is not compliance," Rennie said. "There is a minimum fine of a thousand dollars a day and six months imprisonment for each out-of-spec stretch of track that is not removed from service. The Commission must inspect all repairs and issue a Certificate of Compliance before the condemned sections are returned to service. The Commission may, at its sole discretion, physically remove defective sections of track from the yard. The expenses for track removals will be billed to the railroad, with an added service charge. See the back of the green copy of the order for a full explanation of the railroad's duties and responsibilities."

"You can't do this!" Yard Boss yelled.

Vincent Wójcik stepped forward. "We're putting up red condemned flags at all eighteen spots. And disabling the two defective switches. You'd better go inform anyone working the evening shift."

"You know damned well there's no traffic here after 4:00 p.m.," Yard Boss said.

"Uh, Boss, you forgot," the assistant yard boss said. "You got a crew on overtime for that extra train from Duluth, the delayed one. We better get hustling!"

"Okay," Clarence said. "Let's go put up red flags and disable bad switches!"

Out in the yard, the gandy dancers used their long bars to dig deep holes in the ballast gravel. And put those signs in as tight as a drum. Obie and Jack set up red lanterns at the beginning and end of each condemned stretch of track.

A switcher came rumbling up and stopped. Dewey Kaas climbed down from the cab. "What's going on?"

"You on overtime, Dewey?" Clarence said.

"That extra from up north is coming in late, so yes."

Clarence, Jack, and Obie explained what the Commission had done, what tracks were available, which were condemned.

"We'll work around that, no problem. I'll tell all the crew. But tomorrow, daytime traffic, that's a different ball of wax. Great that you did this!"

Back in the car, Tom said, "This is a helluva story! I'll go up to your pressroom and bang it out right now. Russ, I'll develop your pictures if you let me use a good shot or two for the *People's Free Press* story."

"Deal!" Russ said.

"Tom, that truckload of newsprint from yesterday?" I said. "It is in our building."

"How?"

"We called North Country Paper, bought it."

"You folks are going big-time?"

"Looks that way."

"Anything I can do to help?"

"Keep picketing. And keep writing for us on the sly for now."

"You got it. Sven Oaklock for the *People's Free Press*, signing in here."

"Love that pen name," Russ said, "By the way, you, Karen, talked to Yard Boss like a seasoned attorney who is not to be messed with. No trace of teenager in your voice, Commissioner!"

"It was like speaking a second language. I'm going to practice doing it more."

"I am so proud of ya!" I said. "I knew ya could."

"Even before *I* did," she said.

We heard a loud cheer and then another as we walked toward the pressroom. Sylvia, our legal assistant, was on speakerphone, calling from the courthouse.

"The jury just awarded the Gustaffson family three hundred and thirty thousand dollars," Sylvia said. "The Iversens three hundred and ten. The railroad has to pay the Teen Council ten thousand dollars for legal expenses and a thousand bucks each for financial planners to set up trusts for the families. Lois and Carolyn will never have to worry about money again!"

"Holy buckets! Were they there for the verdict?"

"Lois was laughing, crying, holding Brucie, dancing. Carolyn had to leave for work. She said she'd call you, Russ, on her break, but she didn't expect anything much."

"Heh, heh, heh!" Russ said.

Rennie jumped up and down, hugged me. "See what our little dream turned into!"

"Holy cowbops! Imagine what our bigger dreams will become."

Susie came over to us. "I know I should be at the Teen Council meeting, but I have too much to do!"

"Can I take over some of your stuff, Suze?" Tom Hayes said. "So you *can* go?"

She reeled off a long list of articles to write, edit, approve.

Tom took notes. "Not a problem," he said.

In the corridor, on our way to the Teen Council Meeting Room, Denise came running up to us. "Ka Ka, Paulie, I just registered for my first college class! For Spring quarter! They actually let me take Psychology One. I'm so excited! Been dreaming about this since I was fifteen." She hugged Rennie, then me. "Thanks for making this happen!"

Everyone was there for the Teen Council meeting, even some Nines and Elevens.

"Before we get started," Barb said, "Roger wants to know if he can be at our meeting. I think it's only right since we're talking about his candy invention tonight. Besides, he does volunteer at the warming room."

"You betcha he can!" Laura said. "All in favor? Okay, we agree. Where is he?"

"In the warming room, in case we said no," Barb said.

Laura picked up the phone. "Roger, we'd be pleased to have you!"

"With all of us here, who's staffing the warming room?" Billy said.

"Three of our fall volunteer crop," Daniel said. "Ginny, Neil, and Claudia."

"They are so-o cool!" Bonnie said. "Almost as great as Daniel and Laura."

Roger came bouncing into the room, sat down next to Barb. She held his hand.

Ruka handed out free Hot! Chocolate bars. "Midwest Candy just did our first big production run. My mom named each variety with an African word for freedom. So Hot! Chocolate Black Pepper is an *Uhuru*! bar, to honor the Swahili language. And Hot! Chocolate Ginger is a '*Yanci*! bar, to honor the Hausa language." She chanted, "*Uhuru*! '*Yanci*! Freedom!" Then she said, "You know that vending machine we put in the clinic waiting room? The *Uhuru*! and '*Yanci*! bars have already run out! The regular candy bars? They sell half as fast. So Mama says, 'A huge thank you to everyone!' "

"Calling the meeting to order!" Linda said. "We have so much to catch up on, it'll take at least two hours."

We talked about blue snow and what we had to do to find out if the ever-present multicolored dust from the roofing factory was damaging Creekers' health, Carleton's new employees, the Workers' Market, the *Journette* strike, hiring *Journette* reporters, the judges' press conference, how our community-owned businesses have to be run differently from Fat Cat-owned ones, Burt's offer to fund *People's Free Press*, the Ray Iversen Concert Hall, the Gustaffson and Iversen family court awards, the flood of *People's Free Press* ads, our newsprint delivery, Camden Superette, Cecil's distribution offer for the newspaper, our worries about the pressroom, the Commission's unsafe track condemnation, and our over-all financial picture. It took quite a while to sort through it all, iron out disagreements, figure out how to move ahead and make decisions. But we did it.

"After all this figuring," Linda said, "I hate to put something else on the table, but this is something special. Ruka's book on the history of the Afro-American Shingle Creek community is finished. Can we publish it for her? We've got the presses to do it."

Greg? Coming through the doorway? Sitting down at the back of the room, looking around? He saw me and Rennie holding hands, and frowned, which pissed me off big-time.

Rennie's hand tightened on mine. My snakes attacked. I massaged her palm with my thumb. I hoped he saw that too. His foot began to tap.

"We can print it, yes siree," Rennie said, "but who is it written for, Ruka, 'n' how do we reach them, as far as that goes?"

We had an involved discussion about the audience for Ruka's book, realized it was bigger than just Shingle Creek.

Greg was sighing audibly, shifting in his chair.

"Shit!" Rennie said under her breath.

"Now that I'm thinking about this," Linda said, "didn't the Minnesota Historical Society have books they published themselves? Can we ask them?"

"Holy buckets, you're darn tootin' they did 'n' I make a motion we ask the Historical Society for advice. All hands on deck? Motion passed! Ruka, Linda, you want to go talk to them together 'n' stuff?"

The moment Linda adjourned the meeting, Greg stood up and gestured to Rennie to go. She waved him off, kept talking with people 'til *she* was ready to leave. But the ten-foot-tall seasoned attorney had somehow mutated into an anguished teenager, slouched, frowning, stiff.

Dozer put his arm around my shoulders. "I heard Karen giving that guy hell out in the hallway. She's pissed at him, Paulie. That's good for you."

I sighed. "I suppose. But it is not good for her."

"You're a saint," Dozer said.

"Nope. It is just the right way to be."

When I walked to my car, I was surprised how cold it had gotten. Sheets of ice covered sidewalks and roadways. *They have to drive all the way to the U on this glare-ice. That is bad enough, but Greg might do something stupid because he is angry. Shit! She seemed like she did not want to go with him, and I did not even say anything. I am such a toothless lion. If anything happens to her…*

I walked home, slouched, frowning, and stiff. Fixed myself a plate of leftovers, ate in my room. Then drove to my Finnish lesson with Willi Korhonen.

"At the yard, a wonderful thing you did. Everyone talking about it is. All the time about having a wreck like Frank I worry. His daughter, Frank very proud of is. On his face, his pride you can see but tell people he cannot. Finnish blood he must have."

We were in the middle of discussing different endings on *talo*, the root word for house, depending on whether you are going to his or her house, *taloonsa*, to any house in general, *taloon*, out of any house, *talosta*, or out of my house, *talostani*. I do not know why I suddenly blurted out, "Willi, *muistan sen sanan*! Willi, I remember that word! *Rakastaa*!"

His eyes got big. "*Rakastaa*? Sure you are? *Isäsi rakastaa tytärtäni*?"

"*Kyllä, siinä se*! Yes, that is it. *Isäsi rakastaa tytärtäni*."

He put his hands on his cheeks, rocked from side to side. "So sorry I am, Paulie. Your father my daughter raped it means."

"Raped? Raped?" I said.

"Yo. Yes. Nothing else can it mean. Who to you said it?"

I could hardly get the words out. "My grandpa. My mother's father."

The room was warm, but I was shivering. I stumbled to my car, drove home, went in the side door and straight downstairs. Coat still on, I got into bed, piled blankets on top of myself, shaking so hard I thought my teeth would fall out.

My father raped my mother? I was unwanted? That is why he called me a little bastard?

All night long, I cried out for Rennie. But even in my dreams, she did not come.

CHAPTER 7, MANY MICKLES MAKES A MUCKLE

TUESDAY-WEDNESDAY, FEBRUARY 29-MARCH 1, 1972

WAY BEFORE DAWN WHEN I woke up, the whole world was distant. Everyone was away somewhere, and I was alone, in a hellish country where all I could feel was fury. By the dim night light on the stove, I filled a bowl with rice puffs, raisins, milk. And ate by myself..

Isäsi rakastaa tytärtäni. He raped her. My father raped my mother. I am a little bastard!

I put on a pair of old jeans, a faded work shirt, a shabby sweater, buttoned my coat, pulled a wool hat way down so it touched the top of my dark glasses, stepped outside into a howling blizzard, slogged through six inches of snow to the warming room.

With the lights off, I beat the heck out of the heavy punching bag until my arms grew leaden with fatigue, then trudged through the snow again to Betty Hall for my appointment with Judith.

"Why the shades, Paul?" Judith said.

"The world is a dark and angry place. Out of control."

We talked about my father, my mother, and rape. Went on and on about Rennie. Even when I cried, I did not take my dark glasses off. We got nowhere. I said so.

Judith disagreed. "Your date on Saturday night was an immense step forward."

"Yeah, maybe. But she flat out abandoned me last night."

"Paul! Did you ask her not to go with Greg?"

"She would not have listened."

"You asked her?"

"Nope."

"Did you tell her you're working on your erection problem?"

"She does not need to know about my erection problem."

Judith's right eyebrow shot upward. "You think she doesn't know about it?"

"Horse puckies. I never said boohoo about it."

"Dig it, you didn't have to. She can feel it when you hold her close."

"How do ya know that?"

"Women know. Talk with her about it."

"I cannot do that."

"Then she's going to keep seeing Greg."

"And what about my father raping my mother?"

"It scares the living shit out of you, and rightly so. Understanding it is really important for you. At least you started talking about it."

"Should I tell Rennie?"

"Absolutely! It will help her understand you better and help you cope with it."

"I do not know," I said. But I took off my dark glasses, put them in my pocket.

Outside, the snow had stopped. I headed home to shovel the walk and driveway. The rising sun glared and glinted on new white snow. I put my glasses back on.

I had just started shoveling when there was a big-huge boom. Clouds of blood red haze burst from the roofing factory's smokestack. With my scarf wrapped around my nose and mouth and my back to the wailing wind, I shoveled. The snow slowly turned pink, then red, as fallout from the factory made my world look like a fiery hell.

"Paulie! Look at this red crap," Dozer called out as he walked toward me. "Every week a different color! Li'l Mikey, Laura, Billy, Dad, Linda, Ruka, and Harry are headed to the roofing factory. We're gonna return their lost property."

"I am for it!"

CHAPTER 7, MANY MICKLES MAKES A MUCKLE

"Take your shovel, grab a bucket, let's go!"

Outside the roofing factory, the air was thick with red dust. Susie was there, shooting photos. When we shoveled, there was more red grit than snow. We marched through the door, buckets of red grit in one hand, shovels in the other.

The guard tried to stop us. "Get out! You don't belong here!"

"We're returning lost property to Alastair Tewksbury," Laura said.

"Nobody here by that name," the guard said.

But we knew better. Luke worked there. He had told us where Tewksbury's office was. We kept marching. Opened the door to it.

He jumped to his feet. "Janine, call the cops!" he yelled.

"I am the police!" Gordy said. "We're returning your lost property, Alastair. Please provide appropriate containers for it."

"Get the hell out of here. Now!" Tewksbury howled, swinging a baseball bat.

"Dozer! Mike! Bear hug time," Gordy said.

Dozer grabbed Tewksbury from behind. Li'l Mikey embraced him from the front. The bat fell on the floor. Gordy took the bat, dropped it behind a radiator. We dumped red grit onto the floor.

"You ruined my carpeting! You'll pay for this! I know who you are."

"You didn't provide appropriate containers for your lost property," Linda said.

"Fix your damned equipment, Alastair!" Ruka said. "We're not going to tolerate your stink, smoke, and grit any longer."

Tewksbury raised his hand to hit Ruka. She was so quick, I could not see how she did it, but he ended up sitting on the floor. "I was gentle with you this time because of your age, Alastair," she said. "I won't be next time. Remain seated until we leave."

"Time to get the Industrial Safety Commission in there," Linda said as we walked away with our empty buckets and shovels.

"I'll write this up for tomorrow's *Free Press*," Susie said.

"Gordy, why behind the radiator?" Laura said.

"So he couldn't whack us when we turned our backs to leave. He can get it out, but it will take him some time and effort."

I went home, took a hot shower, ate a second breakfast, joked with Linda about our bucket brigade, began to feel better.

Then I went over to Camden Yard. Trains were backed up on the main line because so many sorting tracks were condemned. Yard Boss was yelling at Clarence, Jack, and Obie, "Remove those damned signs."

"Can't, Boss. Until we fix those tracks," Obie said.

"Well, fix them, damn it!"

"Can't, Boss, without thirty-eight hopper cars of gravel," Clarence said.

"And twelve hundred and sixty-eight new ties," Jack said.

"Plus, new springs and frogs for switches 4C and 9B," Obie said.

"Don't forget the new spikes, base plates, fish plates, and bolts we asked for," Clarence said. "Not worn-out junk that kills people."

Yard Boss tried to pull out one of the condemned signs. Could not budge it. Stalked off. Came back with his assistant and a two-man logger's saw. I pulled out my camera, took photos, walked to my car, used the CB radio to alert Russ.

Fifteen minutes later, Yard Boss had the signs on track eleven cut down. He walked over to Willi's switcher, yelled, "Korhonen! Use track eleven now."

"Not safe it is! To use it I cannot. Rule book violation that would be."

"You refusing a direct order, Korhonen?"

"Yah! Unsafe it is."

"You're fired!" Yard Boss yelled.

Russ's car pulled into the yard. He and Sylvia got out. He pointed to Yard Boss. Sylvia stomped over to him. Obie, Willi, Clarence, Jack, Dewey, and a dozen other guys made a circle around them.

"Yard Boss!" Sylvia bellowed. "In violation of orders from the North-Northeast Minneapolis Industrial Safety Commission and your railroad's rule book, you have tried to place track eleven back in service. As you have been informed, there is a minimum fine of a thousand dollars a day and six months imprisonment for each out-of-spec track that is not removed from service. This is your official notice of non-compliance." She tried to hand him a pink envelope.

He backed away.

"There is also a five hundred dollar fine for refusing to accept an official notice from the Commission," she said. "It is not unknown for a railroad to deduct that fine from a yard boss's salary."

CHAPTER 7, MANY MICKLES MAKES A MUCKLE

"Ooh-ee!" Obie said. "Gonna be hard times at Mr. Bossman's house for weeks if'n that happens! You like rice and beans, Mr. Bossman?"

We laughed our heads off.

Yard Boss took the envelope, cursed.

"We're walking off the job, Boss. Safety violations," Jack said.

"We *can't* strike," Elmer McGill said. "Our contract says—"

"Oh, bag it and sell it as fertilizer," Jack said. "Refusing to work under unsafe conditions is *not* a strike."

"Sez who?" Elmer said.

"Federal law!" Jack said.

A black '61 Ford Galaxie Station Wagon bounced into the parking lot. Marek, four other men, and Aunt Magdalena jumped out, ran toward us, looking grim.

"Awful accident killed our car inspector, Sal Mondadori," Marek said. "Brakeman Wilbur Jones lost a leg—if he lives." He kicked a pebble, sent it flying across the tracks. "Damn you, Minnesota Consolidated Railroad!"

"Paulie, we need a strike meeting *today*!" Aunt Magdalena said.

"Our auditorium is still being built, but we can use it," I said. "Be right back!"

I paged Ma on the CB radio, asked her to talk with Blanche. Five minutes later, she paged me back. Blanche said they would have it usable by two o'clock.

"Okay, folks, we got it. It is not fancy and no heat yet, so dress warm."

Clarence clapped me on the back. "It's finally happening. Finally! I promised Tessie and Kurt they could be there."

"I will bring them," I said. "What are you guys doing until then?"

"Picketin'!" Obie said.

"Laura and The Nines can make ya some signs. I will bring them soon."

I jumped in my car, drove to Betty Hall, explained what we needed to Laura and Lucy. Half an hour later, I delivered signs to Camden and Northeast Yards. On the way back, a bus stopped at 49th and Humboldt. Rennie got out, started walking, bent forward, shoulders slumped.

She does not look happy. I tooted my horn.

She turned around, saw me, trudged over to the car, unsmiling. Opened the door, stepped in, sat down, sighed, did not say hello.

"Are you okay, Rennie?"

"Just very tired."

She must be angry with me about my problem. Because Judith says she knows. I better stick to business.

"Rennie. They just fired Willi."

"Holy buckets, they what? Why, as far as that goes?"

"Yard Boss cut down the condemned signs on track eleven, ordered Willi to use it. He refused. And a car inspector was killed, a brakeman injured at Northeast Lowry."

"Bummer and a half!"

"Strike meeting's at two in our auditorium."

"It's about time, yes indeed."

"Rennie, what if ya called yahr dad, asked him for his vote. Then ya could vote for him at the meeting."

"He's going to yell at me, sure enough."

"I will be right next to ya."

In our office, she put the phone on speaker, dialed, stood slumped. Her hand was limp in mine. "Daddy, they fired Willi. There's a strike vote today."

"Those bastards! How the hell am I going to vote?"

"Daddy, I'll vote for you."

"You'll do that? Ka Ka? You'll really do that?"

Her hand tightened on mine. She stood up straight. "Of course I will, Daddy."

"Thank you, Ka Ka! Oh, my God, thanks!"

Her eyes were teary. She hung up the phone. "Last time he called me Ka Ka...I was ten."

I wrapped my arms around her, held her while she cried. Then she stood up straight, took out her handkerchief, wiped her face. "We have work to do, yes siree! What's first?"

"Helping Tessie with her speech."

In the classroom, the kids were reading and talking about Mrs. Elak's nasty comments in their permanent records.

Burt was sitting in the back, grinning. "I really like it here!"

We pulled up chairs, sat next to him.

"Remember we talked about themes?" Lucy said. "What are they?"

"Ideas that repeat themselves in something you're reading," Charlie said.

"Are there any themes in Mrs. Elak's comments?"

"She thought we were all stupid," Jeffie said. "It wasn't just me."

"She said I was dumb as a rock," Kurt said. "Perfect for a low-wage job just like my dad. He's not dumb, Lucy. The way he has to figure out how to re-align a track takes a whole lot of complicated math."

Kid after kid said Mrs. Elak's notes were about how stupid they were. It made me furious. "She said that about me too," I said. "I think her problem is *she* is too dumb to understand intelligence when she sees it."

"So it takes smart to see smart?" Lucy said.

"Can I make that into a sign for our ideas wall?" Jeanette said.

"Yes! Yes!" the kids called out.

"Here's another theme," Bonnie said. "She said I would be a bad housewife because I was too smart and inquisitive, and I should be punished for reading too much."

"But our mom's very smart," Terri said. "Right, Bonnie? And she's the best mom ever!"

"And our dad says she's the love of his life, so I don't get it," Bonnie said.

"Mrs. Elak said I could read well enough to follow recipes," Tess said, "and I should be discouraged from reading more so I could learn how to clean a house. Like I don't know already."

"Our Tessie is much smarter than that!" Kurt said. "Why do some people think working folks are stupid?"

"And women should be dumb and not think?" Bonnie said.

"Because then women will do what they're told? Workers will do what they're ordered to?" Mamie said. "Even if it's bad for them?"

"Like when Yard Boss tells my dad not to think about safety?" Kurt said.

"And when my old father told my old mother to help him hurt me," Terri said.

"I have an idea," I said. "We are going to have a museum someday, about working people. What if we organized some of Mrs. Elak's notes by themes and saved them for the museum?"

"So people could see what it was like in the olden days!" Ruthie said. "All in favor?" She looked around the room. "All hands on deck!"

"Can I change the subject?" Tess said. "Okay, everyone?"

Lucy saw the kids all nodding. "Sure! What's on your mind?"

"A question for Burt. Why did you give so much money to our Academy?"

"That's a great question, Tess." Burt went to the blackboard, wrote, "Ten Million."

"So first of all, I'm seventy-seven years old. I expect to live another twenty years, and I have ten million bucks. How many days in twenty years?"

Kids pulled out pencils, paper, calculated.

"Seventy-three hundred," Bobby said.

"Not quite, Bobby," Jeffie said. "You forgot leap years. So it's 7,305."

"You're right, Jeffie," Burt said. "But can we round it down to 7,300?"

"Why?" Jeffie said.

"Sometimes it's easier, if it doesn't really affect your results," Burt said. "So, if I have 7,300 days to spend ten million bucks, how much must I spend every single day?"

"Thirteen hundred and seventy dollars," Jeanette said. "I rounded off the cents."

"If I work at spending my money from six in the morning to midnight, that's how many hours a day?"

"Eighteen! But then you'd have no time to enjoy yourself," Mamie said.

"Exactly right," Burt said. "How much would I have to spend an hour?"

"Seventy-six dollars, rounding off the cents," Charlie said.

"After a while, would I have everything I need and want?" Burt said.

"Oh, I get it!" Tess said. "So your problem is what to do with all that money."

Burt nodded, did a little tap dance. "But I found a way to solve the problem! No matter how much happiness you have, you can always use more. Giving away my money so good things happen for people makes me over-the-moon happy. And there's no limit on how much I can spend that way."

CHAPTER 7, MANY MICKLES MAKES A MUCKLE

"Why don't other bosses give away their money?" Terri said.

"Fat Cats *think* money brings them happiness. They're wrong. It's giving it away that gives you genuine pleasure," Burt said. "So I thank you for helping me be joyful!"

There was a moment of silence. Ya could almost hear the kids thinking. And then, a chant broke out. "Bu-urt! Bu-urt!"

Mabel came striding into the room, big grin on her face, two envelopes in her hand. "Excuse me, folks, but this couldn't wait. Daniel and Laura got their letters from art school. Look at this! They both came to *our* house, stuck together."

"Mom! How do you know they're acceptances?" Daniel said.

"I just know!" She carefully separated them.

Silence filled the room. Then the sound of envelopes being torn open.

"Go!! This is intense," Laura said. "I got in! I got in! F-u-l-l, full scholarship!"

"Well, shuckle my boo!" Daniel said. "I'm in, full scholarship too!"

Laura grabbed his hands, danced him around. They whooped and hollered. The kids clapped, cheered. Mabel hugged them both. Rennie took my hand, held it tight.

When everyone calmed down, I said, "I have even more news. There's a strike meeting this afternoon, here in Betty Hall. Tessie, ya still wanna speak?"

"I have to! For Daddy!"

"Was anyone hurt today?" Kurt said.

"Not in Camden Yard. But one guy killed, another hurt over at Northeast Lowry."

Tess wailed, "Somebody else's daddy gone!"

Kurt held her.

"Tessie, we want to help ya with yahr speech," I said.

She said, "Okay," kept crying.

"It takes her a minute or so," Kurt said. "Can I come too?"

In our office, Rennie and I asked Tess to describe what she wanted to say. Helped her figure out how to say it. Kurt's presence seemed to calm her down and give her strength. She did not feel ready, but we knew she was.

Ma opened the door, poked her head in, handed me an envelope. "Sorry to interrupt, but I thought you'd want to see this."

A. Friend at the Communal Association sent me a copy of Archibald Hastings-Dankworth's memo dated yesterday. "To the operations managers of Minnesota Consolidated Construction Services and Railway. It would behoove you to make sure the track repairmen, brakemen, and engineers you had trained at the Sheridan Institute and were kept on standby payments are ready to step in during a strike. Mäkinen and Flynn may be convinced there will not be a strike, but I am not. Do not pay any of them over $1.63. I expect to see your plan for this on my desk by 3 p.m. tomorrow."

"Holy buckets, they *trained* scabs way ahead of time?" Rennie said.

"Russ told me that is what Sheridan Institute is for," I said. "Training guys, getting them jobs in non-union shops or scabbing, forcing them to spy on other workers."

Another knock at the door. Roger poked his head in. "Heard there's a strike meeting today. Can I contribute $250 to the strike fund? Went to the bank today and got the cash."

I hugged him. "You are so wonderful! Ya wanna present it in person?"

He blushed. "I guess. But I have to be at Mabel's at two-thirty to bake poppy seed lemon pies."

"I will get ya on first. Tessie, Kurt, we have ta get yahr coats. The auditorium is not finished yet, so no heat."

It was breathtaking how fast Blanche and her crew had switched from construction to hosting. They had signs in the parking lot, wooden barriers were removed from the emergency exits, tools and materials stacked off to the side, the floor swept. I had no idea where she got the sound system. She even had a table for reporters.

As people streamed in, ushers asked them where they were from and kept a running tally. Besides Camden and Northeast Lowry Yards, we got workers from City Line Yard; Minnehaha Mills Yard; University Yard; St. Paul, Salt Lake, and San Diego Railway Mainline; and Milwaukee, Minneapolis, and Winnipeg Mainline. The bench seating for 500 people and another 100 chairs Blanche had rounded up somehow were full. People stood behind them.

CHAPTER 7, MANY MICKLES MAKES A MUCKLE

Clarence, Jack, Obie, Magdalena, Nelson, Marek, Willi, and Russ sat on stage, next to five empty chairs marked Frank Ahlberg, Sal Mondadori, Wilbur Jones, Ray Iversen, and Arne Gustaffson.

Clarence opened the meeting. "First things first, and before the strike comes the strike fund. The Shingle Creek community has raised fifty-nine hundred dollars toward the railroad workers' strike fund. And we're just getting started!" He beckoned to Roger. "Here is our latest donor. Roger Tornquist just turned sixteen. He earned this money himself."

"I am so happy I can help," Roger said. "My two hundred and fifty bucks is just a drop, but those drops add up. Many mickles makes a muckle!" He handed a stack of ten-dollar bills to Clarence.

The audience applauded, stamped their feet, whistled.

We heard from railway workers, from gandy dancers to dispatchers, engineers to car inspectors, about low pay, hazards, cutbacks. Discussed how we had won big-huge cash settlements for Arne and Ray's families. Heard about the fears so many workers have of losing their jobs in a strike. But a strike vote did not seem certain.

Then Clarence introduced Russ.

"I know the idea of having a nonprofit corporation represent us may sound crazy. But sad to say, the bosses have been very successful at taking away union power. Need to strike for better pay? You have to notify the international president of your union. Then a vice president investigates it and reports back to the president. Who asks the union's legal department for an opinion. Then the union has to give the railroad thirty days' notice. Think you can finally strike? Not so fast! You have to go to a mediator. If you don't like the mediator's decision, then you can strike. It takes months! Meanwhile, the railroad's got scabs all trained and everything ready to break you by the time you start picketing."

"But with Arnray's contract, you get a $2.50 minimum wage, increased for inflation every six months. You're working your asses off? Every six months, your wages are also increased for productivity. So, we start ourselves at a higher wage and it keeps going up—by more than inflation. You don't ever have to strike for higher wages. They're built into the contract.

"Not only that, but you get to elect your foremen and supervisors. That's right, *you* choose them from among your brothers and sisters, and they will remain Arnray members. Don't like what they're doing? Vote to recall them. The law won't let unions do that. Period.

"When a union is really good at getting stuff for its members, the bosses yell, 'Communists!' And that Taft-Hartley law helps the bosses go after your best leaders and hound them out of office, like they did to the Teamsters Union here in Minneapolis. But corporations aren't required to have political tests for their leaders or members. Furthermore, if a union is striking, the law says members of other unions have to cross their picket lines if their boss orders them to. Members of a corporation can refuse to cross picket lines and can take part in a general strike. Union members can't, by law."

As Russ explained Arnray's benefits, I could feel the mood in the room start to shift. When he finished, Clarence said, "Brothers! Sisters! I have a top-secret union organizer here to speak with you."

Rennie and I walked onstage holding hands with Tess.

"Ray Iversen was killed in Camden Yard last year," Clarence said. "His daughter, Tess, wants to tell you something."

"She's just a little kid. What does she know about unions?" Elmer McGill said. "Don't waste our time."

Tess gripped my hand hard. Kurt, sitting in the front row, shifted in his seat, looking worried.

I bent down, whispered in her ear, "It is okay, Tess. It will work out."

"C'mon, Elmer! To listen Ray would have wanted you," Willi Korhonen said, shaking his finger at the younger man.

"Yup, let her speak for Ray's sake. Gosh, I sure miss him," Jack said. "He didn't talk down to me like you do all the time, Elmer."

Elmer frowned, grunted.

I nodded to Tess and Rennie. We all stepped forward.

"Say it, Tess!" Clarence said.

"A lot of you guys knew my daddy. But you didn't know we had a secret special time together. He would tell me stuff while he made breakfast."

"Where was Mommy?" Rennie said.

"Everyone else was asleep. But I'd hear him in the kitchen and run to sit next to him on the high stool by the stove. 'Morning, Bean!' he'd say,

CHAPTER 7, MANY MICKLES MAKES A MUCKLE

patting my head. 'What have you been thinking about?' Bean is his secret name for me. Not even Mommy can call me that."

"What *were* you thinking about?" Clarence said.

"All my questions."

"Like what?"

"Why did Mommy cry when I started kindergarten? Why do you have to go to work when it's still dark out? Why is my friend Ruthie sometimes mean to me? Can I work on the railroad like you when I grow up?"

There was a murmur from the audience. Men who were slumping sat up straight.

"He always knew the answers, even when he was flipping pancakes. You know what he told me?"

"What?" Clarence said.

"I could too be a railroad gal someday."

"Girls working on the railroad?" Elmer growled. "Men cooking? You kidding me?"

"Listen, whippersnapper!" Willi pointed at Elmer. "Too young to remember when women worked on the railroads during the war you are. Darned good at it they were."

"Really, Mr. Korhonen?" Tess said.

"You bet! And you too someday could a railroader be. What else thinking about are you?"

Tess paused for a moment. Then she looked up at the ceiling, hands together like she was praying. "Daddy, you used to say, 'I'll always be here for you, Bean.' And, Daddy, you are—in my heart. But that's not enough for me. Because I have questions for you my heart can't answer. Why did you have to die? Mommy says it's because the railroad wouldn't fix the tracks right. Why couldn't you make them? Mommy says all the railroad men should've gone on strike."

She paused. Tears filled her eyes. She looked directly at Clarence. "Daddy, why didn't they?"

There was silence. Many of the men were blinking a lot. Willie and Clarence looked stunned.

Finally, Obie stood up, took the mic. "Tess, will you be a-castin' your daddy's strike vote?"

"Strike!" Tessie bellowed.

"Frank Ahlberg done broke both legs in a Camden Yard accident," Obie said. "He's still in the hospital. Karen, will you be a-votin' for your dad?"

"Strike!" Rennie roared.

"Sal Mondadori died in an accident at Northeast Lowry Yard today. Vito, you be a-votin' for your dad?"

"Strike!" Vito sobbed.

"Wilbur Jones lost a leg in Northeast Lowry Yard today. He's a-hoverin' at the edge of death. Ananias, you a-votin' for your dad?"

"Strike!"

Willi took the mic. "Up here next do you want your kid for you voting, because dead or in the hospital you are? I, a motion make, we strike! For Tess, for Ray, for Arne and his kids, for Frank, Karen, Sal, Vito, Wilbur, Ananias. For all of us. Strike!"

A chant filled the room. "Stri-ike! Stri-ike! Stri-ike!"

"Raise your hand if'n you vote to strike!" Obie bellowed. "Raise it high!"

A garden of raised hands filled the room. The "Stri-ike!" chant continued.

Obie stood up, raised both hands, the room quieted. "I gotta sing this for you, Tessie! For you, Karen! For you, Magdalena! An old union song. It's about you!" He belted out the first verse. Soon, the whole room was singing about a union lass who stood up to thugs and deputies trying to break up picket lines, stood proud and tall, singing:

Oh, I'm not frightened of you, I'm in the union

I'm a union lady, forever more!

Smiling, tears rolling down her cheeks, Tess gripped my hand hard, sang along. Rennie gripped my other hand, sang and cried.

"A few quick things," Clarence said. "We have a strike hotline starting tomorrow. Call 345-6789 for a recorded update. Listen to KPFP and read *People's Free Press* for news. Please put your name and phone number on the strike rosters at the table by the big doors. Tomorrow and Thursday afternoon at four o'clock, we'll have training sessions here. Find out how

CHAPTER 7, MANY MICKLES MAKES A MUCKLE

to make the picket line uplifting. And safe. Free hot food! Sign up at the big table by the doors."

"We are a-goin' to win! Be part of it!" Obie said.

Wave after wave of applause and cheering filled the room.

"You did it, Tess," Rennie said. "You sure enough did it!"

Tessie ran to her mother, sitting in the front row. "Dad and I are so proud of you!" She took Tess in her arms, rocked her, chanted, "Oh my wonderful daughter, you are just like your father."

Rennie and I talked with dozens of guys, got volunteer strike captains for each yard or mainline, answered questions, encouraged people. When everyone had left, Clarence, Obie, Jack, Nelson, Magdalena, Marek, and Willi came to us, made a circle, linked arms. I motioned to Blanche, and she joined us. I introduced her.

"We did it!" Magdalena said. "Now we have to keep on doing it. Can we have a little strategy meeting, hopefully somewhere warm?"

"How about our conference room, with coffee and cookies?" I said.

Just as we were about to start our meeting, there was a knock on the door. Tom Hayes poked his head in. "Listen, I have great shots of the five kids voting for their dads. Just made these prints for the families."

Rennie's was on top. Tom's photo showed the fury, sorrow, and strength on her face. "Thanks, Tom!" she said. "This will make Dad so happy!"

"I do not want to bring ya down," I said. "But we have information that the railroad is hiring scabs." I read the Stinkworth memo out loud.

"So here's what we need to know," Rennie said. "Why do people scab?"

"My experience," Magdalena said, "they can't get decent work. They're desperate."

"Mine too," Nelson said. "Sometimes they have an alcohol problem. Bosses usually hire drinkers when they don't care if the work gets done. All they want to do is teach their workers a lesson."

"I'd agree with all of that," Blanche said. "But where does that get us?"

"Can *we* employ them?" Rennie said.

Blanche's face lit up.

"What on earth?" Obie said. "What are we a-gonna do with scabs?"

"We need more help to finish our Workers' Market and Auditorium," Blanche said. "We've already hired everyone in Shingle Creek who needs a job. It's really important for us to build a newsroom for *People's Free Press*, but we can't find workers. We get the scabs set up in good jobs, help them get on their feet again, turn them into union workers, and everybody benefits."

"Plus, Camden Yard gandy dancers crew is short-staffed," I said. "Arnray Railroad Safety will need seasoned gandy dancers after the strike is settled. The owner of General Grain, over in Northeast, wants to do a major upgrade of his twelve-hundred-foot siding. He will pay two-fifty."

"But what about your own gandy dancers? Shouldn't they get those jobs first?" Marek said.

"The General Grain owner is a really cool guy," Clarence said. "He's paying two-fifty for the entire Camden Yard crew so they can organize the strike."

"Holy smokes!" Magdalena said. "Never heard anything like that before."

"So we're going to try to get as many scabs as possible working for us?" Jack said. "The railroad won't know what hit 'em!"

"You got scabs, call us! We'll fix them!" Rennie said. "Scabs *can* heal!"

We set up telephone trees, made a list of strike captains, wrote a news release with a complete list of picket lines, made condemnation signs for twenty-three sections of unsafe track, then drove over to Northeast Lowry Yard to serve notice on their yard boss and install signs.

On the way back to Shingle Creek, I asked Rennie to go dancing again Saturday.

"He doesn't own me, no siree." Her face turned redder than the snow in Shingle Creek. "Shit! I didn't mean to say that."

"Own ya? What does that even mean?"

"I don't want to talk about it, to the max."

"Is he giving ya grief?"

"Please, Paavali. Let's just discuss setting up tomorrow's training session."

That night in my room, Rennie clung to me. I could feel she was upset, but I could not get her to talk about it. I wanted to tell her that my father

CHAPTER 7, MANY MICKLES MAKES A MUCKLE

raped my mother, but my snakes would not let me, even though I bopped their heads super hard.

In bed, in the darkness, arms around me, she said softly, "Paavali, you still want to take me dancing Saturday?"

I tightened my arms around her, wishing I had an erection she could feel throbbing against her. "You betcha! It is a date," I said, which made my serpents lose their minds.

We fell asleep, arms and legs entwined, waking each other up when we had nightmares, both of us holding in our wordless pain.

Well before dawn Wednesday morning, I woke Rennie. "The workers at the roofing factory are expecting us. Two months of talking with them is about to pay off."

"You updated Luke Gulbrandsen yesterday, Paavali?"

"I did! He said all but five workers voted to close the plant down until it is safe. After that disastrous strike there five years ago, they are afraid to try a walkout again. So they are kinda relieved we are doing the hard part for them."

At seven-thirty, just before shift change, Rennie, me, Moe Lehtonen, Beth Olson, Harley Blecher, Gordy, Officer Anderson, and nine North-Northeast Minneapolis Industrial Safety Commissioners huddled outside the roofing factory, red dust raining down on us.

"The smell," Beth said, "is probably from polyaromatic hydrocarbons."

"Polyaromatic, huh?" I said. "That means they have many foul smells?"

"You got it!" Beth said. "Nasty chemicals that can make you seriously ill. They stay in the ground and water forever."

"The red is another story," Moe said. "Looks to be colored stone dust. A lot of wasted money is going up that smokestack. Not as bad as the hydrocarbons but causes lung disease over the years. Workers should be wearing masks."

"Luke told me they don't have masks," I said, "and he's coughing all the time."

"We borrowed that cherry picker truck," Beth said, pointing to the street, "from Moe's union buddy. We're going up on the roof to bottle some samples, test them in a laboratory, find out exactly what's in them."

"What action do you think we should take today 'n' stuff?" Rennie said.

"Shut it down!" Moe said.

"It's unsafe for the workers *and* the neighborhood," Beth said.

"What would make it safe?" Clarence said.

"Equipment to capture the hydrocarbons and process them into useful chemicals," Beth said.

"I'd bet the crushing and coating machinery is not working properly," Harley said. "Won't know if it's fixable 'til I see it."

"So here's the plan," Rennie said. "We hit him with a one-two punch. While Beth and Moe get the samples, Gordy, Clarence, Obie, and Jack guard the truck. The rest of us serve notice on Tewksbury and shut the place down. Whaddaya think?"

"What happens to the workers?" Marek said.

"We have enough cash money to pay them for two weeks if they can't get unemployment," I said. "We have plenty of work for them to do."

"All in favor?" Clarence said. "All hands on deck!"

Tewkesbury was not inside. His factory manager was as nasty as he was. Rennie did her ten-foot-tall lawyer procedure, handed him the Commission notice. He erupted like a volcano spewing molten curses. We warned him not to remove our shut-down tags from the machines.

Harley inspected the equipment, turned it off. We followed him, tagging machines as he said, "Condemned! Condemned!"

The manager followed us, still exploding.

"This crushed stone processor needs some new parts," Harley said. "That'll stop the dust eruptions. And save them about five hundred bucks a month in wasted stone."

"Can ya write up a detailed report on that?" I said. "The Commission will charge Tewskbury a fee for it, so ya will get paid for it."

"Sure!" Harley said. "But I'll donate the fee to the strike fund."

I took Luke aside. "Can ya get everyone outside for a quick sidewalk meeting after they punch out? We will catch both shifts that way."

"Been waiting for this day!" Luke said.

With both shifts on the sidewalk, I stood on a wooden crate. "It will take time for the boss to fix the problems. During that time, we need yahr help and we will pay ya."

CHAPTER 7, MANY MICKLES MAKES A MUCKLE

Cheers filled the air.

"We are gearing up for a meeting for all the roofing factory workers tomorrow morning at eight o'clock in Betty Hall Auditorium," I said. "Make a list of all of yahr skills and experience and bring it with ya. Tell yahr friends on the afternoon shift. We want to take care of all of ya."

"Well, that went well, yes siree!" Rennie said when we got back in the mahrove-rove car. "Do we really have enough money to pay them all?"

"I fret about that too," Susie said.

"Burt said not to worry about it. Carleton told me it is okay and we are on the right track, so there is that. But it sure as heck worries me. Just wish we had another source of income so we did not have ta rely on Burt."

We went into the pressroom with Susie. Pam was sorta flying around the room, saying, "I can't believe it! This isn't real!" But everyone was laughing and smiling, so I knew it was not bad.

"We've sold enough ads for this week so far," Pam said, "to pay for that load of paper. And the ink. Which covers us for the next three weeks. And that phone is so hot it looks about to melt! We have to write orders with both hands and our toes!"

A few minutes later, Clarence arrived. "Just came from Camden Yard. They have scabs running trains on condemned tracks. We have to remove bad tracks pretty quick."

Rennie and I grabbed our cameras, got Russ and Sylvia to come with us. Willi, Dewey, Jack, and Obie were picketing out front. Three *Journette* reporters and a pressman were walking with them in solidarity.

"I with you am coming," Willi said.

"Me too! Those gandy dancers are my brothers," Obie said.

We parked by the crew shack, took photos of the pile of chopped up red condemned signs, of trains on condemned tracks, and a small crew of Black gandy dancers trying to fix the dip on track fifteen with no ballast or new ties.

"How many scabs, Clarence?" I said.

"Five gandy dancers, two switch engineers, two brakemen, no car inspectors."

"Holy buckets, two brakemen's four too few for this yard," Rennie said. "Dad told me they need six. Let's talk to the engineers first 'n' stuff, 'cause the yard can't run without them."

We walked over to the feeder track where a switcher was pushing three tank cars toward track four.

"Train doesn't sound right!" Clarence said. He took a close look, yelled, "Willi, Obie, get fire extinguishers! Paul, tell Yard Boss there's a propane leak on a tanker!" He ran up the track, flagged the engineer, motioned him to come down from the cab.

"Brother, you got a hotbox on car one, a slow valve leak on car three." He held up his hand, thumb and forefinger almost together. "You're this close to an explosion."

"Huh? Why?" the engineer said.

"Those tankers are full of propane gas. Gust of wind blows propane fumes toward that hot box, and boom!"

Willi and Obie ran back with fire extinguishers, put out flames shooting from a red-hot metal box next to a wheel on car one.

"We're going to uncouple car one. Don't move your engine!" Clarence yelled. "C'mon, Obie! Willi, guard us!"

"Making sure the engine you do not move I am," Willi said to the engineer. "So kill those men you do not."

Two minutes later, they ran back. Willi climbed into the engine, moved the train backward. There was a loud, screeching noise from tank car one. He stopped, waited for Obie's wave, moved the train forward, leaving car one way down track four, away from the other two cars.

"What the heck?" the scab engineer said.

"Willi, go light a fire under Yard Boss!" Clarence turned toward the engineer. "That's an old-fashioned tanker. The axle bearings are kept cool with grease-packed rags. Grease runs out, the bearings get hot, start a fire that can blow up a propane tanker. And you. Plus, there's a leaking valve on car three. Gadzooks, man! You ever worked in a rail yard before?"

"They didn't teach this stuff at Sheridan," the engineer said. "Who are you guys?"

"Willi Korhonen, I drive that engine when not on strike I am."

"Clarence Björk, a gandy dancer when I'm not striking."

Yard Boss came running up. "Björk, Korhonen, you fix that valve?"

"Yard Boss, we're not car repairmen," Clarence said.

"And on strike we are," Willi said.

CHAPTER 7, MANY MICKLES MAKES A MUCKLE

The assistant yard boss arrived carrying a toolbox, climbed under tanker three, grunted. We could hear him tighten something. The hissing sound stopped.

Russ took Sylvia aside, whispered to her.

"Yard Boss!" Sylvia said. "Your assistant does not have a gas mask on. You do not have any car inspectors or car repairmen working. Your scab gandy dancers do not have proper materials and supplies. And you have railcars on condemned tracks. The Safety Commission is shutting down all operations here. To resume operations, you will need a Certificate of Compliance from the Commission. You will need to have the required three car inspectors and the required six brakemen, strike or no."

"Get the hell out of my yard! All of you!"

"As North-Northeast Minneapolis Industrial Safety Commissioners and their legal counsel, Minnesota law gives us unlimited access to this yard," Sylvia said. "Tankers one and three are out of service until certified repairs are made on them."

"You can't do this!"

"We've heard that one already," Sylvia said.

"The penalty for safety violations like these includes a jail term," Russ said. "You were warned."

"I'm calling the real cops."

"I already called them for ya," I said.

"On what, tin cans and a string?"

"Nope! The CB radio in my car. They are on the way," I said.

Yard Boss stamped off. Assistant Yard Boss climbed out from under the tanker. "Propane fumes are poisonous?"

"Without a gas mask, they can kill you dead. Very quickly," Russ said.

"That son of a bitch said they're harmless!" he said, and walked away coughing, shoulders slumped.

The engineer slouched against the switcher, hands over his face.

"So what's your name, engineer?" Rennie said.

His hands fell to his sides. "Lyle Sund. Now what am I going to do? You make one mistake in life, you never get a good job again. I don't want to scab." He looked down. "But I never get a chance at anything decent anymore."

"What mistake did ya make, Lyle?" I said.

"Beat the crap out of the bastard who raped my sister. Turned out to be son of a rich guy. Did twelve years in Stillwater State Pen."

"And the rich guy's name?" Russ said.

"Bertrand Ainsley. The bastard!"

"The St. Paul furniture Fat Cat?"

"Yeah, him."

"You once had a good job?" Rennie said.

He paced in a tight circle, banging his fists together. "Designed and installed heating systems. I loved my job, but nobody will hire an ex-con, even with my master tradesman's certificate."

"What size heating systems?" Rennie said.

"Large. Industrial plants, warehouses, office buildings."

"Ya actually installed them yahrself?"

"Supervised work crews, worked right alongside them."

"Can you prove all this?" Russ said.

"I got all the papers in my room."

Rennie squeezed my hand.

I squeezed back.

"Holy buckets, if you actually can prove it 'n' you quit being a scab right now this instant, we have a job for you 'n' it pays more than minimum wage." She described the auditorium, pressroom, and newsroom projects, stuck out her hand. "Deal?"

He grabbed it, shook. "De-al!"

"Lyle, man, meet us at ten tomorrow morning. Here is my card," I said.

"And here's mine," Rennie said. "All right then? Bring your papers."

"Yes, ma'am, sir! I'll be there!" He climbed up, turned off the switch engine, jumped down, walked to a beat-up brown '57 Plymouth, waved, and drove off.

The other engineer called us a bunch of pinko commies, told us to go to hell, would not even come down from his cab to talk. One brakeman was glad to talk with us about his cabinet-making skills. The second told us to get lost. We talked with the gandy dancers, explained what was going on, and hired them to work on the General Grain siding.

CHAPTER 7, MANY MICKLES MAKES A MUCKLE

On the picket line, we told Dewey and Jack what happened. They could not stop laughing. "Four guys trying to run that yard!" Jack said. "That's rich."

Gordy drove up in his squad car, rolled down his window. "Rollie wrote up the Commission's complaint against Yard Boss. I'm here to arrest him. I also have a complaint against the scabs for violating safety standards. I'll only use that if I have to." He drove into the yard, parked by the office.

"Will those charges stick?" I said to Russ.

"Ones against Yard Boss ought to because he broke the law big-time," Russ said. "Depends on which judge arraigns him and whether the railroad demands a juryless trial."

In a few minutes, the switch engineer and brakeman came walking out the yard gate. "I'm sure as heck not getting arrested for a buck sixty-three an hour," the brakeman said.

"I'm gone!" said the engineer.

"Is Assistant Yard Boss a decent guy 'n' stuff?" Rennie said.

"Yeah, he is," Clarence said. "And that's why Yard Boss craps all over him."

"Would he make a good yard boss?"

"He just might," Obie said. "Used to be a darn good brakeman. You see the way he done fixed that leak? He's also a competent mechanic."

"Should Arnray talk about hiring him?"

"Now that's something to have a good think about," Jack said.

"What about hiring him to work on the pressroom and newsroom 'n' stuff?" Rennie said.

"Damn good idea," Obie said. "Dependin' on if he comes a-walkin' out under his own steam, or a-ridin' out in the back seat of Gordy's car."

In five minutes, the squad car drove by, Yard Boss in the back, screaming his head off. Twenty minutes later, we heard someone yell, "Screw this job! I'm done. I'm finished," and begin sobbing. "How'm I gonna feed my family? How? How?"

"Hey, Hank!" Clarence said when Assistant Yard Boss dragged himself through the yard gate. "What took you so long?"

"I called all the dispatchers, told them the yard was shut down. Didn't want any chance there'd be an accident, men hurt or killed. You actually know my name?"

"Yeah, you're a decent guy. We all know that. Paul and Karen here want to interview you for a construction job."

"Don't make fun of me, please!"

Clarence put his arm around Hank's shoulders. "We're not."

"The guys said you'd be worth hiring," Rennie said.

As Rennie and I talked details with Hank, he grew taller, his face changed completely. "Yes, you bet I'll be there."

We shook hands. He started walking along 47th Avenue, away from the yard. Clarence ran after him.

"Hank! Didn't you drive to work today?"

"Oh my gosh! Thanks. This has all upset me so much. Yes, my car's in the yard."

"I'll walk you there, Hank," Clarence said. " 'Cause you're an upright guy."

CHAPTER 8, TAKING AWAY THE TRACKS

WEDNESDAY-THURSDAY, MARCH 1-2, 1972

AROUND TWO O'CLOCK, I DROVE downtown to pick up Rennie from her lunch with Judge Haddad but went to the Parks superintendent's office first. Clara, Burt, and twelve senior citizens from Shingle Creek were sitting on the couches and chairs, holding signs demanding Superintendent Hastings-Dankworth resign, senior swimming at the junior high school start again tomorrow, and the Shingle Creek staff be rehired immediately. A TV crew from NBC National News interviewed them.

I recognized Officer Doyle from the Portland Park attack where they killed Fred. At the back of the room, he was stepping from foot to foot. "If you ask me, Captain," he said to a cop with a gold badge next to him, "we should cuff them all and haul them in. Using this," he twirled his night stick.

"Did you get that on film, Mel?" the TV reporter said to the cameraman.

"In the can, baby! Including that cop's remark."

The captain's face got red. "You're a dumbass, Doyle. I warned you, watch your mouth. You just don't mess with a bigwig like Burton Loftus. Or seniors. Just keep your mouth shut now before you stick the other foot in."

"But we did that at Portland Park, even if we only shot one, so—"

"Shut up! I told you the mayor and governor are putting the screws on us."

That is good to know! Hot dog! I am so proud of Clara and Burt!

From the moment I picked Rennie up outside the Orchard Restaurant, she talked a mile a minute. "Badah's getting death threats about her amicus curiae investigation 'n' she used Burt's contacts at the Justice Department in Washington 'n' they promised to investigate 'n' her grapevine tells her they already started, yes siree!"

Then I was speed-talking, and the amount of electricity in the car could have propelled us all the way to Shingle Creek if we had a high-voltage motor.

"Are ya going back to the U tonight?"

"No siree, 'n' enough said about that, 'cause what I want to know is who's making the *mujadara* for the strikers training session, as far as that goes?"

Something is still bothering her. I can feel it! I wish she would tell me. Maybe she cannot, like me with my problem.

"Dina Eldin," I said. "And Mabel surprised us with a big batch of pies. Dahl's Superette donated and delivered paper plates, cups, and napkins."

"Do we have the full hundred people signed up for today's training 'n' stuff?"

"Tomorrow too. Plus a waiting list, so we have ta schedule another session."

We were stopped at a light. She put her arms around me, snuggled up. "Holy buckets, we need another Paulie-Paul or two."

"All for you, or another Rennie for each of them?" I wanted that light to stay red forever. But it changed.

She slid back to her side. "I'd want them all for me, but then again, if I was multiple Rennies, they would all be for me, 'n' your question makes me feel like Alice in Wonderland, but it sure is interesting 'n' stuff."

In the warming room, Laura and two kids were repainting the corner of the mural.

"*American Muralist* is holding the vandalization story until I send them photos of the repainted corner. They also want pictures of Della"—she pointed to a young teen girl—"and Dexter." She pointed to a ten- or eleven-year-old boy.

"Who's covering for you during the strike training today, as far as that goes?" Rennie said.

"Daniel, Claudia, and Neil are doing ice-skating races and games with The Nines and Elevens," Laura said. "I'll help them get started, then come to the training. Imagine me teaching a hundred adults sign language!"

In the auditorium, Clarence, Jack, Obie, Magdalena, Nelson, Marek, and Willi were going over last-minute details. Blanche's crew had put paper tablecloths over the workstation tables, turning them into food serving counters. Dina and her sons brought in four steaming vats of *mujadara*. Mabel and Roger were putting pie slices on paper plates. At ten minutes to four, railroad workers began pouring through the doors. Dozens and dozens of them.

Clarence took the mic. "Brothers, sisters, there's plenty of hot food. Five union kids volunteered to serve you. Let's hear it for Tess, Kurt, Jeffie, Jeanette, and Ruthie!"

Applause filled the room.

"And now, while we break bread together in brotherhood and sisterhood," Clarence said, "Lucy Dahl, our Fourth Grade Freedom Academy teacher, and Diane Ward, from Diane and the Creektones, will sing a good, old-fashioned union song."

Little chills ran up and down my spine as they sang "Joe Hill." *For a hundred years, we have been fighting to get a fair deal.* I took Rennie's hand, held it tight. *I hope, oh how I hope, that this is the start of a big change. That we will win fair wages, safe working conditions, respect on our jobs, and a say in how we do them. That is not asking for much. But it would make such a big-huge difference.*

Clarence started the meeting. "Brothers and sisters, I never expected this. We have with us tonight, eighteen clerks and secretaries from three railroad company offices. They're on strike too! Let's welcome our sisters!"

A thunderstorm of applause filled the room.

"Do we stand with them?" Clarence said.

"Yes! Yes!" the crowd chanted.

"Do we demand a two-fifty minimum wage?"

"Yes! Yes!"

"Do we demand safety standards be enforced at all times?"

"Yes! Yes!"

"Do we demand to elect our own foremen, supervisors, yard bosses?"

"You bet! You bet!"

"Do we demand automatic cost of living increases?"

"Yes! Yes!"

"How are we going to get this? With picket lines," Clarence said. "And the first thing we need for a good picket line is good picket signs. So here's artist Laura Thomá to teach us sign language."

Laura held up a sign with small blue letters on a dark green background. "Is this a good sign?"

"No!"

"Why?"

"Can't read it!"

She held up another. "Same sign, white background," Laura said. "Good yet?"

"No! But better."

"How about this? Same sign, larger letters," Laura said.

"Better! Better!"

"How about enormous letters, like six inches with thick lines?"

People whistled, clapped, stomped their feet.

"So here are the simple rules," Laura said. "Don't worry about remembering them 'cause they're in today's *People's Free Press*, page four. Follow them, and you'll kill it every time."

She held up her forefinger. "One, make a big sign. Eleven by seventeen or eighteen by twenty-four." With two fingers up, she said, "Two, make big, thick letters, five to seven inches high. Three, lotsa contrast. Black on yellow, black on white, dark blue or green on white, red on white, red on yellow. Four, only one simple idea in seven words or less."

She held up a bunch of signs one after another, reading out loud, "Two-Fifty Minimum Wage. No More Safety Violations. We Demand Respect. Scabs Go Home! Locked Out! Let Reporters Write the Truth!" Then she said, "That's it, friends! Just four simple things. Thanks for letting me help you win!"

There was a whooping, hollering round of applause.

Clarence, Jack, Obie, Magdalena, Nelson, Marek, and Willi took turns chairing. They talked about how to make up slogans, chant on the picket line, how to relate to scabs, people passing by, and reporters. Carleton updated them on the strike fund, how much they would get a week, and how to sign up for it.

Magdalena took the mic. "I was just seventeen in 1934 when my dad went on strike with the teamsters. I volunteered to repair the beat-up cars they used to drive around town, looking for scab trucks making deliveries. What I remember most was one man who appeared to be everywhere at once and seemed to know everything that went on. Sisters and brothers, I am honored to introduce that man, Liam O'Farrell, a 1934 Teamsters' Strike and Rebellion leader!"

People jumped to their feet, clapping, whistling, chanting, "Liam! Liam!"

Liam talked about why and how a picketing strategy has to change continuously, reasons to move the picket line to different locations, and how to protect yourself from assaults by scabs, cops, thugs.

"Why did you have an actual hospital in Local 574 strike headquarters?" Obie asked him.

"In earlier strikes," Liam said, "hospitals called the cops when injured people were brought in from picket lines. They got crude medical care and then were hauled off to jail where they were neglected. 'You need your dressings changed? Too bad. Stitches removed? Tough luck!' Injuries that weren't critical became serious, even life-threatening in jail. So we got volunteer doctors and nurses, supplies, and equipment to treat all but the most desperate injuries. We took care of dozens of them, from broken bones to wounds. If you haven't set this up yet, get started now!"

I squeezed Rennie's hand once. She squeezed back.

Lucy and Diane closed the session by singing "We Shall Overcome," "Union Maid," and "Solidarity Forever," teaching the words as they sang, getting everyone to link arms and join in.

When the singing ended, Obie said, "Like Paulie says, this is bigger than me, larger than you. Because it's us and there's more of us than them. We are a-goin' to win!"

That evening as we were getting ready to head to Northeast Lowry Yard for a big-huge strike rally, Clarence and Obie stopped by. They pulled out their jammers, turned them on. Rennie and I already had ours going.

"Don't go to Northeast tonight," Obie said. "Marek has that well-planned. You're not needed there. But we do need you at Camden Yard, nine on the dot. Walk there, but take a roundabout route." He pulled two rubber masks from his pocket, gave me an old lady one, Rennie a young man's face. "Have a borrowed coat in a color you don't usually wear. Paulie, you could maybe borrow Clara's old one?"

"Wear heavy work gloves," Clarence said. "And steel toe Doc Partons. Tell no one where you're going, not even Clara and Ma. We already briefed Susie so the story will be in tomorrow's *Free Press*. Nobody else knows who doesn't have to."

"You may think you see people you know there. You'd be mistaken." Obie winked. "Speak to no one unless you absolutely must. Keep your voices to yourselves. Be ready to pull lots of spikes. We'll meet you at switch 9B, nine o'clock sharp."

"Got a bright flashlight?" Clarence said. "Bring it!"

"Get our drift?" Obie said.

"Yup, and I think yah're on the right track."

"Uh-huh, for sure," Rennie said. "Evening things out on fifteen for Dad!"

I felt really strange in Clara's old, worn maroon coat and matching scarf. Rennie wore a frumpy black down jacket. A group of what seemed like two dozen men and fifteen women flowed together at switch 9B within a minute after we arrived, all with old woman or young man masks.

"We are here to remove the sections of track condemned by the North-Northeast Minneapolis Industrial Safety Commission," someone dressed as a woman but with a man's voice said. "Order 1972-101."

A person in a man's mask and brown coat put a long-handled pry bar in Rennie's hands. It looked a little bit like the claw from a big hammer mounted on a three-foot-long steel handle. "You know where track fifteen is?" a woman's voice said.

Rennie nodded.

"Pull all the spikes between the two red lanterns. We're taking that part of fifteen apart and away. Maroon Coat, hold the light for Black Coat here. When they get tuckered out, you pull. Leave the spikes in piles so they're easier to see when we collect them. When you're done, come back here. Got it?"

We nodded, headed over to track fifteen. I lit the top of a spike with the flashlight. Rennie locked the claw around it, pushed the handle down.

CHAPTER 8. TAKING AWAY THE TRACKS

Spike came right out. Some were harder, but since so many ties were split and rotting, most were easy. I threw them in piles as she pulled them.

At the spot where Rennie's dad had the accident, the ties were especially rotten and splintered. She banged the spike-puller against the rail, made a loud, clanging noise. Even in the dark, we could see the rails were way out of alignment when we shined the flashlight on them. She bent down, pulled out spikes with her gloved hands, shook her head, put a spike in her pocket.

A green coat walked along the side of the track, tossing the loosened spikes into a wheelbarrow. Two black coats took off the fish plates that connected lengths of rail together. In about an hour, we were at the second lantern.

Back at Switch 9B, we could see two people cutting the rails on track eleven. On track seven, a truck with a heavy-duty hoist picked up a rail, drove it to a waiting semitruck. Four people guided it into place.

"The rails are too heavy for our equipment," Brown Coat said. "We have to cut them in half. Doesn't matter. None of them meet railroad rulebook standards. Ready to take out track four's spikes?"

We nodded, walked over, pulled, and piled. Went back to 9B when we finished.

"You might want to see them fix the signals on feeder track C. Really interesting!" Brown Coat said.

The track C signal was bright green. Someone climbed up the signal ladder, unscrewed a panel. Slipped a work glove over the green bulb. Signal went dark. Pulled a lantern battery from their pocket, wired it to the red bulb. It lit up bright ruby red. *Just like in that movie,* The Great Train Robbery! *This is mega-cool! We do not want engineers from other railroads bringing trains into the yard, having a wreck.*

Back at 9B, Brown Coat thanked us. "We're all done. Got it all. Ties too."

As we walked toward the yard gate, the hoist truck headed out, followed by two semitrucks. I saw a small red heart on the cab door of the second one.

I wondered where they were going. And who actually worked with us in the yard. Although I really wanted to know, I was so glad I did not. Sure, everything we did was legal. But in the past, that had not protected working people from punishment. Torture. Even death. *William Hushka. Eric Carlson. Henry Ness. Jack Belor. Say their names.* We were far away from the yard, walking along an empty street.

"Henry Ness! Jack Belor!" I said out loud.

"I know exactly what you mean," Rennie said.

Next morning at 6:15 the bell rang. A man in a trench coat flashed a badge at me when I opened the door. "Mäkinen, agent Gummler, FBI. I have a few questions about what you did last night."

"I have nothing to say to ya, Dummler."

"Who was in Camden—"

"I have nothing to say to ya, Dummler."

"Yard with you?"

I was silent.

"You could face twenty, thirty years in the pen, Mäkinen."

"I have nothing to say to ya, Dummer."

"Make a deal now, we'll cut your prison time down. No hard labor or solitary."

"Goodbye, Dummer. Remove your foot from our house. You're trespassing." I slammed the door. "Make sure we have enough jam with our breakfast," I called out.

The doorbell rang again. Ready to give Dummer hell, I threw it open. Sheila handed me the *Free Press*, called out, "Extra! Extra! Safety Commission Removes Condemned Track from Camden Yard! I can't believe they did that, Paulie!"

"Someone was brave!" I said. "Thanks, Sheila. Yah're doing important work."

At our eight o'clock meeting with the roofing factory workers, Otis Agard, a shingle packer, worried about scabs taking the condemned tags off and restarting the factory.

"Won't happen, Otis," Luke said. "Someone took away track fifteen last night. No supplies, factory can't run. Didn't you see today's *Free Press*?"

"Yea, I did, but I just don't believe it," Otis said. "Nobody could've done that."

"Someone did!" Marcello Fontana said. "Saw it in the paper, went over to have a look-see. *Cavolo*! Everything the newspaper said was true! Must have been real bad dudes to do that."

"So if the factory's shut down anyways," Roosevelt Washington said, "we should strike! It's unsafe. And the pay is crap!"

"We got real bad dudes backing us," Luke said. "Just wonder who did it!"

"Robin Hood? Batman? The Green Hornet?" Marcello said. "Who knows?"

"But how will we pay our bills?" Otis said.

I stood up, waved my hands. "Guys, I was not kidding around. We have ta finish this auditorium, and it will not have rough wooden benches when it is done. Plus, we have not even started work on the big-huge newsroom and pressroom we need for the *People's Free Press*. We want to put all of ya to work, at two-fifty an hour. You can work some overtime if ya wanna, but ya do not have ta. Starting tomorrow."

"Raise your hand if you're interested," Rennie said. "Yes siree, all hands on deck. Paulie, Blanche, Harry, and I will talk with you one by one 'n' figure out where you fit in, to the max."

"If we're working for you, how can we picket?" Otis said.

"Otis, man! We sure as heck can work that into yahr schedule," I said. "No problem."

We divided them into four groups, talked with them, got an amazing list of skills from tile work and structural steel to electrical work, plumbing, and masonry. Most guys had two skills, some had three and four. We asked them to come in at 8:30 tomorrow morning ready to work. Then the four of us planned assignments for them, talked about Hank the assistant yard boss, Lyle Sund the scab engineer, and the scab brakeman with cabinet-making skills.

"I'll take the brakeman and try him out on the spot," Blanche said. "We're short in that department. If he doesn't have issues working with a woman, that will tell us a lot about him. I asked Cliff, the architect, to come by at ten to help us interview Lyle."

We talked with Hank first. Described the newsroom and pressroom projects and the pressure we were under to get them up and running. Showed him the spaces. Asked him how he would organize them.

"First step, I'd talk with the crew. Find out who knows what. Then I'd ask for opinions about the best way to tackle the job so we could learn from each other and come to an agreement. If we think a major change is needed, we come to you to talk it through. And I'd do that every day. Yard Boss used to call me a dreamer, but that way we're more effective than if I tried to order everybody around. That okay with you?"

"We're looking for that kind of leadership, to the max," Rennie said.

"Way I see it now," Hank said, "second step, clear everything out of the construction spaces. Third, make a dropped ceiling with cheap acoustic tile to cut noise, make it easier to heat the rooms. Fourth, put in phone lines and electric. Fifth, build long worktables for the newsroom, use desk lamps to light the area. Can you afford to buy desk chairs? Reporters sit a lot, need comfort."

"Might as well get them sooner than later, as far as that goes," Rennie said.

"All along the way, if the crew has a better way, I want to hear it. I don't know about heat," Hank said. "That's beyond me. Maybe electric space heaters to give you a jump start?"

Rennie gave my hand one strong squeeze. Harry nodded. Blanche stuck her thumb up.

"Yah're hired, Hank. Two-fifty an hour okay with ya?"

He grinned. "That's ten cents more'n I was making! And you didn't call me a dreamer. You bet I'm in!" He pulled a pad and pen from his pocket. "I know the clock starts tomorrow, but I want to start thinking and planning right now. That okay?"

I squeezed Rennie's hand once. She looked at Harry and Blanche. "Yes siree! But are we going to make him work off the clock? Clarence told me he has five kids."

"No way," Blanche said.

"Clock starts right now," Harry said. "You bring lunch with you?"

"I can skip lunch. No problem."

"Nokay! Ya work, ya eat! We will get ya lunch."

"I'm not used to being treated this way!" Hank said.

"Get used to it!" Rennie and I said together.

"One more question," Hank said. "Shouldn't there be a passageway between news and pressrooms? Could we break through the wall separating Betty and Olson Halls?"

"Great question, Hank!" Blanche said. "Our architect'll be here soon. We'll ask."

Lyle Sund arrived wearing a big-huge smile.

Cliff looked him over. "Aren't you the guy who showed me how to save fifty grand on the A&M Insurance Corporation heating system, oh, twenty, twenty-one years ago?"

"Yessir, with hot water radiators instead of steam."

"I used to call you the architect's secret weapon. Always wondered where you disappeared to."

"Long story for another time. You can sure do a lot with this space, uh-huh!"

We took him to all three Halls, showed him our clinic office, explained what we hoped to have there someday.

"How do you plan to heat the auditorium?" Lyle said.

"Dedicated gas furnace," Cliff said. "Hot water radiant heat under the floor."

"What about heat recovery? High ceilings like this, all your heat's going to be up there," he pointed. "An auditorium that size needs a ventilation system to keep the air fresh. You have one planned?"

"Of course," Cliff said.

"Work heat recovery right into that," Lyle said.

"Hadn't thought of that!" Cliff said.

He and Cliff discussed fresh air flows, heat circulation, having individual furnaces for each space versus one big furnace for the whole complex. Came up with a plan, which made a lot of sense. So of course we hired Lyle to work on auditorium and newsroom heating systems.

Lowell Krüger, the brakeman, arrived carrying a toolbox.

Blanche explained our projects to him. "How would you put backs on these benches using the lumber we have on hand?" she said.

"I'd need to bring my router." He pulled a pad from his toolbox, sketched the bench backs, drew the individual pieces. "This is not to scale. That's the next step."

"How do you know this will be comfortable?" Blanche said.

"Good question! Back before I went to prison, I built benches for the army during, you know, the Korean War? Boss at the shop had us make a prototype, get lots of people to sit on it. Also depends on how long people will be sitting for. Short sitters get a different design. This one's for your newsroom, the right height for typing tables. Auditoriums are somewhat different."

Blanche asked him lots of questions. His answers were detailed and clear.

"What did ya go to prison for?" I said.

"I was young and stupid. Drank too much at a bar, slugged a guy. Got two years for assault. But now I can't get a decent job, just odds and ends. So I'm still serving the sentence, you know? I don't drink anymore, ever."

"You have any problem with a woman team leader?" Rennie said.

"From the questions she asked, she knows her stuff. That's all that matters to me."

"You ready to work?" Blanche said.

"Even packed a lunch, just in case."

Blanche looked at us. We nodded. "You're hired!"

As we walked to our office, Rennie said, "Holy buckets, that felt really good!"

"You bet! We are making something from nothing again."

In the mail piled on my desk, I found two more Communal Association memos written by Stinkworth. The first criticized his informant, *Journette* business reporter Hugo Hagnoss, for not being aware the reporters and pressmen were expecting and preparing for a lockout. I showed it to Rennie.

"Okay then, we knew they have spies 'n' Georgia 'n' Tom said they didn't trust him, 'n' we're not hiring him, so this is not big-time stuff."

But the second hit hard. It praised Elmer McGill for trying to hold off a strike and his detailed reports on railroad workers, with a copy of a $600 check made out to him for services rendered. Under his endorsement on the check, McGill had written his driver's license number. A note attached to this one read, "Beware! There are others like McGill!"

"Shit!" Rennie said. "I'm freaked out, no halfway about it." She started to walk back and forth. "I need to think."

"Can Russ confirm that is McGill's actual license number?" I said.

CHAPTER 8. TAKING AWAY THE TRACKS

"Probably, but McGill could claim he didn't write it there, as far as that goes." Rennie walked some more, suddenly stood stock still. "So here's the plan." She took a pad, filled a page, showed it to me.

I wrote a note on the bottom. "Genius in bloom! We will do it!"

She tore the page into little pieces, opened her purse, poured them into an old manila envelope. "For when we light the fireplace tonight." She winked.

Linda came bounding in, face red, sweat on her forehead. "Billy, me, Ruka, Althea, and Neil got eleven hundred kids to walk out of school to protest the war! They're marching on the draft board in Brooklyn Center, gonna sit in! We told kids to bring signs, and hundreds did. Ninety-two are on hunger strike. We got so much done! We need a couple of Gordy's cops with us. And can you call the press?"

"I'll page Gordy on the CB radio," Rennie said.

"Where's Ma? I can't wait to tell her!"

"At Northeast Yard with Clarence and Obie," I said.

"Gorwald here," the CB radio squawked. "What's up FastTalk?"

"Gordy, we need two of your guys to protect a high school march on the draft board. Eleven hundred kids!"

"Where, FastTalk?"

"Historian here, Gorwald," Linda said. "Osseo Road."

"I'm paging a squad car, Historian. Do you read me?"

"Roger, Gorwald. Thanks, old buddy! Over and out."

"Couldn't find a phone to use," Linda said. "Caught a bus up Humboldt, ran the rest of the way here. Phew! Gotta get back to the march!"

"I will drive ya," I said.

"And I'll call the press," Rennie said.

It was a big-huge thrill to see all those kids marching. And I was so proud of Linda. Osseo was a busy road, so they kept to the sidewalk. Motorists saw them, honked, cheered, waved. I wanted to stay and watch, but the CB radio squawked.

"Beagle here, you read me, Mahrove-Rove?"

"Roger, Beagle. But who are ya?"

"Russ. Just chose my CB handle. Ma, Clarence, and Obie are at Betty Hall, need to talk with you."

"Roger, Beagle. Be there in ten."

In the small Teen Council conference room, Clarence, face tight, banged his fists on the table. "We caught McGill ordering the scab gandy dancers to keep working. Jerk was acting like he was their boss."

"He wasn't very good at it," Ma said. "Even I could see that."

"I just plain told 'em, brothers, he ain't your boss," Obie said. "Just a gandy dancer like you an' me. 'Well, why'd that White man say report here today when we was at Northeast Yard yesterday?' one of them done asked me. I told 'em Whitey McGill wants to get you all in trouble and outta here. McGill tried to get me fired 'til Clarence here caught on and beat the tar out of him."

Clarence punched his palm. "I told the guys, when McGill said these are White men's jobs, I saw red. Wasn't going to let him do that to my friend Obie."

"The guys asked, 'Well, who's this lady you're with?' " Obie said. "I told 'em she's good people a-helpin' us organize the strike."

"The guys weren't sure who to believe," Ma said. "Holy moly, can you blame them? So I said, 'Alrighty, see that mill over there? The owner is our friend, really good guy. He wants his siding rebuilt. It's not a scab job. Will you come take a look?' "

"The guys grumbled, but they walked over with us," Clarence said. "Burt had the equipment sitting there, and it didn't say Minnesota Consolidated Construction Services on it. There were piles of ties, heaps and heaps of ballast, mounds of spikes and fish plates, a stack of new rail."

"I told 'em, 'See those ties,' " Obie said. " 'Brand spankin' new. If Minnesota Consolidated even gives you ties, they're in rough shape. This guy has the tools and stuff you need to work with. Now c'mon inside for a minute.' "

"We explained this was only a temporary work site," Ma said, "but the striking workers were demanding a locker room, showers, and a lunchroom like the mill has for all the other rail yards."

"I asked them, 'Who leads your chantin',' " Obie said.

"They said the scab boss wouldn't hire him," Clarence said. "Called him a troublemaker. And they didn't know how to measure track cant, warp, and gradient 'cause their White boss wouldn't show them."

"So Obie and Clarence asked them oodles of questions," Ma said. "Had them do some work on Burt's track."

CHAPTER 8, TAKING AWAY THE TRACKS

"They're good guys and good workers," Obie said. "But they need leadership, and the five of them aren't enough to pull up this track and replace it with new."

"How many more gandy dancers do they need 'n' stuff?" Rennie said.

"Minimum?" Clarence said. "Seven more. We asked Burt what he thought. He said safety was above everything else. Hire what you need."

"But he also pointed out," Ma said, "we already have strikers from five yards and two mainlines. He thinks we can spare some off the picket lines to work with these guys."

"Clarence and Jack can*not* be spared, no way!" Obie said. "They need to be a-organizin' the strike. Besides, they can't lead chantin'."

We went back and forth, looking at all the angles, came up with a plan. Obie would be their chanter and foreman since he knew how to lead, chant, and measure. And we would ask seven more guys from all five yards to work on this crew.

Rennie wrote down our plan for dealing with McGill, showed it around. We had a "discussion" about it on pads, came to a consensus, tore the notes up.

"We're going to toast marshmallows tonight!" Rennie said, pouring the bits of paper into her envelope.

Russ knocked on the door. "Paulie, Karen, Judge Woodruff is about to rule on our injunction request, wants us there."

Rennie put my tape recorder in her bag. We drove downtown. In the courtroom, Archibald Hastings-Dankworth was yelling at the clerk, "You will take me to speak with Judge Woodruff in his chambers this instant!"

Rennie reached into her bag.

"Sir, the judge expressly told me he did not want to be disturbed."

"Do you know who I am? I'll get you fired and him recalled."

"Perhaps you will, sir. But I answer to him, not you."

Stinkworth banged his cane against the court clerk's desk. "He answers to me! Do you understand me? I do not have all day. Hop to it, boy, if you know what's good for you. I'll not take no for an answer."

The clerk pointed to the court officer. "Officer Diebold will remove you from this courtroom if you don't stop your disorderly conduct."

The court officer stood up, walked toward Stinkworth.

"Well, I never... There will be consequences," Stinkworth said, and sat down, his foot tapping, face full of fury.

The moment Judge Woodruff entered the room, Stinkworth, despite his cane, leaped from his seat and strode forward. "Woodruff, I've had enough of this nonsense. Recuse yourself from this case. You've had dealings with Mäkinen and his accessories. You are not impartial."

"I did not call on you," the judge said.

Officer Diebold sprinted across the room, stood nose to nose with Stinkworth. "Sit down and remain quiet until the judge recognizes you, or I'll remove you."

Judge Woodruff stepped up to the bench, sat down, banged his gavel. "Mr. Hastings-Dankworth, this is a simple matter of enforcing a very straightforward law. Minneapolis Civil Service, Section 11.04 requires a disciplinary warning, a written reprimand, and suspension *before* an employee can be fired. Your office could not provide written evidence that any of these steps were taken before you fired Shingle Creek Park's entire staff. There is nothing to be partial ab—"

"You are *not* impartial, Woodruff."

"And you are in contempt of court, *Mister* Hastings-Dankworth. One more outburst, and I will impose a fine."

"Any judge worth his keep would rule in my favor."

"In other words, he would be partial to *you* and you would call that impartial. I hereby order injunctive relief for all of the Park Board's Civil Service employees at Shingle Creek Park. They are all to be reinstated immediately, with full back pay. And you, *Mister* Hastings-Dankworth, are fined a thousand dollars for your latest outburst."

"I'll have your head for this, Woodruff!"

The judge banged his gavel. "You'll pay an additional thousand dollar fine for this new contemptuous outburst. Payment of fines must be made within five days by certified check to the order of Hennepin County District Court. Leave my courtroom right now, or I'll impose jail time."

Stinkworth marched down the aisle and out the door.

The judge banged his gavel again. "In the matter of the Shingle Creek Teen Council vs. the Minneapolis School Board, the regulations for community use of school facilities are perfectly clear. I hereby find the School Board in violation of said regulations and order them to immediately re-

CHAPTER 8, TAKING AWAY THE TRACKS

instate the Shingle Creek Teen Council's senior swimming program and open gym nights, as well as all other school facility uses at Shingle Creek. I will see the plaintiffs in my chambers."

Judge Woodruff stepped off the dais, strode up the aisle. We followed. Once inside, he pulled the jammer we had given him from his pocket, turned it on, sat down, wiped his forehead with a handkerchief. I could see him shaking.

Rennie reached into her bag, turned off the recorder.

"Thank you for coming," the judge said. "That man is terrifying. I would not have had the courage to cross him if you weren't here."

"Your Honor, we got it all on tape, to the max," Rennie said.

Judge Woodruff looked startled.

"I have an idea, Yahr Honor," I said. "Suppose we started yahr reelection campaign now? We could play the tape on KPFP. Then announce, 'Remember this in June! Judge Gannon Woodruff stands up to the Fat Cats. Vote for Gannon Woodruff for District Court Judge.' I bet we could get KPFP to play it daily."

"But judges can't campaign that way."

"You wouldn't have to, no siree, Bob," Rennie said. "We would run one of those disclaimers, 'Paid for by Working People for Judge Woodruff.'"

The judge started chuckling, and that set us all off laughing.

When we could talk again, I took a red loose-leaf binder from my briefcase. "This should cheer ya up even more, Yahr Honor. Yahr press conference clippings."

He looked through it. "*The New York Times*! *Chicago Tribune*! *Duluth Herald*! *Washington Post*! Agency France-Presse! Wow! It goes on and on! No wonder Mr. Hastings-Dankworth is desperate. He used to pressure us behind closed doors." The judge seemed to be thinking for a moment. "Can we really save democracy?"

"Yes siree! It is a job bigger than me, larger than you. But all of us working together, we can," Rennie said.

"You people are amazing!"

That evening, Rennie and I sat on the couch in my room with a pile of books beside her.

"How are ya managing to take so much time away from campus?"

"I'll tell you my secret, Paavali, but it's hush-hush 'n' stuff. I read all the assigned stuff first 'n' then I came up with ideas for original papers by poking around in the professional journals for that topic, with some guidance from librarians. I discussed my ideas with my professors, 'n' holy buckets, every one of them got real interested 'n' gave me some great recommendations."

"But how does that help ya save time?"

"I ask them if I get an A on this paper, can that be my final grade 'n' I explain that I have a demanding job where I need to be away from campus a lot. Two of them said yes right off the bat, 'n' I didn't have to take any more exams either. The other two asked me a whole lot of questions 'n' we had long discussions, 'n' for math, I had to solve some complex problems on the spot 'n' then they said, 'Deal!' So I'm already finished with six classes with straight A's in the bag."

"And the seventh?"

"Biology. The prof said forget the paper 'cause this is a hands-on lab course, 'n' I'll really need that knowledge as a lawyer 'n' she knows 'cause her husband is one, but she gave me a final exam 'n' I aced it, so now all I have to do school-wise is one lab a week 'til the end of the quarter."

"Is Greg upset about that?"

"Oh, Greg!" She put her hands on her cheeks, rocked her head from side to side. "Oh, Greg! I'm seeing him Sunday."

"You do not sound happy about him."

"Like you would say, Paulie-Paul, let's change the channel." She moved closer to me.

I stroked her cheek. My snakes went nuts. "So what are all these books for?"

"To get a head start on next quarter's classes 'cause no halfway about it, all hell is breaking loose here in Shingle Creek 'n' I want to be here for it." She sat on my lap, leaned her head against my chest.

Gee, that felt good! I wrapped my arms around her, punched my snakes in the head hard as I could.

"Paavali, I'm sort of scared about tomorrow."

"Why? Russ said ya have an airtight case."

" 'Cause I read up on it, 'n' whenever there's a sexual molestation case, the attorneys rake women over the coals, lie about them, ask them nasty personal questions 'n' just tear them apart, 'n' Russ says he's surprised Knight's lawyer subpoenaed you 'n' that's really aggressive 'n' stuff."

"Rennie! Remember when ya accused the FBI agents of being Russian operatives and they turned tail and ran like heck? Ya know how to be aggressive. I know it is unpleasant. And not easy. But I also know ya can handle it."

I so badly wanted to kiss her. So I did. She kissed me back, put her arms around me, held me tight.

I kept smashing those snakes' heads, and they quieted down some, but they would not let go of my dick. In my mind, I begged it to get hard. But it could not. *I am going to conquer this somehow, and meanwhile, I am going to enjoy kissing the love of my life, and yeah, that's exactly what she is, even though I cannot say it out loud yet, and screw you, snakes, if my love for her is a problem for ya.*

"I wish we could have sex, Paavali."

"Oh, Rennie, me too. I *am* getting closer to solving it, but my dick…"

"I know. I can feel it. It's okay. Kissing you is just what I need right now."

And I needed it too. She was filling me with energy and strength kiss by kiss.

After about an hour, Rennie said, "Doesn't it feel weird they organized the track removal without involving us?"

"How do I even explain it? Kinda makes me feel left out. Worried things will get outta control."

"Me too, Paavali. I've been talking to myself about it, for sure. But they did a fantastic job."

"But how will we know what is going on?"

"I've been pondering that too. Do we have to know everything 'n' stuff? Why? Do we want to lead? Or control?"

"What if they do not want us to lead anymore?"

"That would be a bummer and a half, yes siree, but, Paavali, isn't that what democracy's about?"

"Yeah, I guess."

"Look it, we all worked really hard to create more leaders, and you did especially, 'n' now, we have them! That's success, big-time, 'n' don't you think everybody knows that? Knock that yammering statue of your mother off your shoulder!"

"How did ya even know about that?"

"Because I *know* you! Just remember, it is bigger than me 'n' larger than you, but if *you* had not been an awesome leader right off the bat, none of this would have started. You done good. You got it nailed. Like you would say, 'get used to it!' "

"I *think* yah're right. Yah're setting me off thinking."

She took me in her arms, kissed my face so many times I lost count. "Those books'll wait, yes siree! I just want more hugging and kissing right now."

I put my arms around her. Kissed her again. Sang a silly song in my head, with a jazz band playing along so loud it was drowning out the hissing snakes. *Yah're winning her back, one step at a time, yah're on the right track, though it's quite a climb! Dooby bop, dooby bop, woo, woo, woo! She's a-getting back together with you!*

CHAPTER 9, POLYCHROME WOMAN RETURNS

FRIDAY, MARCH 3, 1972

Next morning, Rennie, Russ, Clara, and I drove downtown for Theodore Knight's trial for calling her a fifty-cent whore in public. She took four books with her from last night's pile. I had my book about the 1932 Bonus Army demonstration in Washington DC.

"Judge Hanna is quite conservative," Russ said, "but his four daughters are all college grads. He's one of the few judges who sometimes give women a fair shake. Just remember, when the defendant's lawyer asks you an offensive question, hesitate before answering. That gives me a chance to object."

The reporter from *Minnesota Daily* was there, and so was our Georgia, plus Jerome from Associated Press, Perrine from Agency France-Presse, and Nora O'Farrell from KPFP, wearing a particularly elegant outfit. *Great! Local, national, and international coverage!*

The defendant, Theodore Knight, sat next to his father, who looked like him. Rennie had her books piled beside her. Russ put me on the stand first, then Rennie. He asked us routine questions about our heights and weights, how we knew each other, who lived in our house. Then he asked Rennie what happened. It was all straightforward, except the defendant's lawyer kept objecting. And getting overruled. Russ took testimony from two eyewitnesses. Next, two women testified that the defendant had assaulted them physically and sexually. Louise Doscher and Helen Magelby, both of them under five feet tall, had won lawsuits against Knight and had a difficult time collecting their awards. Every step of the way, Knight's lawyer objected and was overruled, until Judge Hanna threatened to hold him in contempt for obstruction of justice, which happened at the perfect time, right before Russ cross-examined Knight.

"Master Knight—"

"Objection!" his lawyer said. "Theodore Knight is over eighteen."

"Sustained."

"Well, I never would have guessed from his demeanor," Russ said. "How tall are you, *Mister* Knight?"

"Six feet, two inches."

"Uh-huh. And how much do you weigh?"

"Two hundred and five pounds."

"I see. So you're sixteen inches taller than Ms. Ahlberg and ninety-five pounds heavier. Is she one of only three petite women you've molested? Or are there more we do not know about?"

Knight turned redder than a rooster's comb.

"Objection!"

"Sustained."

"Mr. Knight, perhaps my question hit home? Why did your face just get so red?"

"Objection!"

"Sustained."

"Where were you on February 15, 1972, at 10:54 a.m., Mr. Knight?"

"I don't remember."

"How convenient! Do you remember you have a History class that ends at 10:50 a.m. on Tuesdays?"

"Oh, yeah, I do."

"Mm-hm. And what comes after History?"

"I guess Chem lecture at eleven."

"And your private limousine takes you from class to class?"

"No, I walk across the quad."

"I see. Who did you see while walking across the quad that day?"

"What day?"

"Tuesday, February 15, 1972. You are under oath, Mr. Knight."

Knight's sudden grin looked stupid. "I couldn't believe it! I'd never seen an actual whore before. What the hell was Karen Ahlberg doing on

CHAPTER 9, POLYCHROME WOMAN RETURNS

campus? She was so sexy, exactly like a twelve-year-old, I just had to grab her and find out how much she charges."

Knight's lawyer rolled his eyes. "Theodore!"

"So you grabbed her?" Russ said.

"A little bit."

"By the hand?"

"No. Where whores like to be grabbed. Between the legs. They like that."

Knight's lawyer held his head in his hands. His father grinned.

"What happened next?" Russ said.

"She slugged me six or eight times, broke two ribs, knocked me down. That's why we're countersuing for a hundred grand."

"So let me understand, Mr. Knight. You said nothing to her, grabbed her crotch, she knocked you down. And you have no idea why?"

"I *asked* her, 'Karen Ahlberg, are you a fifty-cent whore?' She could've said no."

"Oh, of course! You grabbed first, then asked?"

"I guess."

"How did you know Ms. Ahlberg's name?"

"Oh, from *Minnesota Patriot*. It *showed* her being trained for whoring by that guy who testified before."

"Do you know who publishes *Minnesota Patriot*?"

"Minnesota Vigilantes Against Vice, whoever they are. A picture is worth a thousand words, though. I *saw* her being trained."

"What do you know about Minnesota Vigilantes Against Vice?"

"What is there to know?"

"That they are being sued for millions of dollars for libel."

"Objection."

"Overruled."

Russ turned on a slide projector, displaying the photo from *Minnesota Patriot* on a screen at the front of the courtroom. "So, this is the photo you saw, Mr. Knight?"

"Yeah, that's it. Really hot, right?"

"A man and a woman hugging and kissing. How do you know more than that?"

"I thought lawyers were smart. By the caption underneath, dum-dum!"

"So in your brilliant mind, you saw a photo in a publication with no address and no names for editor or writer, the caption claimed he's a pimp and she's a prostitute, and you believed it?"

"Why wouldn't I?"

"If someone put a photo of you in their anonymous publication with a caption, "Theodore Knight wants to have sex with twelve-year-olds in—""

"Objection!"

"Overruled."

"In *your* world, they could do that, Mr. Knight?"

"Objection!"

"Overruled."

"Bastard!" Knight shouted.

"You are in contempt of court, Mr. Knight. One more outburst, and it's jail time."

Russ smiled. "So now that you've just heard Ms. Ahlberg and Mr. Mäkinen tell you they are longtime friends gradually becoming girlfriend and boyfriend, do you still believe she's a prostitute and he's pimping her?"

"It said so right under the photo," Knight said, sounding like a petulant child.

"What's your grade point average in college, Mr. Knight?" Russ said.

"Objection."

"Sustained."

Next, the defendant's lawyer put Rennie on the stand. "How many times did Mr. Mäkinen pay you to have sex with him?"

"We have never had sex."

"But we have this photo of you hugging and kissing him."

"That is not sex."

"But his hand is on your butt in that photo."

"That is my back, Counselor. You don't know your ass from your elbow?"

"Watch your language, Ms. Ahlberg!" the judge said. He looked like he was trying hard not to laugh.

"How old are you, Ms. Ahlberg?" the lawyer said.

"I'll be seventeen in three weeks."

CHAPTER 9, POLYCHROME WOMAN RETURNS

"So you were on campus, cutting school, just to drum up business, Ms. Ahlberg?"

"I am a pre-law university freshman taking twenty-one credits."

"That statement's not credible. You're under oath!" He shook his finger.

"It's on my university transcript. You didn't check it, Counselor? Really?"

The lawyer kept at it. "When Mr. Mäkinen sent you out whoring, how much of your earnings did he keep?"

"Once upon a time, there was a lawyer who made up totally false stories. I am not a whore. Mr. Mäkinen is not a pimp."

"Then how does a sixteen-year-old girl from a dirt-poor family have nine hundred and twenty-two dollars in a bank account?"

"I am the assistant director of Shingle Creek Park. That is a paid position. Dirt-poor families don't own two houses. Mine does."

"But he took money from you every Friday night. May I remind you, Ms. Ahlberg, you are under oath."

Rennie glared at the lawyer. "So are you, Counselor. That statement is totally false. All in your imagination. Your honor, I am only pre-law, so I don't know the answer to this question. Can a lawyer use utter slanders on cross-examination?"

"Mr. Tinworth," the judge said to the attorney, "you have crossed the line of courtroom privilege and presented mere allegations with no proof whatsoever. You are hereby warned! I shall instruct the jury to ignore all allegations that Ms. Ahlberg is involved in prostitution."

Tinworth nodded. "Are you a virgin, Ms. Ahlberg?"

The judge banged his gavel.

"Objection!" Russ said.

"Sustained!"

Tinworth put the two women, Louise Doscher and Helen Magelby, through the same kind of nasty questioning, but the judge's reprimand forced him to tone it down. Russ had prepared them well. With every misleading, false, or inappropriate question, they hit back hard. Russ and Tinworth made their closing statements. The judge instructed the jury, sent them off to deliberate.

"This might take a while," Russ said. "But it looks like you're both prepared."

We opened our books, compared how the Bonus Army was described in Rennie's History text versus my in-depth book. "This is great, Paavali! I have an awesome topic for next quarter's History paper. 'The Treatment of the Bonus March in Textbooks Versus History Books.'"

After two hours and eleven minutes, the jury returned. "We voted unanimously to award Ms. Ahlberg $10,000, plus legal costs of $500," the foreman announced. "Mr. Knight's countersuit is invalid, since Ms. Ahlberg was defending herself."

Knight's father yelled, "This is a phony court. That jury is a bunch of ignorant rabble. We know our rights!"

The judge banged his gavel. "Mr. Knight Senior, I hold you in contempt. One more peep from you, and I will impose jail time. Mr. Knight Junior, approach the bench."

Theodore's shoulders drooped. He dragged himself forward to face the judge.

"I uphold the jury's decision, but I'm adding that you must write a *convincing* letter of apology to Ms. Ahlberg *and* Mr. Mäkinen. You will deliver it to *me* within one week. If it is satisfactory, I will send it to them. If it is *not* satisfactory, you will be fined $500 a week until you write a letter that *is* acceptable. Proceeds of said fines will go to Ms. Ahlberg and Mr. Mäkinen as additional damages. You have ten days to pay awarded damages to Ms. Ahlberg or file an appeal. If you have not complied after ten days, Mr. Knight, you will be jailed for contempt of court. Do I make myself clear?"

"But—"

"Yes or no, Mr. Knight?"

"Okay, have it your way."

"You are dismissed, Mr. Knight."

After Judge Hanna left the courtroom, I heard Knight's father say, "Don't worry, Teddy-boy! Judge Ovington's in my pocket. We'll win on appeal."

Nora O'Farrell was standing behind him, microphone hidden in her shawl. She stepped in front of them. "A pocket judge is absolutely necessary to get justice, right, Mr. Knight?"

CHAPTER 9, POLYCHROME WOMAN RETURNS

"You're damned right! The courts are here to protect society from the great unwashed. This idiot judge failed to do that."

"So sometimes, Mr. Knight, you have to sort of grease the wheels of justice with a little cash, right?"

"It helps, ma'am. It helps."

"You know, Theodore, what you said about twelve-year-old girls is very interesting. Do you have much experience with them?"

"Just my two cousins, Poppy and Victoria."

"What was that like?"

"Amazing! They really put out, went all the way."

"All the way?" Nora said.

"Yes, ma'am. They're on the pill, so it doesn't matter."

"Well, Theodore, good luck to you. You're going to need it," Nora said.

I whispered in Rennie's ear, "Nora nailed him!"

"We'll get the tape into Judge Ovington's hands," she whispered back.

I hugged her. "Ya did a great job on the stand, Counselor! Congratulations! And holy sautéed trash fish! Ya were terrific, Russ!" I hugged him too.

"Karen, that was a clever question you asked about whether lawyers can ask questions based on utter slanders," Russ said. "Did you see the look on the judge's face? Tinworth was starting to really get out of hand, but you made the judge clamp down on him."

In the courthouse lobby, Russ used a payphone to call his office. The grin on his face was replaced with a bigger one. "We have to go to the sheriff's office, Paulie, to pick up *your* slander lawsuit check."

Betty and Bucky were already at the sheriff's when we got there. I showed my driver's license to the clerk, signed a receipt, and she handed me a beautiful, gray check for a million-and-a-half bucks.

"These take ten days for the funds to be clear and ready to use in your account. Don't spend it in one place!" She grinned.

"Carleton said we should deposit them today," Betty said, "and to meet him afterward in the Teen Council conference room."

"All right then," Rennie said, "but we're picking up a chocolate cake at Camden Superette, 'n' I'll call Denise from this payphone here 'n' ask her to make fresh coffee."

Checks deposited, coffee and cake served, we sat down with Betty, Bucky, Russ, Ma, and Carleton.

"This won't take but a minute," Carleton said. "First, you are not taxed on a damage award. But if you put the funds in your account and later donate them to a nonprofit organization, you get a tax deduction. The amounts involved here mean your tax bill for 1972 will be zero." He took a bite of cake, a sip of coffee. "Man, I love this Egekvist fudge cake! Now, here's the important part. During the first ten days, your funds can't be withdrawn but they *are* earning interest. At seven percent, that will be $2,877 for each of you. Personally, I think you should keep the interest, donate the rest. None of you are rich, and this will give you a nice emergency fund."

"I am for it," I said.

"Sounds okay to me," Bucky said. "Whaddaya you think, Betts?"

"Fine, but I also want to give five hundred bucks to each of our kids, including Roger. Everyone okay with that? Ah, all hands on deck!"

"But there's one more thing," Carleton said. "I think everyone who wins a lawsuit with our legal clinic's help should donate half a percent to the clinic. That will provide stable funding for the clinic and help it grow."

"Could we use some of that to pay our interns?" Russ said. "They're working really hard, doing professional-quality work."

"I am okay with that, but wait a minute!" I said. "Half a percent is too small. Three percent is more like it, with a cap at fifty thousand a year. But we should get everything approved at the meeting tonight. In favor? All hands on deck!"

When the meeting was over, Ma handed me two envelopes. The first, delivered by messenger, was a check made out to the Teen Council from Judge Woodruff, for six hundred bucks for Linda, Billy, and Susie's judges' press conference.

"I think we should put it in the strike fund, yes siree, but we'll vote on it tonight," Rennie said. "What's in the plain brown envelope?"

It was a single sheet of paper from a legal pad. A note in blue ink read, "Warning! Gremling is training an armed militia. Ninety men with rifles. Police Department has deputized them. Communal Association is paying for it. They plan to use it against you." There was no signature.

CHAPTER 9. POLYCHROME WOMAN RETURNS

"I'm having a cow, man," Rennie said. "How do we know this is real or how to prepare for it, 'n' I'm totally freaked out."

Suddenly, I could not get comfortable in my chair. "Four million bucks will buy a lotta guns and people ta train us to use them. We have ta defend ourselves."

"Me, I question that," Bucky said. "In the '34 strike, the union collected strikers' guns and knives and put them under lock and key. It would've been more than Belor and Ness dying if strikers had been armed. You have to adjust your gray matter, Paulie."

"Don't have a cow, man," Rennie said. "But remember what Fred told us that day, lying down in the field? The moment they know we have guns, we'll be facing the National Guard and the army, no halfway about it."

"But that militia will kill us," I said. "They will not even spare our kids, I just know it."

"Paulie," Ma said, putting her hand on my shoulder. "I know you want to protect everyone. But I read in that book our Professor Larry recommended that the cops in Philadelphia blew up a house full of Black Panthers after they bought guns."

"Tarnation! They threw a bunch more in jail," Betty said, "for years and years."

"We'd lose a lot of public support if we got into a shooting war," Carleton said, "even if Gremling's army fired first."

"Paulie-Paul, remember how you feel about killing people in 'Nam! Think how upset you'd be if you shot and killed someone here in Shingle Creek. You, who won't even kill ants and flies 'cause they're living beings? It just doesn't fit you right, you're darn tootin' it doesn't."

"Okay, okay! But I flat out wanna bring it up at the meeting. Ya good with that?"

"Hoo, boy!" Betty said. "It's a discussion I think we should have. But! But! If the majority is against us getting guns, how will you handle that, Paulie?"

"Will you be able to change your brain cells around?" Bucky said.

"I would be walloped because I just have a very bad feeling about all of this. But majority rules," I said. "I would have ta go along with them."

Rennie put her arms around me. "You'll think about all this? Promise?"

"Promise!"

When we met with Irene, Ma, Billy, Linda, Rennie, Mabel, Clarence, and Evelyn later that afternoon to plan that night's community meeting, nobody thought we should buy guns. It worried me. I thought we were making it easy for the bosses to slaughter us. Nonetheless, I managed to keep on truckin' and work with everyone to plan a solid team-speak for the meeting's main speech. When we finished, I asked Linda who was leading the draft board sit-in right then. She told me Neil and Althea were. I asked her if she was worried. She said their style was a little different than hers and Billy's, but that was not a concern because in a people's movement, everyone had to work together even if there are some differing opinions. She set me off thinking all over again.

All of us were so busy getting the auditorium ready, we did not have time to make sandwiches for dinner, so I called an order into Camden Superette and picked them up for my family. Rennie and I were eating Finnish *hernekeitto* split pea and pork soup and Archie's Swedish chicken salad sandwiches when Gordy checked in with us.

"Good setup we have here from a security point of view," he said. "We can keep picketers out of the parking lot in back because that's private property. Poor fools are standing in the snow on the empty lot out in front, where nobody can see or hear them, yelling their heads off. Officer Anderson's keeping an eye on them just to make sure."

Even with floodlights, the temporary auditorium was dim at night. It was still unheated and quite cold. Only some of the benches had backs, the tables for soup and rebel cakes were workstations covered with paper tablecloths. Still, excitement filled the air with enough electricity to light up the whole city of Minneapolis.

There was no good space for dancing yet, nonetheless, Diane and the Creektones were playing sweet jazz, the rebel cakes table was overflowing with goodies, the aroma of soup filled the air, and Georgia and Nora sat at a table with three other reporters, pads and tape recorders ready.

On our rough wooden stage, I stood behind the mic. The Creektones did a drumroll and a trumpet fanfare.

"Welcome, welcome, Creekers and friends!" I said. "Look at what we managed to do, all of us working together! Special thanks to Blanche and her crew for—"

CHAPTER 9, POLYCHROME WOMAN RETURNS

Someone in a brown uniform jumped on the stage, grabbed the mic. "This building is condemned by order of Minneapolis Department of Buildings, Order 8JF2134, fire safety class A violation. Emergency doors do not open out. Emergency doors do not have push bars. You must immediately leave these premises."

Our security team, Ruka, Betty, Earl, Clarence, Dozer, and Gordy with two of his cops, came running toward the stage.

I shoved brown uniform out of the way. "We do not have doors yet, fool! Bet ya cannot show me how to put a push bar on a wide-open doorway! *Skitsnack*! *Paskaa*! Bullshit!"

"*Skitsnack*! *Paskaa*! Bullshit!" the crowd chanted.

"We have it in English, Swedish, Finnish. What is it in Danish?" I said.

"*Lort*!" someone yelled.

"Norwegian?"

"*Tull*!"

"German?"

"*Blödsinn*!"

"Chant it in yahr language!"

The crowd chanted "Bullshit!" in eleven languages. Ruka, Gordy, Clarence, Betty, and Gordy's two cops surrounded brown uniform, escorted him outside.

While people calmed down, I looked around. There was that woman again. The one who did not say hello or talk with anyone. I had sorta noticed her at our last meeting, sitting in the back in the shadows, empty seats on both sides, but now she made more of an impression. Huge sunglasses like a barrier. Heavy makeup made her look like an outsider. A kerchief covered most of her too-black hair.

Last time I saw her, she had red hair.

Looking at her made me uneasy. I did not know why. But I was also attracted to her. She looked like Nancy with too much makeup. She was strange but familiar somehow. *Shit! I am getting a hard-on?*

I made myself focus. "As I was saying, look at what we did, all of us working together! Not just here. There is *no* rail traffic moving anywhere in Minneapolis and most of St. Paul. Underwear factory workers are striking for the two-fifty minimum." *Who is that woman?* "Airline cabin attendants and mechanics, nurses, office clerks, truck mechanics all went out on strike this afternoon. Unsafe track condemned by our Safety Commission has been removed from Camden Yard. Hazardous equipment at the roofing factory is condemned and shut down, and their workers are on strike. Minneapolis Teamsters are at a strike meeting right this minute!" *Who* is *that woman?* "Fifty-eight businesses in City Line Yard are shut down by the strike."

Betty and Bucky came bounding onto the stage as planned. "We have news!"

Betty said, "Remember that lawsuit to get back Community Development Funds from Gremling?"

"We got the checks today," Bucky said. "Three hundred and twenty-seven thousand, eight hundred and eighty-four bucks was deposited into the Shingle Creek Neighborhood Association savings account. Same amount to the Teen Council account." The Creektones played a drumroll. "Let's hear it for Russ!"

"Ru-us! Ru-us!"

Betty and Bucky also announced the million-and-a-half buck slander awards in our bank accounts to be donated to the community.

With a drumroll from the Creektones, Clarence picked Russ up, sat him on his shoulders, marched him around the room, the crowd clapping, the band playing "American Hero" by Rosie and the Thornbush, with new words by Diane.

Then, Bucky and Betty raised questions about how to handle the slander awards, took votes, got agreement to our suggestions and some good new ideas. We agreed the funding committee would present a budget for our four-and-a-half million for discussion.

Clarence stepped up to the mic. "This next matter is not as nice. We have been sent a copy of a check for six hundred dollars from the Communal Association made out to Elmer McGill for his efforts at preventing a strike and spying on us railroad workers. In other words, Elmer's been finking on us."

"That's a damned lie!" Elmer yelled. "I've been framed."

"Mr. McGill!" Russ said. "How do you explain the six-hundred-dollar *monthly* deposits in your checking account since September of 1970?"

"That's a lie!"

"Tell that to your bank!" Russ said.

CHAPTER 9, POLYCHROME WOMAN RETURNS

"You can't just search my bank account! This is America."

"You didn't pay taxes on it, Mr. McGill," Russ said. "I investigated a crime."

"I make a motion," Jack said, "we exclude him from meetings and from Arnray membership, ban him from community facilities, plus we do not pay him strike benefits."

"Second!" Harry said.

"Third!" Tessie called out.

"Tessie! Do ya understand what a fink is?" I said.

"A spy. Daddy always told me he thought Elmer was finking on us." She clasped her hands, looked up at the ceiling. "Daddy, you were so right!"

Out of more than six hundred people, only nine voted no.

"You framed me!" Elmer yelled.

Our security team surrounded him, walked him out the door, howling like a wolf.

Then Betty led a discussion about Gremling's armed militia. Nobody agreed we should arm ourselves.

I whispered in Rennie's ear, "Looks like I have ta rearrange my brain cells, huh?"

The team-speak group went onstage.

Irene stepped up to the mic. "Hold up your hands, everybody," she said. "Good! Let everyone see them! These hands built our city! These hands built our nation! Did Marmaduke Percy actually build his flour mill all by himself? Did he cut down trees for lumber, mine gypsum for plaster, smelt steel for machinery? Did he single-handed, build a railroad to ship all this raw material to his land in Minneapolis? And was he a master carpenter, mason, roofer, and machinist all rolled into one superman? No! Way!"

Ma pointed to the crowd. "No? Holy moly! So *who* mined, smelted, and machined the steel for Percy's mill? Tell me who!"

"We did!" the crowd said.

"Can't hear you!" Ma said.

"We did!"

"Who felled trees, milled them into lumber, built the framework of his mill?"

"We did!"

"Who raised the beams, installed the roof, built the chimneys? Percy?"

"No, *we did*!"

"Who ran those mills while Percy played golf and slept on silk sheets?"

"We did!"

"But who got rich from all that work? We didn't! Why not?" Ma said. "Why the hell not?"

" 'Cause *they* did," Billy said. "The bosses. The Fat Cats. They look at us, and they imagine big. 'Let's see how much we can squeeze out of them,' they say. 'They're just pieces of profit-making machinery. Let's use them up, throw them away. We'll set their property taxes high to drain dollars out of their community, so *we* can have trees on *our* streets and in *our* parks and rose gardens by *our* lakes.' "

"Is that fair?" Mabel said.

"Heck no," the crowd said.

Mabel held her hand behind her ear, palm out. "Can't hear you!"

"Heck no!"

"Bossman says, 'We'll send those working folks' boys off to fight wars, so we can make money selling guns and tanks.' Tell me, is that fair?"

"Heck no!"

"Then, bossman says, 'We'll make them pay for all those bullets and bombs with their income taxes.' Tell me, is that fair?"

"Heck no!"

" 'We'll keep pushing prices up, and oh, yes, we'll give them raises but never enough to keep up, so we get richer all the time.' Tell me, is that fair?"

"Heck no!"

" 'And when they protest, we'll smear them with lies, buy off their leaders, suppress their unions.' Tell me, is that fair?"

"Heck no!"

"If ya feel like we are under attack, well, we are," I said. "For almost a century now, the owners have waged war on us, all while demanding we bow down and revere them. How many people here are willing to bend over? So they can aim a good solid kick at yahr butt? All the while claiming yahr poverty is yahr own fault? Bend over volunteers, raise yahr hands!" I

CHAPTER 9. POLYCHROME WOMAN RETURNS

paused, looked around the room. "Bad news, Fat Cats! *No* hands on deck! But better listen up! Because we are the off switch for yahr economy!"

"They think big," Linda said. "Why can't we? Are we still saying, 'We want our fair share?' Hell, no! We're not begging anymore. We *demand* our fair share! You need our hands, our minds, to work for you? You have to pay us our fair share! Or it's no deal! Got that, bossman?"

"We mine the coal and make the steel," Rennie said. "We build the trucks, buses, trains—drive them and fix them too. Try to run the country without us! You can't, Fat Cats! And that's why we *are* a big deal. A *very* big deal." She stamped her foot. "So *we* gotta think big! But they don't like it when we do. 'Cause big thinking could actually stop the great bossman robbery of working people. 'Cause thinking big somehow makes us communists. So does that mean we should not think big? Tell me!"

"Heck no!"

"Look at the almost-finished Workers' Market. Is that small thinking? Tell me, what is it?"

"Big thinking!" the crowd thundered.

"Look at our *People's Free Press* newspaper. Tell me, what is it?"

"Big thinking!"

"Look at the Fourth Grade Freedom Academy. Tell me, what is it?"

"Big thinking!"

"Look at the auditorium fast taking shape around us. Tell me, what is it?"

"Big thinking!"

"Look at every person in our community over age sixteen who wanted a job is now working because of our projects. Tell me, what is it?"

"Big thinking!"

"When you look at all the unions on strike with support from our community, tell me, what is it?"

"Big thinking!"

Clarence stepped up to the mic. "Just before the meeting tonight, someone said to me, 'Paul is too angry!' Well, I am angry too, and here's why. How many of you have kids who want to go to college?"

Several dozen hands went up.

"How many of you can afford that?"

Three people raised a hand.

"Did you get any help with scholarships from the high school?"
People laughed.

"Why was our 1969 high school valedictorian working at Red Owl bagging groceries part-time? Until we got her a job using her skills and smarts? Where she is, by the way, thriving. Why didn't the high school help her get scholarships? Why did the few scholarships they have all go to boys?"

I could see Denise sitting in the audience, tears in her eyes. She stood up. "Yeah! Why?" she yelled.

Rennie said, "They aren't looking out for us, so we have to do that like we did for Denise. Our schools must prepare our kids for a changing job market that demands more education! Our bosses must stop treating us like stupid, ignorant dirt! Does all of that make you angry? Tell me!"

"Heck yeah!"

"Our anger isn't bad stuff," Evelyn said. "It can motivate all of us to get things changed. Always peacefully. Because nonviolence is a far more powerful tool. The goal is not to hurt our opponents or steal from them. The goal is to make them stop hurting us and stop stealing our money and our dignity. And we have the power to do that. The 1934 strike proved it. As Paulie said, there are more of us than them. And when we work together, we have the power of bigger than me, larger than you."

"This has been a great week," I said. "But watch out! The bosses *will* strike back. They always have. We have ta be ready to protect what we have won so far and fight to move forward from here. They are gonna call us reds, communists, bums, pimps, whores, the great unwashed, Joe six-packs, lawless atheists. Do not let that scare ya! Ya ain't done nothing if ya ain't been called a red! And by golly, we are doing a big-huge something. So brace yahrselves! But always remember. We. Will. Win!"

Diane stepped to the mic. "Our Jill taught me this tune she learned from a songwriter named Eliot at the San Francisco Folk Music Club. Sounds like he wrote it just for us!"

Lucy joined the band with her ukulele. She and Diane sang.

Well, you ain't done nothin' if you ain't been called a "red,"

If you've marched or agitated, you're bound to hear it said,

CHAPTER 9, POLYCHROME WOMAN RETURNS

So you might as well ignore it, or love the word instead,
'Cause you ain't been doin' nothin' if you ain't been called a red.

When I was just a little thing, I used to love parades,
With banners, bands, red balloons and maybe lemonade,
When I came home one mayday, my neighbor's father said,
Them marchers is all commies, tell me, kid, are you a red?

Well, I didn't know just what he meant, my hair back then was brown,
Our house was plain red brick like most others in the town,
So I went and asked my momma why our neighbor called me red.
My mommy took me on her knee and this is what she said:
Well, you ain't done nothin' if you ain't been called a red,
If you've marched or agitated, you're bound to hear it said,
So you might as well ignore it, or love the word instead,
'Cause you ain't been doin' nothin' if you ain't been called a red.

When I was growin' up, had my troubles I suppose,
When someone took exception to my face or to my clothes,
Or tried to cheat me on a job or hit me on the head.
When I organized to fight back, why, the stinkers called me red.

But you ain't done nothin' if you ain't been called a red,
If you've marched or agitated, then you're bound to hear it said,
So you might as well ignore it, or love the word instead,
'Cause you ain't been doin' nothin' if you ain't been called a red.

When I was livin' on my own one apartment that I had,
Had a lousy rotten landlord. Let me tell ya he was bad.

But when he tried to throw me out, I rubbed my hands and said,
"You haven't seen a struggle if you haven't fought a red!"

And you ain't done nothin' if you ain't been called a red,
If you've marched or agitated, then you're bound to hear it said,
So you might as well ignore it, or love the word instead,
'Cause you ain't been doin' nothin' if you ain't been called a red.

Well, I kept on agitatin' 'cause what else can you do?
You're gonna let the sons of bitches walk all over you?
My friends said you'll get fired, hanging with that commie mob.
I should be so lucky, buddy, I ain't got a job.

And you ain't done nothin' if you ain't been called a red,
If you've marched or agitated, then you're bound to hear it said,
So you might as well ignore it, or love the word instead,
'Cause you ain't been doin' nothin' if you ain't been called a red.

Well, I've been agitatin' now for fifty years or more,
For jobs or for equality and always against war.
I'll keep on agitatin' as far as I can see,
And if that's what being red is, well it's good enough for me.

'Cause you ain't done nothin' if you ain't been called a red,
If you've marched or agitated, then you're bound to hear it said,
So you might as well ignore it, or love the word instead,
'Cause you ain't been doin' nothin' if you ain't been called a red.

   I could not believe how this songwriter in San Francisco knew exactly what was happening for us. Pulsating clapping, cheering, and whistling filled the room.

CHAPTER 9, POLYCHROME WOMAN RETURNS

Just as the applause died down, Magdalena came running into the auditorium, up to the stage. "Excuse me, can I please tell you all something?"

I motioned her to the mic, introduced her.

"The North-Northeast Minneapolis Industrial Safety Commission just completed removal of all unsafe tracks in the Northeast Lowry Rail Yard and carted them away!"

The Creektones did a drumroll and a trumpet fanfare.

"Magda-lena! Magda-lena!" the crowd chanted. Applause, whistling, foot-stamping filled the cavernous auditorium with a solid wall of sound.

"Can you hold your meeting open another fifteen minutes?" Magdalena said. "We got coded CB radio messages from other rail workers. They're coming to report in."

The band started playing. People chatted, drank coffee, ate rebel cakes. Two men in work clothes come running in, up to me.

"Reporting in from the Minneapolis, Dallas & Houston Mainline!"

I shook hands, invited them up to the mic.

"Steve Rosenquist and Dale Amsel here. We removed seventy-five unsafe track sections from the M, D, and H Mainline. Thank you, Shingle Creek, for your support!"

The band drumrolled and fanfared them. The crowd went crazy with applause.

We invited them to sit down, chat with us. Clarence got them platefuls of rebel cakes, cups of coffee.

"There's Randy Olafsson from St. Paul, Salt Lake, and San Diego Railway Mainline coming in the door!" Clarence said, and waved him over.

"Got our forty-nine unsafe track sections taken out and away," Randy said.

We brought him onstage, gave him a drumroll, a fanfare, applause. Then celebrated, laughing, chatting, eating rebel cakes, and singing along with the Creektones.

"See what ya started," I said to Clarence.

"Me? No way! It was you."

"Yah're the one had the idea to take away the tracks," I said.

"You sure were," Jack said. "Even if you didn't take it seriously. Thanks, buddy!"

"Nah, c'mon! Wasn't me. Next thing, you'll have me running for mayor."

"You betcha. Superb idea!" I said.

Clarence put his hands on his cheeks, leaned forward. "Am I in trouble?"

"Yes, Mr. Mayor, ya sure are. Big-time!"

When Blanche's crew put up the first plywood covering over an emergency exit to start closing up for the night, I saw the sunglasses-and-kerchief woman walk quickly to the left-most door and scurry out.

After most everybody had left, Rennie took my hand. "Paulie, wanna walk home on the Creekside Trail 'n' it's tromped down pretty good so we don't even need snowshoes 'n' there's a big orange moon tonight 'n' stuff, so no flashlight's okay."

"That sounds magnificent," I said.

Just past the doorway, out of the corner of my eye, I thought I saw somebody hiding behind the big wild yew bush about fifteen feet away. I pointed. But a cloud scudded across the moon, the shadows deepened, and nobody seemed to be there.

A few minutes later, moonlight bathed the trail, creek, meadows, and bushes.

"It looks just like a harvest moon, yes siree, but what would we harvest this time of year, Paavali?"

"Big-huge wreaths of success feelings, and gearing up for more, but with a little tinge of fear. Can we take off gloves so I can feel your actual hand?" We slipped one glove off each. I felt a jolt of warmth and energy when I took her hand again.

Deep in a discussion about how so many railroad workers were removing unsafe tracks, we turned the sharp corner at second bend.

The sunglasses woman stepped out of a willow clump? Right in front of us? When she took off her sunglasses, the moon lit up...*my mother, Mildread's face?* My heart was pounding like a dozen gandy dancers driving spikes all at once.

"Paul, please, please listen to me a moment. I apologize for all the awful things I've done to you. I apologize for not being a mother to you. I was so proud of you at that meeting tonight."

CHAPTER 9. POLYCHROME WOMAN RETURNS

Karen squeezed my hand twice, then gripped my right arm tight with both hands. A gust of wind undid Mildread's kerchief, blew it up in the air and away, revealing blonde, brown, and red hair behind the black bangs.

Oh, my God! The polychrome hair woman?

"And everything you've done, you did despite me, without any help or encouragement from me. That wasn't how I wanted life to be. For my children. For me. When I was seventeen, your father dragged me into an empty lot. *Isäsi raiskasi minut.* Your father raped me. I knew his name from school, but I had never talked to him. He got me pregnant. My father had a heart attack, almost died. My mother made us get married. I was forced to drop out of school beginning of my senior year. I hated him. And I hated his children. Felt like you weren't even mine. For the first time in twenty-four years, I haven't been in fear of your father. I can think again. He did a terrible thing to me, but I did terrible things to you. Sandi. And Mark. I can't undo them. I can only apologize. And ask you to forgive me."

For a moment, I felt sorry for her, took a step toward her. Rennie pulled me back with both hands. I looked at my right shoulder, saw the four-inch animated mother figurine giving me the finger. Rage filled me.

"Forgive ya? Ya were never about love! Only anger. And now yah're trying to tell me ya love me? Horse puckies! You and yahr phony grammar rules!" I yelled, "Can't, shouldn't, ain't, won't! And see! I'm not lisping. Ya lied to me about that, and I believed ya. Ya harassed my soul and tortured me for years. I hate ya, and that is that! Stay out of my life. I have nothing more to say to ya."

"I know I deserve your anger. But I'm still sorry," she said, grabbed my left arm and pulled. "Please, Paul, give me a chance!"

Rennie tugged hard on my other arm.

Oh, my God! This is just like in my nightmare. She is not gonna pull me away from Rennie anymore. She is not...isn't...gonna keep me from living my life anymore. She isn't gonna yell insults at me anymore. That meeting's adjourned!

I yanked my left arm free of Mildread's grasp, pushed her away from us. She stumbled backward, let out a wail. The miniature mother statue fell off my shoulder, into a deep pile of snow by the side of the trail. There was a flash, a column of sparks. The snow pile melted. The mother statue was gone.

Mildread turned and ran down the Creekside Trail, her sobbing getting fainter until it was eclipsed by the gentle song of the creek.

Rennie put her arms around me. "Holy buckets, you were super strong, Paavali."

"I'm feeling mostly peaceful."

But then I realized that wasn't true. Why had I been turned on by my own mother? Who I hate!

Rennie's hand was a life preserver. I could not let go of it.

CHAPTER 10, STEPPING ON THE GAS HARD

SATURDAY-MONDAY, MARCH 4-6, 1972

THE WHOLE WEEKEND, WHENEVER I could, I held onto Rennie's hand. Saturday, we worked from seven in the morning to seven at night, snaking wires through metal ducts to bring power to our newsroom, taking five-minute handholding breaks every two hours. Her hand kept me from going under as I tried to swim through the stormy sea in my mind, of *raiskasi* and the polychrome woman I should not have been attracted to.

I could feel from the way Rennie clung back, something still bothered her big-time. But neither of us were able to talk. Not even to Judith.

Although violent waves pounded inside me, I was able to take some joy and a mega feeling of achievement as the newsroom grew around us. Hank, calm and relaxed, smiling often, managed to coordinate everything and inspire everyone, so we worked together like a precision machine with an amazing assortment of parts. Striking gandy dancers worked side by side with locked-out journalists, student volunteers and housewives who'd never labored outside the home before.

"It's an amazing experience, building your own newsroom!" Georgia said. "I don't even know how to put it into words yet. You know what I mean?" she said, turning to Lois Gustaffson.

"You bet! I didn't know I could do this stuff," Lois said as she connected a wiring duct to a junction box. "But Mikey taught me, one, two, three. Maybe when my kids are older, I'll…" She stopped a minute, lost in thought, smiled, connected another duct. "Imagine me, volunteering? I couldn't even leave my house until the Teen Council got me a home aide. Bebee takes really good care of my kids."

Everyone was listening to KPFP as we worked. About nine o'clock, on Keanna's news show, she announced, "Minneapolis and St. Paul Teamsters Locals voted by ninety-three percent to strike for an indexed wage. Union president Conor Brady said, 'We're above the two-fifty minimum, but we want built-in cost of living and productivity raises and the right to elect our own supervisors.'"

A cheer filled the room.

"Teamsters are in? Now we're gonna win this strike for sure," Li'l Mikey said. He turned to Lois. "You're getting really good at this. Can I show you how to connect the wiring to the outlets? Bet you'll pick it up one, two, three."

After work Saturday, we visited the draft board sit-in. There was a rally in front of the building so large, Officer James had to close off the street.

"We still have a hundred kids inside," Linda said. "But we decided to groove up for a better song and called for kids to come from all over Minneapolis. Got just under 5,000 outside here now. It was a very heavy lift, but KPFP made it happen."

After a quick dinner with Clara, Ma, and Burt, Rennie and I drove down to Boogey Barn and danced for hours. Rennie was finally smiling. And so was I.

Sunday morning around eleven at the newsroom, Hank announced, "We got the electric wiring done, people! Light bulbs are in, heaters plugged in and ready. We're going to turn on the juice. One! Two! Three!"

The newsroom was bathed in light and heaters started humming. A cheer rang out.

Hank raised both hands. "Our next task is phone lines. Should we take a half-hour break, or keep going?"

"Keep going! Keep going!" we chanted.

"If anyone *does* need a break, feel free!" Hank said. "You're ready to start now? Gather 'round me." He pointed to a guy next to him. "This here Creeker is Phil Rasmussen, folks. He's going to explain phone wiring. You can find him on bossman workdays, up on a phone pole splicing cables."

CHAPTER 10, STEPPING ON THE GAS HARD

"Except now, when I'm on strike," Phil said. He took us to a metal cabinet only about four inches deep. "This is where the main phone service for the newsroom comes into the building. We have to run three different types of cables from it. Red, yellow, blue. See this blue chalk line here on the wall? Run a blue cable along it. The number 47? That means you'll need a spool with at least forty-seven feet left on it. The number L-100 is the cable number. Be sure that same number is at the end of the line you're following. Hank here helped me make all this easy."

How to keep track of the length of cable left on a spool, the best way to attach the cable to the wall, avoiding common mistakes, and wiring procedures for both ends of the cable? Phil covered it all.

Rennie, Lois, Tom Hayes, and I worked on cable L-121, a thick, blue, two-hundred-and ten-footer. KPFP played Rosie and the Thornbush with some great new songs I'd never heard. Then Keanna announced Nora's story about Theodore Knight.

Nora gave some background, played the tape, discussed what it implied. She ended her story with, "Have Fat Cats ever bought off judges here in Minneapolis? Yes, they have. Do we know if Judge Ovington really was in Mr. Knight's pocket? No, we don't. We *can* say Judge Ovington's decisions on matters impacting the Shingle Creek working-class community have seemed fair and objective to us. We can only hope Knight's claim was an idle boast. But we must make this crystal clear. We *will* find out if judges are being bribed by Fat Cat bosses. We *will* run challengers in the next election against judges who are *biased against us*. And we *will* win those challenges. Our democracy is not for sale."

Rennie let out a big-huge, two-fingered whistle. People applauded. "Nora sure helped me fix Teddy-boy's ass!" she said.

At four o'clock, I said, "Rennie, what time are ya gonna see Greg?"

Her smile disappeared. "Holy buckets, I forgot about that. I'd better catch the next bus down to the U."

"Do ya *want* to see him?"

"Uh-huh. Sort of. I don't know. Maybe not. But I have to. I just don't want to talk about it, all right then?"

"Okay, but I will…I'll drive ya there."

"You don't have to do that, Paavali."

"Yes. I do. Totally."

She was quiet the whole way. No matter how much I tried to get her talking about anything. When I parked near Greg's apartment, she threw her arms around me, gave me a long, passionate kiss. "I'll be back tomorrow morning by eleven." She jumped out of the car, ran off.

Why does it feel like the world is ending?

At seven o'clock, I had just finished working on the newsroom and put on my coat. Someone grabbed me from behind, threw arms around me in a big, backward bear hug. I spun around. "Rennie?" A river of pain ran down her cheeks. "What happened?"

"I don't want to talk about it, Paavali, please, please just take me home and hold me."

In my room, we clung to each other. I kept trying to figure out what was happening to her. I could not. *Couldn't.* My mind seemed to need new spark plugs. My serpents were out of control.

In the still of the night, Rennie's yelling woke me. She seemed to be having a furious argument with Greg. I could not…*couldn't* tell what it was about. Our moonbeam coming through the window lit up her face. Her eyes darted back and forth under closed lids. I stroked her cheek, talked to her. She stopped yelling. Her eye movement slowed, then ceased. She turned toward me, began snoring.

Tired as I was, I could not fall asleep again. Without thinking about it, my hand went down to my dick. It was out cold. As if I were watching a movie, pictures of Maria, Nancy, Dawn, and the other mean, hostile women who had turned me on, flowed across a screen in my mind. My hand moved and stroked. No dice. Nothing.

I am doomed! My dick just does not work anymore. Doesn't. *For anyone.*

I snuggled tight against her, dozing on and off, dread filling my dreams.

Monday morning right at eight o'clock, we handed a tape of Nora's story to Judge Ovington's clerk. "He'll want to be aware of this, if he's not already," I said.

"It was a lot of driving just to deliver it," Rennie said when we were headed back to Shingle Creek. "But holy buckets, it was worth it!"

"Sure was," I said. "We will…we'll be hearing echoes of this for a long time."

We parked in the Betty Hall lot, went up to Russ's office. "Russ, man!" I said. "Ya asked, ya got. Cash money for yahr interns. Approved!"

"Two-fifty?" Russ said, eyebrows shooting skyward.

"Do rainbows have pots of gold, to the max?" Rennie said.

Sylvia, Rollie, and Jason were overjoyed when we told them. They were from working families, living on student loans and whatever their families could scrape together. I was so proud we could pay them.

When we told Hank and Lyle they were getting ten percent raises next week, they thought we were joking.

"Why?" Hank said. "How?"

"Well, we have…we've been fighting for two-fifty minimum," I said. "We just won the first battle. So minimum wage here is two-fifty starting next week. But yah're already there. So we gotta do something for ya. That is…that's the way we are here."

"I'll be making what Yard Boss was?" Hank said. "I'm trying to wrap my head around that one. Thanks, you two."

"I hope the heck I don't wake up from *this* dream," Lyle said.

"That was far out 'n' glorious, to the max," Rennie said after we'd shared the good news with dozens of work groups in Betty Hall, Olson Hall, the warming room, picketers at the roofing factory, Camden and Northeast Lowry Yards, and the gandy dancers working on the General Grain siding.

Back at our office, we met with Dr. Florie Corwin, Fred's wife; Nurse Gwen McCoy, Betty and Bucky's daughter-in-law; and Dr. Marvin Ericson, who took care of me after my father choked me. They agreed to set up a first aid station in an unused office in our mental health clinic and get volunteer medics for our rallies.

Then Debbie Ahlberg, Rennie's other older sister, came to talk about our corner store buying co-op. Debbie worked full time as a checkout clerk at the Crystal Red Crow since graduating almost a year ago. It was a small store, and she was smart, curious, and a question-asker, so she knew all about how it operated. We explained how our co-op would work, what we needed from its manager, and the help she would get from Carleton's bookkeeper, Ronan Flynn, and accountant, Lydia Rivers, as well as Woody Dahl from Dahl's Superette.

"You mean I'd be in charge of the whole thing?" Debbie said, her eyes lighting up just like Rennie's do when she's excited. "And I'd be going out, talking to people too?"

"Yes siree, Debs!" Rennie said.

"Would I get more than minimum wage? A buck eighty, just like Denise?"

"This week," Rennie said, grinning. "But next week our minimum wage here goes up to two-fifty."

"Two-fifty? Two-fifty! Really? Me?"

"For sure!" Rennie said.

"Super wow!" She looked at Rennie, looked at me. "My kid sister is out of sight!" She hugged Rennie, did a little dance with her. "I owe you about a thousand apologies, Ka Ka. Maybe even more."

"Accepted!"

Russ came striding into our office, looking angry. "Just got back from court. I petitioned for injunction against the Buildings Department's shutdown order for our auditorium. Judge Coventry rejected it. He actually said a public space must have doors, not removable doorway covers. That's not in the code or statutes. The Communal Association's big investment in his election campaign is paying off in spades."

Somehow, I didn't get upset. "What is...what's our next step?"

"I already filed an appeal. Let's keep fingers and toes crossed," Russ said.

"Blanche told me the push bars arrived this morning, as far as that goes," Rennie said. "Why don't we mount them on the plywood door covers 'til the doors arrive?"

"And hinge the door covers, so we're a hundred percent in compliance, kinda sorta?" I said.

The three of us laughed all the way down to the auditorium. Still laughing, we told Blanche.

"That's the funniest thing since we made Gremling pay for his soup!" she said. "We'll get right on it, have those push bars in place before tonight's meeting."

Over at the warming room, on the Kid and Teen Achievement Wall, someone had posted a note. First US textile mills strike was led by teen girls, 1834.

"That looks like Tessie's handwriting, yes siree, that extra little loop on the bottom of the g, the star for the dot on the i."

"Joanna told me Tessie has been…Tessie's been asking her about the history of strikes," I said, "reading lots of books about them. Some of them are high school level."

"She talks about strikes a mile a minute. She's really on a kick," Ruka said. "I love it!"

I handed Ruka a letter from the Historical Society. "This just came. I thought ya should be the one to open it."

Ruka removed the letter, scanned it. "They'll be co-publishing my book with the Teen Council? Thank you, Lord. Thank you!" she said. "But we have to edit it, but how?"

"Georgia can do that, or Tom, or both, as far as that goes."

"The Society will design it," I said. "Great!"

"We'll print it, yes siree, Bob!"

"But they'll bind it, which we don't have machines for," I said.

"We'll both distribute it, but I don't understand all this stuff about sales and pricing and royalties," Ruka said.

"We need to meet with Carleton 'n' Russ, 'n' congratulations, Ruka, to the max!"

Rennie went into the office, came back with two small pieces of bright green paper. She wrote two notes.

Our Ruka published a History book at the age of sixteen!

Our Tess, at age 9, convinced the railroad workers to strike!

Ruka posted both on the Achievement Wall. She couldn't stop smiling.

When Laura arrived, Tess was holding her hand, talking at a gallop about the railroad workers' strike.

"Tessie, Laura! Go look at the achievement wall!" I said.

A moment later, Tess came running back, said, "You *did*?" and hugged Ruka.

"And you did too!" Ruka said, doing a little dance with Tess.

Rennie handed Laura a large, tan envelope with Italian postage stamps. "We wanted to look at this together, yes indeed."

Laura opened it, slid out four copies of *Musica Jazz* magazine. A note clipped to the cover read, "*Vedi pagina nove. Grande storia!*"

Kurt sidled up to Tess, linked arms. "What does the note mean?" Tess said.

Ruka said, "Something about page nine and a good story."

"How did...how'd ya know that?" I said.

"Dad taught me stuff about the structure of languages. He speaks eight of them."

Page nine had a large photo of Diane and the Creektones and an article in Italian. We explained the headline to Tess: how Diane Ward helps new jazz musicians get started by playing at community meetings, and told her that Jill's reporter friend, Águeda, wrote it.

Kurt and Tessie were like question machines. It was truly amazing how a genius teacher can make kids so smart.

Back at Betty Hall, we checked in with Susie and Georgia.

"It's so much easier to get all my bases covered working with Georgia and Tom," Susie said. "And Hank told us we'll be in the real newsroom by end of the week."

"Major challenge communicating with sixty-two people all working from home," Georgia said. "With only two phone lines. We're really getting fifty lines?"

"To start with, as far as that goes, 'n' we'll add more if you need them."

"How are...how're ad sales going?" I said.

"Up twelve percent over last Monday," Susie said. "The new guy we hired to help Pam is pretty good. He's still learning the ropes here, but he's showing her some good tactics as well."

"Georgia, how is...how's it going splitting yahr time between here and the picket line?"

"Tom, Susie, and I have it all figured out."

"Got our bases covered and then some," Susie said. "It's like a dream come true."

"For me too," Georgia said. "For me too!"

Rennie looked at her watch. "We have to get to our Commission meeting."

In our office, we worked with Russ, Clarence, and Magdalena preparing notices of fines and fees owed by Minnesota Consolidated Railroad for using condemned track and for our removal of the unsafe track. Since it

CHAPTER 10, STEPPING ON THE GAS HARD

was the first time we'd done this, we had to work out policies, procedures, forms.

"Holy smokes," Magdalena said. "The Commission's going to get a *lot* of money from this!"

"So we will...we'll have a mega budget for factory inspections," I said. "We could actually hire inspectors, if we all vote to do that."

"I would *love* inspecting factories," Magdalena said.

"Personally, I'd say, deal, 'cause you'd be really good at it, but we have to vote once we collect the fines and fees, so start campaigning now," Rennie said.

Every five minutes or so, there was another news flash on KPFP. "Camden Rebar Factory and Shingle Creek Roofing Factory on strike! B&D Manufacturing Partners on strike! Gremling Bug Spray Factory, Veterinary Assistants Local 37, Laborers Local 909, and Locksmiths Local 2100 on strike! Grocery Workers Local 199 picketing now!"

"Holy buckets, it's like a huge wave and getting bigger," Rennie said.

KPFP mentioned one industry after another, many with new union locals, striking for the two-fifty indexed minimum, better working conditions, and respect on the job. Cooks, laundry workers, hotel workers, restaurant workers, bartenders, welders, mill hands. All were out picketing.

"But there's one factory not going on strike," Keanna announced. "Here's why, from Manager Burt Loftus."

"General Grain already pays the two-fifty minimum. Our productivity went through the roof when we raised wages and set up a workers' advisory board. It's just common sense."

"Way to go, Burt!" Clarence said.

"Because General Grain is actively supporting the strike," Keanna announced, "the Teamsters Union is helping their trucks drive along residential streets, selling bread directly to the people. Strikers with union cards get a discount."

Then Todd's voice said, "The following message is brought to you by Working People for Judge Woodruff. Judge Gannon Woodruff stands up to the Fat Cats. Remember this in June! Vote for Gannon Woodruff for District Court Judge."

The phone rang. Woody Dahl told us he was paying the two-fifty indexed minimum, so the Teamsters Union was helping them receive food and make deliveries.

Ma knocked, opened the door, handed me an envelope. "I know these letters from your friend at the Communal Association are by no means your favorite thing, but it's usually important."

Inside was a copy of a check written by Archibald Hastings-Dankworth, made out to Police Chief Jensen for ten thousand bucks. Written the day after Fred's murder. The memo line read, "Good job!"

"Does this look like cash money for murder?" I said.

"Gadzooks! It sure does," Clarence said.

"Do guns shoot bullets?" Russ said.

"I'm wondering about top-level contacts at the FBI," Rennie said. "Does Burt have them? 'Cause that's the only way we're gonna get justice for Fred 'n' we should put those grazies to work for *us* 'n' we better let Florie know about this."

Static crackled on the CB radio. "LedgerGuy here, Mahrove-Rove. Grazy car parked in front of house. Plate MBH-666. We took photos, knocked on car window. Diane kulned them. They left."

"Red Cushions calling in. Four grazy cars drove by my house. I ran after them, swatting at them with a broom. Got one plate, QRS-006."

"Fox's Buddy calling FastTalk. Me, mom, and siblings followed home from mall by grazy car. When they stopped, we kulned them, banged on car with fists. License HKS-445. They're gone."

"Who was that on the CB?" Magdalena said. "What is mahrove-rove?"

"Mahrove-rove is Paulie, because that's what he calls his car. First caller was our accountant. Second was a seamstress, baker, People's Union organizer. Third was my nine-year-old son," Clarence said with a double-wide grin.

"Rail Waltzer here!" Clarence said into the CB mic. "Good work, Fox's Buddy! I'm proud of all of you! Over and out. Man alive! Six different grazy cars. That's a record!"

"FastTalk, it's Henlund One. Grazies stopped me walking home. Asked about meeting tonight. I said 'What're you talking about? No meetings here.' Plate HKS-327."

"Oh, so that's it," Clarence said. "The bosses are scared of our People's Union. Hope you've got something great planned for the meeting."

"Ya know how you railroad folks told us you would…you'd handle the arrangements for track removal," I said. "And we did not…didn't

CHAPTER 10, STEPPING ON THE GAS HARD

have ta be involved? Same thing here. Yup! We're meeting with them this afternoon. But all they want from us is a team-speak to help motivate people and for us to teach their leaders more about how to do their own team-speaks."

"Yes siree! Our classes made a batch of new leaders," Rennie said. "Clear across Minneapolis."

"We are…we're gonna review slides our librarian made for our team-speak," I said. "Ya can stay and watch, if ya want."

"Holy smokes!" Magdalena said. "How'd you get a librarian to do that?"

"She works for us 'n' stuff," Rennie said. "We employed her when the library fired her because she was always helping us, to the max."

"Must be nice to be rich," Magdalena said.

"Just start thinking about what ya would…ya'd like to do in Northeast Lowry. We can help ya do it!" I said.

"I'll start talking it up with folks, see what we come up with," Magdalena said. "The slides? I'll see 'em tonight. Have to get back to Lowry Yard for a meeting."

Just before our meeting with People's Union organizers from forty-four neighborhoods, Rennie put her arms around me. "Paavali, I know you're practicing saying contractions for the first time, but you're hesitating before each one 'n' stuff."

"It sounds bad?"

"Makes you seem unsure of yourself 'n' you don't normally sound doubtful."

I took a deep breath. "Okay, I'll have ta change that."

"Suppose you think of yourself driving the mahrove-rove car and contractions are little hills that need extra fuel, so you push your right foot down against the floor before each one, like you're stepping on the gas hard?"

I tromped my foot down, saw the mahrove-rove car sorta jump forward in my mind. "Okay, I'll give it a try."

CHAPTER 11, THE OFF SWITCH FOR YOUR ECONOMY

MONDAY, MARCH 6, 1972

IN THE CLASSROOM, RENNIE AND I worked with Daniel, Laura, Lucy, and The Nines to move all the desks, shelves, and equipment into the overnight storage area and set up the room for the People's Union planning meeting.

"I'm a little nervous 'cause this seems like the most important meeting we ever had here," Rennie said.

"We can do it!" I took her hand.

She squeezed once.

Soon, chairs and the refreshment table were set up and the room was full of people talking, laughing, sipping coffee, eating cookies. Sarah Nesheim and Vincent Wójcik, the two main coordinators, introduced us to everybody one by one.

"This is expanding our horizons, big-time," Rennie said. "So many new friends!"

Sarah opened the planning session by saying, "Tonight, even if we don't agree one hundred percent, let's work together on what we do agree on. Let's discuss differences and work them out as friends and neighbors. And we vote on *everything*!"

Rennie squeezed my hand once, smiled.

I nodded.

CHAPTER 11, THE OFF SWITCH FOR YOUR ECONOMY

The organizers had a solid agenda, worked out some last-minute details in back-and-forth discussion. We fixed a few problems during our team-speak dress rehearsal.

"I think we're as ready as we can be," Sarah said. "See you all at seven tonight."

"Can Sarah and I see the auditorium?" Vincent said.

"Can we Nines see too?" Bonnie said.

"C'mon with us!" Rennie said.

Blanche and her crew were putting the push bars and hinges on the last few plywood doors. "Won't be as cold with these doors up," Blanche said. "And look over here! Dina and her crew got their red cushions made for twenty benches."

Red corduroy was elegant against light wood benches, now sanded and varnished.

"I borrowed all the chairs I could find anywhere," Blanche said. "We can seat 620. If another 350 stand, we'll fill every nook and cranny!"

On the stage, someone had taped a second microphone beside our usual one, with a little tag on top that read, KPFP.

"It's connected to a phone line so they can broadcast live," Blanche said. "Todd also set up a huge jammer in the storage area. I checked it for him with the CB in my car. Nothing but static on all four sides of our buildings."

Blanche smiled. "Oh, and also, look here! We ran a line in yesterday for more electricity. With doors up, it makes sense to have some heat, so we borrowed the heaters from the newsroom since it's not open yet."

I pressed down on my imaginary gas pedal. "She's one of our heroes," I said, pointing to Blanche.

"And she inspires us girls," Bonnie said.

"Us boys too!" Jeffie said.

"Aw, gee! Thanks," Blanche said. She bent down, hugged Bonnie and Jeffie.

That evening, a flood of people surged through the auditorium doors at seven o'clock. With volunteers from all over the city, our security team was much bigger and able to check everyone's union card. Suddenly, there was a lot of shouting. Four security people ran toward one entrance.

Ruka looked back and forth between a photo and a man and hollered, "You're a grazy. You drive a gray Ford, plate MBH-666, Agent Gummler. This meeting is only for union members, not FBI. Leave now, fink!"

Earl Smith ran through the door. "Found plate MBH-666 parked on 49th Avenue. Single agent sitting in it with a listening device."

They circled around Gummler, marched him out the door. They also ejected Duane Pukari, Virgil Vihainen, Alan Becker, and Mrs. Elak, plus about two dozen other known finks and troublemakers.

One of the organizers from Shingle Creek, Fiona Flynn, opened the meeting, talked about agreeing and disagreeing and keeping our eyes on the prize: a better life for working families. "Let's get right to the main task," Fiona said. "Voting on our platform. Since each of you has only one vote, raise only your left hand. Are we ready?"

"Yes! Yes!" the crowd roared.

"So here's our most important plank, one that brings so many of us here together," Vincent said. "A two-fifty indexed minimum wage. For everyone, no exceptions! Doesn't matter if you get tips. Why should you always have to be hoping for a handout? You work, you get paid, not depending on some rich person's whim."

"By indexed," a guy in blue coveralls said, "we mean our wages go up faster than inflation. And when we produce more, we get more. It's all automatic!"

"All in favor?" a woman in a green coat said. "Put up those left hands and keep 'em up while we count!"

A team of volunteers around the auditorium counted hands, reported back to the tally desk.

"Nine hundred, forty-two in favor, twenty-two opposed," Barb and Roger called out.

"Now this next one," Sarah said, "is a little harder to pin down. How many feel respected at work?"

A few scattered hands went up.

"Who's upset by that?"

A forest of raised hands filled the room.

"How would we make that into a demand we could enforce?"

No raised hands.

"Any ideas?" Fiona said.

"Been thinking about that for a long time," Hank said. "Always wished I could talk about it with someone, but I thought they'd make fun of me."

"I'll talk with you," two women and six men said.

"Will the nine of you be our respect committee?" Blue Coveralls said.

"Yes! You Bet! Sure thing!"

Roger and Barb got their names and phone numbers.

"Meanwhile," Fiona said, "should we vote on it as an idea until the committee comes back to us with some details?"

"Vote it! Vote it!" the crowd chanted. Hands went up.

"Nine hundred and forty-eight in favor, sixteen opposed," Barb and Roger said.

Rennie whispered in my ear, "The organizing committee did a great job, letting folks know the issues. All those *People's Free Press* articles and KPFP programs really did the trick!"

One after another, people added planks demanding no forced overtime; double pay for holidays, weekends, and swing shifts; twelve paid holidays a year; payment for tools, equipment, and uniforms required on the job; and paid disability insurance.

It took some discussion to agree about the right to elect and recall foremen and supervisors. The majority was only 622, with 342 opposed.

"I'm gonna make you folks who voted no a bet," our Dina said. "Six months from now, when you've worked with an elected supervisor, you'll like the idea. A lot. If you don't, start talking to folks, see if you can swing the vote another way. But I'll bet you'll like it! Deal?" She put her hand behind her right ear.

"Deal!" a bunch of voices called out.

We easily passed planks for twelve paid sick days a year, two weeks paid vacation with three weeks after five years, and universal medical insurance, including mental health, dental, vision, and hearing.

The Minneapolis Standard Work Contract took some explaining. But when Bucky said, "It's just a collection of all of our workers' rights planks. We want it approved as law by the city council," it passed by 957 votes.

Rennie thought the plank calling for a chartered safety commission for South and Southeast Minneapolis, completely run by workers elected by the People's Union, would be a tough sell. When Green Coat announced the topic, about fifty railroad workers stood up, raised picket signs reading, "Yes on South Safety Commish!"

"Lemme tell you something," a guy in brown work clothes said. "We had a hell of a time shutting down Minnehaha Mills Yard! Those unsafe tracks are still in place. Worries the heck out of me, railroad will hire scabs and we'll be jobless."

"Me too!" his buddy standing next to him said. "Why the heck can't we have a Commish in South? Yes on the South Commish!"

The plank passed by 960. A roar larger than a thousand lions filled the room, echoed off the brick walls. People jumped to their feet, danced in the narrow rows between benches and chairs. Rennie and I circle-danced with Obie, Clarence, and Jack.

The heaters had warmed the room enough so we no longer saw a little fog cloud when people talked. Coats were unbuttoned, gloves taken off.

A woman in a red jacket asked for the floor. "I'm a machinist at KHA Specialty Steel. Heard about that Arnray Railroad Safety Corporation on KPFP. We need to stand for the right to organize a union *or* be represented by workers' cooperatives like Arnray."

"I don't know enough about Arnray to vote on that," Hank said. "Can someone tell us more?"

Clarence strode to the mic, smiling, hands gesturing, explained how Arnray works. Obie joined him.

"Icin' on the cake?" Obie said. "Our crew of gandy dancers at Camden Yard was way too small for the workload, so when scabs showed up, we watched them, saw they knew the job, and Arnray done hired them away from the railroad, found temporary work for them. When we win the strike, Arnray has a full, trained crew, ready to go! All at two-fifty indexed! Everybody won there. Except the railroad."

"Arnray! Arnray!" the crowd chanted.

"I make that a plank motion," Red Coat said. "The right to organize a union *or* be represented by a workers' cooperative."

"Second!" Tessie yelled so loud it echoed through the auditorium.

"Tessie, come on up on stage," Fiona said. "Tell them why you're for it."

"My daddy, Ray Iversen, was killed in Camden Yard. He's the 'Ray' in Arnray. If we'd had Arnray then, the Camden Yard gandy dancers would've gone on strike before my dad was killed. And I wouldn't have a hole in my heart now."

"How old are you, Tessie?" Fiona said.

"Just nine."

An avalanche of cheers quickly morphed into a chant, "Tessie! Tessie!"

Nobody voted against the motion. Same for the right to organize a workers' council authorized to meet with management, for any work unit, from work team to factory wide.

"This is so cool," I said to Rennie. I pushed my gas pedal down hard. "They're going way beyond what we ever imagined!"

Red Coat asked for the mic again. "Sorry, don't mean to hog the floor. This is important. How many of you ever heard of a woman machinist? Raise your hands!"

No hands went up.

"Dad was a machinist at KHA Specialty Steel. Hated KHA but loved his work. Even had a machine shop in our basement, did side work weekends. He taught me how to use the tools. I adored it! Showed some of my work to his boss. They brought me in for an interview. My parents dressed me up as a man. I got the job. Worked two years posing as a man. Then World War Two came along, so I could stop pretending. Worked there ever since. I've never, ever, met another woman machinist. We need equal opportunities for women. Women shouldn't have to pretend to be men to get good jobs. We need equal opportunity for all races. Ever see a Black or Native American machinist? Me neither. Why. The. Heck. Not?"

"Why not? Why not?" people chanted.

"So I make a plank motion that we demand equal training and hiring rights no matter what sex, race, or ethnicity you are."

"Hold on a minute now," Blanche said. "Magdalena, Dina, Frances, Fiona, and every other woman in this room who works with her hands, please stand up and second this with me."

"Second!" a chorus of women's voices echoed through the room.

"Now our Black and Native American sisters and brothers. Second with me!"

"Second!" a much smaller group bellowed.

When the vote was counted, Rennie said to me, "There were actually a hundred and forty-nine men who voted against it? Shit!"

"Just shows how much education we have ta do yet," I said. "But think of where we were a year ago."

She snuggled up against me on the bench, held both my hands. "I like the way you put that, Paavali!"

A couple of motions totally failed. A young man in a black coat, hat, pants, shoes, made a motion that we seize factories and turn them over to workers' collectives.

Liam O'Farrell argued vehemently against that idea. "People won't support it. The bosses will call the National Guard, even the army and marines if they need to." He put his hand on Black Coat's shoulder. "Son, you wanna make things better for folks right now, or pursue some vague, distant dream that could land us all in prison or dead?"

"I'll never give up that dream!" Black Coat said, stamping his foot.

"Fine. But find a way to put foundations under it," Liam said.

"I make a motion we seize factories with armed force!" Black Coat said.

Another man dressed exactly like Black Coat seconded it. Just twelve people voted for it.

"I want to flip that motion around," Liam said. "I make a motion that we are committed to nonviolent actions to achieve our goals."

"Second!" Rennie said.

A huge majority voted for it. Twelve people voted against.

"Well, how about this to change the subject?" a man in a plaid shirt said. "A plank motion. If a business is going to be closed or moved out of Minneapolis, owners must first offer to sell it to the workers. A paper mill I once worked in, owners closed it, shipped machinery down to Low Wage, Mississippi. Thirty-six years of seniority, gone! Then another paper mill stole my job, shipped their equipment to Even Lower Wage, Mexico."

"He's right!" Green Coat said. "I second it!"

The motion passed 950 to 14.

"Now," Vincent said, "the big question!" He pointed to Blue Coveralls.

"How will we," Blue Coveralls said, "working together, support strikers and the students occupying draft boards in Brooklyn Center and Northeast Minneapolis?"

"South Minneapolis too!" a woman in orange slacks said. She turned to a teenager sitting next to her. "Stand up, honey! My daughter Cecile organized it."

"Kids from two high schools in there round-the-clock," Cecile said. "I learned how to get the press there from leadership class at Shingle Creek."

Another round of applause broke out. "Cecile! Cecile!" people chanted.

"So back to the big question," Blue Coveralls said. "How to support the strikers?"

"I make a motion," Brown Work Clothes said, "every single one of us call TV and radio stations ignoring our strike and our students' sit-ins. Demand they interview us and cover us fairly!"

"Second!" several people called out.

The motion passed.

Brown Work Clothes was grinning. "I never said anything like that before!"

Orange Slacks said, "The president of Twin Cities Heating Gas called our protests a communist plot by lazy buffoons. Yep, on TV news last night. Let's all of us pay our gas bills ten days late and let him know why. That'll hit him in the pocketbook!"

"Second!"

That motion passed too.

"Twin Cities Unified National Bank is a big Communal Association supporter," our Irene said. "They raise money to train scabs and break unions. I make a motion we take our money out of there, put it into co-op credit unions."

"How do you find those?" Hank said.

"We'll publish a list in *People's Free Press*," our Georgia said.

"Second!"

Again, the motion passed.

"I think. I'll tell you what I think," a woman in a thick white sweater said. "We should have a rally in Pulaski Park, Northeast. Another in Shingle Creek Park, North. A third in Como Avenue Park, Southeast. A fourth in Portland Park, South. From the four corners of the city, we march on city hall. Thousands of us!"

"With big, loud marching bands leading us!" a man in a blue work shirt said.

Our Laura, scurrying around taking photos, stopped a moment, said, "And signs, lots of signs!"

"I make that a motion!" White Sweater said. "Can we do it Wednesday?"

"Second!" echoed across the auditorium.

"Nine hundred and thirty-two in favor, thirty-two opposed," Barb and Roger announced. "Volunteers for the rally committee, come to the tally desk."

"And now to change the topic," our Dina said. "Without roots, we can't grow. We look to the past for lessons we can learn about our origins. But for our future, we look ahead. So now, for a team-speak about our working-class past and what's happening today, The Shingle Creek Truthtellers! Bonnie Korhonen, Clara Ahlberg, Clarence Björk, Daniel Anker, Denise Ahlberg, Evelyn Hakkala, Irene Korhonen, Karen Ahlberg, Kurt Björk, Luke Gulbrandsen, Obie King, Pastor Othel Broadwater, Paul Mäkinen, Shirley "Ma" Frisk, Tess Iversen. Give them a hand!"

Creekers started clapping in rhythm. Everyone else followed. Dina waited, then raised both hands. The auditorium quieted. The floodlights turned off. I was surprised when a big, bright light came on, focused right on Clarence, Kurt, and Tess in the middle of the stage. I didn't even know we had one of those.

The rest of us Truthtellers stood to the side.

"Dad?" Kurt said. "Sometimes I'm not sure. Are we really free?"

Clarence, in work clothes, holding his gandy bar, stepped from foot to foot. "I often wonder, son. Right now, the car's not working and I don't have twenty-six bucks to repair it. Doesn't feel like freedom to me."

"Mom said we can't have burgers even once this week," Tessie said. "When she went to Red Crow, they'd raised the price again."

"Does that feel like freedom to you, Tessie?" Clarence said.

She shook her head. "Nuh-uh."

The rest of the Truthtellers chanted, "We demand...the right to eat!"

A photo of a crying child holding out an empty bowl was on a screen at the back of the stage.

The spotlight shifted to Bonnie and Irene.

CHAPTER 11, THE OFF SWITCH FOR YOUR ECONOMY

"Mommy, why is Daddy crying?" Bonnie said. "He never does that."
"The bosses closed the factory, honey. Fired all the workers."
"Why, Mommy?"
"They shipped the machines down to Mexico. They pay workers less there. So bosses make more money."

The screen showed a factory with a sign, "Moved to Mexico."

"What are we gonna do, Mommy?"
"I don't know, honey. Jobs are hard to get."
"Mommy, I thought we have freedom!"
"We demand…our factories stay right here!" the Truthtellers chanted.

Applause rocked the room.

The spotlight focused on Rennie and Luke Gulbrandsen.

"Dad!" Rennie said. "Mrs. Miller said there's no scholarships for girls. I'll just die if I can't be a doctor!"

"I know, honey. I pinched pennies for years, put it aside for you. My hard-earned four hundred and twelve bucks ain't enough, even if you work part-time." Luke bowed his head, covered his face. "I'm so sorry."

"Doesn't feel like freedom to me!" Rennie said.

The screen showed people dressed in work clothes carrying tools, marching up the steps of a college building, holding a big sign. "Let Us In!"

"We demand the right…to education and training!" the Truthtellers chanted.

Wow! This takes our team-speaks to a new level and grabs the audience by the emotions. It's what we need right here, right now.

Denise joined Rennie and Luke in the spotlight.

Luke said, "Are you really free if…"

Denise continued, "A crippling work accident may mean you'll lose your home?"

"That's not freedom!" the Truthtellers chanted.

The screen showed sheriff's deputies carrying a man in a hospital bed from a house, with a sign, "Evicted!" on the headboard.

"Are you really free if…" Luke said.

Rennie continued, "The bosses take money from your pension fund and pocket it?"

"That's not freedom!" the Truthtellers chanted.

"Are you really free," Luke said, "if you work harder than ever, but cuts to your hours, increased taxes, rising prices make you so worried you never feel calm anymore?"

"That's not freedom!" the Truthtellers chanted.

The screen showed a painting of a man's face, hands on his cheeks, howling in agony, flames all around him.

I stepped to the center of the stage, into the spotlight. "I'm gonna tell ya a big-huge secret. About Fat Cat millionaires. Past ten years, there are six hundred and thirty percent more of them. Sucking our blood. Growing fatter. Multiplying."

630% showed on the screen.

"Inflation is robbing *you* blind." I pointed at the audience. "But the rich are getting richer. And it's no accident. It's policy. The Federal Reserve—you ever heard of it? Set up by Congress. It decides how much inflation and unemployment to *create* to squash our bargaining power, keep our wages low. Special tax laws help rich people profit from inflation. Not us."

"The rich get richer," the Truthtellers chanted. "We eat beans."

A photo of the painting in our Daniel's house showed White people in elegant gowns at a ball. But underneath the floor, Black people on their hands and knees, in torn work clothing, held the whole thing up on their backs. Then, a slide of a Fat Cat in a top hat lit up on the screen.

"That's the richest man in Minneapolis," I said. "He doesn't give a shit about ya!"

Clarence, dressed like a Fat Cat, stepped into the spotlight, pushed me aside. "Out of my way, buffoon! Grunt, rabble, failure, dumb, lazy, trash! That's what you are."

Ma, Clara, Daniel, and Pastor Broadwater strode into the spotlight, walked in a circle carrying Two-Fifty Indexed Minimum signs.

The Truthtellers chanted, "Two-fifty minimum! Indexed to inflation!"

Fat Cat Clarence ran offstage yelling, "Communists! Child molesters! Free love freaks!"

Daniel said, "Does history repeat itself? That depends on us. But I say no! Not this time!"

Pastor Broadwater said, "1917. As the First World War killed thousands of working-class fathers and sons, bosses were scared of organized workers and farmers."

CHAPTER 11, THE OFF SWITCH FOR YOUR ECONOMY

Clara continued, "The Socialist Party and the Industrial Workers of the World, known as Wobblies, were strong in Minnesota. The Wobblies had 150,000 members worldwide. They called for one big union."

The screen showed photos of IWW strikes.

"The Non-Partisan League," Daniel said. "North Dakota organization of farmers and small business owners, ran candidates and won the governorship and the legislature."

"The League even set up a state-owned bank," Ma said. "It built a grain elevator, opened a mill, started a railroad, made it possible for farmers to get fair prices for their crops by cutting out the Minneapolis Fat Cats. Then it set up offices in Minnesota."

"Minnesota Fat Cats had kittens!" Pastor Broadwater said. "They passed a law creating the Minnesota Commission for Public Safety in April 1917. It persecuted German Americans and went after the Non-Partisan League, socialists, and Wobblies."

"Was that legal?" Clara said. "Heck no! But the Commission claimed Wobblies and socialists were unpatriotic enemies of the so-called American Way."

"So the Commission," Daniel said, "with a million-dollar budget, hired gun-carrying self-appointed officers. Broke into private homes, made arrests. Without warrants! That's like giving the finger to the Constitution!"

"Or," Clara said, "tearing it up."

We showed photos of Commission officers raiding IWW Halls.

"The Commission worked closely with the Communal Association," Ma said. "And the police. Bridge Square, downtown, was a Wobbly stronghold. The Commission banned bars, pool halls, theaters, clubs—every place Wobblies met and organized."

"They even changed Minneapolis vagrancy laws," Pastor Broadwater said, "so you couldn't have meetings in parks, squares, or on sidewalks. Then they got a hundred and fifty-four towns across Minnesota to pass those laws too."

The spotlight shifted to Denise, Rennie, and Kurt.

"Here's what the Commission did to Wobblies," Kurt said.

"Minneapolis Wobblies had a Swedish language newspaper," Rennie said. "*Allarm*, with two els. It was anti-war."

"The Commission squawked, 'A*llarm* hurts our war effort,' " Denise said.

"They got a grand jury to indict the editor," Rennie said. "Sentenced him to jail. After five years behind bars, they deported him."

"They banned *Allarm* from the US Mail," Denise said. "It didn't last long after that, without its editor and no way to get to its subscribers."

"Freedom of the Press?" Kurt said.

"Not for them! Not for them!" the Truthtellers chanted.

"Are we going to let them do that again?" Pastor Broadwater asked in his booming bass voice that sounded like God calling down from the skies.

Kurt pointed to the audience. "You tell that guy, not this time!"

"Not this time!" the audience thundered.

"Here's what the bosses did to socialists," Kurt said.

"Socialists had a newspaper, *New Times*," Rennie said. "The Safety Commission's Secret Service investigated the editor but couldn't find any evidence of a crime. So, the bosses got US Army recruiters to threaten newsboys, seize their copies of *New Times*."

"Governor Burnquist," Denise said, "told Minnesota sheriffs they should break up meetings where people said anything 'unpatriotic.' "

"In Dale, Minnesota, up near Detroit Lakes," Rennie said, "a bunch of thugs and sheriffs from three counties raided a large socialist picnic."

"They threw banners, signs, and copies of *New Times* into a bonfire," Denise said. "Speakers were arrested and prosecuted."

"Freedom from unreasonable search and seizure?" Kurt said. "Freedom of assembly? Freedom of speech?"

"Not for them! Not for them!" the Truthtellers chanted.

"Are we going to let them do that again?" Pastor Broadwater thundered.

Kurt pointed to the audience, turned his palms up, a question on his face.

"Not this time!" the audience roared.

The spotlight switched to Irene, Evelyn, and Luke.

"The bosses have done it again and again," Irene said. "They destroyed our unions, our publications, our organizations, our political parties."

CHAPTER 11, THE OFF SWITCH FOR YOUR ECONOMY

"They broke up our meetings," Evelyn said. "Made us ashamed of our own cultural heritage, whether it was Finnish, Swedish, African, German, or anything else."

"But back in 1934," Luke said, "when things got really bad, striking teamsters declared, 'No! Not this time!'"

"An army of cops and deputies battered them," Irene said. "With clubs and guns. Two strikers were killed, dozens injured."

"But the strikers won," Kurt said. "We won!"

"Are we going to let the bosses win this time?" Pastor Broadwater thundered.

Kurt pointed to the audience.

"No way!" the audience roared.

"And we back that up with an unbeatable strategy," Evelyn said. "We are nonviolent. We do not attack people."

"But you attack us?" Irene said. "You club or shoot us, our children, our elders? You will instantly lose your war."

"Every single one of us will refuse to work for you," Luke said. "We, people of many nations, Black, White, and Brown, are together. It's not me. It's not you. It's *us*!"

"Don't mess with *us*," Evelyn said. "We are the off switch for your economy."

When the applause, whistling, and cheering tapered off, Daniel said, "See you Wednesday, 8:30 a.m. at Pulaski Park. Or Shingle Creek Park. Or Como Avenue Park. Or Portland Park!"

The floodlights turned on, the spotlight went off.

Nora came running up on stage, motioned Rennie and Denise to come to the mic.

"I want to give a shout out to one of our heroes," Nora said. "Frank Ahlberg, a solid union man, had his legs broken in a Camden Yard accident. Send him greetings at the hospital!"

"Fra-ank, Fra-ank!" echoed off walls. "Fra-ank, Fra-ank!" rebounded floor to ceiling.

"We love you, Daddy!" Rennie and Denise said into the mic.

As people began to leave the room, Rennie grabbed me, danced me around. "Holy buckets, Paavali! It really is bigger than me, larger than you." She looked at her watch. "All right, then, we promised Dad we'd be there by nine-thirty. Where's San—"

Her brother, Scott, came bounding onto the stage, holding hands with Sandi. She held up her left hand. I'd never seen her grin like that before. The stone on her ring sparkled even in the auditorium's dim light.

"She told me I shouldn't buy her a ring, but I just had to!" Scott said.

"I am so happy for you two, yes siree!" Rennie said.

"Me too," Denise said. "May you live in health and happiness forever!"

Rennie's other brother, Anthony, her middle sister Debbie, and Great-Grandma Clara met us in the hospital parking lot.

From just outside Frank's room, I heard him say to Rennie's mom, "That was one heckuva surprise on KPFP, their team-speak and greetings and all. Makes me feel so… I don't even know words for it."

"Wonderful, Frankie?" her mother said.

"More'n that. Lots more!"

"Well, we've got another surprise, Dad!" Scott said as he stepped into the room with Sandi, holding up her hand.

"Well done, Scooter," Frank said. "The sparkle in Sandi's eyes is the only thing brighter than her ring! You're taking a big step up, marrying a Mäkinen." He reached out, shook Scott's hand, then Sandi's.

I noticed the framed photo of Rennie casting Frank's strike vote was on the wall.

"Holy buckets," Rennie whispered in my ear. "It's like Dad from the old days."

"Ka Ka, what're you whispering to Paulie?" Frank said. "You two are next? Gonna have to get your judge friend to bend the rules 'cause Paulie's your brother-in-law now."

Rennie squeezed my hand really hard, her face lit up like a supergiant sun. "I'll file a petition with Judge Haddad when the time comes, Daddy. She's going to look at our family and tell me I'm my own sister-in-law!"

My snakes bit and hissed so loud, everyone must've heard them. I punched them so hard, my knuckles bled.

Anthony poured champagne into plastic cups. Debbie cut an Egekvist fudge cake.

"A toast to Scooter and Sandi," Denise said. "Health, happiness, and may we win this strike, all of us together!"

"Grandma, can you say the toast in Swedish?" Frank said.

I'd forgotten Clara was Frank's Grandma.

Clara's eyes sparkled. "*Ja, det kan jag*! Ya, I sure can! *Hälsa, lycka, och må vi vinna denna strejk*!"

"Dad," Debbie said. "We brought your favorite Camden Superette sandwich."

"Roast beef with horseradish, red lettuce, and fried onions on rye? Really?"

"He hates the hospital food," Rennie's mother said. "Only ate half his plate tonight." She draped a napkin on Frank's chest, helped him eat.

"Thank you, my family, for all of these surprises," Frank said.

Rennie took her jammer out, turned it on, dropped it back in her bag, pulled out the spike from Camden Yard, handed it to Frank. "It's from track fifteen, Daddy. Right where that dip was."

"You mean...Ka Ka...*you* removed track fifteen that night?"

"Can't say I did, won't say I didn't, as far as that goes."

"And, Paulie?"

"Same here, Frank."

"I am so proud of my family!" Frank said. "Including my new son-in-law. Now, I have a surprise for you. Been chewing the fat with a lot of railroading guys visiting me. Remember that idea Ka Ka put in my head, I should run for alderman? They all say I should. So I am! In the June primary."

"I'll vote for you, Dad!" five voices said.

"Me too!" Me, Sandi, and Clara said.

He reached out for Rennie's hand, took it. "Ka Ka, I am proud of you. Everything the guys have told me. The stuff in *People's Free Press*, on KPFP. The spike. That you're gonna be a lawyer and you're already on the way. But most of all, what you did to pull this family back together. I'm so sorry I said those awful things to you. It wasn't right, Ka Ka. It wasn't right." Tears rolled down his cheeks.

Still holding his hand, Rennie wiped his tears away with her handkerchief, began crying.

"All I wanted," Rennie sobbed, "was to have my old dad back again. Now I do. Now I do."

Her father looked at her mother. "Joni?"

Rennie's mom stepped over to her, embraced her.

Rennie was holding my hand again, but not as tight as before.

"I must have been totally insane not to see the fine young woman you were busy becoming. You inspire me, Ka Ka. I had no right to say that phony, stupid stuff about you. Will you forgive me? Please?"

"Yes, Ma. Yes." She dropped my hand.

Her mom embraced her again, held her. Both of them were crying.

As we drove home, I realized my snakes had been silent since my epic punch.

Afterward, in my room, I held Rennie while she sobbed. My serpents were still lifeless.

"It's all those years of pain," she sobbed. "Coming out for good, drop by drop."

"I'll hold ya, Rennie, and help ya through. For as long ya need."

CHAPTER 12, FINDING THE PURPLE THRONE

TUESDAY, MARCH 7, 1972

When the sky was still an inky dark blue, Rennie woke me by kissing my left cheek, nose, right cheek, forehead, chin. "You must be exhausted, Paavali!"

"Nope, slept like a rock."

"But you talked to me in my dreams all night. Helped me deal with lots of stuff."

"Hello, Operator! I wanna make a mind-to-mind dream call to Rennie Ahlberg."

She laughed, rolled on top of me.

My dick tingled for a moment, then went limp. My snakes hissed and bit, but not as much as usual.

"Gosh, I like when ya do that!" I said.

"What?"

"Put a hundred and ten pounds of solid woman muscle on top of me. Just makes me feel so good!"

She kissed my face again. We lay there, my arms around her, chatting, kissing, talking more.

After a while, she said, "If we get a move on, we'll have enough time to work out before our first meeting, yes siree! Deal?"

"Deal! Ya want the bathroom first?"

"Thanks, 'cause I'm about to burst as far as that goes!"

I got the potatoes peeled, onions chopped, grapefruit cut while Rennie showered and dressed. The aroma of cooking bacon, eggs, and home fries wafted through the house. Ma, then Clara, then Linda joined us. Rennie and I put platters of food on the table.

"Amazing how much better stuff tastes when ya eat with people ya love," I said.

The bell rang. When Linda opened the door, I heard Sheila call out, "Extra! Extra! Frank Ahlberg to run for alderman in Ward Four!"

Linda came back with the *Minnesota Patriot, People's Free Press*, and for the first time in days, the *Journette*. She spread them out on the counter.

"Aw, the poor *Journette!*" Linda said. "Someone put it on a diet. Just twelve little pages." She flipped through them. "No news here. All propaganda, no facts. Imagine an editorial supporting Judge Coventry's decision to deny us injunctive relief against the Buildings Department? Calling us amateurs playing with Tinkertoys®?"

"Quick! Check its pulse," I said.

She tapped it with her hand. "Doesn't have one. Too bad, so sad!"

Ma hummed the funeral march.

Linda flipped another page. "But wait! There's more! Claims to be printed by union labor. Don't they know their press operators are still locked out?"

Rennie opened the *Free Press* to page three. "Holy buckets! A photo of Dad! A shot of his locomotive after the crane put it back on the tracks, the whole left side bashed in. And a shot of the rusted-out ghost of a spike I took from track fifteen."

"And Frank's platform!" I said. "Plank by plank, goes beyond the People's Union. 'Community Development Funds to go to neighborhood associations, not businesses; a tax on industries to fund safety commissions, so they don't have ta rely on fines; labor history to be taught from first grade on up; if you're injured on the job, you get full salary until you recover and can work again.' I like Frank's thinking!"

"Best of all," Clara said, "he guarantees he will always support these planks and will resign from office if he does not."

"I knew he could! I knew he could!" Rennie chanted.

"But wait 'til you hear this *skitsnack* bullshit!" Clara said, pointing to a page in *Minnesota Patriot*. "Paul Mäkinen, the Shingle Creek communist

CHAPTER 12, FINDING THE PURPLE THRONE

agitator, was seen at a 5th Street Pawn Shop holding a sack full of five hundred thousand gold Soviet Russian rubles. He sold them all to pay off students duped into sitting in at the Brooklyn Center Draft Board office. Took the proceeds in five-dollar bills and waddled out the door."

"How could I even carry five hundred thousand gold coins?"

"That's about three-and-a-half tons of coins," Rennie said.

"What in Sam Hill can they be thinking?" Ma said. "They're in up to their eyeballs when we sue for libel on this one!"

Clara turned the page. "Oooh! We got them good, yah! Listen to this. 'Our socialist government is persecuting true American patriots again, trying to keep us from reaching hard-working folks like you with our message of hope and freedom. They're trying to prevent us from using *your* personal letterbox or mail slot, that you paid for out of your own pocket, to deliver the *Minnesota Patriot*. We won't stand for this snatching away of yet another fundamental American right! Where we keep our funds is a well-guarded secret, and the postal gestapo will never collect their twelve-hundred-dollar so-called fine. Their extortion attempts will not work on us.'"

"Er, Russ actually knows where they bank," I said. "So it would behoove us to sorta let the Post Office know. Am I on the right track?"

"Yep, you're on the beam, Paulie!" Ma said.

"Yah, *fullkomlig*!" Clara said. "Perfect!"

Breakfast finished, we headed over to the gym room just as the sun was rising. Rennie used the speed punching bag. I worked out on the heavy bag. Then we switched. I spotted her while she bench-pressed the forty-pound free weights a couple of hundred times. Then she spotted me. We got everything set up for the afternoon's activities, walked over to our office. The phone was ringing. Betty, voice shaking, asked what time Russ and the law interns would be in. They had gotten a past-due property tax bill for Olson, Bucky, and Betty Halls. For nine years. A hundred and eight thousand bucks, plus interest.

"Don't have a cow, man. They're just harassing us 'n' stuff 'cause Russ went over all your paperwork when you gave us the building 'n' you *did* have an official tax exemption until 1976, 'n' you don't even own it anymore, 'n' I'll tell Russ the moment he comes in 'n' they can't get away with that crap anymore 'cause we have a law staff, 'n' *People's Free Press* and KPFP to expose their shenanigans."

When Russ arrived, he said he'd petition for an injunction against the assessor's office. With his go-ahead, we called the postal inspector.

"Well, that puts the matter in quite another light," the inspector said. "We don't always have the staff to investigate, but since you did it for us, we can make collecting this a top priority."

When he hung up, Rennie looked at me. "Bingo! That was easy. Now let's—"

The phone rang. Cecil said he had a truckload-sized idea to discuss and could he come by. Half an hour later, he came prancing into the office. "I got tired of the boss yelling at me, so I'm fixing him. Did you know I own the tractor and boss pays me to pull his trailers?"

"That's why ya have a tiny red heart painted on yahr door?"

"You're smack dab on the dot! So, this guy who owns a diner I deliver to in Perham told me his brother's retiring, selling two trailers. One's refrigerated, the other not, plus a tractor, all in great shape. I bought them, two hundred down, a hundred a month for three years. I'll drive one, my brother the other."

"Far out 'n' congratulations 'n' stuff, to the max! How can we help you?"

Cecil grinned. "Long story short, I need to fill them for the trips back from Detroit Lakes. You scratch my back. I'll scratch yours! I know a farmer right outside of Clear Lake, has fifty-four tons of eating potatoes in cold storage. Big corporate buyers offer him less than his cost to grow them. I can deliver them to you for five cents a pound. Farmer makes money, I make money, you make money even selling them at twenty percent off retail. Or more."

"Mega-magnificent! What's yahr minimum order?"

"Forty mesh bags at fifty pounds each. Strike's stopping truck traffic, food's gonna get scarce. Forty bags won't last long, especially with your corner store co-op."

"So, Cecil, do you 'n' your brother make two-fifty minimum doing this 'n' does the farmer 'n' their helpers, as far as that goes?"

"We do. We're both Teamsters Union members. But I'll have to ask the farmer. It's him, his wife, a son, and two daughters working that farm."

CHAPTER 12, FINDING THE PURPLE THRONE

"Definitely sounds like a heck of a good idea, but we need to talk with our store committee and accountant," I said.

"But wait! There's more," Cecil said. "I know a table beet farmer right outside of New York Mills, three carrot farmers near Wadena, all with their crops in cold storage. Why pay more for tasteless carrots shipped in from who knows where when we can buy tasty Minnesota food? Besides, you try to buy milk recently? Can't come in by rail, and non-union truckers are stopped and turned around by Teamster picketers. I can deliver milk, sour cream, butter, cheese, all from a Detroit Lakes co-op dairy owned by farmers. With union workers getting the two-fifty."

"Would you go down south to Hampton to pick up cold storage cabbage and Dennison to get meat?" Rennie said. "We interviewed farmers and packinghouse workers there for our oral history project 'n' they all wished for something like this."

"We could work it out," Cecil said. "When will you talk with your people?"

"Probably today, if not tomorrow. We shouldn't wait on this idea," I said.

"Yeah, this is exploding," Cecil said. "Heard on KPFP on the way over here that masons, bricklayers, and carpenters walked out over safety hazards and respect."

Rennie looked like she was thinking, finger tapping the top of her head, one eye closed. "So, Cecil, are you selling potatoes 'n' stuff to the diners on your route, 'cause holy buckets, if you're not, you should, to the max."

Cecil took a step backward, his eyes got wide. "Now why didn't I think of that? Each of them probably go through a bag or three weekly. They're probably paying a pretty penny for potatoes from Idaho or Washington state."

"Holy cowbops!" I said. "Suppose ya gave yahr diners forgotten recipes featuring Minnesota products, like Swedish spicy whipped carrots with cod, or *raggmunk* Finnish potato pancakes, which are easy to make? Our food editor at *People's Free Press* has been wanting to feature ethnic recipes, and we could make this into a sorta festival, with the diners featuring a different old-country recipe every Saturday night using Minnesota products. Every Thursday, *People's Free Press* could have a list of diners serving that week's featured recipe."

"You people! You are...fan-flipping-tastic! When you get done with me, I'll be making *three* bucks an hour!"

"Here's the plan, as far as that goes. Suppose we help set up small owner-operated or worker-owned trucking companies on major north-south highways in the state 'n' they are based on your model 'n' stuff? And no halfway about it, they all help farmers get a fair price for their crops 'n' they all work together? Dude, would you work with them?"

"We'd all come out way ahead, so you bet I would!"

"Johnson-Meilander Trucking, Amalgamated Foods Midwest, look out!" I said. "Yah're finally gonna get some real competition."

"I'll shake on that," Cecil said, extending his hand. "Talk with you soon!"

Rennie turned on KPFP.

"And the strike news keeps on coming!" Keanna announced. "So much happening so fast, we can't keep up. Intercity Bus Drivers Local 85, KHA Specialty Steel, on strike! Taxi Drivers Local 1980, Plumbers Local 675, Electricians Local 789, Johnson-Meilander Trucking, on strike! Grain Elevator Workers Local 1208SE, Building Inspectors, Stationary Engineers Local 619, Derrick Operators, on strike. Amalgamated Foods Midwest. On strike! Strikers! Let us know, when out *you* go, at 130-0550!"

Hank stopped by. "We've got the lights, phones, and temporary heat working in the newsroom. But only got twenty-one typewriters delivered. Georgia called the journalists we've hired. Forty-eight of them can bring their personal typewriters from home 'til we get the rest of our order in. The wire service guys are setting their connections up. My crew's unpacking desk chairs, office supplies. Only problem is restrooms. Sinks, toilets, and urinals. Supplier said the army ordered 83,000 of them, so we have to wait. How long? They couldn't say."

"But we *have* them all, yes we do," Rennie said.

"What the heck? Where?" I said. "Not on our inventory."

"I thought everybody knew 'n' stuff. In a corner behind the passenger coaches in Olson Hall. Dozens of them, still in cartons. Only thing is, they're bright colors like purple, orange, 'n' turquoise, as far as that goes."

CHAPTER 12, FINDING THE PURPLE THRONE

"Hot dog! Those restrooms will become famous. Hey, I'll be right back. Have ta visit the purple throne. How'd ya know about them, Rennie?"

"The day back in July when I was checking out Nellie the Switch Engine for the first time, I sort of poked around the coaches and locomotives. Had no idea we'd ever need sinks 'n' stuff, so I forgot about them."

We jogged through the new doorway to Olson Hall, climbed around the locomotives, into the corner, opened boxes of shiny red and yellow sinks, purple and green toilets, pink and blue urinals, complete with faucets, fittings, seats. The colors were so bright, I wanted to put on sunglasses.

"These fit yahr specs, Hank?"

"Yes! Yes! Let's grab a forklift, move them to Betty Hall, get them installed. Those colors sure will pop against white tile floors and walls! One color per restroom, or maybe mix the colors all up?" He chuckled.

"Every fixture different?" I said.

"To the max!"

"I'll cancel the toilet and sink contract," Hank said. "Supplier violated contract terms, so no problem. This is far better!"

Hank got a forklift. We loaded ten toilets, eight sinks, and three urinals, hauled them in to the newsroom, started unboxing them in the corridor.

Dewey saw the colors, said, "Howling hotcakes! Bright colors like that, we won't even need lights. Hey, Hank, a bunch of us want to elect our foreman."

Hank's smile vanished. "The crew's not happy with me?"

"Well, we are very happy. You bring out the best in us. So nobody's running against you. But we feel you should be elected."

Hank's smile returned. "Okay, fair enough. I'll run."

"What was that about?" I said when we got back to our office.

"We promised they could expand their horizons 'n' they want to be sure it's real, as far as that goes, 'n' they want to show appreciation for Hank."

For the rest of the morning, Rennie and I met with people helping to teach our ten-week, first ever, leadership class for employees. I was impressed with Ma and Carleton's slide show about where the profits from our work go. Some of our community services, like home aides, were not designed to make a profit. The Arnray Co-op was expected to make a two percent profit to be used for community services. Any additional profit would be distributed to its members. Ma's chart for the newspaper showed a twelve percent projected profit, with half for community services, the rest for employee profit sharing across all of our businesses.

Clarence said he and Hank would start their session on leadership with the question, if everyone is a leader, why do we still have group and project managers?

For Dina and Susie, a big idea behind their discussion of disagreements was, would it seriously slow things down, or cause a safety issue to try two or three different approaches to a problem? What's the potential payoff if a new approach works better?

As I heard each team's design for their portion of the class, I was more and more impressed. *Hot dog! Answers for questions I didn't even know I had!*

At eleven forty, when we got in the car, I said, "I don't feel right being at yahr meeting with Judge Haddad."

"Why, Paavali? She said you should come because she has something she wants to talk about with both of us."

"But it's *yahr* mentoring meeting. I don't want to interfere with that."

"It's very considerate of you to think about it, but she and I both know that would never be a problem, all right then? Something is up because we're having lunch in her chambers. She said Orchard Restaurant walls have ears." Rennie folded both arms across her chest, hands clasping elbows.

I talked about our morning meeting. She answered with only a word or two. We drove all the way down to 23rd Avenue North with her mostly silent.

Stopped at a traffic light, I said, "I feel like something big-huge is bothering ya, and I totally wish I could help ya through it."

She turned, looked out her window. "It's just something personal I'm dealing with 'n' has nothing to do with you, no siree."

"But it's hard for me to see ya this way, because I care about ya and feel for ya. Will ya tell me about it? Please?"

"When you had stuff going on 'n' you weren't ready to talk about it, I respected that 'n' let you alone, 'n' that was hard for me, yes indeed. I can't talk about this stuff, even if Badah asks me about it, which she won't 'cause you'll be there. Please let me be, 'cause I have to box it up and put it away before our meeting 'n' no, don't worry, it isn't something *you* did."

"Okay, Rennie. But ya know I'll do anything in the whole wide world to help ya."

"If I didn't know that, I maybe wouldn't even keep going." She banged her fist on the dashboard.

It's something to do with Greg. I just know it is. And it's serious. It feels like a major pile of rocks has been dumped on my shoulders.

She turned on the radio but didn't sing along. We drove the rest of the way without talking. Just before we parked, she seemed to come to life again.

In the judge's chambers, there was a jammer running. We turned on ours.

"I feel like I know a lot about what's going on at Shingle Creek," Badah said, "listening to KPFP and reading *People's Free Press*. But fill me in on the details. What is it actually like for you?"

Rennie told her how closely the two of us were working together, how wonderful it made her feel, what she was learning from Russ and the legal team, and how she worked it out so she could take twenty-seven credits next quarter.

She did? She can?

"That is amazing!" Badah said. "Eighteen's usually the limit for even the best students. How are you managing that?"

"Well, I wrote a paper on my own, not for a class, on how a community-based law firm should work," Rennie said. "Inspired by the Teen Council Law Clinic. Approached Professor Anderson, who teaches the Sociology of Law class. Asked him to read it. He didn't want to. So, I pulled out a ten-dollar bill, put it on his desk. 'No, it's not a bribe, it's a bet,' I said. 'Ten dollars to nothing, you're going to be impressed with this paper. And no, I don't come from a wealthy background. I worked hard for that ten. I know the value of it. And of my paper too.' "

She didn't tell me about this? Why?

"That's really courageous, Karen!" Badah said. "What happened?"

" 'It's a bet!' he said, took the paper, handed me back the ten. So a few days later, I went to his office. 'You were right,' he said. 'With a few small changes, this paper can be published in *Annals of Legal Sociology*. It's almost equivalent to a master's thesis. I'd give you thirty credits if I could, but the limit for independent study is nine per quarter. The *Annals* editor is an old friend. I can introduce you. Deal?'"

"So I said, 'Maybe, but what are the changes?' He went over them with me. They made perfect sense. I agreed, did the rewrite, 'n' ten days later I met with the editor. He accepted my paper for the June issue. So I already got an A for nine credits for Spring semester. And I'm still on track for law school before I'm twenty."

"I am so proud of you," Badah said. "Published in *Annals of Legal Sociology* as a freshman! Law schools are going to be begging you to enroll."

"Professor Anderson asked me if I had an idea for another paper. I told him about your Maple Grove Program. He said if it has results for at least twenty-five kids over a five-year period, *Juvenile Justice Essays & Ideas* might be interested. So there's nine credits for *Fall* semester."

"That would be quite an honor for you *and* for me!" Badah said. "Maple Grove's been running six years, graduated fifty-three teens. All but two are doing exceptionally well." Badah told us all kinds of Maple Grove background information, had her law clerk copy the documents and reports Rennie needed for her paper.

Every time I think I know how smart Rennie is, I'm wrong. She's smarter!

"Badah, you mentioned there's something important you want to tell both of us about?" Rennie said.

Badah stood up, walked to the door, locked it. "Top secret," she said. "I called the contact Mr. Loftus gave me at the Justice Department and sent her the documentation she asked for about biased amicus curiae briefs. She asked me to fly down there tomorrow to speak with her. There are no flights from Minneapolis because of the strike, so I'll drive to Chicago, fly from there. The Justice Department woman thinks there's grounds for criminal charges against several judges, Mr. Schulz, and possibly Mr. Hastings-Dankworth."

"Holy buckets! Hastings-Dankworth? We have a copy of a check written by him made out to Police Chief Jensen for ten-thousand bucks. Dated and cashed the day after Fred's murder. The memo says, 'Good job.'"

Badah's eyes widened. "Critical circumstantial evidence. They'll want to see it in Washington."

"We'll get a copy to you before you leave," Rennie said.

"I have a question for you," Badah said. "I expect a firestorm of falsehoods aimed at me when the federal investigation becomes public knowledge. I'm up for reelection in June. Can you help me with my campaign like you're doing for Judge Woodruff?"

"Yes, indeed! We'll have our media people, Councilwoman Belinda Frisk and Councilman William Anderson, contact you. Thursday? Friday?"

"Friday sounds good. Shall we eat?" She unwrapped an Orchard Restaurant lunch.

We ate, we talked. The more we told her about building the auditorium, Workers' Market, and the newsroom, the more questions she asked.

"I've never heard of a community doing these things for itself. I think it's just wonderful."

Back in the car, Rennie seemed like her usual self again.

"How come ya never told me about that Sociology paper?" I said.

She turned redder than a cranberry. "I was so exhausted that day 'n' then you told me Willi was fired 'n' things started to happen really fast, 'n' I told Dad I would cast his strike vote for him so I forgot until later, 'n' then I was embarrassed I hadn't told you 'n' the more time went by, the worse I felt about it, 'n' stuff with Greg got mixed in 'n' now it's a big mess."

I pulled over to the curb, stopped, gently put my hand on her cheek. "Rennie, I am so proud of ya, even if ya didn't tell me 'til today. That's not important. What *is* important is yah're getting a paper published! That is astonishing! Breathtaking! Ya really are a genius in bloom."

"Thanks, Paavali," she said, tears rolling down her cheeks.

I turned off the engine, put both arms around her. She leaned her head against my chest, sobbed. But couldn't tell me why. I sang her comforting words that seemed to come straight from my heart.

After a while, she pulled out her handkerchief, wiped her face, blew her nose. "Okay then, we really should start talking about tonight's training session for our new employees 'n' make sure we got it nailed!" We talked all the way back to our office. But when we stopped for a red light, I could still see tension on her face.

That evening, the Teen Council Meeting Hall was jammed. "Holy buckets!" Rennie said to me. "We have this many people working for us 'n' enough to fill the room again three more days?"

"Uh-huh! We're a pretty big deal," I said. "What the chamber of commerce calls a major employer."

Pastor Broadwater took the mic. "Welcome, Shingle Creek employees! I know folks think of me as a pastor. But workdays, I'm a stationery engineer at Camden Rebar, a proud Local 1125 member. And I'm a-walking the picket line like most everyone else here. So when Clarence and Obie asked me to chair this training session, you bet I said yes! For me, what's happening here in Shingle Creek is like a dream. We have a once-in-a-lifetime chance to change our community and our places of work into something happier, healthier, and more rewarding. So we have to learn to work together in new ways to reach a new promised land that's just around the corner!"

He handed Blanche the mic. "Already, we're doing things that haven't been done before. The new Ray Iversen Auditorium will be the largest worker-owned hall in America. Our *People's Free Press* is already America's largest newspaper owned by a blue-collar community. Our working people's museum and sculpture garden, now just a dream, will be the first anywhere in the whole wide world."

"What else can we do?" Pastor Broadwater said. "That depends on what we dream up together. I invite you all to join the dream. Share ideas, no matter how crazy you think they might be. Will you"—he pointed—"and you"—pointing to someone else—"and you dream with me?"

"Yes! You bet!"

"So here's the key," Blanche said. "To make all this happen and keep going, we need a new way of working. Not for a boss. Not following orders. But figuring stuff out together. We're not used to that, and let me say, it's different! Sometimes I have to think so hard, my toes are curling. But I'm enjoying the people I work with so much more!"

"So that's what we're about tonight," Pastor Broadwater said. "How do we best work together as neighbors and friends? Here are Clarence and Hank to start."

"If everyone is a leader," Clarence said, "why do we still have forepeople and group and project managers?"

CHAPTER 12, FINDING THE PURPLE THRONE

Hank clapped him on the shoulder. "When it comes to organizing picket lines and strikes," Hank said, "Clarence is my leader because he knows union history, what works, what doesn't. And he keeps lots of information in his head about the likes and dislikes of every worker in Camden Yard. Including me! I can't see the big strike picture like he does."

"But when we're trying get the newsroom finished really fast," Clarence said, "I don't know the details, who has what skills, how the whole plan fits together, so Hank is my leader."

"When I'm picketing," Hank said, "I always think, *What do I know, what am I seeing, that will help Clarence lead?*"

"And when I'm working on the phone cabling in the newsroom," Clarence said, "and I see an easier, faster way to connect it, I ask Hank if there's any problem doing it that way 'cause he knows. I don't. And he maybe says, good idea, but here's where you can't use it and why. And then we show everyone else how and when to do it faster and better."

"It's called leading from behind," Hank said. "Everyone's looking out for safety hazards, better ways to do things, people problems. I know if there's a problem I don't see, our team has my back. Makes leading easier, more satisfying."

"On our newsroom project team, we have daily meetings first thing," Clarence said. "So we know where we stand, what's a priority, and why."

"Anybody on the team can call a meeting any time," Hank said. "So far, when they do, we get more done afterward, faster and easier."

"The other day," Clarence said, "someone called a meeting, asked, 'Why is Nathaniel installing conduit and Oscar's building shelves, which he hates doing? Nathaniel loves shelf-making!' So they switched, and both of them felt better, worked faster. Meeting took a whole thirty seconds!"

"So let's open a discussion now," Hank said. "How is your team doing leadership-wise?"

We had a great back-and-forth, surfaced problems, worked at solving them, got some great ideas. The one I liked best came from Sam Korhonen. "My Bonnie daughter taught me this. When you're annoyed with someone about silly stuff, think of the thing you like about them most. Tell them that. Often makes the problem just disappear. She stopped bickering with her cousin Mamie that way."

Then, Ma and Carleton showed charts about which workgroups make profits, which don't, and why. That sparked an interesting discussion about whether everyone—male or female, married or single, with kids or without, blue collar or professional, young or old—should be paid exactly the same wage.

As Obie put it, "We don't know. But at least now we have the questions. So let's keep a-talkin', and we'll find those answers!"

I have been wondering why I'm paid so much more than everyone except Lucy. Makes no sense. If I start working for the Teen Council or Neighborhood Association instead of the Park Board, we're gonna have ta review that! Ma and Russ are older than me, but only earn half as much? Doesn't make any sense.

Pastor Broadwater took the mic. "Join us next week, same time, same station, for discussions on working out disagreements and balancing safety, productivity, and job satisfaction. See you all then!"

Rennie looked at her watch. "Holy buckets! It's already a quarter to nine 'n' the newsroom opening party is in fifteen minutes, 'n' are we ready?"

Hank, standing near us, turned and smiled. "Luke's been sending me notes. They did everything and are set to go, green and purple toilets and all! Marcello picked up the cake and ice cream from Camden Market, Eugene has the coffee perking, and there are fifty-nine journalists ready and waiting in the auditorium."

Bonnie, Bobby, Mamie, Charlie, Kurt, Tessie, Jeanette, and Jeffie paraded into the Teen Council Meeting Hall, playing a march on their kazoos. We followed them all the way to the auditorium, up onto the stage, and to the mic.

"Do we have sixty-five journalists?" The Nines bellowed. "Count off!"

"One, two, three…sixty-two, sixty-three," the journalists called out.

"Sixty-four!" Tom yelled, running into the room. "Was finishing a story for tomorrow's paper."

"Sixty-five!" Susie roared, running behind him. "Ditto."

"Hip! Hip!" The Nines hollered, and pointed at the journalists.

"Hurray!" the journalists shouted.

Four of The Nines sang the Shingle Creek welcome song while the other four played it on their kazoos. Then they said, "Follow us, folks!"

CHAPTER 12, FINDING THE PURPLE THRONE

They played the marching song and led the way into the newsroom, a double line of journalists following.

A small oak plaque carved with the journalist's name and beat was on the wall behind each workstation. People hung their coats in the cloakroom, opened desk drawers, found pads, typing paper, carbon paper, pens, clips, tape. Picked up phones, heard dial tones, nodded, smiled. Looked over the small quiet rooms, each with a desk, typewriter, and a door that could be closed.

Susie, Tom, and Georgia clasped their raised hands together, yelled, "We did it!"

The Nines played happy birthday on their kazoos.

"It's our happy re-birthday!" Susie said. "From the ashes of the *Journette*, we are born again! So no candles on the cake until next year." She stood between Bobby and Charlie, held their hands, raised them high. "Ladies and gentlemen, three cheers for the founders of *Shingle Creek News*, now *People's Free Press*!"

"Yipee! Whoopee! Bravo!"

Luke and Marcello served cake and ice cream. People chatted, joked, smiled.

Labor reporter Sidney Felsing came out of the men's room, laughing his head off, spluttering, "Purple! Purple, I say!"

"Purple what, Sid?"

"Go see for yourself, Tommy!"

People went in and out of the restrooms, guffawing and chuckling.

"Orange you glad you used stall three!" the new business reporter, Maurice Feldschuh, said.

Rita Sakala, religion reporter, said, "Nope! Stall one's better for purple prose!"

"Ooh! Went in stall two, now I'm green with envy!" editorial writer K. H. McGuire said.

As the party wound down, Rennie and I stood side by side under the big clock in the center of the newsroom, arms around each other.

"This is gonna show the bosses we mean business!" I said.

"And our march on downtown tomorrow will too, yes indeed!"

CHAPTER 13, MOMMY, MAKE ME STOP DYING

WEDNESDAY-FRIDAY, MARCH 8-10, 1972

THE NEXT MORNING, THE DOORBELL rang while we were eating breakfast. Sheila, ice-crusted scarf over her face, handed me *People's Free Press* and said "Super extra-extra! Every single working person in Shingle Creek either on strike or laboring for the community!"

"Cold out, Sheila?"

"Wind has teeth today! Will be something else marching all the way downtown."

After breakfast, we packed lunches, went to the Teen Council Meeting Hall. Sarah Nesheim from Portland Park was testing three CB radios. "Got them tuned to 2, 11, and 38 'cause they're hardly used. Those are our channels today, pass it on!"

Our antenna, mounted on the Betty Hall roof forty-five feet above the ground, pulled in CB calls from East 62nd Street, sixteen miles away at the southern end of Minneapolis.

"We have command centers at Pulaski, Portland, and Como Avenue parks too," Vincent said, "but this is the main one."

Phil Rasmussen had six phones set up, attached to a cable running all the way back to the newsroom. "I borrowed a few lines for today from *People's Free Press*, you know, for emergency calls. Don't worry. I told Georgia, and all the journalist's phones will work, long as no more than forty-four of them are calling at once."

CHAPTER 13, MOMMY, MAKE ME STOP DYING

Dr. Ericson had a first aid station set up in the office next to Joanna's. "I was also able to get four mobile emergency care stations," he said. "Don't ask how or from who. One's at Shingle Creek, another at Pulaski Park, third's at Como Avenue Park, fourth at Portland Park. They'll travel with the marchers."

"We're inviting reporters from other publications, stations, and the wire services to use our newsroom so they can file their stories fast," Tom said.

A group of about a hundred women were gathered around Ruka, Gordy, and Lola. Gordy deputized them, handed out badges.

"Duane Pukari and his thugs attack us," Ruka said, "we take them down, tie their legs with their belts, hands with these." She gave out lengths of rope.

"And then," Lola said, laughing, "we women put one foot on their chest, and they get their picture taken. Smile, guys!"

We were all guffawing like crazy.

"What happens next?" Ruka said. "We pile them into one of the trucks. Drive them way out to Rum River Regional Park up near the town of Ramsey. Drop them off there, so they can have some quiet time out in the woods, thinking about what they did."

"No buses, no taxis, anywhere near," Lola said. "It's a twenty-mile hike back to the nearest bus stop or payphone."

"That is flippin' brilliant," Vincent Wójcik said.

We went outside, walked toward the warming room. Six stake trucks were parked on 50th Avenue, spaced about half a block apart. Perfect for us, the open backs had low fences around them. Each had benches or chairs and big signs promoting People's Union planks. $2.50 Indexed Minimum, We Demand Respect, Right to Elect Supervisors, Equal Opportunities, Right to Organize a Union, Job Safety Now!

Gordy, Lola, and Ruka came marching up Morgan Avenue from Betty Hall with the deputized women. Parade marshals with red armbands and battery-operated bullhorns were getting four hundred people lined up behind each truck.

People holding signs climbed up, sat down, began chanting their truck's slogan. Two of Gordy's squad cars pulled in to the head of the line. Truck engines started, and we were moving! Rennie and I marched just behind the first truck. We turned right on Morgan Avenue. About midway down the block, four cars pulled into the street from 49th Avenue and stopped, blocking our way. One of them was Duane Pukari's yellow Chevelle. Car doors flew open, men poured out. More men turned the corner from 49th Avenue. They marched down the sidewalk chanting, "Go back to Russia!" Messages on the truck's CB radio said there were carloads of thugs on 50th Avenue too.

Rennie dropped my hand, took a defensive stance.

How could we make such a tactical error? We're trapped!

"Get their women!" Duane Pukari yelled. "Have fun, guys!"

Thugs charged into our parade. Women and girls started kulning, which seemed to confuse the punks. One of them grabbed Laura's breasts from behind. She elbowed him in the privates, spun around, hit his face with a roundhouse punch. He went down, out cold.

A thug tried to punch fourteen-year-old Peri Korhonen. She grabbed his arm, pushed him off-balance. Bonnie elbowed him hard in the gut, kneed him in the groin, he doubled over, and Peri shoved him to the ground, tied him up. Another thug went to slap Ma across the face, but she was quicker. She knocked his arm away with her left fist, smashed him in the mouth with her right, then used his stomach for a punching bag until he crumpled into a blubbering heap.

Betty smashed a thug in the eye. He ran off howling, jumped in his car, reversed out of Morgan Avenue, tires screeching, and sped away. When a thug grabbed Tessie's arm, went to slap her with his other hand, she dodged and Kurt kicked him in the Achilles tendon, Tessie kneed him in the groin, and down he went. Then a thug went after seven-year-old Kimmie Hakkala, which was too much for Rennie. Letting out a great roar, Rennie leaped in the air, crashed down on his toes, kicked his shins. Kimmie made him scream by kicking the backs of his feet, then Rennie hit his stomach with a wicked punch that decked him.

I heard the CB reports going back and forth from parade marshals to each other and to headquarters. There were about sixty thugs at Shingle Creek. Fifty-eight of them ended up on the ground. One ran off. Pukari tried to, but Officer James took the keys out of Pukari's car, arrested him for inciting a gang attack and impounded the car.

CHAPTER 13, MOMMY, MAKE ME STOP DYING

The other parks, where not as many people knew self-defense, reported in with numerous injuries before furious marchers managed to beat the crap out of the thugs. But at Shingle Creek, Dina Eldin had a small bruise on her face. Ellen Lund's cheek was scratched. Twelve-year-old Tommy Hillilä was sobbing hysterically, he was so upset about the thug trying to hurt Laura. And that was it.

When grinning women and girls put one foot on their tied-up thugs' chests, reporters crowded around, shooting photos and film. Rennie and Kimmie both put feet on the thug they took down. Perrine Fournier said, "You know, my dears, your photo will be on front pages around the world. Mademoiselle Kimmie, how did you help Madame Karen bring down this animal?"

"I kicked him hard where it hurt!" Kimmie said with a sweet smile.

Perrine shot another photo. "If I have daughters, I hope they'll be like you two."

Medics from the mobile emergency care unit patched up injured thugs. Laura took thug shots for our records, Georgia for *People's Free Press*. We removed chairs and benches from trucks, piled thugs in.

Tess and Bonnie climbed up on each truck, said to the louts, "Don't you ever come to Shingle Creek again! We won't hold back like this time. We'll put you in chokeholds that'll kill you. Yeah, us little kids. Do you understand us?"

"Yes, Miss," the thugs said timidly.

Four trucks with eight parade marshals headed for Rum River Regional Park, one of Gordy's squad cars leading the way. Rennie and I went to Betty Hall, checked in with the command center, huddled with Sarah, Vincent, Lola, Dina, Herb, Fiona. While *we* could have marched that afternoon, the thug attacks had so disorganized the other three contingents, they couldn't. We set up a speakerphone conference call, decided to postpone the march to the next day and ask some of our women warriors to march with the other parks. Then, Rennie and I joined the People's Union organizing committee, went all around Minneapolis talking with folks who'd been attacked by thugs, asking questions, listening, comforting, making suggestions.

"For sure tomorrow's going to be ultra awesome 'n' the real deal," Rennie said, " 'cause we're all on the same page 'n' even though they did some damage, one way or the other, we all beat the crap out of those hoodlums. They won't be back, no siree, Bob!"

Next morning, Thursday, the sky was a perfect, cloudless blue for the first time in weeks. There was no wind. Temperatures in the high twenties felt almost tropical. We had observers with CB radios in cars along the start of the parade route. There were no reports of thugs in Shingle Creek or at the other parks. The organizing committee asked me to make a rousing speech to launch the march. Even more people than yesterday stood in the big field in front of the warming room, despite a hundred of our women and girls marching elsewhere.

I lifted the bullhorn. "Our crowd is bigger, the sun and skies are smiling on us, our cause is just, and we are strong!" A loud, chopping, thrumming noise started in the distance. "Just remember as we march, we are the off switch of their—"

The noise drowned out my bullhorn. Six helicopters appeared overhead, their thup! Thup! THUP! sound made my whole body pulsate. Flying down low enough for us to see the pilots' faces, doors on the copters' undersides slid open and released a violent rainfall. We were drenched. And suddenly very cold.

Then they dropped dozens of some sorta bomb that blew apart midair, releasing thick whitish-gray smoke as they fell. We started to cough, rubbed our burning eyes. With no wind, the smoke just hung there. I could hear the copters fly up and away, but I could not see them. My eyes were too bleary.

So this is how the Vietnamese felt, except they got burning napalm too. How could we do this to them?

Somebody took my hand, led me away.

"Where's Karen?" I croaked.

"Holding your hand," she wheezed.

"Can ya see? I can't."

"Barely."

A nurse at the mobile emergency care unit on 50th Avenue put us down on the sidewalk, flooded our eyes with water, gave us water to drink. The first aid volunteers made sure everyone's eyes were flushed and they had dry, warm clothes. Including guest journalists. Then, we sat down to talk strategy.

CHAPTER 13, MOMMY, MAKE ME STOP DYING

"They singled us out," Fiona Flynn said. "The other three marches are going along fine, no thugs, no helicopters. Other neighborhoods send their best wishes and want us to resume our march tomorrow. They'll join us."

"Oh, I don't know," I said. "They're just gonna bomb us again. With napalm."

Rennie's hand tightened on mine. She squeezed twice, shook her head.

"We can't, can't give up now," Vincent said. "Paulie, man, I understand how you feel. Yes, what they did to us is scary. But we're just at the tipping point. *If* we keep moving forward."

"My advice," Marek said, "hit 'em hard tonight! Condemn and take away unsafe tracks their scabs just started using again today at City Line Yard. Russ said our North-Northeast Minneapolis Industrial Safety Commission charter allows us to do that if twenty-five workers there petition us. Well, fifty-three did. Clarence, Obie, and I can get the people we need to pull it off."

Rennie squeezed my hand once. I squeezed back. We all voted for it.

"But what about the copters?" I said.

"You know you can take a copter down with a kite?" Herb Anderson, Billy's dad, said. "Now let me be clear, I'm *not* in favor of doing that."

"What in heck is your point?" Sarah said, frowning.

Herb grinned. "We can get a Federal Aviation Administration permit to have a moving kite-flying festival. That closes off the air space. Copters—planes even—can *not* fly there. Period! The FAA enforces it, not us!"

"A permit that quick? And kites?" Sarah said, hands out, palms up.

"I'm a member of Robbinsdale Kite Makers. I get permits for our events. FAA permit guy's my buddy. Give me half an hour, I'll have answers."

"Holy ravioli!" Dina said.

"A genius in bloom, hey?" I said.

Ma came striding into the room. "Excuse me, big news on KPFP. Hastings-Dankworth just fired a bank teller for joining the marchers from Portland Park. Even though he had an approved personal day off. Entire workforce at Twin Cities Unified National Bank just walked out and asked Office Clerks Local 1027 to represent them!"

"Tipping point!" Vincent said.

We voted to approve the kite festival. Half an hour later, Herb called us. "Got the permit! My FAA buddy said those copters were Forest Service with identifying numbers and insignia painted over. Completely unauthorized. He's mad as hell about it!"

For the rest of the morning and all afternoon, Rennie and I, with the People's Union organizing committee, went all around our neighborhood, checking in with everyone, making sure they were okay, explaining tomorrow's strategy.

When we got back to the office, Russ ran up to us. "Some good news, and I'm sure you could use it today! Judge Ovington reversed Judge Coventry on appeal, granted our request! The Buildings Department can *not* close down our auditorium."

I was surprised how teary I got.

Rennie hugged me.

"Thanks, Russ. Yah're the best! It's just been a rough day."

He patted my shoulder. "I understand, Paulie. Bosses are getting desperate. Doing crazy, illegal things. It isn't easy. It won't be easy. But this time, we're going to win! Just get a load of this. Judge Ovington also turned down Teddy-boy Knight's appeal."

Suddenly, Rennie didn't look all weary and sad anymore. And I felt my face relax. She did her little dance, clapped her hands.

"He acted on these extremely fast," Russ said.

"Do ya think it could have something to do with Nora's tape?" I said.

"Heh, heh, heh! Do shoes have soles?"

At midnight, we drove to St. Paul, parked in a deserted industrial area, walked a few blocks, ducked into a dim alleyway, put on our masks and green armbands identifying us as Industrial Safety Commissioners. Waited in the shadows. When we heard someone whistling "American Pie," then "Rock On," we came out of the alleyway, joined a small group wearing masks and green armbands, followed them to two tracks right under a floodlight tower with half the lights burned out. Someone with a woman's voice in a gray coat told us this was the scene of eight accidents since January first. Ties were rotted, fish plate bolts missing, entire rail tie plates gone, no ballast in spots, rails clearly out of line, even in the shadowy light.

To one side, the two tracks branched out into at least thirty. The other way, eight tracks headed off in two directions. Clearly a critical point

CHAPTER 13. MOMMY, MAKE ME STOP DYING

that should've been well-maintained. There was no valid reason for six workers to die there.

Less than an hour later, two hundred feet of track were packed up in the back of a trailer, ties and all. We had big, blinking red lanterns in place, set twenty feet apart, on tracks leading into this junction.

Just as we got in the mahrove-rove car, we heard a locomotive air horn sounding four short blasts. Once. Twice. And again.

"A scab engineer's stopped at one of the red lanterns," Rennie said, "asking for a go signal. Let's skedaddle!"

We pulled off our masks and armbands. On the 280 freeway, we saw St. Paul police cars and a railway cop car heading in the other direction, sirens blaring, lights flashing.

"Jack Belor!" Rennie said.

"Henry Ness!" I said, looking in the rearview mirror, expecting to see red and blue lights following us. The freeway was clear behind us. And ahead.

Finally back in my room, we both fell into bed, exhausted. But helicopters chased me all night long. I woke up screaming. Rennie calmed me. I fell back asleep. *Thup! Thup! Thup!* They were after us again. Dropping clouds of tear gas, showers of rocks, cascades of flames. I was choking, burning, smashed by rocks, screaming myself awake again. Rennie, plagued by *Thup! Thup!* nightmares like mine, held me and cried with me.

Next morning, skies were back to gray. A chill wind blew hard at us, but our coats, hats, and gloves were warm. The wind and kites would be our protectors.

Trucks started their engines. People chanted our plank slogans. Two of Gordy's squad cars led the way, a third brought up the rear. This time we had scout cars radioing back to us before we made any turns, letting us know the way ahead was clear. Almost three thousand of us turned onto Morgan, then into 49th Avenue, and made a right on Humboldt. Hot dog! No thugs. Fifty-three kites up above the clouds gave the finger to copters. People lined Humboldt and Fremont Avenues clapping, whistling, then joining the rear of our parade.

The first group from Northeast merged with us at 42nd Avenue. Forty-three hundred of them, led by a marching band. By the time we got down to Lowry Avenue, our parade marshals estimated we were nineteen-thousand strong with eighty-four kites and people from eight more neighborhoods. At West Broadway Avenue, the second Northeast group, also led by a marching band, joined the rear of our parade. By city hall, with all four marches merged, our marshals estimated 153,000 people were filling the streets and sidewalks downtown.

We stopped marching, the bands stopped playing. "Two-fifty minimum!" we called out. "Fair strike settlements!"

For each demand we chanted, the bells on city hall chimed and big-huge banners unfurled from the belfry, covering the clocks on all four sides. "Fair Strike Settlements!" "We Demand Respect!" "Two-Fifty Indexed Minimum!" "Equal Opportunities!" A great cheer rang out that seemed like it would actually shake injustice loose from these halls of power.

How did they even get up there with banners? Who are they? I turned to Rennie. "It really is bigger than me, larger than you!"

A TV reporter and cameraman from channel four came over to us, interviewed Clara. "The people in power are not hearing us," Clara said. "So we have to raise our voices. Attention, Fat Cats! When one-third of your city is in the streets protesting your policies, you better listen, yah! We are the off switch for your economy!"

There was no open space anywhere near city hall big enough for a 150,000-person rally, so we hadn't planned one. We stood there, chanting, the city hall bells affirming us, for fifteen minutes. The banners on the belfry were pulled back up. When we saw a bunch of people with the banners climb into one of the trucks, the message to head back home came over the CB radio.

Bands started playing, people chanted, truck engines roared, and we were on the six-mile march back home. As we marched, people moved from one section of the parade to another, visiting friends. Bonnie, Peri, and Irene joined us at 31st Avenue North.

"Paulie, I have a question," Bonnie said. "Do professional writers make stories and books about working people protesting like this?"

"Journalists do. That's why you saw so many of them around today."

"But what about plays? And stories? And movies?"

"Not so much anymore."

"They used to?"

CHAPTER 13, MOMMY, MAKE ME STOP DYING

"Back when unions were really strong in the 1930s."

"Can I read them?"

"I know one great one, *Grapes of Wrath*. Joanna can tell you about others."

"Will I be able to write stories about our protests?"

"It will take a lot of work, but yah're more than smart enough," I said.

"How do I start?"

"Keep a diary. Write down everything ya see, hear, think about. And read, read, read everything ya can."

"I'm getting started today when we get home! It'll take a whole lined notebook to fit everything that happened this past week."

"Ya know what, Bonnie? I want a daughter just like ya someday."

Rennie's smile vanished, her hand tightened on mine. Her lips compressed.

"Are ya okay?" I said.

"Uh-huh. Just a thing I was thinking. It's nothing."

We got back to Shingle Creek around 1:30. Tired but triumphant, we gathered in the field outside the warming room. Diane and Bobby used megaphones to lead us in singing "Joe Hill."

A loud, gasoline-powered roar interrupted us. A line of khaki-colored Jeeps? With men holding rifles? Came speeding into our field from the next one up, from behind the tall bushes that flowered yellow every June. The men had Police Deputy badges on unmarked khaki uniforms. Fifty-something Jeeps blocked us, two men in each. Behind us and to our left, the frigid creek cut us off. Gordy and three of his officers were surrounded with us, their squad cars parked on 50th Avenue.

Out of the corner of my eye, I saw Althea slip behind a bush near the creek. Reporter Sidney Felsing followed her. Most journalists had not marched back with us, but Perrine Fournier from Agency France-Presse, Jerry Accardo from Associated Press, and Elżbieta Witkowski from KTCA-TV, plus four *People's Free Press* reporters were there with us. Chatham Jenkins from *New York Press-Journal*, wearing a tan raincoat over an actual suit and tie, kept running to the warming room. Jerry nudged me, pointed to Jenkins, said, "Must've screwed up big, got demoted from his desk job."

Another jeep came speeding into the field, halted right near us. Clyde Gremling, rifle in one hand, megaphone raised in the other, limped out. Richard Prichard stood next to him. "With the authority vested in me by the State of Minnesota, I order you to disperse this illegal, seditious assembly," Clyde yelled.

I raised my megaphone. "It's our park, Clyde, and we have a valid permit."

Gordy yelled into my megaphone, "Gremling, you don't have authority to—"

"Company, shoulder arms," Clyde barked.

"Hands up, don't shoot!" I yelled into the megaphone. "We can't leave, Clyde, ya have us surrounded." I dropped the megaphone, raised my arms.

Everyone put their hands up, chanted, "Hands up, don't shoot!"

Clyde stood there, rifle raised, moving it from side to side with a nasty grin on his face. Some of the deputies looked upset, a few had not shouldered their guns.

One of them yelled, "Mr. Gremling, there's kids here," and pointed his rifle at the ground. A few more deputies lowered theirs.

"Get the Black ones first!" Gremling shouted.

"Oh, no you don't!" Bonnie yelled, stepping in front of Charlie. Dozer moved in front of Daniel. Roger pushed Louie Ward and Brucie to the ground, covered them with his body. Clara jumped in front of Ruka.

"Ready! Aim!"

More deputies dropped their rifles.

Irene ran toward Bonnie. The mobile emergency care unit bounced into our field, behind where Gremling stood.

"Fire!" Gremling yelled.

Shots rang out.

This is not happening. They cannot do this. Please, please, let me out of this nightmare.

I took a frenzied look around me. Bonnie, Dozer, Roger, Clara, Bev, Greta, and Joyce were lying in the snow. Dick Prick strutted around, smiling. Gremling turned, shot at the emergency care unit, so he didn't see Margaret Björk come charging toward him. She grabbed the rifle from him, whacked him in the head with the butt, knocking him down. He lay there, screaming, bleeding.

CHAPTER 13, MOMMY, MAKE ME STOP DYING

Margaret aimed the rifle at the deputies. "Bunch of you are going to die unless you all drop your guns and get the hell out of here! One, two, three!" She shot over their heads.

Guns clattered to the ground. Deputies ran.

Dick Prick aimed his rifle. Margaret shot, knocking the gun from his hand. He turned and ran with the others, blood dripping from his fingers. Engines started up. Jeeps sped away. Margaret shot at their tires, disabling two of them.

"Creekers! Grab the guns!" Ruka yelled into a megaphone. "Pile them in the warming room for now. Guard it!"

Irene, sitting on the ground, cradled Bonnie's head in her lap, stroking her face. "Oh, my precious Bonnie, I love you so much."

"Mommy, make me stop dying. I have poems to write." Bonnie shuddered, closed her eyes.

"Hold my hand tight, Bonnie, don't let go!" Irene yelled.

Dr. Ericson ran to them, tried to stanch the bleeding. Could not. "I'm so sorry, ma'am. She's gone," he said, tears rolling down his cheeks.

Irene's piercing wail sounded like the siren of death.

Laura, sitting, holding Dozer in her arms, begged him not to die. "I can't live without you. I'll never find another love of my life. Nobody else is like you."

Despite his grimace of pain and the steady flow of blood from his abdomen, Dozer forced himself to speak. "Laura! I'm...sorry to...leave you. My...last wish. Do not live your...whole life...just mourning...me. Find...another true...love. Promise!"

The nurse, hands covered in blood, shook her head. "He's going, honey. Talk fast!"

"I promise, Dozer. I promise."

"Goodbye...my sweet...Laura. I love you." He looked up at me. "Paulie-friend."

"Dozer!" she screamed. "Dozer!"

Through my tears, I saw Tommy Hillilä hug Laura. The snow under Dozer was bright red as Tommy, wise beyond his years, talked quietly to her. Ma sat down next to Laura, embraced her. Two nurses rolled Dozer onto a stretcher, covered him with a sheet.

"Can she walk with him to the ambulance?" Ma said.

The nurses nodded. Ma helped Laura stand. Holding on to Dozer with both hands, she stumbled across the field to the ambulance.

"Baby girl," Ma said to Laura when the ambulance drove away. "You want me to take you home?"

"Betty Hall. To the darkroom."

Ma, arm firmly around Laura, led her up the footpath.

Gordy, walking in circles, crying silently, banging his knuckles together, kept saying, "I couldn't stop them. I failed. I failed."

Oh, my God, Clara, Roger, Louie, Brucie, Bev, Greta, Joyce, are they all dead? Is anyone else. Is Rennie okay?

In a frenzy, I ran around the field. Rennie tended to Clara, unhurt but shaken up. There'd been an explosion of feathers when a bullet hit the arm of her new puffy down coat. But only the coat was wounded. Louie and Brucie were unhurt but still frightened and crying. Roger had a wound on his arm. A nurse had stopped his bleeding. Barb kissed his face over and over. Bev and Greta, best friends, needed stitches and wound care. Their dads, Pete and Clarence, took them to the hospital together. Joyce Trockenmann, face scrunched in pain, blood darkening her jeans, clung to Norma Lund.

"You stepped right in front of me, took a bullet for me," Mabel said, holding Joyce's hand. "Why? You don't even know me."

"You're Daniel's mom. I was gonna kill myself. Daniel stopped me."

A nurse cut Joyce's pant leg, pressed a thick pad of gauze to her wound. "I know it hurts like heck, honey," the nurse said.

"I'll never walk again?" Joyce said, voice shaking.

"You'll walk. You'll even run. But now, we have to get you stitched up and dosed with pain meds."

Tears rolled down Norma's face. Mabel's too.

"You're crying for *me*?" Joyce said.

"Yes, precious!" Norma said.

"Then I can stand anything, M…M…Mommy!" Joyce said.

"You want me to be your forever mom?"

Joyce nodded.

"Oh, Joycie! Oh, Joycie! Yes! Of course, yes!"

CHAPTER 13. MOMMY, MAKE ME STOP DYING

The doctor and nurses from the mobile unit did not want to tend to Gremling, who lay screaming in the snow where Margaret had knocked him down.

Althea yelled at the doctor, "He's a human being! Even if I hate his Jim Crow guts. Take care of him, damn it!"

"I don't get it, Miss. He wanted to execute Black people. And he shot at us."

"Two wrongs don't make a right," Althea said. "Look, I jumped clear over that creek to let you know we needed help. So damn it! Help him."

The doctor and a nurse, griping, tended to Gremling, called for an ambulance.

I stumbled around in circles, furious that like Gordy, I had not been able to protect us. How would we live without Bonnie, without Dozer?

It seemed like hours before Rennie found me, took my hand.

"Paavali, I'm taking you home, holding you tight. You have some serious crying to do. I'll do anything to help you through this. You must, have to, un-blame yourself."

"I'm done with all this stuff. We're finished. They won! Dozer's dead. Bonnie's dead. 'Cause I couldn't stop Gremling. My soul is wounded, won't ever heal. I can *not* go on. Can't! Can't!"

CHAPTER 14, UNBLAMING MYSELF

FRIDAY AFTERNOON-SATURDAY MORNING, MARCH 10-11, 1972

CRYING SO HARD I COULD barely breathe, I lay in Rennie's arms. She wiped my tears. They kept coming.

"It's my fault. I didn't plan right. I should have known."

"No way! No way! And no way!" Rennie thundered. "It's *not* your fault, my fault, or our fault, what those bastards did."

"But we knew about the militia. We knew!"

"And what could we have done different, as far as that goes?"

"Guns! We shoulda bought guns!" I punched the mattress, made the bedsprings wail.

"It would've been a much bigger slaughter 'n' we'd all be dead or in prison like the Wobblies in 1916, 'n' you know the vote was against getting guns, 'n' stop blaming yourself 'cause that's what the Fat Cats want you to do."

My body shook. I couldn't stop crying.

Rennie stood up, walked toward the stairs.

"Don't leave me!"

"I'll be right back." Her voice was soothing. "I'm getting something for you."

A moment later, she set a glass of water down on the nightstand. "You have some tranquilizers left. Take one!" She put the glass in my hand, a pill in my other.

CHAPTER 14, UNBLAMING MYSELF

I gulped it down. "Hold me, Rennie. Please!"

For what seemed like hours, she embraced me, talked to me, wiped tears off my face, stroked me. Then the pill kicked in. I drifted into dark, dreamless sleep. When I woke up, she was in the easy chair, reading, tears running down her face.

"Rennie? Why?"

"For Bonnie, Dozer, Roger, Greta, Bev, Joyce. And for you, for the pain you have in your soul. While you slept, I went out 'n' saw everyone's crying, but they are carrying on big-time 'cause that is what we have to do now, 'n' our tears mixed with our tasks is our strength, to the max."

"Everyone like who?"

"Laura's developing photos people took the last three days, crying the whole time but doing it. Joanna's in tears, cataloging all the photos, organizing files for the newspaper and the future museum. Clarence is sobbing but involved in visiting picket lines all over the city, making sure strikers are keeping their spirits up. Lyle is working with his crew, testing the new auditorium furnace, cursing the Fat Cats and wiping tears away. Blanche, Lowell, and Luke, eyes wet, are crafting coffins for Bonnie and Dozer. Russ and his group are hard at work filing wrongful death lawsuits against Gremling and his militia 'n' their eyes are not dry either. Roger, even with his wounded arm, is helping Mabel bake pies, weeping about Bonnie and Dozer."

"I wanna take another pill, go back to sleep."

"No!" She stamped her foot, took the tube of pills, put it in her pocket. "You must carry on too, Paavali. We *all* must keep going forward."

"I can't!"

"Don't have a cow, man, but you can and you must! We all have to."

"How?"

She took me in her arms again. "This is bigger than me, larger than you. People are counting on you, on me, on us. If you can just un-blame yourself, you'll find the strength, I know you will, 'n' you'll get that way by going out 'n' talking to people."

"No! I'm staying right here."

"Okay, but I'm letting you know, Judith's coming to see you in five minutes, 'n' I'd never do something like that normally, but this is an emergency 'n' Judith agreed."

"No! I won't talk to her."

"But *she'll* talk to you, yes she will!" Rennie picked up her book. "I'm going upstairs to let Judith in."

I turned in bed, facing the wall, pulled the blankets over my head. A few minutes later, I heard footsteps that weren't Rennie's coming down the stairs, then the sound of someone sitting in my easy chair.

"Paul? Are you hiding?" Judith said.

I didn't say anything.

"Are you afraid of something?"

Without even thinking about it, I started sobbing again.

"We're all scared. I've talked to twenty-one people since the massacre. The bosses scared the living shit out of us. That's what terrorists do. How is that your fault?"

"It just is," I said.

"Can you look me in the eyes and say that?"

I pulled the covers down, turned toward her. Didn't say a word. Just cried silently.

She pointed at me. "So you're still the little bastard who ruined everyone's lives? Just like your father, Deadwood, said? The idiot, problem-causing child? Just like Mildread said?" She slowly raised her right eyebrow.

My tears stopped. I just stared at her.

"Listen, Paul! You've done a terrific job getting rid of the poison Deadwood and Mildread poured into you. But clumps of it hide in little nooks and crannies in your soul, waiting to ambush you."

"Deadwood and Mildread are making me feel guilty? Still?"

"Exactly! But that's not all. Are you a poorly educated, ignorant, dumb, dirty, failure, so stupid you bring down a heap of problems squarely on your own head?"

"That's what the bosses say. I'm not any of that."

"So you're not responsible for problems Fat Cats create for working people?"

"N-no."

"So, Paulie, why are you blaming yourself?" Her voice was soft, gentle.

I shrugged. "I...don't know."

CHAPTER 14, UNBLAMING MYSELF

"Is it easier to control workers if they blame themselves for their own problems?"

"I guess."

"Is that why so many teachers called you a poorly educated, ignorant, dumb, dirty, failure? Didn't Mrs. Elak call all the kids that? You think that was an accident?"

My fists clenched. "It was planned?"

"You got it! And it comes at you in school, at work, on the news, in movies, even in books. That's why it's so important to challenge working-class stereotypes."

"Bastards!" I hit the mattress with a roundhouse punch. The springs shrieked.

"Good. You're getting angry, which you have every right to be. Nourish that anger. Direct it away from yourself. Let it motivate you. But don't allow it to force out your great love and compassion. They're related, and you need them both. Can you do that?"

"Sure as heck can!"

"I want you to try something else too. Tell Sampaa and Irene, Dozer's mom, Tessie, Roger, Hank, and Karen's dad that you blamed yourself for the massacre. Listen carefully to what they say."

"Why should I do that?" My eyebrows tickled my hairline.

"It'll help you keep your anger directed away from yourself. Will you do that?"

I bit my lower lip a moment. "Yeah, if I have ta."

"You have to!"

"So…Karen was right?"

"Indeed!" Judith nodded. "She's one smart cookie. One more question, Paul. How are you doing with your erection problem?"

I sat up in bed. "Yikes! Dick's totally dead. Even when I think of Nancy or Maria. I'm doomed."

"Actually, that's a sign of progress. Hostile negativity no longer arouses you sexually. You've moved to neutral territory. Are you physically close to Karen a lot?"

"A whole lot."

"Do you feel any signs of arousal, even small ones?"

"Little tinglings. And getting hard for a moment until my serpents stop it."

"Dig it, that's *big* progress. But you're still blocking something. Get it unblocked and you could move into the healthy place where you're aroused by loving positivity."

"And Karen's sexy good looks?" I turned, put my feet on the floor.

"You're finally seeing that?"

"More and more."

"Keep doing what you're doing, Paul. You're on the right track for yourself. And you inspire all of us."

"I'm gonna keep on truckin,' you betcha!"

"Excellent! We'll talk soon. Call if you need me."

I went upstairs with Judith.

Rennie dropped her book, came flying off the chair in the living room, looked at me, hugged me, then shook Judith's hand. "Holy buckets, Judith! Thank you, big-time, to the max!"

"Glad to help. You two going out to talk with folks?"

"Soon as I get my coat on and buttoned," I said.

"I'm going next door to talk with Gordy," Judith said. "It would help vastly if you could talk with Rose. She's been looking for you, Paul."

This won't be easy. Yikes!

Rose, wrapped in a blanket, was shivering. Jeanette's usually rosy cheeks were paler than a winter moonbeam. Emily, Dozer's older sister, held her head in her hands and couldn't look at us.

"My heart aches for yahr family," I said, and hugged Rose. "Dozer has been a light in my world and will always be. I carry him—and you—in my heart."

"Even when I was a little kid," Rennie said, "I could always count on Dozer to look out for me and my friends. He was like one of my brothers."

"Thank you, that means a lot to me," Rose said. "Jeanette, can you take Judith upstairs to see Daddy?"

"Mommy! He'll be angry," Jeanette said. "He told us don't disturb him."

"Not at you, he won't. I promise. Please, Jen-Jen."

Jeanette took Judith's hand, led her upstairs.

"Rose, Emily, will ya forgive me?" I said.

CHAPTER 14, UNBLAMING MYSELF

"What? What for?" Rose said.

"It's my fault. Dozer would still be here if I had—"

"What? If you were Superman or something?" Rose said. "With a magic wand for a left arm? Or Joshua, playing a miracle trumpet that stopped Gremling in his tracks? C'mon, Paul!"

"If I had made sure we could defend ourselves. If I—"

Rose shook her head. "That's bullshit, pardon my French. No way on this green earth you're responsible. I can't believe you and Gordy fell for the same crap. Now you listen to me, Paulie Mäkinen! I'm not forgiving you. There's nothing to forgive."

"But I—"

"Nonsense! You've been Dozer's good friend since kindergarten. He could always count on you. Always!" She came over, stood in front of me, put her hands on my shoulders. "Will you help plan and lead the service? Dozer would've wanted that."

"What Mom just told you, I agree," Emily said.

"You bet I will!" I said.

"Will you tell us memories of him?" Rose said. "We could use that about now."

"We sure could," Emily said. "Let me get the tape recorder, okay?"

I told them about the day when we were picnicking in fourth grade, how I imagined a fruit forest and Dozer wanted to be the one to plant it. About how excited he was when Jeanette was born. And that he had us take branches from a willow tree up at sixth bend, put them in the ground near first bend, and make Jill's willow clump. Some of what I told them they'd never heard before. They hung on every word.

About fifteen minutes later, Jeanette came downstairs.

"Mommy! Daddy took my hand and wouldn't let go. Daddy's feeling like he did something wrong. But he didn't. And I told him."

"I know he didn't," Rose said. "And he really needed you to be there because you know too. I'm proud of you, Jen-Jen."

"Will Daddy get better?"

"Definitely!" I said.

"How can you tell, Paulie?" Jeanette said.

"I had the same kind of feelings. Judith helped me start thinking differently. Your dad will do that too."

Later, when we walked into the fourth-grade classroom, they had a life-sized photo of Bonnie taped on her chair.

"I told the kids they could go home or to the park," Lucy said. "But they want to be here, with me, Daniel, and Ruby."

"I checked on Laura," Daniel said. "She's in the darkroom, crying and printing photos. I offered to sit with her, there or anywhere. She wants to be alone. Shirley…er, Ma, will be checking on her."

"Ruby's really cool," Ruthie said. "Helped us say how scared we are."

"She showed me why," Kurt said, "it's okay to be angry they wounded my sister."

"We didn't know what we'd say to Mamie when we visited her," Charlie said. "Ruby helped us."

"I'm going to visit Jeanette," Jeffie said. "She made me feel better when Roy…" He grimaced. "Now I have to help her."

"But, Ruby," Ruthie said. "What do I say to Terri? She said she should've died, not Bonnie, 'cause she's only adopted and then Irene and Sampaa wouldn't be as sad."

Ruby motioned to her. Ruthie stepped forward, stood beside Ruby's chair. Ruby put an arm around her. "Sweetie, they adopted Terri and Sheila because they're fabulous, lovable kids. Besides, math works differently for parent love." She counted off on her fingers. "I give one hundred percent of my love to my daughter. But I still have a hundred percent left for my big son, plus a hundred percent for my middle son and a hundred percent for my little son. And if a magnificent kid like you, for example, needed a home, I'd still have a hundred percent of my love left for them."

"It never runs out?" Ruthie said.

"Nope!"

"Can I tell Terri if she died, we'd all be crying-sad, same as we are for Bonnie?"

"Wonderful way to put it, Ruthie," Ruby said.

"Paulie, are *you* okay?" Bobby said. "I saw when Karen had to help you walk."

"Just a big-huge sadness in my heart," I said. "And I feel totally awful I couldn't keep Bonnie and Dozer from being killed."

"Oh, man! You blaming yourself?" Daniel said. "The onus is *not* on your anus!"

CHAPTER 14, UNBLAMING MYSELF

I looked at the floor. "I'm trying not to."

"Paulie!" Tessie said, taking my hand. "That's like if I blamed myself for Dad dying because I didn't stop him from going to work that day. That's not right."

"Or it was my fault Roy died in 'Nam 'cause I let him go there," Jeffie said. "Ruby told me that's not helpful thinking. Nobody can protect the people they love that way."

Next, we found Roger, hands covered with flour and dough, rolling out pie crusts in Mabel's kitchen. And crying. When I told him about my guilt, he said, "It wasn't my fault I couldn't stop Father from molesting my sisters. Right? You told me that? Yes?"

I nodded.

He touched my shoulder, left a floury handprint. "Isn't this the same thing?"

Sampaa and Irene said there's nothing to forgive and would I help plan the funeral. Hank told me it's like the way he blamed himself for how Yard Boss treated workers. "It wasn't me who created that horrible workplace, you know."

But when Frank, still in the hospital, said Yard Boss blamed *him* for letting his locomotive fall over, it set me off laughing and I couldn't stop for at least five minutes.

In the car, headed back to Shingle Creek, I said to Rennie, "That feeling, ya know, of guilt, it's just totally gone. Thanks for what you did. I was just so off-base."

"Happens to all of us sometimes 'n' it's no big deal."

"Well, to me it is a big-huge deal. And I'll never forget it."

"Mahrove-Rove! FastTalk!" the CB radio called out. "Not-Nephew here!"

"Denise's new handle," Rennie said. She took the CB mic. "Roger, Not-Nephew."

"Big Three need you here for meeting. Do you read me?"

"Big Three?" I said.

"Teen Council, Shingle Creek Neighborhood Association, People's Union." Rennie clicked the mic. "Read you. Be there in ten, Not-Nephew. Just had good laughs with Dad. He's looking better, yes siree!"

In the parking lot, Burt struggled to unload a big-huge box from his car.

"Burt, I'll get that for you, 'n' what's in it, as far as that goes?"

"Moscow gold!" Burt said, laughing. "Pawn shop couldn't sell it, so they're giving it back to you, Paulie."

We set the box down in the Teen Council Meeting Hall.

"Insulated to keep the bread from getting chilled," Burt said, opening it. "Finnish flat bread, cooled to a perfect taste. Made by Paulie's friends, Lola and Lori. I'll slice it! We have enough for the big meeting too." He set the slices, which looked more like cake than bread, on paper plates, buttered them. "Coffee's ready, bread's buttered, dig in everyone!"

It was the first thing I'd eaten since breakfast, and it tasted mega-magnificent.

Sarah called the meeting to order. "I'm sorry to bother you on such a sad day, but we have some urgent business. Even with General Grain and Dahl's Superette delivering, getting food's a problem."

Cecil stood up. "Got a fix for it right now! I have a trailer load outside of cabbage, beef, and chicken from Dennison and Hampton. Emptied my bank account for it."

"What's your cost per pound and markup?" Ronan said. He calculated our distribution costs and selling price based on Cecil's figures. "Sounds reasonable to me. Woody? Burt? Debbie? Thoughts?"

"Prices are fair," Woody said.

"Agreed," Burt said.

"But how will we distribute it?" Debbie said. "Woody and Burt's trucks are already on the road sixteen hours a day."

"I've got people can staff five more trucks if I only had them," Woody said.

"Let me make a call," Vincent said. "Be right back."

"Me too," said Betty and Herb.

Minutes later, we had nine more trucks. Then, back and forth we went, figuring out who would staff them, working out details. I wrote Cecil a check.

Susie, with Sid Felsing, came through the doorway, grinning. "Sorry to interrupt for a minute, but you have to see this!" she said. She held up an enlarged photo of Althea, arms spread sideways, coat flying out behind

CHAPTER 14, UNBLAMING MYSELF

her, high in the air over the creek. "Spectacular jump! Amazing shot! Three cheers for Althea and Sid!"

Sid grinned, bowed.

Althea stood up, said, "Only way to get help fast. Ran to my house right nearby, called the command center in Betty Hall. Jumped the creek again, ran back to the field."

"You're a hero, Althea!" Susie said. "You'll be front-page tomorrow."

Sid raised high an enlarged photo of Gremling. You could see the bullet emerging from his gun. "Page two tomorrow," Sid said. "Headline, 'Wanted for Murder: Clyde Gremling.' Jerry Accardo from Associated Press shot it. Came over the newswire."

Joanna held up the front page of the Thursday *Chicago Sun-Times* with Perrine's photo of Rennie and Kimmie, feet on the thug. "Out of town papers aren't arriving because of the strike, so probably many more clips. This one came by car with a friend."

"Listen," Li'l Mikey said. "I know today's not the day to discuss this. But it's another way to fight back. Pressroom's almost finished. Auditorium's getting there." He clapped twice. "We have skilled teams that work really well together. Let's think about founding Shingle Creek Builders Co-op. Ask Hank, Harry, and Blanche to co-run it. Lyle to head up the heating and ventilation unit. Ponder on it, okay?"

There was a chorus of yesses.

"Meeting adjourned," Sarah said. "Next up here, a meeting of the Industrial Safety Commission."

"Can I sit in on this?" Mike said. "Heard so much about the Commission. Want to see it at work."

"Sure thing, Mikey, be our guest," Rennie said.

When all the commissioners were there, Clarence said, "Given what happened today, we need to move forward aggressively. I make a motion that we inspect at least one factory every day, six days a week. Condemn and remove equipment in accordance with the law. We've waited the required time for Gremling to repair faulty equipment. He hasn't. Harley inspected it, says it can't be fixed. Removal time!" He pounded the dais.

"Especially since the Teen Council and Neighborhood Association voted to use half the recovered Community Development Funds to replace it," Jack said.

"Second!" Magdalena said.

"Third!" Tessie and Kurt yelled.

We worked out details about who'd inspect which factory when. Russ said his staff would prepare bills for penalties and removal fees at the bug spray factory.

"Short and sweet!" Clarence said, and adjourned the meeting.

Judith came sprinting into the room. "Paulie, Karen, Mike, Susie, Shirley," she beckoned to us. "Been in the darkroom, talking with Laura. Dig it, really not good for her to be by herself right now. We don't want her to fall off the wagon."

I shuddered. "All of us offered to stay with her. But she said no!"

"That doesn't mean it's good for her," Judith said. "Right now, she doesn't know which way is up. And, Mike, she wants you to go tell her dad at work."

"Sure thing, I know where," Li'l Mikey said. "QRS Cabinets up in Coon Rapids. Bastard Boss won't take phone messages, even emergency ones. On my way!"

Judith patted Mike's shoulder, turned back to us. "Will the four of you sit with Laura at the meeting on guns? And come to the darkroom now? That's what she wants."

"Must tell Georgia. Be there in a flash," Susie said, and ran off.

Laura sat on the darkroom floor, sobbing, the red safe light overhead making her look like she was condemned in hell.

Ma sat down next to her, took Laura into her arms. "Baby girl, I know you're hurting something awful."

"Why me, Ma? Why? First Mommy, now Dozer. Why?"

"I know, baby girl. It stinks. My heart is breaking for you. There is no way to explain this, no trick to make it better. All we can do is hurt with you."

"Dozer told me to find another love of my life. But I can't. I want him."

"Of course ya do," I said. "I know yah're feeling awful pain. And we all feel it with ya. But grief is like a current that can pull ya under. Or, let ya slowly drift to a safer place, where ya can manage it. Which is what Dozer would've wanted ya to do."

CHAPTER 14, UNBLAMING MYSELF

Rennie put her hand on Laura's shoulder. "Can Ma and I take you to the ladies' room 'n' help you freshen up 'n' make you feel a tiny bit better, all right then?"

Susie came flying in the door, looked down at Laura, extended her hands. "Can I help you up, Laurie-Laur?"

Laura took Susie's hands, managed to stand. Ma and Rennie led her to the ladies' room. Susie and I waited in the corridor.

"How can we even begin to comfort her?" Susie said.

I was wishing for a magic wand again. "By talking kindly and being there for her. It's not enough. But it's all ya can do."

In the auditorium, Laura sat on Ma's lap, all five feet, eight inches of her. Ma wrapped her arms around Laura, held her tight.

Suddenly, I'm twelve again, we're all twelve, Laura, Jill, and me, in the kitchen in Ma's house. It's before The Mister started beating Ma and she is still talking. Laura, just four-and-a-half feet tall, is sitting on Ma's lap, face tight against Ma's bosom, sobbing. It's only been six days since Laura's mom was killed in a car wreck. Ma rocks her gently, strokes the back of her head. Jill and I, both crying, are holding hands. I want to make Laura feel better, but I don't know how. Every day after school, we repeat this scene. It doesn't end until Laura begins drinking, stops talking about her mom. Or anything else. None of us know what to do, even Dozer. Morning, afternoon, evening, Laura's drunk.

I shuddered, winced. Got up, walked to the mic. "This is a sad day for Shingle Creek. They murdered our Dozer, our Bonnie. So we have ta decide what to do with the sixty-two rifles we captured." *Gosh, Paavali! Ya sound dead and wooden.*

I slapped my hands against my thighs. "Guns! We need more guns! And ammo! We can never let this happen again. We need to learn how to use them. All of us, fifteen and over. It's the only thing Fat Cats will understand."

A murmur that quickly became a roar moved through the auditorium.

Rennie rushed to the mic. Put her arm around me. "I understand why Paulie feels that way, but we are *not* on the same page. I think it would be the biggest mistake he ever made, yes siree! And it's not what we stand for here. For anyone who wants to use guns, I ask you to think about this. How would *you* feel if you killed someone?"

A chill came over me. I was nauseous, my legs felt wobbly. I wanted to agree with Rennie, but I saw Dozer's dying face, heard Bonnie's last words. Rennie's arm urged me off the stage, back to my seat.

"I agree with Karen," Clara said. "We'll always be outgunned by police and the National Guard. They won't give up so easy like the militia did."

"Put a gun in someone's hands," Margaret said, "they do things they'd never even imagine. Hitting Gremling with the gun stock doesn't bother me." She shook her head slowly. "But shooting that other man? All I can see now is that man's hand dripping blood. All I can hear is his scream. Guns are different from your fists. I'm against them. And don't call me a hero. I don't feel like one."

"We can't win with bullets," Bucky said. "Public opinion will turn against us. No path to victory without that."

"Moment we arm ourselves," Betty said, "they'll call sheriff's deputies, the National Guard, every thug for five hundred miles. And wipe us off the face of the earth."

"One of the biggest strikes in Minnesota history," Willi said, "the Wobblies lost. On the Mesabi Iron Range it was. A sad lesson in 1916 iron miners got. From their mistakes to learn we have to."

"I've read up on that one," Clarence said. "Like us, they went out on strike in huge numbers, 15,000 miners. They, too, marched for miles. They, too, cut production and profits way back. For months. Seemed like they, too, were about to win."

"But," Daniel said, "when they threatened to kill three cops for every union death, Fat Cats whipped up fear. Bosses mobilized sheriffs, judges, local police."

"Soon, Wobbly leaders were jailed on attempted murder charges," Clara said. "The Wobblies ran out of money. Strike failed. No wonder a year later, the Wobblies warned members against advocating violence, yah?"

"To the Wobblies' warning," Willi said, "we must listen! To fail we cannot. A motion I make the guns we do not use. Into pieces we smash them."

CHAPTER 14. UNBLAMING MYSELF

Approval resounded through the auditorium. Barb strode to the mic, raised both hands. "And from the pieces, Daniel helps us all create huge statues of Bonnie and Dozer for the entrance to Arne Iversen Hall."

Another thunder of agreement rocked the brick walls around us.

Laura stood up, motioned to Barb, who came running with the mic. "That's the way my Dozer would want to be remembered."

Susie pointed to the mic. Laura handed it to her. "We should invite the press to our statue-making, so the whole world sees we Creekers are law-abiding, peace-loving people. Can you help us make statues, Daniel?"

Daniel, clasped hands raised, shouted, "Yes, I can!"

"In memory of my cousin Bonnie," Billy said, "I second Willi-ukki's motion."

"Third!" Mamie said, holding Billy's hand. "Because guns killed my Bonnie, and I don't want guns here."

I was one of only eleven people who did not vote in favor. *Maybe I am wrong, after all.*

Blanche asked for the mic. "First of all, I want to thank Paulie for his skilled and selfless leadership. Paulie, I agree with you ninety-nine and forty-four one-hundredths percent of the time, as you would say. Even though this is not one of those times, I want you to know, we all love you and respect you."

The room erupted with applause, cheering, whistling.

Tears sprang to my eyes.

After the meeting was adjourned, Daniel came over to Laura and took her hand. "You know, I'd do anything to help you feel better."

"I know. You're a good friend."

"So I have this idea. Would you help me plan the statues? Never did anything this big. I'm kind of terrified. Sure could use your brainpower."

"If I can stop crying long enough."

"I think this might help you."

"Maybe. I'll see tomorrow."

Laura's father came running into the room, frantically searched for her, scooped her into his arms. "I'm so sorry, Lolly."

Li'l Mikey, face red, eyes narrowed, lips compressed, said, "Bastard Boss blocked Timothée's car in so he couldn't leave. Then Boss said I was trespassing, blocked my truck. Had to call the cops. Can we get Timothée a job here?"

"I'll find out right now," I said, and went over to Blanche. "I really appreciated what ya said, Blanche. That was mega-classy."

"Glad we're okay, you and I," Blanche said.

"That makes two of us! By the way, do ya have any need for a darn good cabinetmaker?"

"I have two cabinetmakers for the paneled walls of the auditorium. Need four more. That task begins in two weeks. Why?"

"Laura's dad will probably be fired for leaving work early today."

"But won't he need to spend a lot of time with Laura for now?"

"So maybe we might—" I moved my hand in circles. "I know this is a crazy idea—we might start him with a two-week paid family matters leave."

"This is why we all love you, Paulie!" She looked over at Timothée. "I can't see talking with him right now."

"I can make it short and sweet. Okay with ya?"

"Sure is!" she said.

We stepped over to Timothée, who was still holding Laura.

"Timothée, we don't want ya to worry about work right now. Ya have a job here starting Monday. Yahr full-time *paid* assignment for the next two weeks is to take care of yahr daughter. All ya have ta do *now* is say yes."

His eyes were wide, mouth a perfect circle. "Y-yes! Th-thanks!"

As we walked back to our office, Rennie asked, "Are you angry with me for disagreeing with you in public, as far as that goes?"

I stopped walking, embraced her, kissed her. "I would never want to be a tyrant like that. Not the first time we've disagreed. Just the biggest. And it won't be the last."

She started crying.

I held her close. "Were ya scared to do that?"

"Um, yeah."

"But ya did it anyway! Well, I admire ya for that."

"Oh, Paavali!" She put her arms around me.

I closed my eyes, hit the snakes so hard it seemed like they died. And let myself enjoy her embrace.

CHAPTER 14. UNBLAMING MYSELF

When we got to the office, Jill called to tell us she, Águeda, and Elijah Streeter were flying in to cover the funeral for *LIFE* magazine.

Next morning at breakfast, Clara read aloud an angrier-than-usual article from the *Minnesota Patriot*. "Danger! Warning! The Shingle Creek communists are now armed and dangerous, with enough rifles and machine guns for a full battalion. We demand our governor call up the National Guard now. Arrest Margaret Björk for attempted murder! Arrest Ruka Williams for receiving stolen goods! Jail every last marcher and demonstrator for attempting to violently overthrow the government."

"This is terrifying," Ma said.

"Holy buckets, they're off their rockers 'n' even if they filled every jail cell in the state, they'd only fit about 15,000 people, 'n' it's just more of their scare tactics 'n' stuff."

"I'd like to look at the positive side," Linda said, unfolding *People's Free Press* with Althea's photo on the front page. She pointed to a page-three article by Larry Scarpa on how the Non-Partisan League helped farmers and what our corner store buying co-op was doing to give farmers fair prices. She looked up from the paper. "Susie told me there's a group of volunteers driving all over the state to bring *People's Free Press*, with that article, to farm groups."

"Yah, that is the right thing to do," Clara said. "Also, we can't win in statewide politics without the farmers."

"I called Laura this morning," Ma said. "She agreed to help Daniel figure out a strategy for cutting apart the guns. Paulie, Karen, we should go pick them up."

I had not seen Laura look so pale since her mom died. She sat huddled between Timothée and Ma in the back seat, silent.

At General Grain, Burt was waiting for us. We followed him to the freight elevator, down into the second subbasement, then through a winding corridor. Norman deLuca, one of Burt's six guys, took us to a huge table where the guns were laid out.

Ma and Timothée propped Laura up as if she were a floppy rag doll.

"I emptied the bullets from all of them," Norman said. "Checked barrels and chambers too. But still, never point a gun at anyone."

"Thanks, Norman. Let's talk about the stocks first," Daniel said. "We need to make two blocks of wood at least twenty-four by twelve inches. For the statues' faces."

"Can they be hollow?" Laura said.

"Yes," Daniel said. "But it might be better to fill them with another wood."

"More stable filled," Timothée said. "If we cut this way"—he pointed—"starting at the rifle's butt, we get a nice bunch of uniform pieces."

"And we cut the other way starting here?" Laura pointed to the grip.

"You got it, Lolly."

"Before you start cutting the stock, take all the metal off," Norman said.

"What if we don't have enough wood?" Daniel said.

"These stocks are a nice honey color," Timothée said. "Use a different, darker wood for the statues hair."

"I see where Laura gets her smarts from!" Daniel said. "What about these bullets? Where do they fit in?"

"Can I empty the gunpowder from them?" Norman said. "Before you work with them? Know how from my army days."

"Thanks," Laura said. She picked one up, looked at it closely. "Are they the right scale to make into fingers?"

"I'm just not sure," Daniel said.

"Remember Professor Miller was so cool when he interviewed us for art school?" Laura said. "You do a mock-up from the pieces. I'll take photos. We'll ask him."

Daniel's brow furrowed. "But what if it's not good enough?"

"It will be," Laura said. "I just know that."

Norman helped us take all the metal parts off several rifles.

Daniel looked at them, handled them. "To get pieces for arms and legs, we should cut the barrels longwise, bend them apart, flatten them."

"A lot of people will want to pound those flat, yes siree," Rennie said.

"Arms and legs do not have to be made from a single piece of metal," Laura said. "We piece them together, it says broken, injured, healed."

"Hmm. Good thought! Lenses from the scopes could make eyes," Daniel said, "if they're big enough."

"Or symbolic bullet holes," Rennie said.

CHAPTER 14, UNBLAMING MYSELF

Gradually, piece-by-piece, we figured out various ways to make our statues.

"We all ready for this afternoon?" Ma said.

"As ready as I can be this sad, sad day," Laura said.

"Dozer would be proud of you," Timothée said. "So very, very proud."

"Oh, Daddy," Laura sobbed.

He folded her in his arms, talked to her quietly.

Gosh! I remember when Timothée couldn't be there for her. Wasn't easy for him to learn. What I wouldn't give to have a father who could comfort me like that!

CHAPTER 15, CROSSING JORDON'S RIVER

SATURDAY-MONDAY, MARCH 11-13, 1972

LATE THAT MORNING AFTER PICKING up Jill, Águeda, and Lije from the airport, we placed four extra leaves in the dining room table, borrowed some chairs, put the finishing touches on Swedish caraway cabbage soup and roast chicken, sliced the fresh rye bread Burt had given us, and sat down to a funeral planning lunch with Rose, Gordy, Jeanette, Emily, Laura, Timothée, Irene, Sampaa, the six Korhonen girls, Diane, Pastor Broadwater, and Bobby Lund.

"It's a total Minnesota meal, yah!" Clara said. "Brought direct from the farm by Cecil the trucker and his brother."

"Even the onions in the soup?" Jeanette said.

"Uh-hmm!" Linda said. "And the butter on the bread."

"Mommy, will you read Bonnie's *LIFE* magazine poem at the funeral?" Peri said.

"I...can't. I'll be...crying...too hard," Irene said.

Sampaa, looking down at the table, shook his head. "Paulie, would *you* read it?"

"I'd be honored. Know it by heart."

"What kind of music do you folks want?" Pastor Broadwater said.

"Dozer used to sing 'Swing Low, Sweet Chariot' to me," Jeanette said. "To help me fall asleep." She started crying. Both Rose and Gordy put arms around her.

CHAPTER 15, CROSSING JORDON'S RIVER

"He sang it to me too," Laura said. "To calm me when I had the drinking problem."

"That time we visited your church," Monica Korhonen said, "Bonnie really liked that song. Sang it for weeks afterward."

"Should we open with that?" I said.

There was a murmur of approval, nodding heads.

"We've got five soloists but only four verses," Diane said.

"Not a problem," Bobby Lund said. "I can sing the 'swing low' line solo, twice in each chorus. The choir can sing the 'coming for to carry' lines."

"That works well," Pastor Broadwater said.

"I don't understand," Monica said. "I'm only six and a half."

"Let's show Monica," Diane said. "Pastor Broadwater, Jill, Lije, Bobby?"

They sang the whole song, verses and chorus.

"Bonnie would like that," Monica said.

"Dozer too," Emily said. "He's so sensitive, he'd be tearing up right about now."

"While that's great for the opening," Lije said, "I think we need something different to close. Traditional funeral songs are all like, death is a blessing and they're going to a better place. Well thanks, Bossman! You did them a favor!" He leaned far back in his chair, looked horrified. "Really?"

"I have to agree, Lije," Pastor Broadwater said. "But I don't know of any funeral protest songs."

"Well," Lije said, "we have three songwriters here. Can we write one now? And you all can contribute?"

We had a big-huge give-and-take. Everyone came up with at least a phrase or two. Our song lifted everyone's spirits.

Águeda said to Lije, "This is a story with two big hooks! Funeral protest song *and* community song writing. But for what publication?"

"*Rolling Stone*, for sure," Lije said. "Now, Laura, have you been shooting photos?"

"Lots of them."

"Are you showing?"

The tiniest smile lit her face for just a moment. "Dozer would want me to."

I squeezed Rennie's hand once.

She turned toward me, nodded, said, "Suppose you work with Blanche and Hank to get a space ready and all the tools Daniel and Laura will need for the gun smash. And once Laura shows her photos, I'll take Lije, Jill, and Águeda on a tour of the newsroom, pressroom, and Workers' Market?"

"Aha! On the same page with ya."

Terri came over to us. "Paulie, I feel so good that my words got into the song. Makes me feel like a real part of the family."

"Well, you are, Terri!" I said. "Irene, Sampaa, Monica, Eva, Vanessa, Peri—they're all very lucky to have you in their lives."

At one o'clock, in a vast, empty space next to the pressroom, we had the gun smash. Laura, whose spirits lifted a bit after Lije praised her photos and the new mural in the Teen Council Meeting Hall, worked closely with Daniel like she usually did.

More than a hundred people, all related to Creekers who were shot, took apart, sawed, and pounded. From six-year-olds to seniors, they kept at it until every rifle but one was transformed into statue material. The one, for the museum, we made unusable.

Jerry Accardo, from Associated Press, worked his camera as Daniel and Laura laid out rifle pieces on a big table. They arranged. Laura shot photos. Rearranged. Laura took more. People called out suggestions. They arranged again. Laura caught it on film. Elżbieta Witkowski from KTCA-TV; Perrine from Agency France-Presse; Mikko Ylitalo, *People's Free Press*'s Arts and Culture editor; and a couple of dozen others stood on chairs to get good views, taking pictures, making notes.

Thank heavens we did this! Not having those rifles is a big-huge relief.

"You have a quiet, warm place I can sit and get down my first impressions?" *Art News* writer Marshall Aronowitz said to me.

"You bet! Come with me." I took him to a *People's Free Press* quiet room.

"A typewriter. Comfortable chair. Wow!"

"If you need a darkroom, no problem."

"Really? Color?"

CHAPTER 15, CROSSING JORDON'S RIVER

"Or black and white. Yahr choice. Come with me a moment." I introduced him to Susie, Georgia, Tom. "Ya need anything, just ask, okay?"

"Like?"

"Restroom. Coffee. A snack. Further background on Laura and Daniel. Access to the three Shingle Creek murals. More information on Dozer Walden and Bonnie Korhonen, or why us Creekers were attacked by an illegal militia."

"What is this, utopia?" he said, grinning.

"We're trying to move in that direction," I said.

Georgia came sprinting over to us, grinning wider than three *Alice in Wonderland* cats, tears running down her cheeks. "Paulie, where's Jerry and Perrine? CBS News wants them and me on *Face the Nation* tomorrow morning! We gotta get flights and hotels booked now."

"Zounds!" Marshall said, shaking my hand. "I'm good. Go, run, find them!"

I sprinted to Olson Hall, ran back to the newsroom with Perrine and Jerry, made sure they had what they needed. Arranged announcements on KPFP, alerted the telephone tree to make dinnertime calls, got on the CB radio so excited my voice was shaking. Then, helped Susie gather photos Georgia needed to take to Washington.

When we handed them to Georgia, she said, "Look at this! Jerry's story on the gun smash just came across the AP wire. Willi Korhonen was right on the nose!"

At 3:37 in the morning, Linda woke us. She'd heard the phone ringing. Susie called to say get everyone to come to Humboldt Avenue just north of the tracks.

When we got there, cars were parked up and down both sides of the road, people milled about, pointing at the over-sized, lighted billboard that until yesterday had an ad for *Cola Treat* soda pop. Now it said, in huge black letters on a red background, "Warning! Danger! Active War Zone! Outside Invaders Kill Children Here."

Lije used three different cameras. Sid Felsing stood on top of his car, taking photos. Susie, after circulating through the crowd, told us nobody knew who did it, when, or how. She got a tip from an anonymous caller to the City Desk.

It took Rennie and me hours to fall back asleep. Arms and legs entwined, we lay there, talking and watching our moonbeam travel up the wall behind the bookcase.

"Ya know, I was wrong about the guns. I guess I'm just not perfect."

"Holy buckets, and I'm thankful for that! Perfect people are ver-ry hard to take."

"You saved my butt, Rennie!"

"And someday soon, I might need you to save mine."

"What's bothering ya? Is it about—"

"Let's try to get to sleep now, okay then? We have to be wide awake tomorrow when we take Águeda, Lije, and Jill around to see all the picket lines."

I tried to ask her again, but she kissed my lips shut. "Nothing's bothering me," she said. But she did not sound convincing.

Sunday morning right after breakfast, we had a meeting of the Workers' Market Committee at our house, to go over the final plans for our Tuesday opening celebration. Everything was ready, but we had no canned or frozen foods because of the strikes.

"But," Ronan said, giving a thumbs-up sign, "we have a huge stock of apples, cabbage, onions, potatoes, beets, carrots, parsnips, squash, broccoli, turnips, frozen corn on the cob, you know, all fresh from cold storage."

"Also," Leonard Clausen said, "plenty of wheat flour, bread flour, rye flour, corn meal, popping corn. And Cecil has two truckloads of eggs, four kinds of cheeses, milk, sour cream, butter, ground beef, chuck roasts, pork chops, pork roasts, and chickens coming in tomorrow, so they'll be packed, priced, and ready for Tuesday."

"What about bread, rolls, cakes, cookies?" Ma said.

"Big early morning shipment from General Grain coming Tuesday," Haarald Korhonen said, clapping his hands twice. "Heavy on bread and rolls, lighter on cake and cookies. Burt's mill is out of icing, filling, chocolate because of the strike. Has to use Minnesota beet sugar instead of imported cane. Also, Mabel says Pie Golly! will deliver at least a hundred apple pies."

"How much ice did you cut and store from the lake in Brooklyn Center, as far as that goes?" Rennie said.

"Enough to last until three weeks after the new refrigerated and frozen food cases arrive," Leonard said. "But Harry took the coils and compressors from old deep freezers, fitted them to one of our handmade ice boxes. Keeps it at a perfect zero degrees even with continual door openings. So if those cases are late, it's this"—he moved the side of his hand across his throat—"for the manufacturer!"

"*People's Free Press* is printing strike-winning recipes tomorrow," Debbie said, "using Minnesota staple foods. Joanna found them for us. Quick, easy, tasty."

Just as the meeting was ending, Burt arrived. "Ah, good, good! Was hoping to catch all of you. The two new bakery assistants, Lola and Lori, developed some Strike! Cookie recipes. Using beet sugar and flavored with Minnesota-grown herbs we got dried from Lola's grandpa, the farmer."

He opened a big-huge box of cookies, passed it around. "Green's mint, purple's lavender, fennel is orange, red is rosemary, yellow's cilantro, thyme is blue. Good?"

Gosh they were yummy! They must've used a lot of butter, the cookies were so rich. The flavors unusual but luscious. Lavender and thyme were soft and chewy, the others crisp and crunchy. Sweet, but not overly so.

"Dang, Burt!" Haarald said. "These are habit-forming! How are you packaging?"

"One-pound brown bags for now, 'til we design wrapping and get it made."

"Give me some numbers," Ronan said.

"Retail, fifty-nine cents. Fifteen percent markup for you."

"Wow! Cost far less than famous brands," Ronan said. "Much better markup. Taste way better too. Can you deliver five hundred bags Tuesday morning?"

"Sure can," Burt said. "Denise, your corner stores want any?"

"Let's try a hundred bags. If we run out, when's your next bake?"

"Can do Tuesday late afternoon if you call me before one o'clock tomorrow."

"You must be so proud," Rennie said to me. "*You* connected Lori and Lola to Burt, and now look what they've done!"

"It does feel good." I nodded. "Sure as heck does!"

"You folks want to stay to watch our Georgia on *Face the Nation*?" Clara said. "Starts in five minutes, and I wouldn't want you to miss it, yah?"

We arranged chairs around the TV, refilled coffee mugs, put the cookies into a big bowl. Lije shot a few photos.

After the commercials and the *Face the Nation* theme music played, an invisible announcer said, "Our guest host today is the chairman of the Senate Foreign Relations Committee, New York Democrat Gabriel Sinclair."

"What?" Rennie said. "Why him?"

"Good morning," Senator Sinclair said. "Severe civil unrest in the Minnesota heartland has cost American businesses an estimated two hundred and fifty-seven million dollars, brought Midwest commerce to a standstill, and caused a worldwide reaction that is hurting America's image and our global efforts to advocate for democracy."

"Bastard!" Clara said. "That's all he cares about?"

"We go behind the scenes now with four journalists covering the situation as it unfolds," Senator Sinclair said. "Chatham Jenkins, *New York Press-Journal*; Jerome Accardo, Associated Press, Georgia Giordano, *Minneapolis People's Free Press*; and Perrine Fournier, Agency France-Presse. Mr. Jenkins, how would you summarize the Minneapolis havoc?"

"Why him first?" Ma said. "Just because he's from the biggest paper in America? Wouldn't even talk with people, just watched with that hoity-toity look on his face."

"After nearly two weeks of widespread strikes and three days of demonstrations attempting to shut down city streets, the City Militia finally had to intervene to quell an unpermitted demonstration—"

"That demonstration *was* permitted. Get your facts straight," Georgia said.

Jenkins shook his head. "The demonstrators at Shingle Creek did not produce a permit on demand. Did not disperse when ordered to. Caused millions of dollars in damages."

"They had their hands up," Jerry said, slapping his thigh. "Rifles were shouldered, aimed at them. Fired. Before anyone could show a permit. A nine-year-old girl and a nineteen-year-old gardener, shot dead. Four kids under age eighteen, wounded."

CHAPTER 15, CROSSING JORDON'S RIVER

"Damages?" Perrine said. "That crowd did not cause damages. I was there the whole time, not running off to warm myself every ten minutes like you, Jenkins."

"I didn't see damages either, because there were none," Georgia said. She pointed at Jenkins. "And they *did* have a permit. I saw a copy of the original filed at the Park Board office."

"They completely removed railroad tracks," Jenkins said, "in dozens of locations. Planned to steal machinery from a factory, and—"

"Pretty sloppy reporting for a newspaper of record," Jerry said. "Hazardous railroad tracks were removed by a Minnesota-chartered Industrial Safety Commission in accordance with state law."

Jenkins frowned. "Two City Militia Jeeps were fired upon and captured by the mob, along with enough rifles and machine guns to arm a battalion. That mob is now armed and dangerous."

"Can we allow workers to take over like this?" Senator Sinclair said.

"I want to set the record straight before I answer your question, Senator," Georgia said. "City Militia, which by the way had *unmarked* Jeeps, did not have machine guns. Yes, after they were fired upon, workers did capture sixty-two rifles."

"But the moment—"

"Excuse me, Mr. Jenkins, you left the scene early and did not see every one of those rifles destroyed in a public ceremony honoring nonviolence," Perrine said.

Jenkins waved his finger at Perrine. "The moment Margaret Björk grabbed that rifle, shot at the militia, the strikers lost all legitimacy. Shooting the Militia captain—"

"She hit him with the rifle butt," Jerry said. "I saw that, got it on film, and reported it in my story on the AP wire. Accuracy, please, Mr. Jenkins!"

"But she shot a man's hand off and shot at two Jeeps."

"Yes," Georgia said. "When a militia man pointed a gun directly at her, she shot in self-defense! And by the way, her eleven-year-old daughter was shot in the leg just moments before."

"So, Mr. Jenkins," Perrine said. "You didn't mind an armed militia shooting at US citizens and journalists at a permitted rally? But you're fuming when one of those citizens defended herself and her neighbors?"

Senator Sinclair shifted in his seat. "But Margaret Björk attacked a legally sanctioned law enforcement agency."

"No!" Georgia pounded the table. "It was *not* legal! The US Constitution, Second Amendment calls for, quote, a well-*regulated* militia, unquote. Not a private body accountable to no one. Clause sixteen gives *Congress* the power to organize it, not a private entity. And clause fifteen gives *Congress* the power to suppress insurrections, not a non-government institution. A permitted rally is not an insurrection. You should know this, Senator!"

"Furthermore," Jerry said, "Northside-Northeast Police was not informed this so-called militia would be assigned there. The nineteen-year-old killed was the son of the police commander, Lieutenant Walden."

Senator Sinclair looked like he would explode. "Have the three of you always been so incredibly biased?"

"Do you mean, Senator, everyone who reports this accurately and factually is biased toward workers," Georgia said, "but Mr. Jenkins, who reports falsehoods, based on talking points from a right-wing commentator, is not? If that's the case, everyone's biased. Impartiality's a myth. And it boils down to, 'Which side are you on?'"

Jerry stood up. "Senator, when you're looking down the barrel of a gun simply because you're doing your job, let's just say your perspective changes."

"But back to your concern, Senator," Perrine said. "Can the United States be an effective advocate for democracy on the world stage, if children of striking workers are shot dead? *Sacrebleu*! In France, we would say *no*!"

Senator Sinclair pounded the table. "Can we allow workers to take over like this?"

"You mean to compete and win in the free market?" Georgia said. "To decide who they will or will not work for and under what conditions?"

"They have stolen the workers and advertisers from two major newspapers," Jenkins said, "forced them to shut down."

"Mr. Jenkins!" Jerry said, taking a step toward him. "The *Minneapolis Journal* and *Gazette* locked its union workers out. The Shingle Creek community took the initiative to hire those locked-out journalists. Advertisers

CHAPTER 15, CROSSING JORDON'S RIVER

saw a good thing, jumped on the *People's Free Press* bandwagon. When capitalists do that, you call it free enterprise."

"Free enterprise cannot survive this kind of assault," Senator Sinclair thundered.

Perrine laughed. "Senator, you're saying there's no freedom in free enterprise? Workers don't have a right to choose employers or compete in the marketplace?"

"Employees must have some responsibility to the people who provide them with jobs," Senator Sinclair said. "Or we'll have communism and anarchy."

"Senator, *Face the Nation* brought us all the way here from Minneapolis to report on the strikes," Jerry said. "We have first-hand accounts, photos, documents, and information. Will you let us share it, or is the free press a myth too in your book?"

"Keep it factual, Mr. Accardo," Senator Sinclair said.

Jerry sat down. He, Georgia, and Perrine managed to present solid information about Shingle Creek and the People's Union, despite sniping from Jenkins and the senator. They showed photos of Bonnie, Dozer, Roger, Bev, Greta, and Joyce, the Workers' Market, the *People's Free Press* newsroom, the gun smash, the *Journette* picket line, the mental health clinic.

As the show's theme music faded in, and the credits rolled across the screen, Lije said, "All in all, that was a remarkable achievement. You folks should be proud. This is going to bring the bosses to the bargaining table, mark my words! And Georgia talking about Bonnie and Dozer being killed because they protected Black people..." He shook his head, moved his hands from side to side. "Mmm-mmm-mmm! That took guts!"

"It looked like the senator was about to hit her," Águeda said.

"Georgia, Perrine, and Jerry are the real deal, to the max, 'n' what an ultra job!"

"Holy moly! I think they have become our Jerry and our Perrine!" Ma said.

"What about Georgia?" Águeda said.

"Why, she has been for quite a while," Ma said.

"So you refer to members of the community as 'our,' " Lije said.

"Yes indeedy!" Ma said. "We're sort of like a big family here. And you've become our Lije and our Águeda, you know."

"Second that motion," Jill said.

After a day of visiting picket lines all over Minneapolis with Jill, Lije, and Águeda, we sat down to dinner.

Linda tuned the radio to a commercial news station. "Let's see what they say about us."

"Now, here's KOBA-Radio Sixteen-Sixty's Gilbert Randle with the Sunday Evening News Six O'clock Roundup."

"Good evening, Twin Citians! Thinking about putting off your gas bill payment? Better think again. KOBA Sixteen-Sixty News recorded this statement tonight from Twin Cities Heating Gas President and CEO Joost de Vries."

"It has come to my attention communists and thugs are conspiring to prevent law-abiding citizens from paying gas bills. That illegal action would prevent us from paying our wholesalers and force shut down of the entire Twin Cities gas system. In this emergency situation, we are obligated to require full payment of all gas bills, plus a hundred-dollar advance deposit, by four p.m. Wednesday, March 15th. Failure to pay by the deadline will result in immediate shut-off of gas service."

Randle continued, "De Vries explained the hundred-dollar deposits will allow Twin Cities Heating Gas to accumulate emergency funds so wholesalers can always be paid on time and paying customers will always have access to heating gas."

"They've gone bonkers!" Jill said. "Can they actually do that?"

"No siree! 'N' state law forbids cold weather shutoffs 'n' the bills aren't even due until the end of the month, all right then?"

"So how do you handle that?" Águeda said.

"We organize a phone tree asking people to complain to the Public Utilities Commission," Linda said. "Our legal staff gets a permanent court injunction so the gas king can never do any of that. And they also file an equal time petition with the station, demanding we have free airtime to explain our side of the issue."

"Wowzers!" Jill said. "My kid sister learned a ton of stuff since Christmas!"

CHAPTER 15, CROSSING JORDON'S RIVER

"Groovin' up for more to come!" Linda said.

"Lije, we can do an article on how to fight city hall," Águeda said. "I've never heard of a community using these tactics before."

A couple of words on the radio caught my ear. I put my finger to my lips. "Have ta listen to this one!"

"…will enforce a five-dollar weekly limit on cash withdrawals and a fifty-dollar weekly limit on all checking accounts. Mr. Hastings-Dankworth explained in this recorded statement."

"Twin Cities Unified National Bank is the cornerstone of the Twin Cities economy. Communist agitators using the slogan, 'we are the off switch for your economy,' are organizing an attack on our bank, designed to make us fail. Anyone attempting to withdraw cash or write checks totaling above those limits is subject to arrest by the Communal Association's City Guard armed deputies. One or more of our forty-eight patrol units will be stationed at every Unified National Bank branch."

"*Dios mio*! This really is a full-scale war against you," Águeda said.

"He really should be talking about how his bank will serve its customers with its entire staff on strike. But he's just given us some big-huge information," I said. "If he has set the limits so low and he's willing to flout the law, it means he's terrified because he doesn't have enough cash reserves. So he probably can't pay to bring in scabs unless he's willing to sell some of his prime farmland in Wisconsin. Which he'd never do. And he's probably in violation of state and federal banking law. Isn't the first time he's been in that boat."

"So what do you do next, Paulie?" Lije said.

"Our budding attorney here"—I pointed to Rennie—"knows better than me."

"Holy buckets, Hastings-Dankworth and his bank have been huge, long-term, financial supporters of the Communal Association that bought the Jeeps and rifles used to illegally attack us. Probably financed by Unified National Bank. Probably in violation of the law. So we attack. The enemy is weak now. Let's bring it down hard!"

"Won't that crash the Minneapolis economy?" Águeda said.

"Checked that out with my economics professor," Rennie said. "He's an adviser to the Minnesota Department of Commerce, which regulates banks. Short answer, 'No way.' Long answer, 'No way in hell. You can quote me on that.'"

Which set us off laughing. Then Rennie outlined an attack strategy on the local, state, and federal level.

Hot dog! I was so proud of her!

After dinner, Lije said, "You know, it was a tough day today, getting my mind wrapped around the massacre. I need to sing, get some of my emotions out. That okay?"

Jill's face went from tired to wide awake in two seconds flat. "Great-Grandma Clara, okay with you?" she said.

"Much more than okay, yah! Lije, you play piano?"

"I do, I do!"

We went into the living room. Lije sat down, played a slow and sad melody I remembered hearing once when I was a kid, on a hot summer Sunday, coming through the open doors and windows of Jericho Baptist church as I walked slowly by. It made me cry then, and it made me tear up now. I didn't know why.

"Who else plays piano?" Lije said.

"I do, yah," Clara said.

"Come, sit down next to me. Let's play together. I'll show you."

When Clara got the hang of the melody, Lije embroidered it on the piano and started singing, tears rolling down his face.

Deep River

My home is over Jordon

Deep River, Lord

I want to cross over into campground

Deep River

My home is over Jordon

Deep River, Lord

I want to cross over into campground

Oh, don't you want to go

To that gospel feast

That promised land

CHAPTER 15. CROSSING JORDON'S RIVER

Where all is peace

Oh, Deep River, Lord

I want to cross over into campground.

His bass voice filled the room, reverberated inside my soul. *I want to cross over into campground, wherever that may be, and come and get you, Bonnie and Dozer. Bring you back, across that deep river, back here with us, to your real home. But that river has no bridge, I have no boat, oh, if I had wings to fly, you wouldn't be gone, gone forever.*

Rennie looked at me, saw my tears, put her arms around me. Lije played an interlude, sang more. We sang with him, Jill weaving her voice around his.

"Lije, I'm not sure how to ask you this," Rennie said, "but am I missing something? You said you didn't want songs that say we're going to a better place after death. But this one makes you cry."

Lije turned to face us. His voice was soft, soothing. "You *are* missing something, and it's not your fault. The context is different for Black people, going back to slave days. You were crying, Paulie. Do *you* know what I mean?"

"Wish I did. The feeling in the music made me cry."

"The key words," Lije said, "are campground and Jordon. Some slaves, sometimes, were allowed to go to camp revival meetings held in big tents where they could sing religious songs, express their anger and sorrows, and feel free, if only for a few hours. Of course, they couldn't just say out loud what troubled them, so they used religious imagery as camouflage. Master's plantation was the gates of hell. The promised land, over Jordon, was where they wanted to be, free of slavery."

"They wanted to die?" I said.

"Lord have mercy, no. Not if they could help it! The River Jordon was the Ohio River, a boundary between slave-state Kentucky and freedom in Illinois, Indiana, Ohio." He pulled out his wallet, took out two photos, passed the first around. "What do you see there?"

"A Black kid's hair with some sort of design in it," Ma said.

"Look at this second one."

There was a line drawn in that zigged and zagged, following a path in the design across the child's head.

"That child's cornrows didn't look like anything special to a plantation overseer or master," Lije said. "But they were a map to a shallow, narrow part of the Ohio River used by thousands of slaves to reach freedom."

Linda stamped her foot, face bright red. "Why didn't they tell us that in school?"

Ma, Jill, and Rennie teared up.

"*Cielo santo!*" Águeda said. "I *have to* write about that."

"Will you teach about it in your Freedom Academy?" Lije said. "I can give you a whole series of large photos with complete explanations."

"I am for it," I said. "We'll push for it, right, Linda?"

"Absolutely!" Linda said. "Will you write a book, Lije? I can ask the Teen Council if we can publish it. Ruka might want to help edit it."

Lije hugged Linda. "Yes! Please ask."

"I'll second that motion," I said.

"So, Lije," Ma said, "what does 'over Jordon' mean to you now?"

"First, I think about how my ancestors suffered and died under slavery. Second, how brave they were to escape, which mine did. Third, how us Black folks all still yearn for a home over Jordon, where everyone views us as human beings. And if we're angry, we can say so without worrying about being lynched. And we have as much chance to succeed as everyone else." He clasped his hands. "Lord, Lord, that asking for so much?"

"No," Clara said. "It's only right you should have that."

"Shall we sing some more?" Lije said. "And wash away at least a tiny bit of our sorrow? Because there'll be a whole fresh flood at the funeral tomorrow."

We sang for hours.

Next morning, the sun came up bright and golden-red, as if to mock our day of mourning. I stood on our front lawn, looked up at a perfect blue sky, gritted my teeth. *Do not mock us, sky! Cloud over! Snow! And blow, wind, blow!*

"You have the pruning shears, Paulie," Jill said when she came outside wearing the pink snow jacket from her high school years.

I patted my pocket, nodded. She took my arm. We headed up the sidewalk, toward 50th Avenue.

CHAPTER 15, CROSSING JORDON'S RIVER

"How is Joe doing?"

Jill's face lit up brighter than sun on a snow-covered field. "Out of this world! He finally talked about *why* he felt he didn't deserve me." She stopped walking, turned to face me. "He told me I could spill the beans to you and only to you."

"I won't say boohoo to anybody. I'm totally…" I put my forefinger over my lips.

"He blamed himself for his parents' death." A big-huge cloud came over her face. "Said he killed them. At age ten—"

"What? How? Why did he ever think that?"

"Get this! He forgot to remind his father to check their car's brake fluid."

"That was *his* responsibility?"

"Oofdah! Exactly what I said. That's the nutshell version. It took weeks for us to work it all out. He has a whole new kind of smile on his face now."

"That is pure joy to hear. And you, Sis, are a genius in bloom!"

"Thanks, Paulie. I'm still not exactly sure how I did it." She took my arm again. We walked up Oliver Avenue, toward the school.

"How are you and Karen doing?"

"I keep taking steps forward. Not totally there yet. But I have ta tell ya, it's so close I can taste it. Except…"

"Except what, Bro?"

"Something big-huge is bothering Karen. And she won't talk."

"Wowzers! I got the same feeling. Be patient with her, Paulie."

"I sure as heck will. I'm hoping if I get my problem solved, it'll help hers."

"It will, for real, Paulie! Majorly."

At a corner of the school building, the chokecherry bush Jill and I had planted with Ma when we were six stood tall and proud, covered with snow.

"It's so whoppingly big now," Jill said. "Just six inches high when we planted it."

We shook it, sending snow flying every which way, chose two hefty branches full of dormant buds.

"Good-sized cuttings," Jill said. "They'll root well."

"I called the cemetery," I said. "They'll have holes dug in just the right places."

When we got to Iversen Auditorium, the room was warm and comfortable. But the two polished wood coffins at the front of the stage made me feel cold and shivery. Thank heavens, they were closed. I just couldn't...

I tore my gaze away from them, looked at all the benches complete with backs and cushions and the two pianos Blanche had somehow found.

Jill tried them, nodded. "Wowzers! They're in tune. A Steinway and a Boston. Really good pianos."

Elżbieta Witkowski was at one KTCA camera, her colleague at the other. The press seats were filling up, including some journalists we didn't know. When Georgia arrived, the press gave her a standing ovation. Hundreds of unionists wearing caps with their local number filed in. Tess, Kurt, Ruthie, and Jeffie showed people to their seats.

We went onstage. Elijah and Charlie sat at the pianos. I was on the side. Rennie sat on the opposite side. Jill, Diane, Bobby, Ruka, Daniel, Althea, Pastor Broadwater, Ndidi, and Carleton clustered into a choir.

Stay focused, Paavali. Ya can't cry 'til later. Everyone's counting on ya.

The room quieted. The lights turned down. I nodded to Lije and Charlie. The pianos filled the room with melody, then Bobby sang in his sweet, high voice, "Swing low, sweet chariot," and the choir answered him with, "coming for to carry me home."

Jill, Diane, Pastor Broadwater, and Lije sang their solos. Bobby and the chorus did call and response.

I was panicking. *When this is over, Dozer and Bonnie are gone forever. Stop them, Paavali, don't let them get away! Open the coffins. And hold them tight. For eternity!*

I moved to the mic. "Remembrances of Bonnie Korhonen. Sampaa, her dad."

"My Bonnie always made me think really hard. She's the one told us to index the $2.50 minimum wage to productivity. Gremling took away our shining star, our diamond, our..." Sampaa was sobbing uncontrollably.

Willi, Sampaa's father, stepped onto the stage, put his arm around his son, lead him away.

"Charlie Ward, Bonnie's friend."

CHAPTER 15, CROSSING JORDON'S RIVER

He came up to the mic, holding hands with Ruthie. "When Gremling said, 'get the Black ones first,' Bonnie stepped in front of me. 'Oh no you don't,' she yelled. And then she died. To save my life." Tears rolled down his face. "We were supposed to be friends forever and always. It's not fair!"

Ruthie, arm around Charlie's shoulders, led him offstage.

"Terri Korhonen, her sister."

"When the Korhonens fostered me, Bonnie asked her sisters and all The Nines to do a ton of nice things for me. Because she knew I was very sad then. Bonnie was so kind to me, I asked to become a Korhonen."

Billy took Mamie's hand, led his little sister to the mic.

"Mamie Anderson, Bonnie's cousin, the other Anderhonen twin."

She was silent for a moment. "BonBon was my twin sister. We even look alike. Half of me is gone," she sobbed.

Billy helped her walk off stage.

"Walt Trockenmann, Bonnie's friend."

"Nobody wanted to be my friend. But one day, Bonnie did. I didn't have lunch. Bonnie shared hers, without me even asking. Being her friend turned my life right-side up. She's my angel, forever."

"Mr. Andreas Bidstrup, Bonnie's friend."

"Bonnie and a gang of kids rang my doorbell. I was sure they were up to no good because those snow shovels they carried could be used as weapons. 'Mr. Bidstrup, can we shovel your walk and driveway?' she said. 'Well, how much will you make me pay?' She told me, 'Two smiles, Mr. Bidstrup. We don't accept cash.' 'Well, okay, I guess.' But I still thought they were up to no good. So those four kids set to work, cleared everything off in no time flat. I couldn't help smiling, and Bonnie said, 'Oh, Mr. Bidstrup! You smiled three times. I owe you change!' Been years since I laughed like that."

"Irene Korhonen, Bonnie's mom."

"Bonnie loved the song, 'Joe Hill,' but she didn't agree with 'Don't mourn, organize!' She said it should be, 'Mourn, of course! Then, organize!' It's hard to think about going forward now. But Bonnie would want us to keep on."

"Bonnie was an inspiration," I said. "Someday, I hope to have a child like her, who thinks a hundred and fifty miles an hour about how to be unusually kind to people. Her parents asked me to recite her poem, 'Oceans of Love,' which was in *LIFE* magazine."

> Mommie, Daddy, whenever it gets dark for me,
> And I am crying afraid of cold mists shivering and shaking me,
> Together you call out the sun, you call out the moon,
> Even through clouds, even through storms,
> And surround me with light that calms, warms, soothes.
> Your love for me is like a river, always there, always full.
> But even though I'm small, I have oceans of love for you.

"Let us bow our heads in a moment of silence for our Bonnie."

Lije played some soothing music. I was so glad he thought of that.

When Lije stopped, I said, "Remembrances of Gary Dozer Walden. Laura Thomá, the love of his life."

"In kindergarten, he was really big! And I was tiny. We were partners, and he held my hand so gently. Once when I fell, scraped my knees, he hugged me 'til I stopped crying. Then one day, middle of winter, he came to school with a single rose in a tiny vase. For me. Told me he loved me. The teacher even cried."

"Rose Walden, Dozer's mom."

"Spring when Dozer was five, he asked for flower seeds. For Laura. Gordy and I helped him plant Zinnias, Marigolds, Daisies. But that wasn't enough for Dozer."

"Joanna Pajari, our librarian."

"This sweet, tall kid, looked about nine, asked me for a book on growing flowers. When I handed it to him, he said, 'But there's no pictures.' Was I surprised when he said he was five! He looked up at his dad, said, 'Daddy, you have to teach me to read it.'"

"Gordy Walden, Dozer's dad."

"I was amazed, but I read to him, showed him sounds and words, and he caught on real fast. He fussed over his flowers, picking off bugs, watering them. He was so proud of his first bouquet for Laura."

"Here's how he got his nickname," I said. "In first grade, Mikey told him, 'Hey, Gary, you're as big as a bulldozer.' 'Comin' to git you!' Gary

CHAPTER 15. CROSSING JORDON'S RIVER

said. 'Dozer, Dozer! Vrrrroomm! Vrrrroomm!' and he chased Mikey, tackled him. The two of them, laughing their heads off, wrestled on the grass like little kids love to do. After that, he wouldn't answer to Gary. 'Nah! Gary's some little kindergarten kid.'"

"Jeanette Walden, Dozer's kid sister."

"He always looked out for me. He'd be playing with his friends or talking with Laura, but if I needed something or a kid was bothering me, he'd be right there. And he watched out for my friends, 'cause he said he liked us little kids. Winter when Jeffie and I were four, Dozer pulled him out of the creek when the ice broke and Jeffie went under."

"Mike Blecher, Dozer's close friend."

"When I was twelve, I had a crush on Vickie Smith. I told Dozer I was too ugly for her. He listened, said, "Nobody else thinks you're ugly. She sure doesn't. Look at how she pats your shoulder and takes your hand when she talks with you.' So I asked Vicky to be my girlfriend. We were together for six years. I could talk with Dozer about anything."

"Daniel Anker, Dozer's friend."

"You didn't have to do that, Dozer, step in front of me. Take a bullet for me. That says it all, doesn't it? Oh my God, Dozer, Laura, I am so sorry."

Laura hugged him, then turned toward the mic. "My mom died when I was twelve. By thirteen, I was an alcoholic, trying to blot out the pain. Dozer tried everything to comfort me. He was always by my side, even when I was drunk and angry. I couldn't have gone sober if it wasn't for Dozer's love."

"Let us bow our heads," I said, "in a moment of silence for our Dozer."

Lije played another musical interlude. I managed not to cry.

Bobby strode to the mic. "We remember our martyrs!"

Lije said, "Killed in the fight for a better life for working people everywhere."

"Or slain in needless work accidents," Diane said.

"We thank you, we mourn for you, we pledge to keep fighting for you. We say your names," Jill said.

A line of fifteen children, all relatives of our martyrs, slowly walked on stage. Rennie and I lit the candles they were holding.

"Adam Linwood, Steel Worker," Peri Korhonen said. "Say his name."

"Adam Linwood," the audience said.
"Eric Carlson, Bonus Army," Terri Korhonen said.
"Henry Ness, Striking Teamster," Eva Korhonen said.
"Bonnie Korhonen, Strike Marcher," Monica Korhonen said.
"Alison Krause, Peace Demonstrator," Mamie Anderson said.
"Gary Dozer Walden, Strike Marcher," Jeanette Walden said.
"Fred Corwin, Park Superintendent," Tess Iversen said.
"Raymond Iversen, Gandy Dancer," Robin Iversen said.
"Arne Gustaffson, Gandy Dancer," Brucie Gustaffson said.
"Darlene Hillilä, Teenage Artist, rape victim," Tommy Hillilä said.
"You have been taken from us," Bobby Lund said. "But we remember your passion, we share your dreams, you are forever part of us."

Lije and Charlie played loud, jarring, dissonant chords on the pianos. The choir sang, almost like they were yelling.

No-oh! No-oh! I don't wanna go-oh!
No-oh! No-oh! I don't wanna go-oh!

The piano chords stopped. Jill sang.

I have to go away, dear Mama, bossman's telling me I must

I have to go away, dear Papa, but it really isn't fair and just

They tell me I'm a-riding on a glory train

But it all makes zero sense to my unhappy brain

'Cause my ticket is a bullet from a bossman's gun

And there's no way I wanna make this run.

Then the chorus chimed in again.

No-oh! No-oh! I don't wanna go-oh!
No-oh! No-oh! I don't wanna go-oh!

Lije sang.

I have to go away, dear sisters, it makes me angry and so sad

CHAPTER 15. CROSSING JORDON'S RIVER

I have to go away, dear brothers, but the deal I got was really bad
Bossman's bullet is my ticket, and the wound is hurting still
Evil smile upon his face, he sure was aiming for a kill
He not only slayed my body, he wiped out my spirit too
And there's no way I wanna see this through.

No-oh! No-oh! I don't wanna go-oh!
No-oh! No-oh! I don't wanna go-oh!

Diane sang the next verse.

So gather 'round, dear Mom and Papa, hear the words I have to say
My sisters, friends, and brothers, don't let the bossman lead you astray
If they take away your children with a bullet to the guts
They've called an all-out war against you, no ifs or ands or buts
You work another day for them, they'll just do it all once more
Grab your picket signs and march right out the door!

The pianos stopped playing. The chorus changed its tune.

Make a sign, form a line
This is not the point to linger
Time to act, it's a fact
So give bossman the finger!

I couldn't believe how Jill sang the word "strike," starting on a super high note, gliding way down to a note so low it seemed to come from her toes. Then, she chanted, "Stri-ike! Stri-ike!" The crowd stood up, chanting as they headed for the doors, chanting in the parking lot, waiting for Bonnie and Dozer's coffins.

Bonnie's family was so large, and all The Nines wanted to be pall bearers, so Blanche, Lowell, and Luke made a special, extra-long coffin platform with many handles. When the coffins came through the doorway, the crowd quieted. Dozer was carried by his family, four guys who worked with him, Timothée, and the Teen Council. A hundred and seventy-one cars and three of Gordy's squad cars headed to Humboldt, then over to Penn Avenue, down to Serene Lake Cemetery.

Irene had asked for Bonnie to be buried next to Dozer, so she'd have a big brother to look out for her. When coffins were lowered into the graves, everyone was crying and hollering, the pain was so awful. Rennie stood on one side, arm clamped to mine, and Ma on the other, her arm around my shoulders, mine around hers, right below Jill's.

Finally, Rennie, me, Jill, Mikey, Laura, and Ma pulled ourselves together, planted a chokecherry bush at the head of each grave behind where the headstones would go.

"You used to get so excited about that bush, Jill," Mikey said.

"Still do," Jill said. "The silvery bark with crimson patches peeking out, red buds and white flowers, leaves turning scarlet in the fall, juicy purplish-black berries, all the birds flocking to eat them."

"That bush got Dozer interested in gardening," Laura said.

"Remember when the school janitor wanted to dig it up?" I said. "Dozer got so angry, the janitor stepped away from him backward, tripped and fell?"

"And we got sent to the principal's office for it," Laura said.

"I handed the principal his head on a paper plate," Ma said, laughing.

"You got the coolest Ma of the month award for that," Jill said.

"Those were happier days," Laura said. "Happier days."

CHAPTER 16, THE FOREVER NINES

MONDAY, MARCH 13, 1972

Even though Rennie and I were feeling really down, we went to our office to try to pull ourselves together for our four o'clock mystery meeting.

Neither of us could concentrate. We had KPFP on the radio, half listening, when Rosie and the Thornbush faded out and Keanna announced, "Sorry to interrupt, but we have breaking news. Twin Cities Heating Gas workers, Local 3756, walked out today, demanding all People's Union planks. Local President Alice Rosander said a small crew of union workers will make sure gas keeps flowing to customers, but union members will not read meters, process bills, or turn off service to customers during the strike."

"Holy buckets, well that makes me feel a little bit better, as far as that goes."

A couple of men in suits knocked on our open door. "Excuse us," the guy with a blue tie said, "Tim Thomá said we should see you. We've been at Dozer's funeral."

"Worked with Tim going on twenty-two years," the guy in a red tie said. "Heard all about Dozer ever since he bought Laura that single rose. Just feel horrible for Tim and Laura."

"How'd you guys get Bastard Boss to let ya off work?" I said.

"Oh, he screeched like a wounded rat when I called in this morning," Blue Tie said. "Fired me for the sixty-third time. Literally! I'd like to take him up on it."

We took them over to see Blanche. Hired them. Back at our office, they called Bastard Boss on the speakerphone, told him they're quitting. He threatened to sue them, blacklist them, have them arrested for theft. We got it all on tape.

"Man, he really had a cow 'n' stuff," Rennie said, " 'n' I'll bet our Susie could write a really interesting story based on it, you know, for *People's Free Press*, if that's all right with you guys."

Red Tie nodded. "Bosses need to know they can't treat workers like crap because we'll spread the word and nobody'll want to work for them. Do you folks keep a blacklist of bastard bosses?"

Rennie's eyebrows shot way up.

I clapped my hands together. "I have ta tell ya, that's a magnificent idea. Hot dog! We're gonna do that."

I turned the radio back on. Our Linda's voice said, "When teens get in trouble. Punish? Or help them? Judge Haddad says, 'Help them!' " Billy's voice said, "Judge Haddad, helping troubled kids become responsible adults. Vote line C in June!"

"Badah will love this one 'n' they've really gotten good! But, Paavali, I don't know how to prepare for our meeting 'cause we don't know what it's about."

"Well, all Sarah said is it's important and who we should have here."

The phone rang. "Jyri Tuomi, from L&M Federal Credit Union's here to see you," Denise said.

"Guess we'll have ta wing it," I said.

A tall man wearing overalls, who was so big he made Dozer and Li'l Mikey seem tiny, came walking through the doorway. "You folks did a really nice job with the funeral this morning. Never saw anything like it in my life. Feel like I know you, Paul and Karen, after *LIFE* magazine and that TV show about Shingle Creek."

Carleton, Ma, Betty, and Russ filed into our office.

"Well, what can we do for ya, Mr. Tuomi?" I said.

"Please call me Jyri. Don't mean to be presumptuous, but I think I can do something for you."

CHAPTER 16, THE FOREVER NINES

"Have a seat, Jyri, 'n' can we offer you coffee and Strike! Cookies?"

"Strike! Cookies, hey! That's pretty classy. You bet!" He sat down. Tasted a cookie. Nodded his head, smiled. "These are go-od!" Munched for a minute, took a swig of coffee. "I'm going to cut right to the chase. Twin Cities Unified National Bank is causing big problems for working people. Depositors can't pay their bills, get to their money."

"My daughter Brenda can't pay her rent," Betty said. "I had to loan her money."

"We can fix that," Jyri said. "Our credit union has over fifty million bucks in assets. Enough spare cash to loan Unified National a fair amount of money."

"Isn't that risky for you?" Carleton said, leaning way back in his chair.

"Not with our plan."

"Oh?" Russ said. "Please explain."

"When a Unified National customer pays a bill, the business that gets the check deposits it in their bank. That bank sends it to the official check clearinghouse, which reroutes the check to us. We pay that bank the funds and send a bill to Unified National."

"You'll never collect from those crooks," Russ said, moving his hand side to side.

Jyri nodded twice. "You're right! We won't. But the check clearinghouse is the Minneapolis Federal Reserve. And they will."

"They trust Hastings-Dankworth?"

"No way. They forced him to sell some prime Wisconsin farmland, deposit the cash as collateral. He had to or they'd pull his federal charter."

"Holy minced dogfish!" Russ said, eyes wide. "Because his staff is on strike?"

"No, sir. The Fed is no friend of labor. It's because he spent bank funds equipping his City Militia, and on donations to the Communal Association, and paying for farmland that he put in his name, not the bank's. And now Unified National's seriously short of funds."

"*You* figured that out, Paulie!" Rennie said, putting her arm around my shoulders.

"Well then, Paul, you're smarter than the Federal Reserve," Jyri said, "because it was right in their face. They didn't see it until we pointed it out to them."

"Why are ya doing this, Jyri?" I said.

"L&M used to be called Loggers and Miners. My grandpa was a logger, fierce union man. Helped found it. L&M did a lot for workers in the old days. A bunch of us, kids and grandkids of founders, want to make Loggers and Miners go back to its roots."

"I don't get it," Ma said. "How will this move help working people?"

"Keep Unified National from ever giving money to the Communal Association again or funding monstrosities like City Militia. We'll help working people with accounts at Unified National. Put pressure on Unified National to settle the strike and—"

"Settle in accordance with all People's Union planks?" Sarah said.

"Absolutely. Besides, L&M will be authorized by the Federal Reserve to charge Unified National a twelve percent handling fee, plus interest."

"Why would the Fed let you?" Betty said.

Jyri clapped his hands. "Fed doesn't like banks failing, runs on banks, unstable banks, or worst of all, armed thugs telling customers they can't withdraw their money."

"What happens to the interest and handling fee?" Russ said.

"After we take out our expenses, the rest goes to our depositors as a special dividend. Ninety-two percent of our depositors are working people, five percent professionals, three percent small businesses."

"Sounds interesting," Carleton said. "What do you want from us?"

"Endorsement." Jyri held up three fingers. "From People's Union, Shingle Creek Neighborhood Association, the Teen Council."

Rennie pointed at him. "And if we don't endorse you, as far as that goes?"

"The plan is dead."

"Suppose we want to modify?" Carleton said, leaning forward. "For example, half of the special dividend is donated to the People's Union?"

"We'll talk with you until we come to an agreement. Or abandon the idea."

"Looks like the Big Three need to meet 'n' we better get a move on, to the max."

After Jyri left, Russ said, "Seems like he's on the up-and-up. But I'd like to do a little poking around just to be sure. Okay with all of you? Can I ask Joanna to help?"

CHAPTER 16. THE FOREVER NINES

"That's exactly what we should be doing," Sarah said.

We took a vote, made calls to schedule meetings of the Big Three for that evening.

At four o'clock, we drove to the bug spray factory with Clarence and Obie, met the other Industrial Safety Commissioners in the parking lot. Officers James and Anderson arrived in their squad cars. There were twenty guys on the picket line. Sid Felsing, our labor reporter, was shooting photos.

"Heh-heh-heh," Russ said. "Gremling'll flip when he sees this in the *Free Press*!"

Two box trucks drove up. Beth jumped out of one, Moe the other.

"Good, they're twenty-six footers," Harley said. "We'll only need one trip."

"We storing the machinery somewhere?" I asked.

"No point," Harley said. "Not repairable. Selling it all for scrap, by the pound. We'll deduct the proceeds from their fees and fines bill." He opened the trunk of his car, took out three boxes. "Dismantlers and movers, step up! I have goggles, masks, gloves."

Clarence handed Rennie and I power saws. We followed Harley into the factory.

"Never heard it quiet in here before," Harley said. He stepped up to the security guard. "Jared, we have a Commission Order to remove all the machinery. Don't make it hard on yourself, man."

"Mr. Gremling didn't give me an okay."

"Mr. Gremling has no say on this. The law is the law."

"He's going to fire me if I let you."

"Jared, you've known me for years," Harley said. "Do I always tell the truth?"

"Yeah, you do. But…" He wrung his hands.

"Replacement equipment's arriving in about three weeks, so don't worry," Harley said. "Picketers told me you let them use the toilets behind Gremling's back. You're a good guy. It might not be here, but I will make sure you have a job. Don't worry, okay?"

"What the hell's going on here?" someone shouted.

"Ah, Gremling Junior, so pleased to see you," Harley said.

Clarence and Obie took cameras from their pockets. Rennie reached into her handbag, turned on the tape recorder.

"Get out! All of you!" Gremling Junior yelled.

"Under the laws of the State of Minnesota, the North-Northeast Minneapolis Industrial Safety Commission has ordered removal of hazardous and non-repairable machinery," Russ said. "Here's your copy of the order and your receipt for the mechanisms and equipment."

Gremling Junior pushed Russ. Russ stumbled backward. Junior raised a hand to hit him.

Officer James grabbed Junior from behind, took him to the ground, cuffed him. "You're under arrest for assault and interfering with official procedures. You have the right to remain silent."

"You'll pay for this! Kiss your job goodbye, Off-fucker James."

Officer James grabbed his arms. "Stand up, Junior." Brought him to his feet, marched him out the door, Junior yelling all the way. The squad car door slammed shut, car started up, revved up, drove off.

Harley sprinted from machine to machine, explaining how to dismantle them. "Drill holes on X marks, cut along lines," he said, painting marks on the equipment.

We put our saw blades into the drilled holes, cut, cut again. Metal fell to the floor in wheelbarrow-sized pieces. The insides of the machines were crusted with chemicals, patches on top of patches, more corrosion than metal. Sid took photos as we worked. With eight people cutting and twelve more taking out bolts and sheet metal screws, it took less than two hours for the wheelbarrow crew to get every last piece of machinery loaded in the trucks. Officer Anderson's squad car followed the trucks out of the parking lot, down 49th Avenue, and out of sight.

"Holy buckets, that made me feel so much better, yes siree," Rennie said as we drove home for dinner.

Next morning when Sheila handed us *People's Free Press*, there we were on the front page, Rennie and I, side by side, cutting apart a mixing vat. Sid's shot clearly showed corroded holes. "Perfect photo. Tells the whole story," I said.

Rennie pointed to the *Minnesota Patriot* lying on the doormat. "Oh, ish! I have to touch that?"

CHAPTER 16, THE FOREVER NINES

I picked it up, shook the snow off, carried it in. "Let's look through this horse puckies first. Then use *People's Free Press* as a big-huge antidote."

"Okay, then," Rennie said. She sat down, looked through it quickly. "Whoa! The most incredible batch of crap yet. Get this! 'We take our mission to protect hard-working Americans seriously, especially in areas with corrupt police departments. So when our intelligence officers discovered that five militant Black Panthers are living underground in Shingle Creek under assumed names, to avoid prosecution for murdering police officers in cold blood, we arranged for the City Militia to arrest them.'"

"What in Sam Hill are they talking about?" Ma said.

"*Skitsnack*!" Clara said. "It's the old trick of trying to get Whites and Blacks fighting each other instead of the bossman."

"Who are these so-called Black Militant cop killers?" Linda said.

"Hang onto your hats," Rennie said. "Daniel Anker, Mabel Anker, Charlie Ward, Louie Ward, Ruka Williams. 'Louie Ward got his degree from a so-called college with questionable accreditation.' Holy buckets! Five years old, and he has a college degree?"

"Uh-hum!" Linda said. "From Jill's Shingle Creek Preschool. Last year!"

"It gets worse," Rennie said. "'These five thugs used hard-working White people and a nine-year-old girl as human shields while a hidden Black gunman shot Militia Captain Clyde Gremling's jaw off and Assistant Captain Richard Prichard's hand.'"

"Who's going to believe this crapola?" Ma said.

"Well, Chatham Jenkins from the *New York Press-Journal* did," Linda said. "That paper's read by millions of people."

"The *Patriot* must've given Jenkins an advance copy, as far as that goes."

"We have ta keep on truckin'," I said, "and counterattack in *People's Free Press* and KPFP. Plus, another libel suit against *Minnesota Patriot*."

"And the *New York Press-Journal*, if they printed that shit," Rennie said.

"Let's eat breakfast and start calling," Ma said. "We'll try to get a counterattack strategy meeting set for 8:30 in the a.m., so we finish before the Workers' Market opening celebration."

"If we move as fast as we did last night, approving L&M Federal Credit Union's proposal," Clara said, "we'll have no problem."

I called Susie, told her to come in her Teen Council role, not as a reporter.

"Plus, you need Sid and Georgia too," Susie said. "Billy and Linda know about approaching the media, for sure, but Sid and Georgia have years of experience."

"But this meeting's off the record," I said.

"Not a problem," Susie said. "We'll be there as workers, not as reporters."

What a difference they made! They outlined a whole public relations campaign, explained how we could use our newswire memberships to distribute stories; said they'd have no problem getting stories from Jerry, Perrine, and Elżbieta; described the best news hooks for getting coverage in unsympathetic newspapers; told us that Jenkins was a known scab, widely hated in the industry and successfully sued twice for libel. Sid, right out of his head, listed labor reporters at the dailies in the biggest twenty-seven American cities.

"We'll give Harrison Barrow at *Hennepin Afro-American* a call," Georgia said. "He can tap us into the African American newspaper and radio networks. Everyone'll want to interview the five-year-old college graduate!"

"We should also contact union newsletters and alternative magazines like *The Progressive, The Nation*, and *Dissent*," Joanna said. "I'll put together a list."

"Of course we'll sue," Russ said. "Can't wait to get my hands on the latest issues of *New York Press-Journal*! But what Jenkins said on *Face the Nation* is a good start."

"Well, we sure are cooking with gas!" Ma said. "Anything else? No? Nice going! Now let's go moving right along to celebrate Workers' Market!"

"Okay," Georgia said. "I'm turning my hat inside out from worker to reporter. C'mon, Sid! Let's go gather some *good* news!"

We had to go out into the parking lot to get to Workers' Market from Betty Hall. The lot was full and there was a long queue of people waiting to get in. Harry walked up and down the line, thanking people for coming, letting them know the doors would open in a few minutes, reassuring them there was plenty of food on the shelves and in our warehouse. Inside, Paz's conga band was already playing. A big table had free coffee, Strike! Cookies, and Midwest Candy samples. The cash registers were filled with small bills and coins to make change.

"Testing! Testing!" Ronan's voice said on the speaker system. "Paulie and Karen, please meet Judge Woodruff at the register area."

"Paul! Karen! Wonderful to see you," the judge said. "This is magnificent! What an achievement."

"Now if we only had canned goods," I said. *Why did Ronan just grin?*

"Can I take you on a tour?" Ronan said.

"Yes, please," Judge Woodruff said. "I want to see it all!"

In the back, butchers were cutting and packing pork roasts and ground beef and a woman was unloading apples from a huge washing vat, which made them look even tastier. In the front of the store, near each cash register, a display held twelve varieties of Midwest Candy and General Grain's Roger's Chocolate Coffee-n-Cake snack.

As we turned into the first aisle, Ronan said, "Look what Debbie Ahlberg did!"

The shelves were completely full of canned food.

"Holy buckets! How?"

"She worked with the teamsters and our wholesaler so they could make deliveries. All their warehouse workers were raised to the $2.50 indexed minimum. Teamsters got thirty-five cents an hour over their regular wage."

"Like they settled the strike, as far as that goes?"

"First employer to settle!" Ronan said. "Progressive Wholesalers signed the Minneapolis Standard Work Contract at six o'clock this morning and delivered at seven. You folks must've been busy. KPFP's been announcing it since eight-thirty."

"Congratulations!" Judge Woodruff said. "The beginning of a big victory."

"Mega-magnificent!" I said. "Is Progressive delivering anywhere else?"

"Only to Dahl's Superette. Every other supermarket's still on strike. For most of Minneapolis, the General Grain and Dahl food trucks, corner stores in our buying co-op, or a trip out to the suburbs are the only ways to buy groceries."

"I know that for sure," Judge Woodruff said. "The Red Crow near me is completely closed, so I brought my shopping list with me."

We went outside, onto a small platform with a mic. "Creekers and friends!" I said. "Welcome to Workers' Market. I'm honored to introduce Judge Gannon Woodruff!"

"I know you're all eager to shop," Judge Woodruff said. "So I'll make it quick. Congratulations, Creekers. You out-crowed the red bird! Now come on in, there's plenty of food, free Strike! Cookies, coffee, candy, and a jazz band, all waiting for you."

The doors opened, waves of people flowed in. The band played, shoppers filled carts, some even danced. Because we built the shelves with service aisles behind them, the store's staff was restocking the moment they were empty. Ronan, Debbie, Haarald, Eugene, and Leonard sprinted around, checking here and there, answering questions, solving problems. Checkout lines moved quickly, but the queue outside didn't get any shorter. More cars kept entering the parking lot.

"Just look at my sister Debbie," Rennie said. "Wearing that big grin! Isn't she terrific? I'm so proud of her, to the max."

"Let's shop, hey?" I said. We loaded our cart, got in line behind Judge Woodruff. He had bread, butter, chicken, carrots, and potatoes in his.

"These are like luxury items right now," he said. Then he lowered his voice. "You know there's something…I feel badly about. Off the record, okay?"

"You bet!"

"Yes siree!"

"I cut the jury award in the Gremling libel case because the man threatened me with violence. I told Judge Ovington about Gremling's threats, and thank goodness, he undid the damage on appeal. But I think your influence is changing things. Mr. Hastings-Dankworth's two-thousand-dollar contempt fine? Paid at the last minute, but paid. You're helping me put teeth back into the court. I'll never let any of them intimidate me again!"

Back at our house, the moment we put the bags of groceries on our kitchen table, the phone rang. Rennie jogged into the living room to answer it.

CHAPTER 16, THE FOREVER NINES

"Whoa! Holy buckets, Billy! Agreed. We'll handle it, for sure, to the max!" She yelled, "Paavali! The sheriff arrested Ruka at school, 'n' Billy 'n' eight friends barged into the office, demanded to use the phone to let us know 'n' he thinks he'll be suspended for doing that, 'n' we should use People's Union Emergency Plan Four, 'n' you put the food away 'n' I'm calling our Big Three leaders right now."

By the time I put the groceries away, Karen had a consensus and began activating the phone calling trees. I selected channel two on the CB, called for a Plan Four action at one that afternoon, made the same announcement on channels 11 and 38. People began responding immediately.

The doorbell rang. Greta? Was standing there, alone, crying? I helped her limp inside, calmed her. She told me her mom was driving her home from a doctor's visit when a sheriff's car pulled them over, arrested Margaret. And left Greta sitting in the car, by herself, on 49th and Morgan.

I made her tea, gave her some Strike! Cookies, checked the bandage on her wound. "We're getting thousands of people for a protest caravan downtown. We'll make them set yahr mom free."

"Can I come?" Greta said.

"If it's okay with yahr dad. Ya want to tell everyone what happened on the CB?"

Rennie sat down with us. We helped Greta figure out what to say, explained how the CB worked, how to hold the mic.

"Sheriff arrested Margaret Björk, my mom," Greta said. "Because she stopped Gremling from killing all of us. Sheriff left me sitting in the car, alone, even though I was wounded. We need a Plan Four." She repeated the message on the other CB channels.

"Rail Waltzer here," Clarence said on the CB. "Where are you, Grety?"

"Paul and Karen's house."

"You okay?"

"Just scared, Daddy."

"I'm on my way, Grety. Obie's driving me. Ten minutes."

The phone rang. Sarah said, "Fifty-four carloads so far. Three stake trucks for Far North high school kids. Working on more."

We tuned in KPFP. Man, Todd was fast. He heard Greta's message, recorded the repeat, was playing it now. Greta sat up a little bit straighter when she heard it.

Clarence arrived, comforted Greta. "Paulie, who's making the payphone call to the mayor? When we get downtown?"

"I got appointed to do it."

"Could I do it?" Greta said.

Clarence smiled, nodded.

"Actually, Greta, yah're the best possible person. Can we practice?"

By one o'clock, we had fifty-one hundred and thirty-two cars and a hundred and twelve trucks lined up, ready to descend on city hall from four directions. Not as many people as our marches the week before, but the cars took up more space, made the impact bigger, and left other people free to continue picketing, working on neighborhood projects, and carrying out the other parts of our plan.

From 12:30 on, thousands of people called our Plan Four list—their alderman, the mayor, county attorney, state representative and senator, newsrooms at all thirty-nine radio stations and the five TV channels. Their message was simple. "Free Ruka Williams and Margaret Björk immediately!"

Our caravan stopped at the high school. Kids climbed aboard the twenty-two stake trucks, then we moved on. Four caravans joined us from Northeast as we went.

Vincent Wójcik's sister-in-law, who worked in the City Traffic Department, had told us the narrow downtown streets could only handle thirteen hundred cars an hour. Coming all at once, we filled the four streets surrounding city hall. And stopped. Traffic was backed up for miles. No cars could get into or out of city hall, The Grain Exchange, the county courthouse and jail, or the Fat Cat's Minneapolis Club.

I don't know how she managed it, but Blanche was standing next to a parking spot for me right in front of city hall and next to a pay phone. I had a very long cord plugged into the CB radio and attached to a little gizmo Todd made with a suction cup on top. I spit on the rubber cup, pushed it against the phone receiver, dropped a dime in the payphone slot, and holy cowbops! It was live and on the air.

Greta stepped up to the phone, Clarence holding her hand. I dialed the mayor's secret direct number and...he answered!

"Mr. Mayor, this is Greta Björk," she said in a sweet, innocent voice. "I'm here to pick up my mom and my friend Ruka." She changed her

CHAPTER 16, THE FOREVER NINES

voice, sounded much older. "With thirty-four thousand friends! We're not leaving without Mom and Ruka!"

"What the hell do you think you're doing, little girl?" the mayor said. "This is an emergency number!"

Fifty-two hundred and forty-four CB radios turned up loud, echoed the mayor's voice back and forth along downtown's streets.

"You're on the air, Mr. Mayor," Greta said. "And this *is* an emergency! Look out your window. You can see us."

High up in city hall tower, we saw a window blind raise up.

"I'll get right back to you, Miss Björk." the mayor said.

"Let's chant, folks!" Rennie said into the CB mic.

"Free Ruka and Margaret now!" roared through the streets.

Twelve minutes and thirty-seven seconds later, one of Judge Hanna's clerks came out of city hall, looked around, saw Rennie and me, smiled, came over, shook hands. He looked at Greta. "Ms. Björk?"

"Yes, sir?"

He shook hands with her. "We'll have your mom free in about twenty minutes. You were great on the phone. Everybody in the whole building heard you!"

"Thank you, sir!"

"Judge Hanna can't dismiss the charges without a trial, so he'll release your mom and Ms. Williams on fifty dollars bail each. Can you cover that?"

"No problem," Rennie said.

It was the quickest arraignment I'd ever heard of. The county attorney accused Margaret of assault with a deadly weapon and attempted murder. Ruka was charged with conspiracy to hide stolen goods. They pleaded innocent.

"Bail is set at fifty dollars each," Judge Hanna said.

"What are you doing, Your Honor?" the county attorney growled. "These are dangerous criminals. You can't let them loose to commit more crimes."

Judge Hanna glared at him. "Careful, Dudley! There is such a thing as truth."

"Who do I make the check to?" Rennie said.

"Hennepin County Court," Judge Hanna said.

She wrote the check, handed it to the clerk.

"The court hereby orders Margaret Björk and Ikuruka Williams released. Trial is Friday, April 14th, in this courtroom at one o'clock, unless dismissed. You are free to go, Ms. Williams and Ms. Björk. Ms. Ahlberg, can I see you in my chambers?"

Margaret came running to us. "Is Greta okay? Where is she?"

"She's okay, right outside with Clarence, waiting for ya. She hiked to our house, and we took care of her."

"Was my Greta really on the phone? How'd you make it so loud?"

"Wasn't she the real deal? Todd worked out a contraption so all five thousand plus CB radios played that call loud, yes they did!"

Ruka stood still, expressionless. I stepped over to her, hugged her. "Ya okay?"

She sorta collapsed against me.

I had to hold onto her to keep her from falling. "Let's sit down for a moment, ya good with that?"

"Okay, Paulie. Will you be taking me home?"

"Of course, right to yahr door. I understand how ya feel. Been arrested twice. It makes ya a little nutso afterward. It's okay to feel that way."

Rennie came out of the judge's chambers with a manila envelope and a big grin. We each put an arm around Ruka, walked her slowly out of the building. With every step, she seemed a little stronger.

"Does my mom know?" Ruka said. "She's at the factory."

"You want her to come home and be with ya?"

Ruka nodded. "Uh-huh."

"We'll call the office on the CB, ask Denise to call your mom 'n' you should sit with us up front, not all alone in the back seat, no siree."

"Thanks. I've never been so embarrassed in my life. Jail? Me?"

"Yah're a hero. Heroes get jailed more often than average."

She shifted in her seat. "Hero? I don't think so. Feels like I did something wrong."

We talked about guilt and how she had both Fat Cats and Jim Crow telling her, "Blame yourself!"

"Uh-huh, that's what my dad says. But it's hard to get the shame and sinful feeling out of my head."

CHAPTER 16, THE FOREVER NINES

"Ya have ta keep working at it. Doesn't happen snap! Like that. Still catch myself feeling guilty I couldn't stop Gremling's massacre."

"What, Paulie? Really? Why?"

As we talked, Ruka's face relaxed. Finally, she said, "I have to do some deep thinking."

"That's what it takes 'n' stuff, no halfway about it."

"Karen, what's making you smile so much?" Ruka said.

"What the judge gave me, as far as that goes. Letter of apology from the bastard who called me a fifty-cent whore 'n' groped me on campus 'n' a check for damages from him for ten thousand, five hundred bucks. And the judge said he admired my spunk."

"Oooh! How will you spend it?"

"Nine thousand strike fund, a thousand law clinic, five hundred for me."

"Do you get the bail money back?"

"Yes siree, Bob, 'n' you quit worrying, Ruka, 'n' go back to being the way you were before you became a hero."

"Don't know if I can. Just don't know."

"Will you feel differently when the courts award you with a million bucks in libel damages 'n' still more for false arrest?"

"They never will. I'm Black."

"Yah're a People's Union hero, 150,000 folks strong, and we say they will!"

"I hope so," Ruka said. "If we ever truly get over Jordon. Know what I mean?"

"Yes indeed! On the other side of the deep river, at campground, 'n' Lije explained it to us, to the max. Jim crows can't fly there 'cause they fall dead into the bottomless waters, never to be seen again. But the river wasn't bottomless for slaves 'n' they could walk across it 'n' stuff."

"He said that Jim Crow stuff?" Ruka said.

"No siree, I did."

Ruka smiled, sang "Deep River."

We joined in. Waited with her, still singing, until her mom arrived. Rennie and I learned four new spirituals. It was mega-astonishing how much better we felt.

Outside our office in The Nines classroom, they were reading the first chapter of *Grapes of Wrath* in honor of Bonnie. Joanna could only find four copies, so they took turns reading out loud, discussing it as they went. Jeffie was holding Jeanette, Terri holding Mamie. Tess held Kurt's hand. Bobby had his arm around Charlie.

"We voted today," Mamie said, "to call ourselves the Forever Nines for the rest of our lives, so Bonnie can always keep up with us."

"Aw! That is flat-out magnificent. Yah're the best, Forever Nines!"

Sid Felsing came into the room, stood beside us, pointed to the Forever Nines, smiled, put his thumb up, pointed toward our office. We stepped inside with him.

"I'm embarrassed to ask," Sid said. "That purple toilet? It's somewhat magical, know what I mean?"

"Not sure we're on the same page," Rennie said.

"Um, it helps a lot." His face turned fiery red. "With the constipation problem."

"Glad to hear it," I said.

"Could I..." He shoved hands into pockets. "You know, buy? One for home?"

I squeezed Rennie's hand once.

"Dude, we have forty-nine more purple ones 'n' I have to check with the Teen Council and Neighborhood Association just to make sure, but I think it would be okay, yes I do, so I'll find out 'n' let you know."

"I could pay up to twenty-five bucks."

Rennie squeezed my hand twice. Pointed her chin downward.

"Aha, that flat out seems to be too high to us. Yah're not exactly rolling in cash money, are ya? Besides, what about installation?"

"Oof, yeah. That."

"How about we look into it and let ya know. Personally, I'm all for it."

"Thanks. You two are the finest!"

Susie came flying into the room, waving a yellow sheet from the Associated Press wire. She spread it out on our table. "Get a look at this!"

"Minneapolis Postal Inspectors Attach Bank Account to Collect Fine. Minneapolis, MN, March 14 Associated Press. Postal Inspectors collected a $1,200 fine levied on a publication titled *Minnesota Patriot* for improper and unauthorized use of postal facilities, Inspector H. W. Munsen announced today."

I jumped straight up in the air, yelled, "Hot dog!"

Rennie did her step dance. "They can't just go around breaking the law, no siree!"

"Can I quote you, Karen?" Susie said. "We're doing a story for tomorrow."

"Yes indeed!"

Late that afternoon, Ronan called us. "As of three o'clock, Workers' Market gross sales are thirty-nine percent above projected. We made two bank deposits and ordered more of everything for us, Dahl Superette, and the Corner Store Co-op. Cecil found ten tons of amazing cold storage winter radishes, white outside, deep red inside, taste great! He brought us a hundred pounds to try out. Sold out in less than fifteen minutes. We'll have a half-ton delivered tomorrow."

Rennie hugged me. It felt so good to hold her close, with success finally blooming all around us.

Russ skipped through the doorway, wearing a big smile, his winter coat, scarf, and gloves still on. He looked at us, said, "Oops! Am I interrupting something?"

"Nope! Just heard from Ronan. Hot dog! They have ta reorder everything. Way above projections. Celebrating with a hug! Never saw ya skip before."

"Been nosing around downtown, taking care of business. One of the grapes on my vine says Judge Ovington is suing Teddy-boy Knight's old man for slander. For ten million. Ovington's pissed, so he deliberately arranged for the trial to start in September, to have it hanging over Knight's head as long as possible. And a little bird told me he wants to give Knight the chance to hide assets so it becomes a criminal matter."

"Bingo!" Rennie said. "We got that one nailed."

"And!" Russ said. "And! Child Protectors began investigating Teddy-boy's abuse of his girl cousins. So more nailed than you thought, Karen!" He took a document from his briefcase, spread it on our table. "Court order reinstating nonprofit status of our building and acknowledging that tax *is* paid for portions rented to commercial entities. And! And! An injunction prohibiting heating gas turn-offs until May, signed by Judge Woodruff. So de Vries can't hire scabs to do that! The judge also threw out the hundred-buck advance payment."

"Did ya let the gas workers' union know?" I said.

"Do dogs wag their tails? Next task, we have to file fairness doctrine complaints with the Federal Communications Commission."

"How do they work 'n' stuff?" Rennie said.

"Radio and TV stations are required to air contrasting opinions on major issues. How many stations aired *our* story?" He held up his hand, counted off four fingers. "We'll file grievances on the others. Can we step up our complaint calls? What we're doing is annoying them. But it's not enough pressure."

He went into details, helped us figure out how to take our battle with the broadcasters to the next level so we could lay out a plan, get it voted on by our Big Three.

Suddenly, the grin left his face. "By the way, I really appreciated your including my dad's name in the funeral service." His eyes teared up. "I just can't tell you…" He shook his head, wiped his eyes.

I put my arm around his shoulders. "It was the right thing to do, Russ."

"No two ways about it," Rennie said.

Laura knocked on our door. She had the tiniest smile, a magazine in her hand. She opened it, put it down on our table. "*American Muralist* came through!"

There were photos of Laura, the two kids who helped her repaint the warming room mural's corner, Laura's original color-pencil sketch, and the restored part. And Laura's article about Prichard's vandalism with her byline.

"Dozer would be so proud! And Dad…he's just crowing! Blanche said Dad can use her lathe to make a frame, and Dad said we'll hang it in the living room."

"We have a huge supply of window glass over in Bucky Hall 'n' you could use a piece for your frame, as far as that goes."

"Thanks, Karen. And thank you both for getting Dad a job here. Gol! I've been wishing he could quit QRS Cabinet for years, and that's the t-r-u-t-h, truth!"

The phone rang. Rennie answered it. "Hey, Debs, what's up? Sure, c'mon over." She hung up, grinned. "Debs needs a ten-minute meeting." A few minutes later, Rennie hugged Debbie and said, "Holy buckets, look at you! That big-time grin, your cheeks all pink like they used to be."

Debbie blushed redder than a rose. "Thanks, Ka Ka. So Ronan, Lydia Rivers, and I looked over our sales figures as of four o'clock, including the corner stores. Spoke with Cecil on the CB radio. So grasp this! Even if sales go down by half when the strike is settled and we're competing with Red Crow and other big supermarkets, Cecil's farmers don't have enough food in cold storage for more than a month, except potatoes."

"Is that both Route 10 up north *and* Route 52 down south, as far as that goes?"

"Correct. We're okay on milk, but not eggs, sour cream, meat, and chicken."

"Aren't we in tip-top shape with flour, corn meal, baked goods?" I said.

"Norm deLuca at General Grain said they're getting beet sugar and all the stuff we need from new sources, delivered by small truckers paying two-fifty indexed."

"Debs," Rennie said, "you're looking mapes, 'n' what's up your sleeve?"

"Mapes? What the heck does that mean?" I said.

"When your good news shows on your face," Debbie said. "From when we were kids. One of Dad's original words."

"Debs, are you talking 'n' stuff?" Rennie said.

Debbie grinned wider. "Cecil's looking for more farmers with food in storage. The *People's Free Press* farm reporter's writing a story about farm-to-store opportunities. That should help us find more. But we also want to set up new truck routes."

"Similar to Cecil's, as far as that goes?"

"Precisely. Cecil met an independent trucker, Patsy Blumhardt, means strong flower in German. She supports her disabled husband and four teen-aged kids. Her sister's a widow with six kids. They have two refrigerated trucks, not enough business. Cecil thinks they should set up a route like his on Minnesota Route 65 north up to Bethel, Grandy, Mora, McGrath, McGregor, then US 169 to Hibbing."

"He's familiar with 65 and 169?" I said.

"Cruised them in his car a couple of Sundays, talked to diner and gas station owners. Many are unhappy with suppliers. Most of them know farmers." Debbie clapped her hands. "So, here's what we get from this. First, *People's Free Press* distributes to more diners and gas stations. Second, rural allies. Third, a bigger supply of locally grown food, including buckwheat, barley, turkey, and duck. Fourth, a market for canned goods and other groceries, so we can make bigger orders to our wholesalers, get lower prices."

"And what do we risk 'n' stuff?"

"Nothing," Debbie said. "Although, unlike Cecil who has savings, we may need to pay the Blumhardts for big food orders ahead of time."

"Dynamite. I am for it, but only if they have cargo insurance. Rennie?"

"Yes siree, Bob. Let's recommend it to the Teen Council and Neighborhood Association. Debs, you coming to the Big Three meeting 'n' you've never been to one 'n' you should know what's going on 'n' I'm asking Denise to come too, 'n' she can 'cause she's not scheduled to work tonight, as far as that goes."

"You mean me and Denise are big deals?"

"Bingo!" Rennie nodded. "It starts at five in Arne Iversen Auditorium."

"I'll talk with our team, make sure they can spare me then."

Just before the Big Three meeting started, Denise and Debbie, arms linked, smiling, came into the auditorium. Rennie, Russ, Ma, Sarah, and I reviewed the day's events for everyone, got our new media coverage plan and the Blumhardts' truck route approved, voted to sell Sid Felsing a purple toilet and matching sink for fifteen bucks, and took care of an astonishing amount of small but important stuff.

"We got a boatload of business done just now," Dina said. "But once upon a time, we had soup 'n' sandwich meetings. With rebel cakes. Every single time. And the Creektones playing dance music. I know we've been, shall we say, a bit distracted. But I miss the music, the rebel cakes, the soup, the chance to have a meal with your neighbors. Yeah, there's a lot more people at meetings now. But we can do it!"

The discussion went back and forth. Dina volunteered to chair a music and food committee. Eugene Drass, Norma Lund, and Harley Blecher said they'd work with her.

CHAPTER 16, THE FOREVER NINES

Then, Ma took the floor. "There's something else been missing from here recently," she said. "We used to do it at every single soup 'n' sandwich meeting before the Fat Cats went berserk on us. I make a motion we start retelling our big dreams of the future, with Karen's Nellie story and Paulie's Fruit Orchard one."

"Second!" Harry called out.

"Third!" Mamie hollered. "Bonnie used to love those stories."

"Never heard of a third," Sarah said.

"Alrighty, it's a Shingle Creek tradition," Ma said. "Started as a joke, but turned into something we all love. Only Forever Nines can third a motion."

"That is so sweet," Sarah said.

"All in favor?" Rennie said. "I see nobody opposed, but a lot of people aren't voting. Those who didn't vote, is it because you've never heard these stories?"

Lots of hands went up.

"Will you try them on for size?" Rennie said. "I guarantee you'll like them."

The hands stayed up.

"Once upon a time..." Rennie said.

Her Nellie story got a standing ovation. I told my fruit forest story, and once again, got applause, cheering. People said these stories filled them with hope and things they could dream about. A woman in a green coat who'd spoken at past People's Union meetings suggested we air the stories on KPFP and ask other communities to come up with their own myths.

Right after the meeting, we sat in on the employees' leadership class. Two of our counselors, Ruby Ominira and Al Mikkola, showed people how to work together more effectively, exactly the way Joe once showed the nine original Teen Council members.

Just when we were about to turn off the lights in our office and head home, the phone rang. "Mr. Mäkinen, Miss Ahlberg," a woman's voice said, "you have a call from Algernon H. H. Bobellon. Please stay on the line."

Rennie pushed the speakerphone button, grabbed the tape recorder, put in a fresh cassette. She looked at me, saw the question on my face, wrote "CEO of AHH Bobellon-Carter, Inc." on a piece of scrap paper.

"That Bobcart company?" I wrote back.

She nodded. "How long does he think he can keep us waiting?" she wrote. "Full professors only get ten minutes."

I held up five fingers, was just about to hang up when he came on the line.

"Mr. Mäkinen, Miss Ahlberg, this is Mr. Bobellon, AHH Bobellon-Carter, Inc. These strikes are costing me a great deal of money. They must be settled. I am not affiliated with the Communal Association. They're rigid and old school, never negotiate. You call off your dogs, and we'll make sure there are real negotiations."

I got so angry, I stood straight up. "Dogs? Ya think working people are dogs?"

"It's just a mere expression."

"Are you comfortable being called Bastard Boss? Just a mere expression," Rennie said.

"No, it's demeaning. I apologize. I had no idea I was being offensive."

"*Mister* Bobellon," I said. "We cannot order our friends, neighbors, and fellow workers to do anything. We vote. Every last one of us. On everything. Have ya—"

"Mr. Mäkinen—"

I raised my voice to talk over his interruption. "Have ya negotiated with the unions representing yahr workers?"

"That's *your* first step, Mr. Bobellon," Rennie said. "The second is to sign Minneapolis Standard Work Contracts with them."

"Now see here! I'm holding off the Communal Association, which plans mass arrests. You people know you've broken the law. It could go very hard for you. Ask your lawyer. If he's any good, he can lay it all out for you. That so-called standard contract isn't worth the paper it's printed on."

"Can ya explain then, why two of yahr competitors signed it already?" I said.

Rennie wrote on the paper, "Don't name them!"

"Oh really? Who might those be?" Mr. Bobellon said.

"I'm sure, Mr. Bobellon, yahr superb competitive intelligence unit can lay that all out for ya," I said.

"He's not ready, right?" Rennie wrote on the paper.

I nodded.

"Mr. Bobellon, you are not ready for serious talks about a settlement," Rennie said. "We'll send you a comprehensive list of our demands from the People's Union, Shingle Creek Neighborhood Association, Shingle Creek Teen Council, Arnray Railroad Safety Corporation, and North-Northeast Minneapolis Industrial Safety Commission. Call us back when you're fully prepared to get down to brass tacks."

"What kind of joke is this? You're telling me I have to negotiate with a bunch of teenagers, a non-existent commission, a two-cent slum improvement cabal, a union with no locals, and a private corporation?"

"I would suggest," I said, "ya have yahr intelligence unit brief ya. Or more simply, go to yahr local library and read coverage of these entities in back issues of *People's Free Press*."

"Good evening, Mr. Bobellon," Rennie said, and hung up the phone.

"How come ya called it a settlement?"

"They have to settle with us 'n' holy buckets, we don't give in 'n' we don't negotiate, no siree!"

"Heavy duty. I have ta think about this one!"

Russ was sitting in his office, talking with Judith. They looked exhausted. They listened to the tape, congratulated us. Said Bobellon was bluffing and agreed we should send him the demands, a copy of the Minneapolis Standard Work Contract, and nothing more.

"But we must," Russ said, "*must* have a settlement strategy meeting tomorrow."

"Ya mean, this is coming to a head? We're gonna win?" I said.

"If we handle it right? Pay dirt!" Russ said.

"If not?" Rennie said.

"We get very painfully unhorsed," Russ said.

CHAPTER 17, TURNING NIGHTMARES INSIDE OUT

THURSDAY-FRIDAY, MARCH 16-17, 1972

THURSDAY MORNING, RENNIE WAS SILENT at breakfast, face blank. "I'm sorry, Paavali, bummer and a half, but I can't be at the meeting with Hazel 'n' I know it's important because she wanted it here for privacy, but I have to go to the eight o'clock bio lab 'n' it's my last chance 'cause I missed all the other sections since we were so busy, 'n' I'll be back as soon as I can."

"What's bothering ya?"

"Nothing." She looked down at the table. "Just tired."

"Can I drive ya?"

"I need to study on the bus 'n' stuff 'n' you have to be here for the meeting."

I followed her to the closet, put her coat on her, wrapped her scarf to keep her neck and ears warm. She stood there passive, just letting me do it. Then she shambled out the door, shoulders bent forward.

She must be big-huge upset. Normally, she wouldn't want me to do that.

Back in the kitchen, Linda was washing the breakfast dishes. "My gosh, what's irking Karen? Couldn't get a word out of her."

"Wish I knew!" I said. "She sure as heck has me worried."

"It's not like her," Linda said.

I banged my knuckles together. "I'm gonna fret 'til she comes home. Darn!"

CHAPTER 17, TURNING NIGHTMARES INSIDE OUT

Russ arrived, stamped the snow off his shoes, sat down with us at the kitchen table. "Not just one but four little birds told me if Hazel runs a decent campaign, she'll be the next county attorney. Dudley Courtenay has lots of enemies. The Communal Association's shaking in their boots. And Chief Jensen's terrified Hazel will open an investigation into Fred's killing."

"Daughter's revenge," I said. "Powerful stuff!"

Hazel and Billy joined us. We turned on our jammers, got down to brass tacks.

"How are you doing with your fairness doctrine campaign?" Hazel said.

"Just getting started," Linda said. "But can you believe it? We've had Georgia, Karen, Paul, Clarence, Vincent, and Sarah on the air already."

"And!" Russ said. "And! We coached Sherri Anselm, leader of Northeast Junior High Kids for Peace. She and her friends have already been on four stations."

"So," Hazel said, "let's use the Fairness and Equal Time doctrines to the utmost."

We went back and forth, developed the outline for a complete campaign, from door knocking and candidate forums, to radio spots, newspaper ads, talking points.

Meeting over, the house empty, I sat on the couch, reading about negotiation strategies. After about an hour, I heard the front door open.

"Great-Grandma?"

Rennie sounds really upset. I put down my book, called out, "Are you okay? Great-Grandma's picketing the underwear factory with Burt."

She came shuffling into the living room, crying silently, took off her coat, threw it on the easy chair with her handbag, sat down next to me. I moved my arms toward her. She collapsed against me, on my lap, face tight against my chest.

"Rennie, honey, what's wrong?" I couldn't believe I let "honey" slip out, but that's how I felt. My serpents made a fuss. I knocked them silly.

Wailing louder than a wounded she-wolf, Rennie tried to talk, couldn't. I rocked her gently, she curled herself into a ball. Arms around her, I wanted to create a safe, sheltered space for her. They weren't long enough to do that, but I tried.

"It's all over for me 'n' Greg said it's my problem 'n' he wasn't going to let me interfere with his future 'n' he just walked away 'n' now when you're just about ready for me 'n' calling me honey, it's too late 'n' I'm losing you too, 'n' I just don't want to go on anymore 'n' if I had your tube of pills with me, I would have ended it already, 'cause I know you won't be holding me anymore."

"No way yah're losing me!"

"Paulie, I'm pregnant."

Never before had I heard her sound totally defeated. I tightened my arms around her. "I'll stand by ya no matter what. We'll work everything out."

"But it's not your baby."

"So. What?" *Yah're doing okay, Paavali. But what do ya say next? Think! Think!*

The hands on the cuckoo clock moved, moved again.

"How do ya even know yah're pregnant?"

"No period. Six weeks late." She wailed again.

I rocked her gently in my arms as she cried.

Ya need to protect her, Paavali. But from what? She's as strong as ya physically. A better fighter than ya by far. A lot smarter than ya. But her feelings… That's it! Ya never knew anyone with emotions that strong, not even Jill. That's what ya have to protect! Her feelings! Her hopes! Her ambitions! Because there are men in this world who will try to squash her just because she's a woman.

She said she's not ready to be a mother yet, and how would she go to law school with a baby and who would support them. I said I understand. It will work out okay. I said it again. And again. "I'll stand by ya. Great-Grandma will stand by ya. Ma will stand by ya. Susie, Linda, Ruka, Laura, Li'l Mikey, and Daniel will stand by ya." I rocked her, chanted to her, "It will be okay. You will be okay." Then I sang. I didn't have any idea where the words and melody came from. I didn't have a great voice like Jill's, but that wasn't the point.

I'll make myself into a covered bridge for ya,

Lift ya high above the roiling angry waters,

CHAPTER 17, TURNING NIGHTMARES INSIDE OUT

Keep ya warm, safe, and dry 'til the storm is through,
Be the most ardent of yahr supporters.

She stopped crying, turned her head, cheek leaning against my chest. I opened my arms, stroked her forehead, her face began to relax. I kept chanting, continued rocking and stroking. I was ready to do it for as long as she needed me to.

She opened her eyes. They were a distressed steel gray. She looked down at my shirt. "I'm sorry. I snotted on you."

"I'll wear it as a badge of honor."

For a moment, a blue glimmer was back in her eyes. Then it was gone.

"What should I do? I'm knocked up!"

"Do ya have regular periods?"

"Um, no."

"Are ya nauseous after breakfast?"

"Never."

"If ya want to keep the baby, I'll be there for ya. If not, we'll get ya an abortion."

"How? They're illegal."

"An underground group in Chicago called the Janes. I know how to get in touch. But first things first! Let's go get us a pregnancy test."

She slapped the couch. "It will take two weeks. I can't wait that long. I can't!"

"Two hours is all."

"How do you know?"

"Judith took me to a secret abortion training session."

"Oh, Paavali!" she said, resting her head against my chest again. "Just hold me. I'm not cried out yet."

"Not knowing's always worse than knowing, Rennie. This isn't the end of everything. C'mon! We should wash the tears off yahr face." I took her hand, led her to the bathroom, stroked her face with a warm washcloth.

"You're so gentle with me, Paavali. You're not angry?"

"Only angry at myself."

"And I'm furious with myself."

I kissed her forehead, put her coat on her, guided her outside to the car. "I'll make a deal with ya. If ya forgive yahrself, I'll forgive myself."

"Deal!" she said.

A huge weight lifted off my shoulders.

She sat so tight against me, I thought even a pry bar couldn't pull us apart. When she turned on the radio, Keanna's voice filled the car.

"And now, the latest from singer-songwriter Jill Frisk, written on the plane home to San Francisco, her newest song, *The Real Deal*. Jill dedicates it to her beloved Joe, light of her life, and two of her nearest, dearest relatives."

A pulsing beat on Jill's concertina, a sweet melody, then Jill's voice.

If he's the right guy,

He'll know just how you feel

If he's the right guy,

And he's the real deal

He'll stand right by you

When things get hard and rough

Know what you've been through

And why it's been so tough.

"It's for us, yes siree!" She sang along on the choruses. "Jill knew, just the look on her face that time she saw me upset. She tried to get me talking, but I couldn't say much 'n' she even used my words in the song, the real deal."

At the Free Clinic, Rennie's face turned bright red, her hand clamped mine.

"Can we get a Wampole two-hour," I said.

"Sure, no problem," the guy at the front desk said. He looked at Rennie. "You can use your real name here or a made-up one."

"Magaly McGuire," Rennie said.

"You from the neighborhood, Magaly?"

Rennie's blush deepened. "N-no."

"Well, you've got two hours before the results. You might want to walk over to the river to pass the time. Nice sunny day today, not freezing, no wind, lots of great views to occupy your mind, if you know what I mean."

CHAPTER 17, TURNING NIGHTMARES INSIDE OUT

"Big-time!" Rennie said.

The test itself was no big deal. "There's the restroom, here's a cup, go pee in it." They asked her if she wanted birth control, explained the different types and the insertion procedures for IUDs. Gave her some pills to make insertion easier.

"Whaddaya think, Magaly?" I said. "A walk by the river?"

"To the max!"

"Magaly McGuire! How'd ya ever come up with that name?"

"I have no idea 'n' she's a superhero 'n' maybe I'll write stories about her."

We walked down to West River Road, arms entwined, then over to the river. Barges filled with iron ore and wheat from up north floated by. A few early songbirds made sweet melodies. And Rennie was belching. Loudly. And often.

"Yahr stomach upset from the tension?"

"Yes siree, B—" which blended right into a belch and set us both off laughing.

Back at the clinic, Rennie sat on my lap, face against my chest. A nurse called her. I helped her stand, entwined my arm around hers. We went into an exam room.

"You're not pregnant, sweetie!" the nurse said.

"You sure?"

"A hundred percent, Ms. McGuire."

Rennie's face went from bright red to its normal color. Laughing and crying, she took my hands, did her two-step boogie, danced me with her. "Now I can go to law school!" she sang.

"You sure can, and Lord knows, we need some women lawyers! Now let's get you set up for the insertion. Sir, can you have a seat in the waiting room?"

"I want him in here! Holding my hand," Rennie said.

The nurse looked at me. "Well, okay, I guess. Sure you won't faint?"

"Nope, not a chance," I said.

"Righto. Ms. McGuire, take off your jeans and undies, climb up onto this table, feet in the stirrups. I'll be right back with the doc." She closed the door behind her.

Yikes, I have never seen Rennie naked before. I can't stop looking! I was so wrong! She's no little girl! My dick tingled, stood up, saluted. But the serpents brought it down again. I whomped their heads. My dick stood up, the snakes tackled it again. I had a seesaw in my pants.

"Paulie, why are you staring at me?"

"Sorry, honey." It slipped out again. My serpents were furious. "Yah're so gorgeous down there. Like a thick golden bush with a single, perfect blossom below it. I never knew a woman could be that beautiful."

"Up here too?" she said. She pulled up her shirt, undid her bra.

Those are not a little girl's breasts! Holy cowbops! My dick's at attention again. "They're gorgeous. And sexy. And the muscles in your legs and thighs! Gosh, yah're stunning."

She redid her bra, moved her shirt back down. "Come, hold my hand! These are happy tears again!"

She has periods. She's not a kid. She's a woman inside, outside, in her body, in her mind. Those beautiful labia, like an intricate flower! Why didn't I realize all that before? What was standing in my way? Is it still? I'm holding her hand even tighter than she's holding mine.

The nurse came back, looked at me. "You sure you're okay?"

"Yup, I'm fine now."

She explained the procedure, told us exactly when there'd be pain.

"I may scream, yes siree, but I can handle it."

A woman came into the room. "Hello, I'm Doctor Bucek, your galnecologist."

Rennie laughed. "All. Right. Then! I wouldn't want some strange *man* poking around down there."

"That's why I went to medical school! Let's get your health history, Ms. McGuire." She asked a bunch of questions. "Okay, all sounds good. Mostly this insertion is easy. You'll have some pain, but it's over in seconds. I'll warn you when it's coming."

Three different times, the doctor said, "Pain alert," Rennie screamed, crushed my hand. I cried, I was so upset for her. Afterward, I pulled out a clean handkerchief, mopped her brow, then mine.

"Okay, Ms. McGuire," Doctor Bucek said. "You may have some pain today and tomorrow." She handed Rennie a small bottle. "Take these if you do. Don't have sex for forty-eight hours. And come back for a checkup

CHAPTER 17, TURNING NIGHTMARES INSIDE OUT

right after your next period, or in two months, whichever comes sooner. Have you ever considered hormone treatment?"

"N-no. For what, as far as that goes?"

"To help your body get on a regular schedule for periods. Think about it, and let's talk about the pros, cons, and diagnostic procedures when you come back."

Gosh! Women have a lot more stuff to worry about than men!

"You can stay in this room for a while to recover your wits," the nurse said, and closed the door behind her.

"Rennie! Did ya forget something?"

"Huh? What?"

"Happy birthday!"

"Holy buckets, I did forget!" She hugged me. "What a wonderful birthday present you gave me today 'n' it's the best possible one in the world."

"I baked ya a Swedish sticky chocolate cake. Had just enough cocoa powder left. We're having a special dinner for ya tonight."

"How about lunch 'cause I'm starving!"

"Ever been to Vito's Ristorante in Dinkytown?"

"No siree, Bob! You?"

"When I bought my big dictionary, I poked around Dinkytown, ate there, really liked it. And I, er, took…" I put my hands over my face.

"Nancy there?"

"Yeah, that mistake."

"We're forgiving ourselves, remember?"

"Thanks. I'll be needing reminders. Wanna try it?"

"Sure. Dutch?"

"Heck no! It's yahr birthday."

"Guess I have to get unused to Greg Dutch-Treat Overgaard. I treated him a couple of times 'n' he never treated me once."

We put on our coats, she took my arm, we walked toward the car. "Now I'm only two years younger than you, Paavali, not three!"

I took her in my arms, kissed her cheeks, sang a line from one of her favorite songs. "Yah're not too young, and diffident, for me-ee!"

We got a booth off in a corner. It was past lunchtime, the restaurant was almost empty. Rennie scooted in, motioned to me. I sat down next to her.

She moved toward me. "I just want to be close to you, Paavali."

The waiter put menus, a basket of bread, glasses of water on the table. "No hurry. Wave me over when you're ready to order."

She stroked my cheek. "I used to cry after sex with Greg 'n' I had no idea why 'cause he turned me on 'n' I really enjoyed it, so I asked Judith 'n' she said I really wanted to be with you 'n' not him 'n' could never be close to him like I am with you, 'n' she was so right, yes she was."

"I'm not sure how to say this, so here goes. Did ya...ya know, come?"

"Holy buckets, did I ever! Sometimes two or three times 'n' it's not something you're supposed to talk about, especially women, 'n' Greg always told me that, but how can you work things out if you don't discuss it 'n' stuff?"

"Did ya scream and moan?"

"Um, no. Neither do any of the women I know when they're having real orgasms, 'n' it's more like grunts and sighs 'n' usually women make a lot of noise when they're faking orgasms to please a man, as far as that goes, 'n' did Nancy?"

"Yup, real loud, right when I was coming. I sorta thought it wasn't real."

Yahr seesaw is going up and down. And up again. Holy cowbops, ya can learn a lot about sex from her!

"Did ya..." My face was burning. "Er, let him eat..."

"My deal with him was, he sucked and licked me down there, which I love more than any other kind of sex, then I'd blow him, 'n' I actually like that, even the taste, especially when we kissed right after." She took my hand. "What else, Paavali, 'n' there's nothing to be ashamed of 'n' you can ask me anything."

"Did ya..." I shook my head, covered my face with my hands.

She gently took them off, held them. "What, honey."

She never called me that before. Gosh, I love it! I bit my lip. "Use hand signals with him?"

"Paavali! No way I used *our* hand signals. Or any others. No way."

Tears ran down my face. "Thank heavens! I couldn't bear that."

CHAPTER 17, TURNING NIGHTMARES INSIDE OUT

She squeezed my hands gently. "That is so sweet! I wish I'd known how to ask you more about what was happening to you 'n' helped you through it instead of running."

"Please, don't blame yahrself. Please! Ya have needs too, not just me."

"Well, I'm asking you now 'cause I can sort of tell you've been dealing with it, but I want to understand what's really going on, 'n' be there for you like you've always been for me, 'n' I won't judge you, as far as that goes, all right then?"

"I know that from my nose to my toes."

We ate, we laughed, we talked, we hugged. I told her about my serpents, my psychotic dick, how I went out dancing looking for an answer, and what Judith had to say about it. And I told her about the seesaw, what I thought was keeping the snakes alive, how I was fighting with them. And winning, inch by inch.

"It's like combat on two fronts, the war against the Fat Cats 'n' the war against your own demons, yes siree, 'n' we're winning them both, you and me!" She put her arms around me, moved close, her nose touching mine. "Paulie-Paul, talking about it really helps 'n' please, let's carry on doing that."

"Dynamite! You betcha!"

On the way home, we turned onto North 2nd Street, listening to The Creektones on KPFP.

"The following is a paid political announcement," Keanna's voice said.

"An illegal Fat Cat militia commander shot Margaret's eleven-year-old daughter," Linda's voice said.

"But the county attorney charged Margaret with a crime. Not the commander. Not his troops," Billy's voice said.

"Hazel Corwin-Pokorny says, 'Fat Cats must pay when they break laws,'" Linda's voice said. " 'Not their victims.' "

"Vote Hazel Corwin-Pokorny for county attorney, line C in June," Billy's voice said. "Your vote counts!"

"Paid for by Corwin-Pokorny for county attorney," Todd's voice said.

"Holy buckets, they worked fast 'n' how'd they do that 'n' still go to school?"

"Same like you. They use smart strategies and shortcuts."

We got back just in time for the Big Three meeting on negotiation demands. First, we made a list of all three hundred and forty-nine suggestions. Cut out duplicates. Voted on everything. Got the list down to two hundred and twelve. Russ and his staff would spend the next day making the language bulletproof. Then we'd have all members of the Big Three vote on them.

As we walked home from Betty Hall, arms entwined, I said, "What are we telling our family about today? It's totally yahr decision."

"Well, they all know about Greg 'n' I don't see any big secret except that you're far more wonderful than I ever could've imagined, to the max!"

I felt myself blush. "Even Billy knows?"

"How could he not 'cause he's seen Greg pick me up late at night, so rather than have him turn to his imagination, Linda asked me if she could tell him 'n' I was on the same page, no halfway about it."

The six of us cooked a tasty Swedish-Finnish feast. When Rennie talked about today, Ma, Clara, and Linda said they were relieved because they knew something was very wrong. We lingered over coffee and Kladdkaka Swedish sticky chocolate cake, talking about negotiating strategies.

Just before we started cleaning up the kitchen, Clara hugged me. "Thank you, Paulie, for taking such good care of my älva-Karen. *Du är en unik, märklig kille.* You are a one of a kind, remarkable fella, just like my Torkel was."

"Holy buckets, Great-Grandma, last time you called me your Karen-elf, I was six!"

"Yah, but I always think about you that way. All my kids and grandkids are still *små älvor*, little elves, deep in my heart."

Later, in our room, I sat on the couch, Rennie on my lap. She stroked my cheeks, kissed my face, kissed it again. My seesaw went up, down, up, up, down.

"Thanks for being you, Paavali. Awesome, far out, glorious, the real deal. Words just can't describe how wonderful you are. Will you sing to me again?"

"I can't really sing, ya know."

"Well, whatever you did today, it went clear to my heart and soul."

CHAPTER 17, TURNING NIGHTMARES INSIDE OUT

I sang her favorite tunes from the radio, several songs by Jill, and a few I made up on the spot, rocking her gently.

She looked into my eyes the whole time, face relaxed. "I can barely keep myself awake," she whispered.

"Want me to help ya get ready for bed?"

She nodded.

I undressed her, put on her pajamas. Picked her up, carried her to the bed, tucked her in, sat beside her, stroked her face. "More songs?"

"Uh-huh."

I said goodnight, sang softly. Her breathing got slower, deeper. Everything about her fascinated me. I counted her freckles. Thirty-seven on her nose, a hundred and two on her left cheek. Loved how her hair cascaded over the pillow. And her cute ears. When I finally put on my pajamas and turned out the light, I watched our moonbeam move across her pillow and bathe her face with luminous silver.

In the middle of the night, her sobbing woke me.

She sat up in bed, yelling, "No! No! Let me out!"

I bolted upright, held her. "Rennie! I'm here for ya. What happened?"

"I don't wanna be in this room all the time. You know the one. Tall windows, bright red drapes 'n' they don't let me out of it 'n' you come here all the time."

"Honey, yah're still dreaming. Yah're in our room in Great-Grandma's house."

"There's dozens of gorgeous women, all tall, with big tits, 'n' you come in once a day, chat with me a few minutes, pat me on the head." She sobbed harder. "Then you listen to them insult you, 'n' you take one of them by the hand and leave with her without even saying goodbye to me, 'n' two women take her place, 'n' my whole body is pulsing inside, I want you so badly, 'n' I don't wanna be here locked away from you!"

I reached over, turned on the lamp. "Rennie, honey, open yahr eyes! Yah're here, with me." I stroked her face.

Her eyes fluttered, went wide. "Holy buckets, Paavali, I hate that nightmare!"

"I'm so sorry. I didn't mean to hurt ya that way. I big-huge care about ya. And I don't care for anyone else. But I've been so scared."

She put her arms around me, held me for a long time. "Scared of what?"

"I don't want to break ya."

"How would you break me? I don't get it."

"I wish I understood. I have nightmares about it. But never remember them. Only the awful feeling."

We fell back asleep holding each other. But somehow, I was in a familiar, very small room with no windows, and a ceiling way above my head. The walls were dark-brown stone, floor was stained, splintered, dirty planks. A smoky torch in a holder on the wall couldn't fight off darkness and shadows. There was no door, nothing to drink, no way to bathe. My skin was caked with dirt. Rennie, in an intricate, long white dress and a bridal veil flowed right through the wall. I wasn't clean, but she begged me to kiss her. Terror filled me. I embraced her, she shattered into a million little gray bits. Her eyes melted, oozed along the floor, the liquid changing from blue to black, disappearing into a crevice.

"Rennie!" I screamed. "Oh God, I killed her." I fell to the floor, wailing.

Deadwood stormed through the wall, grabbed me by the neck. "Now look what you've done, you little bastard!" He turned me over his knee, whipped me with his belt, making sure he hit my balls. The pain was horrific.

I woke up screaming, Rennie stroking my face. She held me while I shivered, shuddered, sobbed.

"Tell me, Paavali! Tell me!"

"The dream. Every damned night."

"Tell me!"

My voice shaking, I described the dungeon. How the walls moved, closer and closer, when she wasn't there, and it got so hot I couldn't breathe.

She got out my pills. I took one. Then she held me 'til I stopped trembling.

"I'll talk with Judith tomorrow. I'll get rid of all that fear that's keeping me from you. Forever. I promise you, Rennie! You and me, we're gonna break out of our nightmare prisons."

My snakes were hissing, gnawing my insides. I felt like I had to vomit, went up to the bathroom, kneeled, head over the toilet, dry retching while Rennie held me.

"The snakes, the damned snakes. I. Can't. Get. Them. Out."

"It's gonna happen, darn tootin' it will, 'n' you're closer than you've ever been."

Next morning at 7:00, I was telling Judith about my shattered-Rennie nightmare.

"Hmm. That *is* a significant dream. Was your mother kind and loving to you?"

I stamped my foot. "No way!"

"Was Nancy? Would Maria or Dawn have been?"

"No, they wanted to make me feel small, like they feel."

Judith stood up. "So you've been turned on by women just like your mother? Someone who's unkind to you? You're attracted to them? So you can have the same kind of angry, depressed, family as the one you came from? A whole new family who would be happy to send you marching off to die in 'Nam? Who actually *want* to break you?"

"My parents almost did! Nancy, Maria, Dawn all sorta enjoyed slamming me."

"Is that why you were attracted to them? Because they were like your mother and your father too? And your parents are supposed to love you, so that's what you've come to believe love is? It breaks and shatters people?"

"Judith, is…is…that why my mother turned me on?"

Her right eyebrow pointed skywards. "What do you mean?"

I described the night Mildread appeared in disguise in the back row, looking like a mixture of almost every woman who ever aroused me. "When she turned me on, my serpents hadn't bitten or hissed. The moment I realized who she was, my hard-on wilted."

"Was it your mother who turned you on? Or a symbol of hostility?"

"No, no, not my mother." I banged my fist on her desk, was quiet for a moment. "A symbol. So…I shouldn't feel guilty?"

Judith sat down. "Exactly! If we've been abused, we're attracted to people like those from childhood who abused us. If our childhood was shaped by people who ripped apart our self-esteem, we are probably attracted to nasty people who will keep us in a familiar place. Anxiety. Pain.

Fear. Insecurity. It's a horrible place, but it's comfortable. We're familiar with it. Anything else—even if it's wonderful—is terrifying."

I turned my palms up, fingers spread apart. "What the heck? Why?"

"You're not used to it. Don't know how to handle it. You have to actually give up your old identity. And build a new one. So, Paulie, close your eyes and think for a moment about who you really are *now*. Are you the guy who takes no shit about standing up for the love of his life in a crisis?"

I clapped my hands twice. "Yup! I did that."

"And you go so far beyond what most guys could do, it sounds like a fairy tale. But it's real?"

"I guess that *is* me!" I closed my eyes, looked at it every which way. "The only way I could shatter Karen is by not dealing with this and not being the love of her life."

Judith nodded, smiled. "You got it!"

"Then why am I feeling so nauseous? I have ta…" I sprang to my feet, ran out of her office, out of the clinic, across the hall to the men's room, barely holding it down. Kneeling in front of the toilet, I closed my eyes and vomited. There were little plipping sounds, then big splashes. I rinsed my mouth out, washed my face. Went back to Judith's office.

"What just happened, Paul?"

"I puked!" I said, and started laughing so hard I couldn't speak. Tears rolled down my cheeks. Finally, I was able to say, "The serpent came out. With all her not-so-little babies. And all the poison pellets. I flushed them down seven times over. To make sure. Slammed the lid down and sat on it."

"What are you feeling now, Paul?"

"No more snakes. No more anxiety. A big-huge head-over-heels love for Karen. I'm going right home to tell her. She's waiting for me."

"Congratulations, Paul!"

"Am I on the right track?"

"Absolutely. As nobody else ever could be. Because Paul—you *are* the real Paul Mäkinen!"

There was a loud series of knocks on the door. It flew open. "Sorry!" Gordy said. "Paulie, City Militia's after you. They arrested Karen. Come with us. Fast!"

CHAPTER 17, TURNING NIGHTMARES INSIDE OUT

Officer Anderson handed me a balaclava that covered my face and a pair of dark glasses.

All Gordy said was, "We're taking you to a safe hideout."

We ran into the classroom storage space, through a door, across space full of lumber and bricks, behind the newsroom, through the pressroom, and into the room with Nellie and the railroad cars. In a hidden nook behind piles of boxes, a '65 black Plymouth Fury, windows tinted dark, was waiting, bright red and blue lights flashing from under the front grille.

When Gordy opened the trunk, the bottom was covered with pillows. "Sorry, Paulie, hop in. It's not a long ride."

The trunk lid clicked shut. I was in darkness. I tried not to worry about Rennie, but she was all I could think about. The siren went on. Tires squealed. We were moving mega fast. I counted the turns, tried to figure out where we were. Couldn't. Siren went off, the car slowed.

After what seemed like forever, we stopped, trunk lid opened. I climbed out. We were in an industrial garage.

"Sorry, Paulie! City Militia was hot on your tail. They tried to stop us when we barreled out of Olson Hall, but we were too fast. We're at General Grain now. We may see people you know. Say nothing, except to Burt, and only if he's alone. Keep your voice to yourself, shades and hood on until we're in the dorm."

I looked around, saw nobody. "Is Karen okay?"

"Don't know yet. I'll tell you soon as I find out. They also got Nelson but not Sarah. Have to run. More people to rescue."

Norm deLuca came through a doorway, shook hands. "I don't want to know who you are, Buddy, but welcome. Dorm's an okay place, spent many a night there during winter blizzards. Come, follow me."

We walked down a long corridor. Norm opened a door. We stepped into a large room with about two dozen beds. One of them had sheets and blankets. Norm pointed. "All yours, Buddy. We have blackout curtains up so you can have lights on at night. There's a radio, a CB, and a phone, but you can't use the phone."

I spread my hands out, palms up.

"Phone's probably tapped. You eat breakfast?"

I shook my head, rubbed my stomach.

He took a pencil from behind his ear, paper from his pocket. "Write down what you want. We'll get as much of it as we can. Be back in about twenty minutes."

I hung my coat on the rack, laid down, buried my face in the pillow. Too numb to cry, I tried to control my thoughts, couldn't, jumped up, looked around. Saw a clean bathroom with showers and stacks of towels. Books about working-class history in a corner with couches and easy chairs. A kitchen and a dining room with a CB radio.

The door opened. Lori walked in. "Hello, Buddy. I have pajamas and slippers for you and clean underwear for tomorrow. A mask that's easier to take than your woolen one. We'll have a personal care pack later." She handed me a young woman's mask. "And don't worry. With Paul Mäkinen's leadership, we're gonna win this strike fast!"

This is, what's that word? Surreal! Or trippy, like Dozer used to say.

I reached out, shook hands. Figured Lori and I would have a good laugh about this sometime soon.

After I ate, Todd arrived with a microphone attached to a box. "Hello, Buddy," he said into the mic. "Not supposed to know your name." It made him sound like a machine. "Plug this cord into the CB port here"—he pointed—"and your voice on the air is disguised. Don't use this on the phone. Calls can be traced quickly. CB is much more difficult."

Soon, Gordy and Officer Anderson arrived with seven more people, all in balaclavas and dark glasses. Norm and Lori got them set up, left us alone. We sat down at a table in the dining room. Masks came off. I was with Clarence, Obie, Sarah, Dina, Fiona, Magdalena, and Vincent.

"They got my nephew Marek," Magdalena said, shaking her head.

"And"—my voice caught—"my Karen."

"And our Jack," Clarence said.

"And my Nelson," Sarah said, her face scrunched up.

"And our Herb Anderson," Fiona said.

"Me, I'm a-thinking we need a strategy," Obie said.

"Agreed," Fiona said, "but let's get an update from KPFP first."

"We have two radios here," I said. "Suppose four of us listen to KPFP, the other four to MSP News Network 1100."

What we found out was critical. Only KPFP was talking about the arrests. A half-dozen companies announced they were ready to sign

CHAPTER 17, TURNING NIGHTMARES INSIDE OUT

Minneapolis Standard Work Contracts. But their workers were holding back.

KPFP ran a clip from Grain Elevator Workers Local 1918 President Vance Amundsden, who said, "Signing Standard Work contracts is a good first step. However, until all People's Union demands are met, the strike isn't settled."

But 1100 News Network had propaganda clips of three Fat Cats saying Shingle Creek communist agitators won't settle the strike 'til they've destroyed all the factories.

"What we have to do is clear." Dina shrugged. "How, is another story."

"If yer askin' me," Obie said, "I'm a-thinkin' we go ahead and put our strategy to paper. By the time we done finished it, we'll know how we're a-gonna do it."

Magdalena patted his shoulder. "Obie! How'd you get so smart?"

Obie grinned. "Well, I don't have much schoolin'. But sixty and five years in the college of hard knocks done taught me some serious shit."

I laughed for the first time since Gordy's door knock.

We were working away, starting with Local 1918's statement, building from there. We heard the outside door open, grabbed our masks, put them on.

Burt walked into the room with someone in a young man's mask and a blue coat. "I brought a friend of yours," he said. "You can all take your masks off."

"Linda! What the heck?" I said. *She doesn't have a blue coat.*

"City Militia got Billy at school," she sobbed. "Cuffed him. Took him away."

I stood up, put my arm around her shoulders. "Oh, Linda! I'm so sorry. We'll get him freed, sure as heck."

She wiped her eyes with a tissue. "A militia man grabbed me, but I pushed him hard against the wall, ducked and dodged, ran like the wind, out the door, no coat. Lizzie Paske ran after me, caught up with me around the corner, put her coat over my shoulders, said, 'Keep running like hell!' I didn't know Lizzie gave a damn about anyone. So I put on Lizzie's balaclava from her coat pocket, sprinted up the alleyway between Penn and Queen 'cause I didn't think the militia would look there. Ran across all those railroad tracks in the yard, no trains moving 'cause of the strike, and clear up to Ma's office. She hid me in that old boxcar in Betty Hall while the militia searched. Then Gordy came for me."

Linda looked around. "Paulie, where's Karen?"

"Shit." I shook my head. "Shakopee Prison."

"What are we gonna do?"

"We're working on that," I said.

"This is gonna be a very heavy lift," Linda said.

"We can do it, Sis! We have ta," I said.

Burt raised his hand. "Can I update you folks a bit? I've been using my grapevine to check on our captured heroes. Karen is okay, hasn't actually been charged. A grape on my vine says they're going to accuse her of attempted murder. You too, Paulie."

I jumped to my feet. "What the hell?"

"They allege you and Karen tried to kill Richard Prichard in the warming room, using a jump rope. Russ's grapevine says they don't have a shred of evidence and they haven't made anything up yet. Marek, Jack, Herb and Nelson are in high-security in Stillwater. They weren't hurt during capture. They haven't been charged. An old friend of mine at the Atkinson Collins Law Firm is working with Russ to lay down the law."

Linda gripped the edge of the table. "Wh...where's Billy?"

"Lino Lakes Juvenile Prison. He's okay."

"What the heck," I said. "Nobody was arraigned? Sent straight to prison instead of county jail downtown?"

Burt slammed his hand down on the table. "It's plainly illegal! Russ and Corey Atkinson filed habeas corpus writs demanding everyone's release. City Militia has no authority to arrest. Or exist."

"Isn't Atkinson a Fat Cats' lawyer?" I said.

"That doesn't mean he exactly loves them. He's a firm believer in the law, says some of the Fat Cats are breaking it left and right. It infuriates him. Besides, Karen interviewed him for a paper she's writing. He was thoroughly impressed."

Somehow, with Burt there, we became intensely focused. He didn't say much. When he did talk, it was right on target. And he had a calming presence.

After about an hour, Linda said, "Can I sum up? I think we have three main tasks." She counted off on her fingers. "One, formulate conditions the Fat Cats must meet before we'll settle. Two, get a vote on the demands and our strategy from every working person in Minneapolis."

"Even beyond People's Union members?" Fiona said.

"Uh-hmm. We don't want the Fat Cats saying it was just a vote by a radical minority. Which we're not. But if we reach just a bit further and publicly declare what we're doing, it'll help make our case."

We took a quick vote. Everyone agreed.

Linda continued, "Three, decide how to step up our protests to put even more pressure on the Fat Cats."

I started clapping, stomping my feet, whooping. Everyone joined me. For only ten people, we sure made a racket. "Linda, yah're a genius in bloom!" I said.

"Second that motion," Fiona said. "And if Ruthie was here, she'd third it."

"All hands on deck!" Linda said. "Now, can we tackle part one?"

"Not so fast!" Burt said. "It's getting toward lunchtime. Lola and Lori need access to the kitchen to prepare it. Our usual local restaurants don't have much in the way of food because of the strike, but Lori went shopping at Workers' Market, and they'll put together a nice lunch. Personally, I think those ladies are a hundred percent trustworthy. What're your opinions?"

Sarah nodded. "I'll vouch for Lola, my daughter's best friend. Known her since she was knee high to a grasshopper. From a union family. Sure knows which end is up."

"And I'll endorse both women," I said. "I've talked with them at length, helped Lola build the Portland Park teen and youth councils, and know how much our organizing means to Lori personally."

"Could we trust them as couriers too?" Burt said.

"Definitely!" I said. "The whole shebang!"

"Shebang!" Sarah said. "That's it!"

Burt went off to get them. Didn't take us long to decide our conditions. Until the bosses dropped charges and released all their hostages, seized the assets of the illegal City Militia, charged its members with murder, and granted us an hour of daily airtime on each of the twenty largest radio stations, we would not talk about settling.

"But there's one more thing," I said. "Karen insisted last night we make them sign a guarantee that negotiators won't be arrested or freed hostages rearrested."

Vincent shook his head. "Not worth the paper it's printed on. What do I say, 'But, Fat Cat, you promised?' And he says, 'Tough shit, Wójcik,' like they always do?"

"Agreed!" I said. "They have ta back it up with a million-dollar surety bond. They default, People's Union gets the cash money. Snap!" I clapped my hands. "Like that!"

"Whew!" Obie said. "Our Karen is one smart woman. Second that motion."

"All hands on deck," Linda said.

When Lori and Lola wheeled a cartful of groceries toward the kitchen, Lori said, "Something else, huh? Nine people all have the name Buddy!" Which set us off laughing.

While they made lunch, we figured out how to ratchet up our strike by organizing walkouts at the businesses that were still operating; flooding corporate switchboards with calls; getting people to pay bills two days late; having everyone make appointments with their elected representatives including judges, one after another, every five minutes; and mass-picketing the state legislature and city council.

"How do we do that from here?" Linda said.

We went back and forth, realized we still had Ma, Clara, Margaret, Blanche, Eugene, Barb, Willi, Ruka, Daniel, and a couple of dozen other seasoned organizers. With Lola and Lori as couriers, we could tackle all this and get everyone's input. If we were off target, they'd let us know and we'd get back on track.

"Me, I think, we done did it!" Obie said. "I'm a-goin' for a ten-minute walk back and forth around the dorm. Anyone else a-comin'?" He stood up, sang a marching tune.

We followed him, singing along, laughing. But underneath, I thought about Rennie and the other captives. I knew everyone else did too.

Lori and Lola made yummy chicken vegetable soup, served it with rolls hot from the mill ovens, with Strike! Cookies for dessert.

We tuned the radio to KPFP. "Afternoon Labor News with Nora O'Farrell. Unions in Albany, New York; Monroe, Michigan; Youngstown,

CHAPTER 17, TURNING NIGHTMARES INSIDE OUT

Ohio; and Milwaukee went on strike today to demand a two-fifty indexed minimum wage, Minneapolis Standard Work Contracts, and in support of the Minneapolis General Strike. So far, it's only a few unions in each city, but our contacts tell us it could spread fast."

I jumped up, clapped my hands once. "Hot dog! We're gonna win! Best way to put the screws on the Fat Cats ever."

We carried on so loud, the mayor coulda heard us all the way downtown.

Burt, grinning, nodded his head. "I'm so glad we're using the dorm this way. Kind of poetic justice, you know. Father had it built back in 1902 just after the big wave of Minneapolis strikes. Used it in the 1903 flour loaders strike for scabs and several times after that. Didn't look like this back then. No sofas or easy chairs. Privies outside, no toilets or sinks even. Beds were stacked three high, ends touching, rows just thirty inches apart. Workers got eight hours to sleep, then another guy used that bed."

"Did you build the dining room and kitchen later," Linda said. "Back in '03, the mill owners had a restaurant in a separate building."

"You know your history, all right," Burt said. "Father added them in 1922 so he could keep crews here and the mill working during blizzards. Those men had no choice. Today, we shut down the mill in a big storm and ask for volunteers for the snow-clearing crew. It's a tight-knit group does that now, and they consider it their privilege."

That night at dinner, Lola brought us a cassette tape from Ma. "She said it's feedback on your strategy, just a few small suggestions. You look just like her, Linda!"

It felt so good to hear the voices of our relatives and friends. When Laura said she and her dad were going to visit Billy the next day and Ma told us she and Clara would visit Rennie, Linda and I both cried.

We resolved the questions they had, recorded our comments. Then I said, "Please, Ma, Clara, tell Karen I love her. I got everything figured out. I'm hers forever."

Clarence shook my hand, clapped me on the back. "Congratulations, man!"

After dinner, we played Scrabble, which I'd never actually done before.

"I'm a-telling you," Obie said, "Paulie has a dictionary in his head!"

It felt strange and somehow wonderful, telling eight other people goodnight. When we turned out the lights, with just a dim night lamp on top of the bookshelf leaving the dorm almost completely dark, I thought I'd wait up for the moon, realized the windows were blacked out, pulled the blankets up to my chin. Thought of Rennie. I imagined she was kissing my face, my dick sprung to attention. I braced for the snake attack. Didn't happen.

"Paavali, I want you so much!" she said in my mind.

"I'm yahrs, Rennie. All yahrs. Now and forever!"

Gently, I took off her clothes. Even in the dark, I could see her gorgeousness perfectly. My whole body throbbed.

Ya can't touch yahrself, Paavali. Ya can't move or make any noises. Ya don't wanna disturb anyone here! Or embarrass them. Clasp yahr hands together, keep them above yahr belly button!

In my head, Rennie took off my shirt, left a trail of kisses from my neck to my navel and back up, her body quivering as our tongues caressed. My heart was going a couple of hundred miles an hour. Then, slowly, I slid down under her, kissed her breasts, said, "I love ya, Rennie!" As I sucked her nipples, she tightened her legs around me.

"Rennie, ya want yahr favorite?"

"Please!" Her voice was vibrating as hard as her body.

In our bed, in my mind, I pivoted under her, licked her as I went, her belly, her thighs, all around her vulva, then deep inside, savoring her aroma and flavor, then back around the outside and toward the top. Her body tensed, she made a little grunt, tensed some more, another grunt, fluid warmed and caressed my face, I licked her more. *Gosh, the taste is wonderful. I can't get enough of it. Pleasuring her is a big-huge turn on. Ohmygod, I love her so much! Hold back, Paavali, make sure she gets where she wants to be!*

Suddenly, her body relaxed. I took a deep breath, held it, and I came, longer, harder, more intense than ever, but totally quiet. Rennie's image faded from my mind. My hands were still clasped over my abdomen. I allowed myself one deep sigh. A wave of joy and intense love for Rennie washed over me. *Ya did it, Paavali! Ya made love with Rennie! Ya freed yahrself of the snakes!*

CHAPTER 17, TURNING NIGHTMARES INSIDE OUT

I whirled around and around, into astonishing relaxation and a deep, healing sleep.

But... Then I was in my dungeon again.

"Horse puckies!" I shouted. "I'm outta here!"

Deadwood, coming from nowhere, charged at me, swinging a hammer aimed to hit my head. There was a loud clang! The hammer shattered into bits. He pulled his arm back for a roundhouse punch, but midway, his fist jerked back toward him, his fingers all twisted and broken.

A City Militia jeep drove through the wall, right at me, smashed into something I couldn't see. The whole front was battered. A wheel fell off. Gremling and Prichard pulled themselves from the wreckage, aimed rifles at me. The bullets sounded like they were hitting glass. First Prichard fell to the ground, then Gremling.

Ah! The ricochet!

I stepped up to the wall, put my hands against it, pushed. With a loud roar, the stones crumbled into dust. Over the rubble I stepped, into a sun-drenched clearing amidst a forest of plum and apple trees, birds singing, leaves and ripe fruit on the trees. My filthy rags transformed into a tuxedo. From around a bend in the footpath, Rennie came running toward me in a long white dress with a bridal veil, arms wide open.

CHAPTER 18, THROWING FAT CATS OFF-BALANCE

SATURDAY-WEDNESDAY, MARCH 18-22, 1972

Early Saturday morning, Russ sent us a note that blank arrest warrants with no charges had been issued for the nine of us. Then Lori brought us a message from Ma and Clara. Rennie had been moved from Shakopee Prison. She was in shackles, with two armed guards, on a public bus to the high-security women's prison for felony convicts in Billings, Montana, twenty-two hours away. The warden's office at Shakopee said Rennie was a flight risk and there were no secure women's prisons any closer.

Clara was furious, said she was driving right to Billings. I desperately wanted to go with her, but Gordy sent us a tape saying I'd be arrested, and we couldn't risk that. The nine of us talked about who could go with Clara. Everyone was overcommitted, but we finally decided to ask Sandi and Scott.

Then, another message came that Laura and Timothée were told Billy had been moved to the high-security unit in Stillwater Prison. They went to see him there but were turned away because he was not approved for visitors. Corrections Department officials were not available when *People's Free Press* reporters called. The *Free Press* ran a huge front-page headline, "Disappeared!" with photos of Rennie and Billy.

I was crazy with worry, terrified Rennie would be beaten up or molested, or both, imagining her trying to sleep on a sheetless mattress

CHAPTER 18, THROWING FAT CATS OFF-BALANCE

stinking of urine, in a tiny, dark, cold, high-security cell. But I tamped it down because I knew the only way to free her was for us to act fast and aggressively, so I had to stay focused.

The American-Built Automotive car assembly factory in St. Paul was still operating, but we'd heard workers there were tired of forced overtime, workplace injuries, and disrespect. Willi, Betty, and Barb went to talk with Assembler's Union Local 655 on Saturday afternoon. They voted to strike Saturday night.

An organizing group at Cloud Ten Refrigerator Factory upstate in St. Cloud contacted People's Union for help. We sent Li'l Mikey, Norma Lund, and Bucky up to visit them. Workers, who called the factory "Finger Chopper," were ready to strike over safety hazards, just needed encouragement and advice. They voted to walk out Sunday.

Cecil and his brother helped grain elevator workers in Becker and machinists in Big Lake vote to strike. Stories came over the Associated Press and United Press wires about the strike in Milwaukee spreading from factories to breweries and new strikes by oil refinery workers in Houston, as well as Pittsburg steel workers.

We finished our citywide vote, got approval of our demands by just about every working person in Minneapolis, and their endorsement of our settlement committee.

Late Sunday afternoon, Lori brought us a telegram from Clara.

KAREN OKAY VISITED TWICE
LOVES YOU TOO PAUL CLARA

A huge burst of energy made me skip around the room, jumping over beds and doing handstands, whooping my head off, all while everyone clapped and laughed.

Monday morning, Warehouse Workers Local 1944 announced a strike, teaching and research assistants at the University of Minnesota walked out, ten thousand people picketed the state legislature, six thousand the city council.

Before nine in the morning, we had a package ready for Algernon H. H. Bobellon with our conditions for settlement talks, our demands, and a copy of the Minneapolis Standard Work Contract. We wrote a news release. Our pressroom printed copies.

"We can't send this out until the Fat Cats call us," Clarence said. "Would make us seem too eager."

"Agreed!" Linda said. "We gotta be groovin' up slowly."

So we waited.

Judge Coventry denied our habeas corpus writs. Russ filed them with the US Attorney, along with a request for a criminal complaint against the Minnesota and Montana Corrections Departments.

We listened to Russ's tape that Lola brought us. "Here's the criminal complaint strategy. Karen's a minor. They transported her across state lines. Jailing someone with no charges and removing them from the jurisdiction that would arraign them, making arraignment and a trial impossible, is immoral *and* illegal. This is a clear violation of the Mann Act. And! And! Mann Act penalties are a fine up to ten thousand dollars and up to ten years in jail. You have a Mann Act conviction? Kiss your career goodbye.

"But wait, there's more. Heh-heh-heh. I went nosing around to see what I could find on this Richard Prichard person. Wait'll you hear this! He's Hastings-Dankworth's great-grandson. Been fined six times and jailed twice for perjury. Holy roasted minnows! Will a jury believe his lies? Do pigs have wings? Let's file a libel lawsuit against him for claiming Paulie and Karen tried to kill him. And maybe a little bird is going to sing to us about who was in on the decision to kidnap Karen."

About 10:30, Lori brought us a tape from Judge Haddad. She'd just gotten a call from the Justice Department with a heads-up. At noon, the Criminal Division would announce an investigation of the Communal Association's role in the falsified amicus curiae briefs. And Fred's assassination. Just before twelve, we sat around the radio waiting for the big announcement.

"This is Keanna with what might be the biggest newsbreak of the year. A Justice Department investigation reveals Hennepin County Hospital Director of Social Work Arthur Schulz wrote more than a thousand fraudulent amicus curiae briefs over a ten-year period. These briefs, from people who have a "strong interest" in a case but no legal connection to it, are intended to influence the court's decisions. And they sure did.

CHAPTER 18, THROWING FAT CATS OFF-BALANCE

"The investigation found Schulz wrote 1,147 briefs, starting in 1957, with claims that were completely false. These falsified briefs were always for trials of Black and working-class people. Cases involving Schulz briefs had ninety-two percent conviction rates, longer sentences, bigger fines. But here's the most amazing part," Keanna's voice said. "The investigation found memos from the Communal Association to Schulz telling him which cases to write briefs for. And why! This morning, US Marshals arrested Schulz, Hennepin County Judge Haskell Coventry, and Archibald Hastings-Dankworth, Communal Association chairman. More arrests are expected. We'll have details as we get them."

"Look what you started, Paulie!" Linda said. "Schulz never should've messed with you."

"Brace yahrselves!" I said. "This'll bring the Fat Cats to the bargaining table."

"You started this, Paul?" Sarah pointed at me. "How?"

"Well, it all began when I realized I had to help Roger turn his life around." I went on, told the whole story.

"No wonder Keanna calls you St. Paul," Vincent said.

"On the radio?" I said.

"Yep. More than once."

I felt my face burning.

Linda patted my shoulder. "Get used to it, St. Paulie."

I'd gotten used to a whole bunch of stuff, but I couldn't imagine ever being comfortable with sainthood.

At 12:25, Ma paged us on the CB radio. "Certainly here. Do you read me, Historian and Mahrove-Rove?"

"Roger!" we both said.

"Bobcart guy says he's ready to talk turkey. Details soon. We need a bread delivery. You copy?"

"Roger, Certainly."

"Over and out," Ma said.

"On my way," Lola said.

"I don't get it," Magdalena said, hands turned upward, stretched out in front of her. "Who's Certainly? Why a bread delivery?"

"Certainly is Shirley," Linda said. "Ma's real name. Shirley, Surely, Certainly."

"A bread delivery means use a Mill box truck, not a car," I said. "Because they think they're being watched and followed."

"And pull into the Workers' Market loading dock," Lori said. "Actually bring a couple cartons of bread inside, which they always need, they're selling so much."

"Got it!" Magdalena's hands went back to her lap. "Smart thinking."

The CB radio came to life again. Ma told us State Senator Erik Callio, US Senator Jensen, Chamber of Commerce President Bartholomew Holmes, and seven other CEOs wanted to negotiate.

We finished getting our settlement packets ready, prepared the distribution lists. We'd deliver our packet to every politician, the CEOs who asked for it, and the chamber of commerce. With an added news release, it would go to all newspapers and broadcasters. We'd give *People's Free Press* a head start.

"I sure am glad we got different cars to use today," Lori said. "Last two days, I feel like I've been tailed. Thought about it last night. Hold on a moment." She went into the kitchen, came back with a hat with big-huge ear flaps. Put her long, red hair up in a bun, hat over it. Added steel-rimmed dark glasses. "Plus this man's work coat was my dad's before he died." She slipped into it. "Do I look like a guy?"

"The baggy coat and work pants sure do help," I said.

"Your voice is low enough to pass," Magdalena said. "Now walk. No swaying!"

"Sir, do you always carry a handbag?" Sarah said.

Lori blushed. "Oops!" She took some things out, put them in her coat pockets.

"Those pink gloves," Clarence said. "Nope!"

I handed her my gloves.

"You got it now," Dina said. "Remember, you can't go into the ladies' room, sir!"

"And don't open your coat," Fiona said. " 'Cause you're not exactly flat."

"But otherwise you're okay, sir," Linda said. "You got your marching orders!"

CHAPTER 18, THROWING FAT CATS OFF-BALANCE

Todd's voice came over the CB radio. "Attention, Creekers and People's Union Members! Big breaking news on KPFP in three minutes. Tune in now!"

We tuned in, listened to the end of a bluegrass music program. Then Keanna said, "Breaking News! Hennepin County District Court Judge Badah Haddad today called the arrest of one of her campaign managers 'a deliberate attempt to sabotage my reelection.' Here's Judge Haddad with the story."

"No charges have been filed against William R. Anderson. He hasn't been accused of a crime. But he's been held in isolation for three days, with no visitors allowed, including his lawyers. My other campaign manager, Belinda M. Frisk, managed to avoid arrest by going into hiding. She isn't accused of a crime either. This is un-American and totally illegal. I have petitioned the federal court to order the immediate release of Mr. Anderson and the other imprisoned People's Union organizers, none of whom have been accused of any crimes."

When Lola brought the Fat Cats' tape, there were no surprises. The senators, the chamber of commerce guy, and CEOs sounded imperious, demanding, angry, impatient.

"Which probably means they're terrified!" I said.

"They're seeing the strike spread hour by hour," Vincent said. "Now we're hitting up north and across the country and a judge is standing up for us, so yeah, they're scared. Shitless."

"Do you think we could just go...see them?" Dina said.

"No way!" Magdalena said, clapping her hands together twice. "We have to be stubborn, strong, elusive, and more demanding than they are. We have the upper hand. Let's keep it. Until they drop charges, release all hostages, seize the City Militia's assets, charge its members with murder, sign a million buck surety bond, prove to us they have the authority to make a deal, and grant us daily airtime...We. Don't. Talk. Settlement!" She pounded the table with each word. "And we keep escalating our strike!"

"Sorry," Dina said. "You're right. Just wishful thinking."

Lola looked at Lori, grinned, nodded. "I'll disguise myself a different way." She opened her purse, pulled out a mirror, lipstick, makeup. Quickly, her eyes got bigger, her face longer, her mouth wider until she became a different person—older, closed, hard, remote. It was sorta amazing.

"Do I know ya?" I said.

"Never saw you before, buster," she growled, grin conflicting with her new face.

"Ready to roll!" Lori said. "I'll feel rich all afternoon driving a '66 Mustang."

"Me too," Lola said. "That '64 Barracuda they got us looks hot!"

"Hard to believe they were junkers 'til our Beth's crew fixed them up," I said.

After they'd left, Clarence said, "You know the bosses won't just agree to our conditions right off the bat. How about we record a message so we have it ready. All hands on deck?" He looked around. "Agreed! Now what do we want to say?"

"It's not a heavy lift," Linda said. "How's this? 'If you can't agree to these modest terms, you're not serious about settlement talks. Call us when you're ready to be sensible.' And then each of us say our name and titles. And that's it!"

"Ya aced it!" I said, putting my thumbs up. "Can Ma, Margaret, Willi, Ruka, Russ, Susie, Betty, Bucky, and Li'l Mikey add their names?"

"Yeah! Yes! Yup! Good idea!"

Just after three that afternoon, Bert brought us a tape from Ma.

"First of all, Paulie, Linda, Clarence, I want you to know Walt just stopped by my office. He was worried I'm lonely without my family here, which holy moly, I am. So he said he could come have dinner with me. I said, 'Yes, indeedy!' I just love that kid. Now here's the response from Bobellon. Stand firm, okay?"

I nodded as if Ma was in the room and could see me.

There were a couple of clicks and then, "Mr. Bobellon here, AHH Bobellon-Carter, Incorporated. Senator Kallio, Mr. Holmes, Mr. Corbyn, Senator Jensen, Representative Rinder, Mr. Bailey, Mr. Palmer, Alderman Ose, Mr. Kingsbury, Mr. Meilander, and Mr. Fitch all concur. Your conditions are onerous and quite unreasonable. We must talk, face-to-face, without these stipulations that only serve to inhibit a productive discussion. We invite Mr. Mäkinen and Miss Ahlberg to sit down with us at 9:30 tomorrow morning at the Minneapolis Club Imperial Room."

CHAPTER 18, THROWING FAT CATS OFF-BALANCE

"Horse puckies!" I said, making a motion as if I was throwing a handful at Bobellon. "How tone-deaf can ya get?"

"And how out of it?" Dina said. "He doesn't know Karen's been kidnapped?"

"Let's add a couple of sentences to our tape," Clarence said. "Mr. Bobellon! You don't know Ms. Ahlberg was kidnapped by the Minnesota Department of Corrections? You haven't heard she was shackled like a wild animal and taken to a jail in Montana? You have no idea there were no charges filed against her?" He held his hands out, palms up. "What do you think, friends?"

We all nodded.

"I want to add more," Sarah said. "You've no clue a Mann Act criminal complaint has been filed with Minneapolis federal court? That'll put some fear into them."

"And one more," Obie said. "Invitin' Ms. Ahlberg to a mornin' meetin' tomorrow is a cruel joke."

We added to the tape. Burt brought it to Ma, came back with a tape from Vance Amundsden, president of Local 1208 Grain Elevator Workers. "We've gotten an urgent request for help from a union organizing committee at Lake States Fertilizer & Seed. Their entire committee of fourteen people was fired. Anything we need to know?"

"That's easy," Dina said, nodding. "Yes! Help them organize a strike today, if possible. Kingsbury, their CEO, is on Bobellon's negotiating committee."

"Beautiful!" Vincent said, laughing.

Todd's voice came over the CB radio. "Creekers and People's Union members! Major announcement in three minutes on KPFP! Tune in now!"

We turned on the radio. Paz's band was just finishing a rollicking dance tune, so I jumped up, motioned to Linda, and we danced for two-and-a-half minutes.

"We interrupt 'Dancin' With Paz' for a special news bulletin," Keanna said. "The National Labor Relations Board announced this afternoon, Minnesota Consolidated Construction Services was guilty of unfair labor practices when it didn't pay gandy dancers at the rates their contract specified for straight hours and overtime. They ordered the company to pay their workers the difference plus interest and a penalty of a thousand dollars per worker by March 27th. Congratulations to our hard-working gandy dancers!"

Paz started up a new tune. This time, it was Clarence and Obie bouncing off the walls, then Obie dancing with Magdalena, Clarence with Sarah, and the rest of us waltzing away too, switching partners on each new tune so everyone got a turn.

"We flat out won't hear anything more from Bobellon and crew until tomorrow," I said. "So hot dog! Let's enjoy ourselves!"

We'd only gotten four dances in when Keanna stopped the music. "Sorry to interrupt your dance time again, but we have another major bulletin. Here's Jyri Tuomi, Community Affairs and Heritage Coordinator at L&M Federal Credit Union."

Jyri's booming voice filled the room. "Our Board of Directors voted this afternoon that L&M Federal Credit will immediately donate three hundred thousand dollars to a strike fund for workers at Lake States Fertilizer & Seed Company, American-Built Automotive, and AHH Bobellon-Carter, Inc."

We whooped, cheered, and hollered louder than before, fingers in the air with the V sign.

Jyri continued, "Plus another three hundred thousand dollars to the Shingle Creek Strike Fund. We will administer the Lake States, American-Built Automotive, and Bobcart fund ourselves, which will issue benefit checks to strikers starting tomorrow and personally deliver a certified check to the Shingle Creek Citywide Strike Fund tomorrow morning. Any unused strike fund moneys will be donated to the People's Union once the strike is settled. Good luck, fellow workers! You deserve a break!"

"Holy cowbops! Hot dog! This is too mega-magnificent. It's gotta be a dream!"

"Me, I am a-hopin' it lasts right on through settlement talks so we'll be a-knowin' how to do it when we wake up!" Obie said.

"Groovin' up fastly," Linda said. "Let's dance!"

A few minutes later, Lola and Lori pushed the kitchen cart into the dorm with a basket of Strike! Cookies, a pile of Roger's Chocolate Coffee-n-Cake packages, carafes of coffee and tea.

"Burt congratulates you on your victories," Lori said. "Sent this all up to you. Can we party with you?"

"Two of my favorite dance partners!" I said. "Course ya can! Right?" I looked at my sister Linda, my friends.

"Let's boogie!" Obie sang out.

We had just finished our refreshments and danced to a few songs when Keanna broke in again. "This is the day for hot, breaking news, all right. Police Chief Jensen, Lieutenant Colding, and Officers Doyle, Jacobsen, Jaarvinen, Latvala, Lindgren, Madsen, and Meyer have been arrested by US Marshals for a murder-for-hire conspiracy to execute Parks Superintendent Kincaid (Fred) Corwin III. Doyle, Jacobsen, and Meyer, who allegedly fired the shots that killed Corwin, are also charged with first-degree murder."

"That's like sending Bobellon a note," Clarence said, "We ain't just fucking around! Pardon my French."

"Yes, indeed!" Obie said. "Bet we'll be a-getting' some Fat Cat action tomorrow, bright and early."

The CB radio crackled. "HospitalStories, Certainly here. Horseback ride time!"

"Roger, I copy," Lori said. "Saddling up now. Over and out." She turned toward us. "Shirley must have a tape or something. Goody! I get to drive the mustang again!"

Linda pointed at Lori. "Why that CB handle?"

"Saturdays I volunteer reading stories to kids in the hospital downtown."

"Watch out! They're gonna be calling you St. Lori soon," Linda said.

She shook her head. "Not even close, Linda! Not even close."

Lori, there and back in half an hour, handed us a large envelope and a small one. "Shirley says don't even look at the large envelope first. Tape in the small envelope needs attention right now. Mike's standing by, waiting for an answer."

We played the cassette. "Hey, Paulie, Linda, friends. Remember we voted a big yes about starting a Shingle Creek Builders Co-op? Both in the Council and Association? Now's the time to do it! We can steal a whole bunch of strikers from some big corporations and use the L&M strike fund to pay them. And get started on our dreams for Scandinavian Restaurant, International Kitchen, Mabel's Place, Shingle Creek Health Clinic, and the Working Class Museum. Say yes, and I'll get an approval vote on this end and get ahold of L&M to make sure they're okay with it. Let's get it rolling!"

I switched to record so Mike could hear our discussion. "A genius in bloom!" I said. "We announce that tomorrow, we'll scare the living daylights out of Bobellon and friends. Ya good with that?"

Obie stood up. "Me, I got one condition. There's a lot of young Black guys would kill for a construction job but never had a chance to get on-the-job experience. I'm a-wantin' fifteen Black trainees hired."

"All guys?" Linda said. "Houston, we have a problem!"

"You're right! Gals too," Obie said.

"Let's break this down into steps," Clarence said. "First, do we agree that now's the time to announce and start this from a strategy point of view?"

"Darn right it is," Vincent said.

Everyone else nodded.

"Next, should we use L&M to fund the wages?" Clarence said.

We talked it out and agreed.

"Third, do we all vote for fifteen Black trainees?"

"Fifteen minimum," Fiona said. "Five of them Black women, minimum. Another dozen White women, minimum. Depending on how many workers we'll need, which we haven't figured out yet, we may well want more."

We voted to approve, start getting people in for interviews, begin doing a lot of fast figuring with Blanche, Hank, and Harry about hiring needs.

I got on the CB. "Mahrove-Rove here. ShortyMike, ya read me?"

"Roger, Mahrove-Rove."

"It's a yes! Details coming. Okay to start. We'll announce tomorrow early."

"That is big-ass awesome, Mahrove-Rove. I'll get L&M's approval. Over and out."

"Aw gee!" Linda said. "I could've danced all night! I guess we have to be heavy into getting the announcement ready."

"Me too!" Clarence said. "We finish early enough, let's dance some more. Need to work off some of that nervous energy."

Inside the large envelope, *LIFE* magazine had a cover photo of Bonnie and Dozer in open coffins before the funeral under the headline, "Tragedy

CHAPTER 18, THROWING FAT CATS OFF-BALANCE

at Shingle Creek." Inside was a two-page photo spread of the funeral. Tears came to my eyes. I thought about Rennie, began sobbing. Magdalena took me aside, talked to me, almost like Clara, Ma, or Carleton would. Told me again and again Rennie would be freed soon. I finally calmed down, washed my face, pulled myself together, was able to take part in the escalation strategy discussion.

Mid-morning next day, we heard a news update on KPFP. "Two more strikes declared this morning," Nora's voice said. "Electric Power-Minneapolis Locals 33 and 209, on strike! Local 209 Vice President Delphine Bjorhus said today that 'no meters will be read, no bills sent out, no shut-offs done until the strike is settled. We demand the two-fifty indexed minimum and the Minneapolis Standard Work Contract.' But here's the real whopper. All five unions at Lakes State Fertilizer & Seed voted to strike this morning. 'Never been a strike at Lakes State,' a combined union statement said. 'But we've put up with starvation wages and disrespect long enough. We demand the Minneapolis Standard Work Contract!'"

"Gadzooks!" Clarence said. "This will put J. H. Kingsbury's feet in the fire! It'll be easier to negotiate with him now. He'll see we mean business."

"So they've got, what, eight CEOs on their negotiating committee?" Vincent said. "And all but three have strikes on their hands? Feet in the fire, Clarence? I think it's another part of the anatomy!" He broke out in laughter so contagious it caught all of us.

"From his cell in Stillwater Prison," Nora's voice said, "where he's being held without any charges filed or any arraignment or possibility of bail, People's Union organizer Nelson Nesheim today announced he's running for state senate against twelve-term incumbent Republican Butch Larsen, Senate President."

"Holy cowbops!" I said. "We're going after almost their whole negotiating team."

I started feeling optimistic again. But then, we got a tape from Russ. "Minneapolis Federal Judge Luther Godwin just granted our habeas corpus writs. Federal marshals are at Stillwater Prison, arranging for Billy, Nelson, Herb, Jack, and Marek to be released tomorrow. But the marshal who went to Shakopee Prison called in to say there were no records for Karen. Judge Godwin was furious and ordered the marshal to arrest the warden and open an investigation. Hang on, Paulie! It's going to be a bumpy ride, but we have a federal judge on our side."

Wednesday morning, things moved at the speed of light. We got a CB radio message from Russ. The million-dollar surety bond had been signed. The federal attorney charged City Militia's members with murder and attempted murder. Gremling and Prichard faced sedition charges for forming an unconstitutional militia. Federal marshals began arresting them. Gremling was in the hospital's prison ward.

But it wasn't fast enough for me. My Rennie was still behind bars. Despite everyone's support and assurance, I was terrified, furious, angry, sad. In the morning, when I wasn't needed for strategizing, I walked in circles around the dorm room, hands in my pockets, my feet pounding so hard I thought I'd crack the concrete floor.

It helped when Russ finally let us know we could come out of hiding.

Lori and Lola drove us all back to Shingle Creek. A crowd welcomed us in the Betty Hall parking lot. Half The Nines played the Shingle Creek welcome song on their kazoos, the other half sang the words. We all got lotsa hugs.

Russ's car bounced into the lot, the doors flew open, he and Sylvia ran over to hug all nine of us.

"We must—*must!*—talk about this proof of authority to negotiate," Russ said. "The CEOs are pressing for a late afternoon meeting today. Let's go get prepared."

Russ and Sylvia trotted toward the entrance. We followed them to the meeting room. The Council, Neighborhood Association, and People's Union leaders were with us, except for the hostages.

The moment we sat down, Rollie strode in. "Just got their commitment of free airtime. A messenger's on the way here with details and the signed document. It's a mix of big and small stations, pretty close to what we demanded."

"Big five included?" Russ said.

"Four of them," Rollie said. "No surprise there. You folks get on it. I'll monitor KPFP news."

"Here's the deal," Russ said. He passed out a bunch of contracts. "Ninety-two medium-to-large corporations signed binding agreements to accept their negotiating committee's decisions. So far, so good."

CHAPTER 18, THROWING FAT CATS OFF-BALANCE

"The hitch," Sylvia said, "is that we're demanding legislation. These agreements don't mention that. A court could rule that by signing them, we gave up our right to demand legislative action."

"Take a moment. Read through them," Russ said. "Pay close attention to the 'sole remedies' clause."

The room was quiet for a few minutes. Then Obie said, "Clear as day to me. They're a-tryin' to hand us the shitty end of the stick!"

"So what do we do about it?" Mike said.

I closed my eyes. *What would Rennie do? And why?* I almost felt like Rennie was speaking directly to me. Eyes still shut, I stood up. "I have ta tell ya, we demanded *they* provide proof to *us*. We did not agree to sign these. So thanks, Fat Cats, these are what we needed to hold yahr feet to the fire. Or as Vincent says, some other sensitive part of the body. But *we* never agreed to sign *these*!"

"See, Paulie," Magdalena said. "I knew you're really tough!"

"Holy moly," Ma said. "Let's make copies of these, file them away in two different safe places. Nice going, everyone!"

"Can I be the one to tell them?" Linda said, "Too bad, so sad, we didn't ever agree to sign *these* documents. Now let's get down to the matter at hand!"

The mood in the room lifted several notches.

"Let's take a vote," Clarence said, "Because gadzooks, we need to move on."

"But what if they walk out when Linda too bads them?" Mike said.

"Not a chance," Fiona said. "Mike, I understand why you're worried, with all we have at stake here. But look at what they've already done! Charges *have* been dropped. City Militia members *have* been arrested. The million-dollar surety bond *has* been signed. Agreements to negotiate *have* been signed. We never thought they'd do that stuff, and they wouldn't have if they weren't desperate to settle. We can never forget that!"

"Yeah, you're right, for sure," Mike said. "Thanks! I needed that reminder."

"We all did," Vincent said.

The vote was unanimous.

Rollie poked his head in the doorway. "Reviewed the airtime grants. They meet all our criteria." He handed the packet to Russ.

Susie ran into the room holding a yellow sheet from the AP newswire. "Extra! Extra! Federal marshals just seized forty-eight Jeeps and twelve dozen rifles from the City Militia! They're hunting for more at Hastings-Danksworth's Wisconsin farms."

"Thanks, Suze! Is that a front-pager?" Russ said.

"Unless some bigger news pushes it to page two."

We reviewed the Fat Cats' free airtime proposal, approved it, had just finished drawing up a plan for who would speak on which station each of the next five days when Rollie came running in, radio in his hands, cord dangling behind him. "KPFP major news alert on the CB, 'bout two minutes!" He plugged the radio in, set it down.

Jill's voice filled the air, singing the "Union Maid" song. Then Keanna said, "Another hot news day! Federal Judge Luther Godwin just announced a grand jury has indicted City Militia members, as well as Clive Gremling and Richard Prichard. This means there *will* be a trial. Congratulations, Creekers and People's Union members! One more step forward for all working people!"

Rollie unplugged the radio. "I'll bring it back if there's more news breaking."

"Congratulations to us!" Russ said. "Now let's all take a deep breath and keep our hands on the plow. We need to talk about the meeting venue."

"Could you lay out the issues?" Barb said. "Why not have it at Betty Hall?"

"We couldn't walk out if we needed to," Mike said.

"We want it in a neutral place," Sylvia said. "Better for us emotionally. You know, we don't want to feel like we're dealing with hostile invaders or a hostile environment."

"And!" Russ said. "And! If we need to have a quick private session to make last-minute hush-hush strategy decisions, we must be certain it's not bugged and doesn't have secret chambers or closets where spies can listen in on us despite our jammers. Do the Minneapolis Club's walls have ears? Do cats, skinny or fat, hear stuff?"

"How about our church," Obie said. "Willow Avenue AME. I could call my pastor. We have four classrooms. Soundproofed."

"You ever seen a Fat Cat there, Obie?" Clarence said.

He shook his head. "Nope."

"I like that idea," Sylvia said. "Throws them way off-balance from a psychological point of view and forces them to recognize the Black community too."

"We have to make the Fat Cats pay the church," Mike said. "They have expenses too, you know."

We voted in favor. Obie made a quick call from my office. The pastor agreed. Russ called Bobellon's private number. He muttered and spluttered but agreed we would meet at four o'clock at Obie's church.

I closed my eyes again, stood up. "About the legislation issue. We simply tell them that we require their agreement be backed up with legislation. If they say no, we leave. And keep escalating the strike. Are ya good with that?"

"Why didn't we see that before?" Linda said.

"Because Karen's not here," I said.

"Yeah, what's going on with that?" Clarence said.

Rollie popped in again. "Just got a phone call from Brenda. She has Billy, Marek, Jack, Herb, and Nelson in the car, leaving Stillwater, heading right here. Says they're hungry after five days of prison grub. We have thirty minutes to plan a welcome."

"Russ, would Atkinson know what's happening to Karen?" I said. "Can ya call him?"

"Yes, yes. Been checking all day, but he might have an update now."

I nodded. "Russ, Ma, Linda, Clarence, Obie, Magdalena, can ya come to my office, so we can take care of Karen? The rest of ya, can ya organize the welcome and food? All hands on deck?"

Russ sat at Rennie's desk, dialed the phone. Didn't say much. Listened. Hung up. "He's on the phone with his associate in Billings. His assistant says the situation's complicated. About ten minutes and he'll call back."

Seemed like the longest ten minutes of my life before the phone rang. Russ put it on speaker.

"My apologies," Atkinson said. "Here's what's going on. Montana Corrections insists their contract with Minnesota Corrections requires delivery of Ms. Ahlberg back to Shakopee, so Montana won't release her in Billings despite the Minnesota federal court release order. But Montana prison guards won't accompany Karen back to Minnesota because they're afraid of being charged with a Mann Act violation. Minneapolis Federal

Judge Luther Godwin was beyond furious when he heard that. He called Montana Federal Judge Finley Campbell, an old Harvard Law School buddy. Judge Campbell will look into this tomorrow."

I was slumped down in my chair so far my chin was almost on the conference table.

"That's the bad news," Atkinson said. "On the other side of the ledger, Judge Godwin just decided to hold Montana and Minnesota Corrections officials in contempt because his court order for Ms. Ahlberg's immediate release was violated. He has issued bench warrants for the prompt arrest of the Minnesota officials and extradition of Montana officials to Minneapolis. Is Mr. Mäkinen on this call?"

"Yes, sir," I said, sitting up straight.

"I understand this is personally very hard for you," Atkinson said. "I am so sorry. I want you to know, Karen's family, plus my associate in Billings, Samantha Gladstone, are visiting Ms. Ahlberg twice daily, updating her, making sure she's okay, bringing her law journals to read, chocolate, and personal items."

"Thank you, Mr. Atkinson. This has been like torture."

"Of course it has. You'll have her back very, very soon. We're pushing. Hard!"

"May I ask, sir, how they got the goods on Tewkesbury and Pukari?"

"You bet! Duane Pukari, looking for a plea bargain, spilled the beans the moment he was arrested. Judge Godwin has him speaking to the FBI. Looks like the Justice Department will be involved. And between you and me, Algernon Bobellon will not take this well at all."

"Thanks, Corey," Russ said. "We all really appreciate your help."

When we walked into the reception area of Iversen Hall, it was full of people. Blanche gave me a bear hug. "Welcome back, Paulie! I sure as heck missed you."

"Well, I was comforted to know yahr common sense and steady hand were holding down the fort here." I looked around. Tables had platters of Strike! Cookies, Roger Cakes, and Hot! Chocolate bars, urns of coffee, paper cups, plates, napkins, all in place. "How'd ya get all this together so fast?"

CHAPTER 18, THROWING FAT CATS OFF-BALANCE

"Russ warned us ahead of time. We took some staff off work crews. We have hot soup and Camden Superette sandwiches for the hostages. Seems they didn't eat as well as you folks did in hiding."

Bobby Lund came running over, arm-in-arm with a teenage girl holding a trumpet. She played a quick fanfare. The room quieted.

"On behalf of the Forever Nines, I declare," Bobby said, "Paulie, we sorely missed you! Without you walking through our classroom every day, talking with us about stuff, it was just sort of blah."

I bent down, hugged him. "You, Bobby Lund, are one of our treasures."

"This is Tina, our new fanfareist." Bobby said. "She's from Brooklyn Center, but she wants to volunteer in the warming room. Laura and Daniel say they'd like to let her."

"Why wouldn't we?"

"Remember you once explained to me about tax money supporting us?"

"That's true. So if we get more than a few Brooklyners wanting to join us here, we'll talk to their mayor, work something out. So yeah, Tina, welcome aboard!"

Pretty soon, there was a longer, more elaborate fanfare. Bobby welcomed the hostages home. Billy was holding Linda, crying in his arms. I was so happy for them but felt so sad inside.

"You're missing Karen right now. I can see it on your face," Ruka said. "You thinking about crossing over into campground?"

I nodded. She wrapped her arm around mine. Chatted with me. I told her about wanting wings.

"Yeah, I get that." She sang, "To fly you high, like a sacred dove, over the prison wall, to the woman you love. It's an old Black folk song going way back to slave days." She motioned to Bobby. "Can you play this on the piano for us? I think Paulie needs to sing just about now."

Bobby played. I sang, changing the words slightly.

I'm gonna grow wings,

Like a sacred dove,

Fly over the prison wall,

To the woman I love,

I'm on my way,

My Rennie honey,

I'm on my way.

I'll bend the bars apart

On your cold, dark cell,

Fly ya away on my back,

From those gates of hell.

Ruka and Bobby sang along on the chorus.

I'm on my way,

My Rennie honey,

I'm on my way.

Across miles of prairies,

And over the lakes

I'll keep flyin' ya home

As long as it takes.

I'm on my way,

My Rennie honey,

I'm on my way.

People gathered around us, joined in. Nora asked if she could record.
"You bet! So Rennie can hear it too."
"Rennie's your love name for her?" Nora said.
"Well, I guess the secret's out," I said, feeling myself grinning wider than the Mississippi River.
Nora smiled. "Congratulations, Paulie! Can't wait to see you two reunited."

CHAPTER 19, ROCK AND A HARD PLACE, BAM BOOM!

WEDNESDAY-THURSDAY, MARCH 22-23, 1972

JUST BEFORE WE LEFT FOR the negotiating meeting, Russ called us together for a quick huddle. We chose code words so we could communicate. *Maksapihvi*, which means liver steak in Finnish, signified we must make irate objections. *Fulang*, Swedish for ugly field, and *makeiset*, Finnish for candy, meant time to walk out. The German word for potato, *kartoffel*, meant they can but don't want to, so they don't actually know they can. To indicate we all agreed on something, we would say *kukat*, for flowers in Finnish.

"Remember," Russ said. "These are *not* our friends. We don't want to be nicey-nicey. Do that, and they'll turn on us in a heartbeat. We must be strong. And unyielding. Never let them off the hook!" He punched his palm with his fist.

Gordy, Officer James, and Officer Anderson drove us there in their squad cars. We timed it carefully so we arrived at exactly five to four. There were already thirteen limousines in the church parking lot. We stood there for a moment, staring at them.

A uniformed chauffer opened a limo door. A man in a dark suit and red tie stepped out, leather briefcase under his arm, looked at us, frowned, flared his nostrils. "You arresting some trouble makers, Lieutenant?"

"Allow me to introduce you to the People's Union negotiating team," Gordy said with a hearty laugh. "And who do I have the pleasure of meeting?"

The man took a step back, stuck both hands out in front of him. "Montgomery Q. Palmer, chief operating officer and chairman of the Board, Atlantic & Pacific Trust Bank." He stood there like a deer in the headlights of an onrushing car. Finally muttered, "But, Lieutenant, they're all wearing work clothes."

"Well," I said, "we *are* workers."

Without having to say a word to each other, we formed a line in front of him, none of us smiling. I held out my hand. "Paul Mäkinen, Shingle Creek Park Director, Chair of the Shingle Creek Teen Council, Shingle Creek Industrial Safety Commissioner, Member of the Hennepin County Court's Troubled Youth Advisory Board, Arnray Railroad Safety Corporation Director."

His face tight, his body rigid, Palmer shook my hand. It wasn't a particularly cold day, but his hand felt like glacial ice.

We all used our titles. Everyone had at least three.

Obie led us inside the church.

Look at how uptight Palmer is, off-balance, just like we want him. And he's letting us lead him inside! Wearing work clothes was a genius idea. Thanks, Willi! Forming a reception line was too. Thanks, all of us!

In a large room decorated with children's artwork, twelve grim men in suits were seated along one side of a long table. Palmer sat in the empty chair next to them. They all had name signs on the table in front of them. About five feet away was another long table with fourteen chairs for us, facing the Fat Cats, and three more chairs behind ours for our police bodyguards. As we'd asked, the church had not made name signs for us.

Obie led us between the two tables. We stood there about two feet away from the Fat Cats, silent, expressionless for what seemed like forever. Finally, Obie said, "You all a-goin' a come introduce yourselves, or your mama didn't teach you manners?"

Several of them looked startled. Two blushed. All of them seemed stiff, frozen. Finally, State Senator Erik Kallio walked around the table to Obie, introduced himself.

CHAPTER 19, ROCK AND A HARD PLACE, BAM BOOM!

Obie shook his hand. "Obie King, Gandy Dancer, North-Northeast Minneapolis Industrial Safety Commissioner, People's Union Board Member, Arnray Railroad Safety Corporation Director."

Senator Kallio moved up the line to Linda. Bartholomew Holmes, CEO of East-West Materials Corporation, stood up looking so rigid I thought his joints would squeak and creak when he moved. He shook hands with Obie. One by one, they introduced themselves. Not an ounce of warmth from any of them. Even less from us.

Everyone else sat down. I remained standing. I saw Linda and Magdalena reach down, switch on the tape recorders hidden in their large handbags. "The proof you offered that you have authority to negotiate was a start, but only a start," I said. "We need legislation at the city council and state legislature level to back that up. I'm sure competent politicians like you, Alderman Ose, Senator Webster, Representative Rinder, Senator Kallio, can push that through before we sign any agreements."

"Impossible!" Bobellon said. "Never heard such an asinine thing. Can't be done!"

"*Kartoffel!*" Mike called out.

"*Kartoffel!*" we all responded.

"Ah, but it can!" Burt said. "What happened to you, Algernon? You were such a big thinker way back when. Your mind got frozen up with age? Mucked up with money? We just get a commission charter, and bang! We've got all the authority we need!"

"That's ridiculous," Increase Fitch, CEO of Amalgamated Foods Midwest, said, slamming his hand on the table. "State commission law is now being misused on the North Side. That was a wartime national security law meant solely for the creation of the Minnesota Commission of Public Safety in 1917, not meant for laypeople to use."

"That's not what the law says," Russ said. "Read it!"

Grant Bailey, CEO of Manufacturing Partners, thundered, "Patriotic citizens around our great state are organizing to repeal that commission law. Every chamber of commerce in the state is supporting them. We're going to put an end to your little game, Mäkinen. You damn well better agree to it if you want to achieve anything here."

"*Fulang!*" Betty called out. Which literally means ugly field in Swedish, but to us it meant, time to walk out.

Bailey looked confused.

"*Fulang!*" the rest of us echoed.

Ma got up, walked across the great divide between tables, stood in front of Bailey, quietly said, "If the first thing you demand takes away the power of working people to insure our own safety, then you're not serious. Guess you don't want to settle."

We got to our feet.

"Call us when yah're ready to be genuine," I said.

"Serious? Of course we're serious," Bobellon said. "Here's the best offer you're going to get. We'll agree to a $1.79 minimum wage."

"Indexed?" Carleton said.

"That's a *ten percent* raise," Bobellon said. "More than inflation."

"Doesn't even keep up with the past two years' inflation," Carleton said. "Indexed?"

"Indexing is pure communism," Bobellon said.

"*Fulang?*" Linda said.

"*Fulang!*" we all repeated.

"Too bad, so sad," Linda said. "Good day. Call us when you're ready to talk turkey. Pay the Church's invoice on your way out."

Melvin Meilander's face turned beet red. "But we must settle this strike! Johnson-Meilander Trucking can't continue with no revenue."

"You've clearly told us to do that you are not ready," Willi said.

"You'll be ready," Betty said, "when the legislature and city council pass actual laws that an agreement on your part is binding."

"And when you show us," Linda said, "a valid commission charter that legally empowers you to sign a binding agreement."

"And when," Mike said, "the legislature and city council pass laws affirming the North-Northeast Minneapolis Industrial Safety Commission is legal."

"And laws," Sarah said, "setting up South-Southeast Minneapolis, St. Paul, Iron Range, and Duluth Industrial Safety Commissions."

"That was *not* one of your demands!" Holmes yelled.

"So what?" I said. "It's on yahr table now! Along with our two hundred and twelve original demands, which you must consider individually."

"*Fulang!*" Willi said. He led us out of the room, out of the church.

CHAPTER 19, ROCK AND A HARD PLACE, BAM BOOM!

As we drove away in Officer James's squad car, Mike said, "Those fools are just bluffing, hard as they can."

"Sure does look that way," Linda said. "It's out of whack with what they did to comply with our pre-meeting conditions."

"But Meilander's letting the cat out of the bag," I said.

"And it's some cat," Burt said. "His working capital's way down."

"What does that mean?" Ma said.

"His company's running out of money," Burt said. "The strike is pushing it right toward the edge. There may be bargains for sale soon. Or good workers we can poach. Or how about Shingle Creek-Meilander Trucking?"

Back at the office, Blanche greeted us. "Harry, Hank, and I talked with sixty-four striking workers today, from Lake State Fertilizer & Seed, Johnson-Meilander, B&D Manufacturing Partners, and American-Built Automotive. About fifty have good skills. More coming tomorrow."

"So Lake State walked out?" I said.

Blanche slapped her hands together. "While you were meeting."

"You're going to need cash handy for all kinds of stuff besides salaries," Burt said. He handed us a check. "Here, for the offices, clinic, museum, whatever."

"Thanks! But we have ta get approval first," I said. "Before we take yahr money."

"If you don't get approval, return the check. But please! Help me meet my giveaway quota for this month. I'm falling behind. Again."

"Okay, Burt. I won't argue. Unless I don't get authorization."

That evening at dinner, I could barely hold myself together. "They lied. They didn't release Karen. Even with a million bucks at stake. They're never gonna let her free. Just try to buy me off with a pile of cash. But I ain't buying! I want Karen!"

The room seemed to be spinning. I felt drunk even though it had been months since I'd had a drink. I cried so hard I couldn't catch my breath. "They promised! Those bastards promised!" Slumped forward, half on my chair, half on the table, my face down on my hands, the room seemed like a wobbly, high-speed merry-go-round.

Ma moved right next to me, put her arms around me. She talked to me. Linda talked to me. Billy talked to me. But no matter what they said, I could not shake off dread and anxiety. All I could think of was Rennie. My stomach was in knots. I couldn't eat.

When the phone rang, Linda went to answer it, came back a few minutes later. "A. H. H. Bobellon called, wants to have another settlement meeting tomorrow. Claimed they're ready to reach a settlement and said they've done everything we demanded. I told him we'd vote and get back to him. Paulie, you want me to take the vote?"

I lifted my head a moment, said yes, kept crying.

Next morning, I woke up in a towering rage, went outside, cut a bouquet of thorny branches from Clara's roses.

"What're those for?" Ma said.

"Corsages for the Fat Cats." I put them in a Workers' Market brown grocery bag.

We deliberately arrived at the church five minutes late, filed into the room in silence, stood in a line, facing them.

After a couple of minutes, I said, "Ya have defaulted on yahr surety bond."

Chip Corbyn, CEO of Nicollet Super Stores, jumped to his feet, face bright red. "We did *exactly* as it specified." He slammed his hand down on the table. Reached forward, tried to grab me.

Officer James stepped between us. "Sir! I will not permit violence here. I'd suggest you sit back down."

"Mr. Corbyn," Linda said, "you seem to have forgotten about Ms. Ahlberg."

"She was released yesterday with the others."

"Then why, Mr. Corbyn," Carleton said, "is Federal Judge Luther Godwin still working on getting her freed? Perhaps you know something the judge doesn't?"

"I was told she was discharged."

"Who told you?" Russ said. "A little bird? Well, that sparrow was sadly mislead."

"I have to check with my secretary," Corbyn said, stamping out of the room.

"You have five minutes," Magdalena said.

"Aren't you going to take your seats?" Mr. Meilander said.

"We are *not* taking this sitting down," I said.

CHAPTER 19, ROCK AND A HARD PLACE, BAM BOOM!

We stood there, silent, expressionless.

Corbyn came back, spluttering, "They charged me ten bucks for a local call. Thievery, I say!"

"Oligarch Economics 101," Burt said. "When something's scarce and valued, raise the price."

"So, you found out," Betty said, "that Ms. Ahlberg really *has* been released, Mr. Corbyn, and we were all wrong?"

"She's *going* to be released."

"Which means," Clarence said, "you need to write a surety bond default check for one million dollars."

"How would an uneducated laborer like you begin to understand this?" Fitch said.

"Uh-huh," Clarence said. "Wizardry, nothing but. And I also understand we need your replacement surety bond to guarantee Ms. Ahlberg will be freed by 11:59 a.m. Central Standard Time tomorrow and further guarantee there will be no arrests of the strike settlement committee, or rearrests of anyone you took as hostages."

"And since a million-dollar surety bond you didn't abide by," Willi said, "one for five million you must provide."

J. H. Kingsbury from Lakes State Fertilizer & Seed tore a sheet off his notepad, crumpled it into a ball, threw it at Willi. "Outrageous! We made every effort to release Ms. Ahlberg. It's just a bureaucratic glitch."

"Bureaucratic glitch my foot!" Linda said. "There are consequences when you arrange to transport a minor across state lines in violation of the Mann Act."

"Which was *arranged* by the Communal Association," Russ said. "You, Mr. Kingsbury, have been a dues-paying member for at least five years."

Kingsbury's face looked like a red balloon, about to burst.

"So let's reiterate," Sarah said. "This is what we need to continue working on a strike settlement. One, the surety bond default check. Two, a new five-million-dollar surety bond."

"Three, statutes passed by the legislature and city council," Mike said, "that make your agreements legally binding. Four, a state statute authorizing a general strike settlement commission."

"Finally," Betty said, "laws affirming the city and state's agreement that North-Northeast Minneapolis Industrial Safety Commission is legal and authorizing South-Southeast Minneapolis, St. Paul, Iron Range, and Duluth Industrial Safety Commissions."

Senator Johnsrud, smug smile on his face, snake oil in his voice, leaned way back in his chair. "You laypeople just don't understand the checks and balances of the legislative process. We have to go step by step, deliberately, carefully following our time-honored procedures and avoiding the siren calls of demagogues. Anything less is a threat to democracy."

State Representative Rudolph Rinder shook his finger at us. "Absolutely right! It's a matter of policy, not legislation. We're sticking with our policies, inasmuch as our policies actually address the need to continue to address this challenge."

"*Maksapihvi!*" Obie, Willi, and Linda called out. Which in Finnish means liver patty but to us meant horse puckies! We need to object loud and clear.

I stood up. Glared at them in silence for a good ten seconds. "Go slow? We started that way. You owners ruthlessly attacked us. Libeled us. Slandered us. Broke your contracts with us. Killed our Bonnie, our Dozer, our Fred. Wounded our Roger, our Bev, our Greta, our Joyce." I reached into my grocery bag, pulled out the thorny rose branches, scattered them on the Fat Cat's table. "*You* pushed us to this point, and *you* didn't go slowly. Well, we won't either. *You* made this bed of thorns. Now lay down on it!"

Bailey waved his hand as if to dismiss us. "Guess it's time to call in the scabs. Mr. Fitch, we have the full force standing by?"

"Trained and ready to go," Fitch said.

"*Maksapivi*," Willi said.

"Please, do that!" Magdalena said. "You know what we do to scabs, don't you, Mr. Bailey, Mr. Fitch? We recruit them! At two-fifty indexed."

"Like we did to the scab gandy dancers," Clarence said. "They work for us now."

"And the scab roofing factory workers," Linda said. "Now on our payroll."

"We have hundreds of two-fifty indexed jobs open right now," Ma said.

CHAPTER 19, ROCK AND A HARD PLACE, BAM BOOM!

"Workers are hard to find," Mike said. "Please! Bring us in a new supply from out of state. We'll welcome them with open arms!"

"Warning!" Obie said. "We're a-coming after your corrupt flunkies! Chief Jensen, Lieutenant Colding, Stillwater Prison Warden Van Alst, all City Militia members, Clyde Gremling, Richard Prichard, Minnesota Corrections Commissioner Pembroke, Alastair Tewkesbury, Duane Pukari, Arthur Schulz. Ooh-ee, they all done been arrested!"

"Your power base is crumbling fast," Ma said, the first time one of us smiled.

"*Makeiset?*" Sarah said, which means candy in Finnish but for us meant bye!

"*Makeiset!*" we all responded and stood up.

Meilander called out, "Wait! Stop! Let's keep talking."

"Do yahr homework first, Mr. Meilander," I said.

"Call us when you're really, truly ready," Ma said. "No more shenanigans. Don't waste our time again!"

And out we walked, leaving them sitting there spluttering.

When we got in the car, Ma said, "Personally, I think those Fat Cats are terrified."

A couple of blocks up Emerson Avenue, the CB radio crackled. "Breadcakes here," Burt said. "Urgently need meeting moment we get back. All here agree. Over."

"Beagle here, Breadcakes," Russ said. "All here agree too."

Linda picked up the CB mic. "Historian here. Count us in. Over and out."

"A baker, a lawyer, and a historian walked into a bar," Mike said. "But what's the punch line?"

Which set us all off laughing. By North 39th Avenue, laughter had transformed into a discussion about strategy. We had ideas but no clear answers yet.

When we sat down in the Teen Council conference room, Burt said, "Can we ask Joanna to join us and order in lunch? It's going to be a long meeting!"

Ma called Archie at Camden Market, placed our orders. I talked with Joanna, asked her for a list of Minnesota Senate and House of Representatives committees. I took out a package of lined pads, a bunch of pens, put them down at everyone's place, then got out paper plates and stuff for lunch.

Joanna came into the room, said, "I just talked with my friend who's an assistant to State Senator Larsen. The governor's and the legislature's top priority is to settle this strike. My friend said you should expect a phone call from Larsen."

"Holy cowbops," I said. "He's the senate president. Staunch Republican."

"His favorite oligarchs are hurting big-time, demanding an agreement," Joanna said. "His constituents are calling nonstop, insisting on a pro-labor strike settlement."

"Rock and a hard place, bam boom!" Mike chanted.

Burt jumped up almost as nimble as a teenager, started pacing. "Those poor Fat Cats are all shook up worse than Elvis ever was! The strategies they, their fathers, and their grandfathers used for almost a century aren't working anymore. They literally have no idea what to do. So *we* have to tell them!"

Clarence rested his chin on his hand a moment. "Let's break it down into steps, huh? If we got the legislature to put all our demands into an actual law, wouldn't that be the best protection?"

"You bet," Carleton said. "And we wouldn't waste time starting a commission."

"Clarence, which is easier to handle?" Russ said. "One huge piece of legislation covering two hundred and thirteen things—"

"Nope!" Clarence said. He shifted in his seat. "Organize them all into ten or fifteen main topics with legislation for each topic. Much easier."

"Karen told me bills go to a committee first," I said. "We should organize them that way. All in favor?" I looked around. "All hands on deck!"

"Isn't the first step to get the legislature to agree to fast action?" Clarence said.

"Maybe an all-night session," Carleton said. "Give it the top priority it deserves."

Russ shook his head. "I'm not sure we should do an actual end-run around the eight Fat Cats. Sure, we could get the wheels rolling in the legislature. But let the Fat Cats feel like they're in on it too and that we've

CHAPTER 19, ROCK AND A HARD PLACE, BAM BOOM!

just made their job simpler. Good for us, because it's easier to pressure them and let them pressure the legislature."

We took a series of votes, worked out a bunch of details, were about to eat lunch when the phone rang. Ma answered it, listened, waved her arms around, said, "Russ, Paul! Corey Atkinson's calling you."

Russ jumped up, put it on speaker.

"I have good news," Atkinson said. "Judge Godwin issued a court order requiring Karen's release at or before 11:59 a.m. tomorrow, Mountain Standard Time. The court also ordered Montana and Minnesota Corrections to pay for airfare back to Minneapolis for Karen, Clara, Sandi, and Scott and transport costs to get Clara's car back home. Since Minnesota airline mechanics and cabin attendants are on strike, there are no commercial flights, so Minnesota and Montana corrections were ordered to arrange and pay for a private flight to Crystal Airport. Judge Godwin called Federal Judge Campbell, his friend in Billings. Campbell agreed to send two federal marshals to enforce the court order at Montana Women's Prison and two more at Montana Department of Corrections in Helena, two hundred and fifty miles from Billings.

"One more thing. The four top officials at Montana Department of Corrections are on their way, in handcuffs, to Judge Godwin's courtroom in Minneapolis. I've never heard of anything like that before! Major sign of a big win for you!"

It was a good thing Ma had ordered extra food. After Atkinson's call, my stomach unknotted. I polished off three sandwiches, a pile of Strike! Cookies, an apple, a pear, and a Hot! Chocolate bar.

We soon got calls from Senator Larsen, Speaker of the House Biber, and the eight Fat Cats. Organized our demands into fourteen topics. Forwarded them to the Fat Cats and the appropriate legislative committees. Then we recruited Hazel Corwin-Pokorny, Badah Haddad, Lester Jeppesen, and Gannon Woodruff as volunteers to work with Russ and Rollie, reading the legislation with us as it was proposed and again when it was ready for voting. Sylvia would be monitoring the senate for us, Jason the House, making sure nobody pulled a fast one.

Even so, we kept increasing the pressure. Margaret and Bucky worked with an organizing committee at East-West Materials. Their manufacturing unit went on strike that night. So did clerks and secretaries at the chamber of commerce and checkout clerks at Chip Corbyn's Nicollet Super Stores. Jack, Marek, and Vincent signed up thirty-nine scab office clerks from Bobellon's company to work for us. The eight Fat Cats were angry. We didn't care. We just kept pushing them to keep the legislation machine moving.

Just before dinnertime, we received a copy of the new law from the city council, mandating that the state legislation would be binding on the city. All evening, into the night, we checked off each demand as it was incorporated into law. Jason and Sylvia called us when bills passed milestones.

We did find a few times when the Fat Cats tried to deceive us. Their original bill called for the Minneapolis Standard Work Contract to take effect five years from now. The next version left out the productivity index. And the bill authorizing Community Development Funds for working people's neighborhoods didn't say where the funds were coming from.

Each time, we told them, "If we agree to that, you'll be negotiating with someone else. Because we'd lose all our friends if we betrayed them like that."

At midnight, Obie started dancing around. "Ooh-ee! We're a-gettin' most everythin' we been a-fightin' for!"

At one a.m., Senator Larsen called. "I'm sure we can work out a small problem with the Minneapolis Standard Work Contract."

Horse puckies! Here it comes.

"The Minneapolis Chamber of Commerce says that would give St. Paul and suburban businesses an unfair advantage. Can we please compromise?"

"How?" Sarah said.

"Rename it the Minnesota Standard Work Contract?"

Clarence stood up, put his finger across his lips. Wrote in big letters on a pad, "We must vote first!" Showed it to everyone.

We all nodded.

"We'll vote on it and let you know, Senator," Clarence said.

I couldn't believe what I'd just heard. "Holy cowbops! We just actually won the Standard Work Contract for all of Minnesota? Somebody, please, pinch me!"

The conference room was too small to dance in, so we went into the old pressroom and waltzed to the tunes of victory playing in our heads. Then we called the senator and agreed to "compromise."

At three in the morning, Senator Larsen begged for a five-hour break with no more walkouts called, no more scabs or striking employees stolen. We "conceded" on that one as well. But the next morning at 7:30, we were back at our command post, checking and double-checking. By nine o'clock, we were up to our elbows again.

A messenger brought us an envelope with a certified check for a million dollars for the surety bond default. I was so pre-occupied worrying about Rennie and everything we had to do, I just brought it to Lydia for deposit, went right back to my tasks.

At 9:27, a Western Union messenger came into our office, asked for me, Ma, and Linda, handed us a telegram.

MONTANA CORRECTIONS HIRED PLANE FOR US LEAVING 1245PM, ARRIVING CRYSTAL AIRPT 8PM MINNEAPOLIS TIME TONIGHT KAREN CLARAKTA SANDISCOTT.

Linda, sitting next to me, pointed to the word *Clarakta*, raised her eyebrows.

"Swedish for Genuine Clara," I said. "She once told me how the bosses were sending phony telegrams, trying to fool strikers that their union had settled the strike."

At a quarter past one that afternoon, Senator Larsen called us, predicting the last bill would be signed into law around five o'clock. Bobellon called to confirm that.

Todd's voice came over the CB radio at 1:30. "Creekers and People's Union members! Major announcement from Governor Johansen on KPFP in three minutes!"

A moment later, Todd called. "Johansen's going to announce the strike is over. Paulie, stand by to respond when he finishes. We're hooked in to eighteen other stations."

Rollie came running with the radio. Everyone was shaking their heads.

"Not 'til the last bill is signed into law *and* all of us vote on it," I said.

"Way to go, Paulie!" Todd said.

Everyone in the room put their thumbs up. We waited on the edge of our seats.

"Good afternoon, my fellow Minnesotans!" Governor Johansen said. "I am pleased to announce, at long last, the strike which has had such a heavy cost to our prosperity, and whose impact has spread across this great nation, has been settled. Now, it's time to get back to work making Minnesota a showplace of democratic prosperity. I call on every Minnesota working man to report for work this very afternoon. Even half-a-day's labor can help us all pull out of this frightening slump. We're all in this together!"

"Thank you, Mr. Governor," Todd said. "And now, a comment from strike leadership committee member, Paul Mäkinen."

"Thank ya, Governor Johansen, for the big-huge effort you, the legislature, and the business community have made toward settling this strike. But ya have forgotten one word, that simple word, *almost*! As Senator Johnsrud says, 'We have ta go step by step, following our time-honored procedures and avoiding the siren calls of demagogues. Anything less is a threat to democracy.' We are *almost* there. Once the last bill is approved by both the legislature and the People's Union Settlement Committee, final ratification by a vote of all working people in our great city is still required.

"We expect to have that vote finished early this evening. Then, and only then, if the vote is to approve, will we whole-heartedly ask every working man and, Mr. Governor, every working woman, to negotiate a return to their jobs with their bosses in accordance with our new laws, and that every boss grant them the respect they need to be the most productive workers possible."

There were only fourteen of us in that room, but the applause, cheers, and whistles made us sound like a huge crowd.

"Thank you, Mr. Mäkinen," Todd said. "And now back to Keanna for some good, old-fashioned union songs. Don't be bashful! Sing right along!"

The music started. "You were fabulous, Paulie!" Todd said on the phone. "Sorry for no heads-up. Our dear governor sprung it on all of us broadcasters with three minutes warning. Gotta run! Talk soon!"

"Did anyone record that?" I said.

"Yes indeedy!" Ma said.

CHAPTER 19, ROCK AND A HARD PLACE, BAM BOOM!

" 'Cause I can't believe I actually said that!"

"Awesome stuff!" Mike said. "You talk just like a politician when you need to, *Senator* Paulie. Sure put that big-ass fool in his place!"

"Can I hear it?" I said.

"It's a doozy!" Ma said, and pressed the play button.

I felt myself grinning wider than the rings of Saturn. *Holy cowbops! That sure as heck is the real Paul Mäkinen!*

"We are so proud of you," Linda said. "You grooved it up just the right speed!"

Our judge friends, still helping us read bills and statutes, shook my hand.

"Mike is right," Gannon Woodruff said. "You have what it takes, Paul, if that's what you want."

"I second that motion," Badah said.

"I don't actually know," I said. "Kinda sorta someday, maybe?"

The afternoon flew as we read final bills, caught errors, demanded changes, avoided problems, and also set up that evening's vote and the victory celebration. At 5:45, we approved the final bill.

"Fat Cats made it easy for us," Magdalena said. "Instead of having everyone vote on two-hundred-plus demands, we just have to agree it's okay we lost on six of them!"

We activated People's Union Emergency Plan Seven. The calling tree's first tier notified neighborhood associations, which called block captains, a teen and an adult for each block. They went door-to-door getting votes. Since almost everyone was striking, and we announced the vote on the radio, most people were home, waiting for their chance to vote.

When all their block captains had called in, the neighborhood associations let us know their totals. We had the final tally at 7:05. The settlement was approved by an overwhelming ninety-two percent margin.

"*Voiton suloiset kukat!*" Willi yelled. "Sweet flowers of victory, approve I do!"

Calls of "*kukat!*" filled our conference room.

CHAPTER 20, GETTING BACK OUR STOLEN BOOTSTRAPS

THURSDAY, MARCH 23, 1972

At 7:20 that night when we entered the auditorium, Carly, in a stunning red dress, came running up to me with Merrill, Lola, and Corrine beside her. "Did we get some money, Paulie?" she said.

"Enough to get your dad the best medical care and let your family live in comfort."

She hugged me, started crying. Thanked me six times. "And thank goodness Judge Haddad bought me this dress. I was so embarrassed in that ragged yellow one."

"Looks elegant on ya, perfect for TV," I said. "Will ya announce yahr family's settlement for us?"

"Me? Really? Dad will be so proud! And soon, he won't be in pain anymore! *This* is like a nightmare ending for us."

"It's three hundred and fifty thousand for yahr family."

Her eyes got bigger than harvest moons. "Oh, my gosh! Oh, my gosh!"

"Al, one of our counselors, will work on getting yahr dad proper hospital care tomorrow morning."

I helped her figure out what she wanted to say on the air. Showed her where to go up on stage. Got seats for her, Merrill, Lola, and Corrine next to Judge Haddad. I smiled, said, "I hope someday, I have a daughter just like ya, Carly. I'm so proud of ya!"

CHAPTER 20, GETTING BACK OUR STOLEN BOOTSTRAPS

The Creektones were playing. Diane, Bobby, and Jill, who'd flown in for the victory celebration, sang.

Elżbieta Witkowski ran up to me. "Airtime's in eight minutes! National hookup."

I looked at the stage. Our settlement committee was waiting. "Thanks! We're ready." I gave the thumbs-up to Todd. Said hello to Gilbert Randle from KOBA-Radio Sixteen-Sixty, Kirby Kenworthy from *TC-News Six*, and Minnie Olander from *Channel 8 Morning News*. Went onstage, sat down, felt myself smiling.

At exactly seven-thirty, the band stopped playing. Bobby, in his booming voice, said, "Introducing Paul Mäkinen, Chair of the Shingle Creek Teen Council and Lead Strike Settler, with an overview of the Minneapolis General Strike Settlement."

Tina and the band played a fanfare.

I stepped up to the mic. "Thank ya, friends, neighbors, family. I am honored to have with us Roger Tornquist, Greta Björk, Bev Hakala, and Joyce Trockenmann, shot by the illegal City Militia, still recovering from their wounds. Alas, Bonnie Korhonen, also shot, will be forever nine, and Dozer Walden, forever nineteen, may you rest in peace. We must never forget this settlement was paid for in *blood*."

Slides of Bonnie and Dozer showed on the big screen onstage.

"Never again will we permit safety hazards on the job that killed and maimed so many working people for the last century. Ray Iversen, Arne Gustaffson, Sal Mondadori, we will always honor and remember ya.

"Two of our railroad workers, Frank Ahlberg and Wilbur Jones, are recovering from devastating accidents." The spotlight focused on Frank and Wilbur, onstage in their wheelchairs. "They have ta learn how to walk all over again. But, Frank, Wilbur, I know ya will be up. And running. Fast! Give 'em a cheer, folks!"

A great, roaring hoorah! filled the room.

"But from now on, empowered by the new law just passed by the Minnesota legislature, working people will have our own safety commissions. We'll inspect workplaces. Demand hazards be fixed on the spot. And shut down unsafe workplaces. No ifs, ands, or buts. All over Minneapolis. St. Paul. Duluth. The Iron Range. And for workers injured in past workplace accidents, we didn't forget ya."

In a swirl of red fabric, Carly ran onto the stage.

"My name is Carly Ranum, and I'm fourteen. Dad was almost killed at KHA Specialty Steel Company. Been bedridden five months now. His wounds aren't healing. We only got a few hundred dollars from KHA. Our savings are gone. I was gonna drop out of school and go to work so we could pay the rent. But tonight Paulie told me KHA settled for enough money so Dad can go to the hospital for proper treatment. And we can pay the rent and have meatballs with our spaghetti. Thanks, Paulie! And thanks to Russ, our lawyer. And to my judge friend who bought me this amazing dress." She bounded away in another red flurry.

"For months now," I said, "we've been looking for workers injured on the job who didn't get proper compensation. We found a hundred and thirty-eight of them. Got them fair settlements. And we didn't end this strike until we had checks in our hands for them. Our couriers will hand-deliver those checks tomorrow."

Clarence stepped up beside me. "Not to change the subject, but...most of us Creekers know, Karen Ahlberg is the love of Paul's life. But she's not here tonight. Wait 'til you hear why! Karen was kidnapped, illegally taken across state lines, never charged with a crime, held in a high-security Montana prison." Rennie's photo flashed on the screen. "The Fat Cats and bureaucrats responsible have been criminally charged, arrested, indicted. Right now, Karen's on an airplane somewhere over western Minnesota, on her way here. How are you going to welcome her, Paulie?"

"Say something I've never said before!"

"What?" Clarence said.

"You'll see!" I grinned, nodded.

Ruthie scampered onto the stage, juggling four balls as she ran. She came up to the mic, still juggling as we talked. "My hands are all better, Paulie. Don't need physical therapy anymore!"

"Tell us what happened," I said.

"Before we got a really great new teacher, the old one was mean. She beat my hands and Bonnie's. All bloody. With a steel-edged ruler. Because she didn't like the free-verse poem Bonnie wrote. And I said I liked it."

"Ya needed stitches?"

"Yeah, and it hurt so bad I thought I was dying."

"Yahr hands were in bandages?"

CHAPTER 20, GETTING BACK OUR STOLEN BOOTSTRAPS

"For weeks! Like Bonnie said, 'I never knew how important fingers are in life!'"

"Why are ya juggling?"

"Because Bonnie did. But Fat Cats shot her dead."

"Ya just now learned juggling?"

"Yeah, to honor our Bonnie. Don't let us have a mean teacher ever again!"

"Yah're safe now, Ruthie! The School Board just signed a contract with us. From now on, *we* get to choose the teachers, long as they're licensed."

"Is it true we won the money lawsuit?"

"Ya sure did. Twenty-five thousand dollars to ya, the same to Bonnie's family. We'll be giving out the checks tomorrow."

"Now I can go to college for sure!" Ruthie juggled her way offstage.

"Friends and neighbors, Ruthie Flynn. Member of the Forever Nines. Named themselves that so Bonnie can always be part of them."

Mike stood up, came over to us. "So, Paulie, what's the bad news?"

"Well, honestly, Mike, not a whole heck of a lot."

"But there *is* bad news?"

"Okay, let's get it over and done with. Six things we didn't get." I held up my hands, counted on my fingers. "One, the legal right to elect and recall foremen and supervisors. But we can still negotiate that with individual bosses."

Linda came over to us. "And? What else?"

I held up another finger. "If workers quit a job because of disrespect, they *don't* get three months' severance pay."

"Houston, we *don't* have a problem!" Linda said. "Shingle Creek has created so many new jobs, there's a labor shortage. Respect us or too bad, so sad, we're gone!"

I had three fingers up. "We didn't get free medical care for everyone."

"But we did get some steps in the right direction," Mike said. "By law, the state has to set up and pay for low-cost medical clinics in Shingle Creek, Willow Avenue on the Near North Side, Broadway Park in Northeast, Wentworth Park in South."

"But can workers afford them?" Clarence said.

"Just one buck for an appointment," Linda said.

Magdalena joined us.

I held up my fourth finger. "We didn't get the right to organize workers' councils authorized to meet with their bosses."

"It would've been wonderful to get that," Magdalena said, "but we'll work around it. Minnesota Consolidated Railroad signed a contract with Arnray. All their railroad workers in Minneapolis and St. Paul work for Arnray. The contract calls for workers councils."

"Uh-huh. Big deal," Clarence said. "That's only one company. Just playing devil's advocate here."

"We figure workers councils will raise productivity at least ten percent," Magdalena said. "Money talks. We just need the proof so it can do the talking. And that goes for the fifth thing we didn't get too."

"The right," Linda said, "to be represented by a workers' cooperative. Highly cool, we actually *did* win that with Arnray. So same strategy! We show the Fat Cats it increases productivity, we let the cash do the convincing."

With my sixth finger up, I said, "This last one is a little harder to take. If a factory was up for sale, we wanted workers there to have first rights to buy it and low-cost loans to pay for it. But no dice."

Ma came up to the mic, took Clarence's place. "Remember a year ago when the stove factory in Champlin moved down to West Virginia because minimum wage down there was only $1.20? And the bottle factory over in Diamond Lake was packed up and shipped to China? That crapola is going to happen more. We don't want the smashed dreams that come with it."

"So that means," Sarah said, "we have more work to do to extend our rights. But let's take a close look at what's in the settlement we voted for, 149,837 to 192. Because it's a humongous, giant-economy-sized victory!"

"Strange but true," Betty said, "we demanded a *Minneapolis* Standard Work Contract, but the Fat Cats agreed to…"

The Creektones and Tina played a fanfare.

"…a statewide contract. With all of our terms. For all of Minnesota! Which all bosses must sign, by law."

Cheers filled the room.

"Do we with all the details to bore you need to?" Willi said.

"Bore us! Bore us!" the crowd chanted.

CHAPTER 20, GETTING BACK OUR STOLEN BOOTSTRAPS

The Creektones drummer played a roll.

"A two-fifty minimum wage indexed, no exceptions!" Obie said.

People jumped up, whistled, yelled, applauded. The Creektones played a dance tune. Folks waltzed in the aisles.

"Pay raises one percent over inflation twice each year there are," Willi said.

"Productivity raises every six months," Carleton said.

"Paid hundred-thousand-dollar disability insurance," Russ said. "No forced overtime, double pay for swing shifts, twelve paid holidays a year. And! And! Payment for tools, equipment, and uniforms required on the job. All striking workers must be rehired when a strike is settled. Benefits for part-time workers. No forced changes in shifts or schedules."

"Equal training and hiring rights for all sexes, races, and ethnicities," Ma said.

"They done agreed to two weeks paid vacation after a year," Obie said. "Three weeks after five years. And ooh-ee! *Five* weeks after nine years, yes indeed! Even if you ain't a-workin' full-time, you'll be a-getting' part of it. So what do you all think of that?"

Folks jumped up, clapping, cheering. The Creektones played boogie music, everyone was bopping. The spotlight found Frank moving his wheelchair back and forth in time to the beat.

"Friends and neighbors," I said. "In the spotlight, we have an honest candidate for alderman in the June primaries. Everyone knows him. Call out his name!"

"Frank! Frank!" the crowd yelled.

The spot highlighted Clarence.

"And look who's running for mayor!"

"Clarence! Clarence!"

"They both support the People's Union platform!"

"Dah-dah-dah-dee-dah-dah!" Tina and the band played.

I raised both hands.

The auditorium got quiet.

Obie said, "Now I'm sure everyone wants to know exactly what done went on in that church classroom on Willow Avenue. So we done made you all a tape!"

We played the part where they threatened us with scabs, which set the whole room off laughing. And the part where Obie asked if, "your mama didn't teach you manners?" We guffawed even harder.

When we'd laughed ourselves out, I said, "So ya wanna know what happened with Minnesota Consolidated Construction Services?"

"Tell us! Tell us!"

Carleton stepped forward. "Judge Woodruff ordered it closed down since its only purpose was to screw workers. Owners appealed. Judge Ovington refused to hear it. So did the Minnesota Supreme Court. All happened in two days. Who says government can't move fast when it has to? Who says justice has to take six years longer than forever?"

"Who's putting back the tracks?" Gandy Dancer Steve Rosenquist called out.

"Gadzooks! We are," Clarence said. "At two-fifty, indexed. Time-and-a-half overtime. With all new materials. To industry standards. Using full-sized crews."

"Who's paying us?" Steve said.

"Arnray!" Clarence said. "Railroad pays Arnray. Arnray pays us. Railroad workers all get to vote on Arnray's work rules and policies. And red baiters can't come after our strongest leaders with that danged Taft-Hartley law 'cause Arnray ain't legally a union!"

"You ask me," Magdalena said, "Arnray is a *super* union!"

"Shhh!" Obie said. "Don't be a-tellin' no one."

One of the Black gandy dancers we'd hired away from the railroad stood up. "You White folks gonna keep us on like you promised?"

"We're a-countin' on you guys," Obie said. "But your crew ain't big enough, so you'll be a-working together with White guys. No more of that separate shit!"

"And we get two-fifty indexed?"

"Same as everyone else!" Magdalena said.

"A couple more things there are," Willi said. "The railroad's check for Safety Commission fines and fees for track removal we have. Everyone who the tracks removed at night, time-and-a-half pay from the commission will get. Checks in three days ready will be."

CHAPTER 20. GETTING BACK OUR STOLEN BOOTSTRAPS

"Willi-ukki!" Mamie came running up onto the stage. "Willi-ukki! Now can you take Nellie the Steam Engine out on the tracks and all us kids for a ride?"

Willi's voice caught. He took Mamie's hand. "All the way down to Edina on the West Route and across Northeast to St. Paul on the east we can. Every day up to thirty times the new law says."

"When, Willi-ukki?"

"A lot of work to do we have first. Busy we will get!"

"It really will happen?" Mamie said.

"In the law, written it is. And in our hearts!" Willi said. "Come, Määmiliini. A seat next to me on the stage for you there is."

I motioned to the band for a fanfare.

"Announcing honest candidates who support the People's Union platform," I said. "For County Commissioner, Ndidi Williams! County Attorney, Hazel Corwin-Pokorny!"

The spotlight found them, the crowd cheered.

"And now," I said, "Russ and Sylvia with the legal side of our strike settlement."

"Well, we sure hit pay dirt," Russ said, "so there's a lot to talk about! Charges against Ruka Williams and Margaret Björk? Dropped! Lawsuits for false arrest? To be filed Monday!" Charges against Jill Frisk? Dropped! But Duane Pukari has already been indicted for assaulting her."

"Ruka, Margaret! Margaret, Jill! Jill, Ruka!" the crowd roared.

Two teenagers approached the mic, holding hands.

"My name is Sherry Anselm. I'm thirteen."

"And I'm Cecile Wagner, age fifteen. Jeffie? Can you come up here with us?"

Jeffie came sprinting onto the stage.

Sherry and Cecile raised their joined hands high. "We organized junior high and high school kids," they said together. "Demanded an end to the draft, an end to the war."

"We made all the draft board members so ashamed, they quit!" Sherry said.

"The new state law we won," Cecile said, "won't let the governor replace them."

"So," Sherry said, "those draft boards are closed for business."

"Shut tighter than a miser's grip," Cecile said.

"No more big brothers forced to go to 'Nam?" Jeffie said.

"No more!" Sherry said. She hugged Jeffie. "Roy would be so proud of you!"

"Chant with us," they said together. "No more war! No more war!"

We chanted long, we chanted loud, until the Creektones played "Ain't Gonna Study War No More" and we sang along.

Then Russ said, "Gremling has been indicted for theft of Community Development Funds. He'll be in four separate trials, one after another. And! And! The governor forced the county attorney to charge Police Chief Jensen for making a death threat against our Gordy."

Sylvia and Russ held their clasped hands high. "Remember," Sylvia said, "when someone cut the electric power during the soup 'n' sandwich meeting in December? We knew who did it all along. County Attorney Courtenay played dumb. Well, the governor got on his case about that too. Courtenay finally filed charges against the cable cutter today. Now, our Laura and Irene have some news."

"After helicopters dumped freezing water and tear gas on us," Laura said, crying, "and deputized bastards killed our Dozer, our Bonnie, we demanded justice."

"We knew copters from the US Forest Service were used without permission," Irene said. "We knew the City Militia was deputized by the police in defiance of the law."

"But the county attorney played dumb again," Laura said. "Now, the governor is heading the investigation. And the new law says the Minnesota Attorney General must bring charges before Labor Day."

Irene clasped her hands together, raised them, looked upward. "We did it, Bonnie! Took your advice. Mourn, of course! Then, organize!"

Diane, Jill, and Bobby, arms around each other, began singing "Joe Hill." All of us, arms linked, sang along, swaying to the rhythm.

Hazel, along with her mother, Florie, approached the mic. "My name is Florence Corwin. Fred, the Superintendent of Parks, was the love of my life. He was executed by the police on Saturday, February nineteenth." Her face crumpled, she couldn't talk.

Hazel hugged her, stepped toward the mic. "The camerawoman from KTCA-TV caught the cops murdering Dad on film. With dozens of eyewitnesses. But when I went to the county attorney's office demanding those cops be prosecuted, do you know what they said? 'You can't prove that.' Did they take witness statements? No! Preserve evidence? No!"

Florie wiped her face with a handkerchief. "So we went to the Justice Department in Washington with Circuit Court Judge Badah Haddad. Today we can announce, the FBI is investigating Fred Corwin's murder. *And* the county attorney's lack of action."

"We will never forget our Fred," I said. "His kind and gentle guidance is why we got where we are today. Let's bow our heads in a moment of silent remembrance."

The quiet was potent.

"I'm only here today, helping you, because of Fred," Russ said. "There was no money in the budget for a lawyer, but he found a way. And he started something bigger than him, than me, than even a hundred of us. He helped us unleash our power. And that power has finally triumphed in court."

"Trials for five lawsuits we filed were actually held," Sylvia said. "But for each one, right after the juries' decisions, the verdicts were mysteriously sealed." She zipped her finger across her lips. "We just found out a few hours ago it was Judge Coventry who sealed them, on the order of Archibald Hastings-Dankworth and the Communal Association. Why? Hastings-Dankworth wanted to discourage us Creekers until he had us under control. His great-great-nephew, Duane Pukari, let the cat out of the bag."

"Did we win those secret trials?" Russ said, stepping from one foot to another. "Do bees make honey?"

"So, trial number one," Sylvia said. "The Shingle Creek Teen Council and Neighborhood Association sued the *Minnesota Patriot* for claiming our mental health clinic is really a state-funded indoctrination center for communist propaganda units, built using stolen materials. We didn't think we'd get more than a few grand, but we asked for five million each. We actually got it! Those checks are already in the Teen Council and Neighborhood Association bank accounts!"

"Won't they appeal?" Russ said. "No, ma'am, sir! We tied up the *Minnesota Patriot's* leaders in a boatload of lawsuits and investigations. They've been arrested and indicted. The court actually ordered these checks be issued immediately because the Fat Cats were so terrified we wouldn't return to work."

There was a surge of applause, whistling, cheering.

Sylvia raised both hands. "Remember when Paulie and Karen sued owners of the *Patriot* for libel because they claimed Paulie's a pimp and Karen's a whore?"

I jumped up in the air, clicked my heels together. "We won? We actually won?"

"Four owners of the *Patriot*," Sylvia said. "Pukari, Tewksbury, Archibald, and his wife Cressida. Five-million bucks from each for you and Karen. Now you can buy a castle on a tropical island, live in luxury!" She chuckled.

"Horse puckies! I'd be bored in about ten minutes. I can't speak for Karen, but every penny of my part goes to the Council and Association. I don't want to be rich. I want to be happy here with my friends and neighbors, working together to make *all* our dreams come true!"

"Paulie! Paulie!" the crowd roared.

I raised both hands. The room quieted. "I've always said we should think big. But with that kind of money, we need to think even bigger! The other cases, Sylvia? Russ?"

"Case number three," Russ hollered. "The *Patriot* claimed Jill was a communist organizer and that *she* assaulted Pukari. Jury award? Two million!"

The Creektones played a fanfare, then a drumroll. Jill scat-sang a rising wave that lifted us all up to a peak where she crooned, "Every penny of it shall go, I say with great elation, to the Teen Council and our Neighborhood Association!"

"Case number four," Sylvia thundered. "The *Journal* repeated the *Patriot's* claim we built the mental health clinic with stolen goods. Jury award? Two million each to the Council and Association. The checks have been deposited."

"Case number five," Russ roared. "Shirley, Harry, Beebe, Gloria, and I sued the *Journal* for claiming we're communists. We have checks for half a million bucks for each of you."

CHAPTER 20. GETTING BACK OUR STOLEN BOOTSTRAPS

"I don't know," Harry said, hands on his cheeks. "This all makes me uneasy. We really deserve all that dough? What in the heck are we going to do with it?"

"How many other folks feel unsettled, like our Harry?" I said.

About a hundred hands went up.

"I think we gotta talk about this! Okay with ya?"

A small chorus of yesses.

"Can we ask Judith?"

A large "yes" chant.

Judith trotted up to the stage. "Harry, you remember what happened in the fifties? With unions?"

"I'd prefer not to." He shuddered. "They took away our power step by step."

"Who else remembers?" Judith said. "How they did that?"

Frank came rolling toward the mic. Willi joined him. So did Magdalena.

"You up here with us come, Harry!" Willi motioned to him.

"How?" Magdalena said. "They called the best union organizers communists."

"And blacklisted them," Frank said. "I couldn't get a job anywhere."

"Or me," Willi said.

"Same for me," Magdalena said.

"Dang! Me too!" Harry said.

"So with a single loaded word, they knocked the crap out of unions?" Judith said. "And isn't that what they just tried to do to us all over again? How much did it cost us working people over the last twenty years? Can you even measure it?"

Kurt and Tessie bounded onstage. "If we started counting up the millions and millions of bucks today," Kurt said, "I'd be a grandpa by the time we finished!"

"Even if we counted by tens," Tessie said. "Our teacher Lucy, who taught us that, was blacklisted too."

"So now," Judith said. "Only those folks who weren't sure we deserve all that bread, are we entitled to it?"

It was only about a hundred voices, but the *yes* vote was like a roaring lion.

"Now, let's talk about Harry's second question," Judith said. "If the Fat Cats had not been able to steal our bootstraps, if the unions had stayed powerful and forced them to pay us what we're worth the whole time, what would we have now?"

"My kids would each have their own room, like rich people," Pete Hakkala said.

"Better schools! Better houses! Trees on our streets!" Dina Eldin said.

"Our own small businesses! Like the knife-sharpening van I always wanted," Roosevelt Washington said.

"Big factories maybe even we could buy," Willi said, "and into workers' cooperatives turn them."

"Aha! Aha! So exactly how we'll spend our money is a big-huge discussion we need to have very soon," I said. "And then? We'll all vote on it!"

"Just put my part in the Council and Association accounts," Harry said.

"Me too!" Ma, Beebe, and Gloria said.

"Thanks," Carleton said. "But the money has to go into *your* accounts first. And don't forget the rule we all voted for. You *must* keep a thousand bucks for yourself."

"Why? What do I need that's more important than our community?" Gloria said.

"Keep it for emergencies," Mike said. "Case you get sick, your car goes kaflooey, your furnace goes kaput, stuff like that."

"You're wise beyond your years, Mikey," Gloria said.

"Just a chip off the old block," Mike said.

"A few more tidbits," Russ said. "We filed better than a dozen lawsuits that haven't been heard yet. The legislature passed a law forcing them to go to trial before Labor Day. Will we win those? Do carrots grow from carrot seeds?"

"Last but not least," Sylvia said, "District Court Judge Badah Haddad has some good news for us."

Badah was sorta dancing around in front of the mic. "Working with Judge Jeppesen, Paul Mäkinen, Florie Corwin, Hazel Corwin-Pokorny, and Burtram Loftus, I was able to get the Justice Department in Washington to investigate a terrible injustice to workers and Black people. The head of

CHAPTER 20, GETTING BACK OUR STOLEN BOOTSTRAPS

the County Hospital Social Work Department, Arthur Schulz, was paid by the Communal Association to make up information that sent hundreds of innocent people to prison. Schulz and Judge Coventry have been indicted. Judge Jeppesen and I will be finding all 1,147 of those victims to get them the legal help they need for justice to finally be done. Thank you, Paul, Karen, Russ, and Burt, for helping us with this."

Otis Agard, a roofing factory shingle packer, yelled, "He did that to me! I was sixteen. Back in '59. Schulz claimed I was a burglar. Reality? I danced with a White girl. Fast dance, didn't touch nothing but her hand. Got four years at Lino Lakes, and a record."

Badah motioned to him. "Please, sir, talk with me!"

He went, sat with her off to the side, talked. I'd always liked Otis. What they'd done to him, way back when, made me seethe.

"Introducing Stella Dahl," I said. "Honest candidate for State Senator, daughter of the Forever Nines' favorite teacher, our Lucy!"

The Creektones played a fanfare.

"And our Irene is running for School Board Member. Give them both a hand!"

"Stella! Irene! Stella! Irene!"

I looked around the auditorium, spotted Earl and walked over to him with the mic, long cord trailing behind me like an extended, fat worm. "Earl, have ya been wondering how they're going to find the cash money to pay for all this?"

"You got my number, Paulie! Don't want to be a party-pooper, but don't want all our raises going for taxes."

"I don't blame ya for worrying. But that flat out won't happen. The new law freezes sales, income, and property taxes for five years *if* ya earn less than twenty-two grand a year and your savings and house are worth less than fifty grand. For farmers, the first hundred acres are exempt."

Earl shrugged. "So where's all the money for this great stuff coming from?"

"Heh-heh-heh," Russ said. "I'll tell you where! From the Fat Cats! Big new taxes on stocks and savings. Whopping increases on income and property taxes. Just like Franklin Roosevelt did back in the thirties. Fat Cats survived then. They'll manage this. Don't listen to their yowls! Look at their lifestyles, houses, limousines, yachts."

"Do you all wanna start the celebration now?" Obie said, "Or are you all a-wantin' us to bore you with more details?"

Greta called out, "We're making history! This is what I got wounded for!"

Joyce yelled, "I got shot for this! C'mon, everyone, chant, it's not boring!"

The room erupted again. Greta and Joyce stood, grinning, flashing the V sign.

Walt just ran up to Joyce, hugged her? She hugged him back? Wish I could hear what they said! This is big-huge!

Our settlement committee formed a semicircle next to me, Susie, Laura, and Daniel with them. Keanna and Todd joined us too, holding hands and grinning.

Betty raised her hands, quieted the room. "Every working-class community in Minnesota, for the next five years, gets Community Development Funds. By law now, all community members get to vote on how they're used."

"How'd they define working class?" Gene Drass said.

"Average income under seventy-five hundred a year," Carleton said.

"That's us!" Gene said. "Way under. How much cash we getting?"

"Goes by population," Betty said. "For us, it's five hundred and six grand yearly."

"Moving on," Carleton said, "the city is forbidden by law from condemning Betty, Bucky, and Olson Halls."

"That new law," Clarence said, "rezones our buildings to allow stores, restaurants, offices, manufacturing. It also permits up to four liquor licenses, but the Neighborhood Association and Teen Council both must approve them."

"And there's super fab news for *People's Free Press*!" Susie said. "We're now the official newspaper for business, state, and city legal notices, by law. Only others are the Duluth and St. Paul dailies. So we get more income and a status that protects us."

"Susie! Susie!" we chanted.

"You know how hard it is to get the chamber of commerce to give even a single penny to working people?" Daniel said. "You know they had to be feeling the heat because, shazam! They gave us five million pennies,

CHAPTER 20, GETTING BACK OUR STOLEN BOOTSTRAPS

that's a cool fifty grand, for a working-class sculpture garden! Here, at Shingle Creek!"

"Do we have the check?" Ruka said. "Are there strings attached?"

"Russ set up a separate account for it," Daniel said. "Money's in it. Conditions? Only one. Has to be open to the public."

"That's it?" Ruka said.

"The long and the short of it!"

"Without KPFP, it would've been a *lot* harder to win," I said. "Todd, what'd the Fat Cats do for our favorite spot on the dial?"

"Passed a law making us an official community station. We have the state's check for fifty thousand in Community Development Funds. That pays for better equipment, our license application, and staff salaries for the first year at two-fifty minimum indexed."

"We don't have to worry about being busted anymore," Keanna said. "Always keeping a lookout, moving the studio truck in a hurry, even while we're on the air. Todd's an equipment genius"—she kissed his cheek—"but we need the real stuff!"

"Wanna know a secret?" Todd said, pointing to Keanna. "She's the real stuff!"

"Something else we got that none of us knew to ask for," Mike said. "When they were worried we wouldn't accept a statewide Standard Work Contract, they offered this. There's a new agency for environmental protection in Washington. They're gonna come here, to Camden Yard, looking for poisonous chemicals. You think they'll find some?"

"*Cavollo*! Plenty from the roofing factory," Marcello said.

"A whole lot more from the bug spray factory," Harley said.

"Coal ash from the old steam engines is pure poison," Mo said.

"So? They find that stuff," Ron said. "Then what?"

"They'll dig it out, haul it away," Mike said.

"And put it where?" Beth said. "Keep it safe, how?"

"Smart questions," Mike said. "We'll have to find out. Don't want to burden some other community with our garbage."

"Ours, or the Fat Cats'?" Clarence said. "Maybe that gunk belongs in Kenwood!" He grabbed an invisible bucket of goop, heaved it toward the southwest.

"That's another big-huge discussion we need to have," I said. "But, friends, for now, can we go on?"

"Go on! Go on!" the crowd said.

"The Minnesota Historical Society," Laura said, "announced today something they've been planning for a while. They will exhibit artworks from the Darius and Mabel Anker residence here in Shingle Creek. At the Historical Society in April." Laura hugged Daniel. "Congratulations to you and your family!"

He looked embarrassed, pleased, and worried all at once.

"What an honor to our community!" Ma said, and she hugged him too. "Daniel, your dad would be so proud of you!"

"Ah, you guys!" Daniel said.

"Now, this next one's small," Carleton said. "But we've been begging for it since 1950! We will have a mini Post Office at the Workers' Market customer service counter. In a bigger win, we now have it confirmed by law, Gordy and his six officers answer to and are paid by our Safety Commission, with funds coming directly from the state, enough for two more officers."

Sarah stepped to the mic, bowed. "Those of us who aren't from Shingle Creek are very happy to hear about all the wonderful things your community has won. You've gone beyond the beyond, helping us figure out what *our* communities need, and supporting our fights for it. Thank you, Creekers, for what you've done for all of us."

"Up in my Northeast neck of the woods," Magdalena said, "we got a much-needed, state-funded mental health clinic at Pulaski Park, including youth and teen advisers. Been asking for this for years! Thank you, Creekers, for offering to help us set it up. We're counting on you!"

In a second whirlwind of red, Carly led Lola, Corinne, and Merrill onto the stage.

"We begged for teen and youth advisers for years," Lola said.

"Mr. Prichard just laughed at us," Corinne said. "Since I was thirteen."

"We got a grant for one, but he's so busy already, you can't get to see him," Merrill said.

"Now other kids don't have to go through what I did," Carly said. "We also got a mental health center! With people who'll actually listen to us teens and help us!"

CHAPTER 20, GETTING BACK OUR STOLEN BOOTSTRAPS

"And we done got one for the south end of the North Side," Obie said. "Down at Morgan Park."

"Legal clinics," Betty said. "We got them at Portland Park, Wentworth on the far South Side, Pulaski, and Southeast Como, just like Shingle Creek's. All of them, including ours, with guaranteed state funding."

"A free childcare center," Mike said, "at Stinson Park in Northeast for babies and toddlers. So women there can work outside the home."

"On the Near North Side, there's lots of small groceries," Linda said, "owned by people from the community. But they don't carry fresh produce, meat, seafood, or whole grains. So the Morgan Neighborhood Association got Community Development Funds to set up a small markets subsidy program. It pays for shelves and refrigerated showcases and subsidizes healthy foods, so small markets can make a profit on them. Shingle Creek will help them get it started. Workers' Market will buy for them."

Willi placed his hand over his heart. "A wonderful and unusual one here is. Marshall Park over in Northeast funds for a Syrian-American Museum got. The first one in America we will have, here in Minneapolis. Congratulations! Tahanina, Syrian neighbors! Right I said it?"

Badah stood up. "Thank you, you said it perfectly! This is something our community has wanted forever."

Ma said, "Southeast Como got development funds to turn a large empty lot into a community vegetable garden this spring."

Betty, shaking her finger, said, "On a very different note, something has been going on between General Grain and Midwest Candy. We know they're rivals, but really? Ndidi, Burt, come up here and explain yourselves!"

"Do you know what she did to us?" Burt said, trying hard to look stern. "You won't believe it!"

"Well, after what you did to *us*, you deserved it!" Ndidi said.

Around the room, people moved to the edge of their seats. Both TV cameras moved in close.

"Ndidi Williams knew full and well we'd been working hard to get a national distribution contract for our treats," Burt said. "Without telling us, she went and got one for Midwest Candy."

"That's right," Ndidi said, "Hot! Chocolate candy bars will be distributed nationwide! I got a late afternoon call from one of my sorority sisters, works for Three Coasts Distributors Corporation. 'Hey, Nididsi! Just heard I'll be in Chicago tomorrow for a trade show. Can you come with samples?' I was stunned. Been working on her almost two years!"

"And she didn't even tell me," Burt said.

"Had to pack in a hurry, get last-minute hotel reservations, drive like a bat out of hell down I-94 because the strike shut down planes, buses, trains. It was worth it! Had a great meeting with her team."

"Tell the whole story!" Burt said.

"Truth?" Ndidi said. "I told her I have a sister company. How they make yummy cookies and snack cakes. How Burt gave us thousands of dollars to develop our brand. Of course, I stopped at Workers' Market on the way out of town and got a shopping bag full of General Grain snacks and Strike! Cookies for samples."

"See!" Burt said. "Didn't I say you wouldn't believe it?"

"So General Grain got national distribution too?" I said.

"Sure thing!" Burt said. "Ndidi Williams is the best!"

"Nuh-uh!" Ndidi said. "Burt Loftus is the best!"

"How will they ever settle that one?" I said, chuckling.

They held their clasped hands high. The band played, "Dah-dah-dah-dee-dah-dah!"

"And now, friends," I said, "an honest candidate for District Judge in Coventry's old seat, our Sylvia Hansen!"

Tina and the band played another fanfare.

"And for State Senator, People's Union Activist, Nelson Nesheim!"

The band played once more.

Laura came to the mic, linked arms with me. "Paulie, what about Dozer's favorite story? The one you've been imagining since summer after fourth grade? Did we get Park Board permission for a fruit forest?"

I did a little two-step and sang:

We got approval, bop-a-doo!

And we got money, bop-a-woo!

And they'll even buy us bees to make us honey!

Where'd those words come from?

CHAPTER 20, GETTING BACK OUR STOLEN BOOTSTRAPS

Jill, with a big-huge grin, played a melody on her concertina, and the band joined in. "Sing it, Paulie!" she called out.

Oh, my gosh! Here come more!

It's so uplifting, bop-a-doo!

It's so exciting, bop-a-woo!

And they put every last detail down in writing!

They'll work right with us, bop-a-doo!

To help design it, bop-a-woo!

And help us as we're working to refine it!

Folks were dancing in the aisles again, singing, clapping along to Jill's melody.

Linda stood before the mic, raised both hands, waited for quiet. "We got so much taken care of with the Park and Library Boards. All staff who were fired at Shingle Creek and Portland Parks back in February, officially rehired with back pay? Check! It's in the new law. Joanna Pajari rehired to work at Betty Hall for the Shingle Creek community? Check! Paid for by the Library Board? Check!"

"What about our seniors swim exercise classes?" Monya Pedersen said. "I'd just convinced Mr. Bidstrup to come with me when that idiot Dankhead canceled them."

"They start again Wednesday," Linda said. "Now, how about union organizing training? And labor history classes? At all parks in the city, when ten people sign up, they'll have training, they'll have classes!" She pointed to Hoops and T.K. "You're on!"

"My name is Rosie, but they call me Hoops at Portland Park where I'm from. I'm a shelf-maker, but we live in an apartment, so no good place to work my craft. But now, Portland Park got a storefront community workshop, with power tools, workbenches, lumber, paint, hardware. Any community member can build or fix stuff there. Thank you, Creekers, for hatching that idea!"

"And I'm T. K., age fifteen, same as Hoops. Been working with her organizing a Teen Council. Our last park director didn't give a hoot what we had to say. But the new law says Teen Councils, Youth Councils, and neighborhood associations work *together* with directors to run the parks. Isn't that the way democracy's supposed to be?"

"Yes, it is! Yes, it is!" the crowd chanted.

I pointed to the Creektones. "Dah-dah-dah-dee-dah-dah!" Tina trumpeted.

"Honest candidate for reelection, Civil Court Judge Badah Haddad!" I said.

Tina trumpeted again.

"Honest candidate for County Sheriff, Our Lieutenant Gordy!"

The spotlight found Badah and Gordy. The crowd chanted.

Billy emerged from backstage, sprinted up to Linda, handed her a note.

"Karen and everyone landed," Linda whispered in my ear. "Denise picked them up in Frank's car. We're patching in their CB radio in about nine minutes, when they're at 49th and Queen."

My heart started beating so fast, it felt like I was running a marathon even though I was standing stock still. I gripped the mic stand. Got my voice under control. "We have won tremendous victories. Tonight, let us celebrate!"

The loudest applause I'd ever heard inundated the room. The walls seemed to be vibrating. I waited, then clasped my hands, raised them. "But tomorrow morning, we have ta start planning and working so nothing can be snatched away from us. In 1900, workers in Minneapolis won a hundred and forty-two strikes. But three years later, the Fat Cats ran the unions right out of the flour mills. We. Can't. Let. That. Happen. Again!" I put my hands in front of me, palms facing out. "No, Bosses! You ain't doing it! Not this time!"

"Nuh-uh, nuh-uh," Jill played on her concertina.

"We have ta keep our newspaper interesting, helpful, and strong. Make our Workers' Market out-compete Red Crow. Get paid bookings for Arnray Auditorium. Now that we have the money to build our dreams, we must plan strategically so the fruit forest, working-class heroes sculpture garden, blue-collar museum, Scandinavian and World Dining Room, Mabel's Place, and the Nellie Railway are all on solid foundations. We must build businesses that treat workers well and generate enough income to support all the things we want to do here in Shingle Creek. In

CHAPTER 20. GETTING BACK OUR STOLEN BOOTSTRAPS

Minneapolis. And all over Minnesota. And we can! Because *we* are true Ameri-cans!"

"You tell 'em, Paulie!" Frank yelled out.

"Tell 'em, Paulie!" everyone chanted.

I'd never before felt this strong, this focused, this sure we were on the right track. "We have ta reach out and help other working-class communities and together build our power base so these victories cannot be snatched back by greedy bosses. Because they *will* try to take away what we have, and we must be ready to defend it. And go for even more big wins. So this evening, we are not finished. We have just begun. We will fight like lions, like panthers, like a huge pack of wolves, to defend what we've won with our tears, sweat, and blood. And extend justice for working people into every corner, every nook and cranny, of America, our home, sweet home! Defend and extend! Chant with me!"

Once again, chants inundated the auditorium.

I drank it in, looked at my watch, looked behind me, saw Billy and Linda signaling me to wrap it up. I raised my clasped hands. "For me personally, the biggest news comes next. Our Karen, the love of my life, has been freed! She's in her dad's car, with her sister Denise, Great-Grandma Clara, brother Scott, and my sister Sandi at…"

"49th and Queen!" Rennie's voice called out over the sound system.

People jumped to their feet, clapping in rhythm. The Creektones drummer picked up the beat. Jill and Diane improvised scat-singing, sax and horn wove a melody in.

"Just crossed Penn!" Rennie announced. A moment later, "Oliver Avenue!" Then, "Newton Avenue. I'm coming, Paulie!"

The crowd was scatting along, using whatever nonsense words came into their heads, many of them dancing.

"Parking lot!" Rennie said. A moment later, she burst through the doorway, running faster than I'd ever seen, up onto the stage.

I opened my arms wide, ran toward her.

She leaped up, wrapped her legs around me.

I hugged her tight, danced around. "I love ya Rennie! I'm yahrs forever!"

The women chanted, "Paulie! Paulie!" The men called out, "Karen! Karen!" The band played, Jill and Diane scat-sang.

Rennie kissed my face again and again. I was throbbing. The whole world was throbbing.

I made a superhuman effort to tamp it down. Back to the mic I danced. "Here's our biggest hero, folks. We wouldn't have won if not for her. When I wasn't sure which way to go, I closed my eyes, said, 'What would Karen do?' And I could hear her, telling me the way. She may have been in prison 800 miles away, but she helped lead us to victory! Let me tell ya the other victory Karen won. She won my heart. And I'm going to tell ya what I just told her face-to-face for the first time—'I love ya Karen! I'm yahrs forever!'"

"I love you, Paavali!" she said. "We did it! You! Me! All of us!"

Still glued to me, she was laughing, crying, and kissing me, with the cheering, singing, dancing crowd surrounding us. And then I felt two more sets of arms on my back. Mike and Clarence were guiding us off the stage, through the crowd, which surged with us, cheering and clapping, like a sea of love, floating us out the door.

"See here, you two," Mike said. "Me, Ma, Daniel, Clarence, Obie, Blanche, and all have the victory celebration under control. Go home! 'Cause you have some big-ass catching up to do."

"Let's give 'em a hero's ride!" Clarence said.

Mike gently pried Rennie off me, lifted her up on his shoulders. Clarence picked me up like I was a bag of feathers, put me on his. Bobby came running up with Tina and her trumpet. The Creektones horn and sax joined her, playing a marching song, the cheering crowd following, all the way to Clara's house.

Clarence and Mike stood side by side. I leaned toward Rennie, gave her a long, deep kiss.

"Karen and Paulie up some trees, k-i-s-s-i-n-g," Ma said with a chuckle.

"Elevator going down!" Clarence said, lowering me gently to the ground.

Rennie and I stood, holding hands, waving to everyone as the parade headed down Knox Avenue, turned left at the corner, and disappeared, the singing and cheering getting softer and softer.

She tightened her hand on mine. "Paavali...?" Her voice was sultry, silky, like I'd never heard it before.

CHAPTER 20, GETTING BACK OUR STOLEN BOOTSTRAPS

We moved through the side door still holding hands, down to our room, two steps at a time. She unbuttoned my coat, tossed it high. It landed gently on the couch with a ploof! I unzipped hers, flipped it onto the chair.

"Rennie!" I smiled so wide it tickled my ears, wrapped my arms around her.

She looked up at me, her eyes the brightest blue I'd ever seen them. "Can I tell you a secret?" she said.

I bent down toward her, wondering what she was going to murmur in my ear.

"I love you," she whispered. She licked my ear and sucked on my earlobe.

My dick bulged against my pants, my whole body pulsing so hard I was dizzy, and I knew, for certain and for sure, that she is the woman of my dreams. I caressed her cheeks gently, looked right into her eyes. And said it again. "I love ya, Rennie. For real and forever."

"Why?" she said, moving a step away.

I didn't expect that question. But it made sense. I'd never really told her in words. "Because ya're mega-smart."

"And?"

"Tough."

"And?"

"Ya can beat me in arm wrestling."

"And?"

"Kind."

"And?"

"The big-huge, magnificent ideas ya have."

"And?"

"How ambitious ya are."

"And?"

"Yahr enthusiasm."

"And?"

"Ya're so pretty and sexy and gorgeous! The way yahr freckles swirl across yahr cheeks and over yahr nose. I want to kiss every square inch of ya."

She moved back against me, stroked my face. "And?"

"Did I say how smart?"

"Yes. And?"

"Yahr eyes, like dancing blue flames! My guiding light, Rennie. That's what ya are. My guiding light." It felt so good to say all this!

"And?"

"When I'm with ya, I feel so wonderful. I feel like…"

"The real Paavali Mäkinen?"

"Yup! That's it! The real Paavali Mäkinen is finally here!"

She hugged me mega-tight. "The real Rennie Ahlberg will never let go of you!"

"Oh, Rennie, Rennie, I'm not going anywhere! I'm yahrs forever."

She kissed and licked my cheeks, my forehead, my nose, my chin.

I worshipped every part of her face, her neck, and her ears with my tongue, my lips, my fingers. I didn't think it was possible, but my dick got even harder.

"Yes, Paavali! Yes! Yes! I want you, Paavali! Make love with me!"

Blouse, shirt, bra, belts, pants, underwear, slipped off, tossed to the side. Her tongue opened my lips, gently sucked mine into her mouth. She shimmied against me. I moved with her in a slow, hot dance, kissed her face, held her tight.

The whole world was throbbing. This time, I didn't have ta tamp it down.

She took my hand and led me to our bed.

THE END

WHAT HAPPENS NEXT?

This is, indeed, the end of *Getting Back Our Stolen Bootstraps*. But it's *not* the end of Shingle Creek Sagas! Find out what happens next when the upcoming Shingle Creek Saga, *Shirley, Victorious!*, is finished!

Right now, *Shirley, Victorious!* is just a concept and many pages of notes about the plot, subplots, characters, and events.

Jill, Linda, and Paul's beloved Ma, Shirley, is inspired and empowered by the Creekers' huge victory and Paul and Karen's love story. She can no longer deny how much she craves a romantic relationship. As she becomes increasingly involved in running the community's many successful ventures, Shirley realizes she's finally ready to start looking for love—even though that terrifies her.

In *Shirley, Victorious!*, you'll read all about:

- The Fat Cats' sinister new plot to wipe the Shingle Creek community off the map.
- Biggest challenge Creekers face when their Scandinavian Dining Room opens.
- Dirty Fat Cat tricks that provoke a second general strike.
- How the family stays together when Burt and Clara get married—and even takes in two new members.
- Who Shirley has her first love affair with. Big surprise!
- How Creekers' successful business ventures lift wages for everyone.

- Where and how Shirley meets the love of her life. And what happens to her ex-husband after she does.
- Shirley's smart solution when Creekers complain Scandinavian Dining Room is too expensive.
- Unusual, highly-profitable businesses Creekers start that attract workers from all over the country.

You can get free sneak previews of scenes from *Shirley, Victorious!* as I write them. Just sign up for a free subscription to *Yale's Novel News*. Every first Friday of the month, *Yale's Novel News* will help you get inside this writer's mind. It's a quick read, but full of information.

Sometimes you'll get juicy tidbits from the cutting room floor that just didn't fit in but are still good reading. Plus, inside tips about the craft of novel writing. And updates about my novels and other publications. All on just one page.

Subscribe FREE now and get a secret ending scene I had to cut from my novel *Becoming JiJi*. I'll tell you why I cut it and what replaced it. It's not available anywhere else online or off.

https://bit.ly/4-YalesNovelNews

Curious about how the Creekers changed themselves from being defeated and depressed into a powerful force for social change? Get the whole story in the earlier Shingle Creek Sagas, *Becoming JiJi, No Free Soup for Millionaires,* and *They Break the Laws We Must Obey.*

More information at https://davidryale.com.

A NOTE FROM THE AUTHOR

Can I Count on Your Help?

I hope you enjoyed reading *Getting Back Our Stolen Bootstraps: The Third Paul Makinen Novel*. I'd like to ask a small favor. I don't have a huge publisher behind me, so I need your help to let the world know about the heartwarming story of Paul, Rennie, and the Creekers. Here are some quick ways you can help:

- ✓ Write a review of *Getting Back Our Stolen Bootstraps* on your favorite bookseller's website, your blog, social media, or your union or progressive organization's website. It doesn't have to be long. Just a couple of sentences will do it!
- ✓ See if your union or progressive organization would be willing to post a link to the *Getting Back Our Stolen Bootstraps* eBook on their website for FREE distribution to members. The link gives free access to members of qualifying organizations, but advance permission is required. Tell them to contact me for information at https://DavidRYale.Com/Contact
- ✓ Ask your local library to order copies so your whole community can read it!
- ✓ Buy me a coffee. You'll get a surprise free gift. And you'll help me keep writing and keep giving free eBooks to unions and progressive organizations. Visit me at buymeacoffee.com/DavidjxQ

✓ Wondering what it was like before Joe and Jill started the Teen Council? The strategies Joe taught Jill to save Ma from deadly depression? How Jill courted Joe after he suddenly moved to San Francisco? And how she helped him conquer crippling guilt using counseling techniques *he* had taught her? The first book in the Shingle Creek Sagas, *Becoming JiJi,* tells it all. It won first place for contemporary fiction in the 2018 *Writers Digest* self-published eBooks awards.

For more information about all my books, please visit:
https://DavidRYale.Com.

To sign up for *Yale's Novel News,* please go to:
https://bit.ly/4-YalesNovelNews

Thanks for all you do!
David R. Yale

ABOUT THE AUTHOR

Known for heartwarming portrayals of ordinary people, David R. Yale has been influenced by Charles Dickens, John Steinbeck, Jo Sinclair, Marge Piercy, and Barbara Kingsolver. Living and working in blue-collar communities in Brooklyn, Minneapolis and rural Arkansas, as well as a socialist utopian community in New York, have also shaped his narrative.

His first job was as a preschool teacher. In the 1970s, David was the recreation director at Shingle Creek and Bohannon Parks in North Minneapolis. He has taught writing at the University of Minnesota and The School of Visual Arts. Until his recent retirement, he was an international direct mail marketing consultant.

David's fiction and poetry have been published in *Midstream, Response, Newtown Literary, Blue Collar Review, Pangolin Review*, and *Which Side Are You On? Labor Day 2023 Poetry Anthology*. His short story, *The Front Room*, won a *Writers' Digest* second place award. Yale's book, *HomesPun Humor*, was a finalist in both the 2014 Indie Excellence® and USA Best Book Awards.

His first novel in the Shingle Creek Sagas, *Becoming JiJi*, **won First Place in the 2018** *Writer's Digest* **Self-Published eBook Awards Contemporary Fiction category and was a quarter-finalist in the** 2019 *ScreenCraft* Cinematic Book Competition. A short story excerpted from *Becoming JiJi* was long-listed for the *Lascaux Prize for Short Fiction*.

David has read from his stories at Union College, Claremont College, The Mendota (Minnesota) Jazz Emporium, and UCLA.

With a blue-collar, working-class outlook, Yale writes about one of the most overlooked communities in the contemporary fiction scene.

For more information about David,
visit https://davidryale.com/

THE FACTS BEHIND THE FICTION

While the characters and events in this novel are fictitious, the cultural and political history is based on research and facts. Yes, there really was an organization similar to the Communal Association. You can read about it in William Millikan's book, *A Union Against Unions.* (Minnesota Historical Society Press, 2001)

The 1934 Minneapolis Teamsters' Strike was, indeed, highly organized. Farrell Dobbs, one of the strike leaders, gives you the inside view in his book, *Teamster Rebellion.* (Pathfinder Press, 1972)

Was there actually an active chapter of the Ku Klux Klan in Duluth, Minnesota? Richard Hudelson and Carl Ross tell you all about Klan activism and early 20th Century strikes on the Mesabi Iron Range in their book, *By the Ore Docks: A Working People's History of Duluth.* (University of Minnesota Press, 2006)

For a helpful overview of American labor law, I relied on *Labor Law for the Rank & Filer*, by longtime lawyer and activist Staughton Lynd. (PM Press, Oakland CA, 2011)

In addition, for information on everything from Scandinavian cuisine to kite-flying height limits, rail yard operations to IUD insertion pain, I studied more than 300 articles and websites.

ACKNOWLEDGMENTS

My heartfelt thanks to the ten people who encouraged me, read or listened to me read parts of *Getting Back Our Stolen Bootstraps* as I was writing it, pointed to inconsistencies and problems, and supported me when I had doubts.

Barbara Kay Rolnicki, Hannah Garson, Jim Kousoulas, Judith Lukin, Kelsey Laing, Rita Plush, Robert Lerose, Suhong Chen, Terry Riccardi, and Tom Pope, I couldn't have done it without you!

CHARACTER LIST

MAIN CHARACTERS ARE IN BOLD-FACE TYPE

First & Last Name	1972 Age, Description
Águeda Nomancebo	23, Joe and Jill's journalist friend from San Francisco, writes *LIFE* article
Alan Becker	43, strike breaker, cut electric cables during community meeting
Alastair Tewksbury	55, Fat Cat on boards of Minnesota Consolidated Railroad and Construction Services companies, owns roofing factory, active in Communal Association
Algernon H. H. Bobellon	43, CEO of AHH Bobellon-Carter, strike negotiator
Albert (Al) Mikkola	37, counselor at mental health clinic
Alexander Doyle	42, South Minneapolis corrupt cop
Althea Lewis	17, Teen Council, works in warming room
Alton Lindgren	37, South Minneapolis corrupt cop
Ambrose Anker	13, Daniel's brother

Andreas Bidstrup	84, grumpy old man who loves roast duck, Bonnie's friend
Annie Nordness	23, Barry Olson's wife, music teacher, plays violin
Archibald Hastings-Dankworth	94, big Communal Association supporter, controls Minnesota Vigilantes Against Vice and TC Unified National Bank
Archie Pfeiffer	60, owner of Camden Superette
Arden Winchester	57, owner of Club Nicolette, hires Jill for gigs, supports Creekers
Arne Gustaffson	(died 1970 at 25) Brucie's dad, killed in a rail yard accident
Arthur Schulz	50, head of social work at hospital, helps corrupt judges frame working-class and Black defendants
Ashford Havemeyer, Judge	68, judge, enjoins police from enforcing non-existent curfews
Aurelius Hanna, Judge	66, judge at Karen's slander lawsuit vs Theodore Knight
Badah Haddad, Judge	47, Roger's judge, Creekers' ally
Barbara Olson	15, Teen Council, preschool assistant, skilled mechanic at parents' shop, Betty and Bucky's daughter
Bartholomew Holmes	66, Chamber of Commerce president, strike negotiator, East-West Materials Corporation CEO
Beatrice Blecher (Bebee)	43, Li'l Mikey's mom, Gustaffson Family home care aide

Becky Hakkala	11, Susie's sister
Beth Olson	19, Betty and Bucky's daughter, college student, she and boyfriend involved with air pollution control
Betty Olson (Betts)	47, Bucky's wife, co-owner B&B Repair Shop, community leader
Beverly Hakkala	12, Susie's sister
Billy Anderson	17, Teen Council member, Willi's grandson, Linda's boyfriend, becomes a Teen Council leader
Blanche Drass	57, Czech soup cook, skilled cabinet maker, becomes work crew manager for community
Bonnie Korhonen	9, Mamie Anderson's cousin, Willi's granddaughter, class leader
Brenda Olson	22, Betty and Bucky's daughter, full time at B&B Repair Shop
Bobby Lund	9, co-owns *Shingle Creek News*, singer, announcer, class leader
Brucie Gustaffson (Brucie Woosie)	6, everybody's favorite little kid, misses dad, Arne, killed in rail yard accident
Bucky (Bucyrus) Olson	48, Danish, Betty's husband, co-owner of B&B Repair Shop, community leader
Burtram Loftus (Burt)	77, CEO/owner of General Grain and Flour Corp., Clara's boyfriend
Carleton Ward	37, owns small accounting firm, community leader

Carolyn Iversen	34, Tess's ma, husband Ray killed in rail yard accident
Charlie Parker Ward	9, co-owns *Shingle Creek News*, pianist, Carleton and Diane's son, class leader
Carly Ranum	14, Portland Park teen Paul helps, dad critically injured in steel mill accident
Cecil Nilson	52, independent trucker, helps expand and win the strike
Chatham Jenkins	59, reporter for *New York Press-Journal*, slanders Creekers on national television
Chip Corbyn	47, CEO of Nicollet Super Stores, strike negotiator
Chief Jensen	53, Minneapolis Chief of Police
Clara Ahlberg	87, Karen's great-grandma, longtime union activist
Clarence Björk	32, Camden Rail Yard gandy dancer, Kurt's dad, Margaret's husband
Clayton Madsen	45, South Minneapolis corrupt cop
Clifford Ruona	56, architect Burt hires to help design Ray Iversen Auditorium
Clinton Meyer	39, South Minneapolis corrupt cop
Clyde Gremling	77, bug spray factory owner, Communal Association leader
Corey Atkinson	43, lawyer who volunteered to help with Karen's legal problem

Cressida Hastings-Dankworth	59, Archibald's trophy wife, Clyde Gremling's cousin, Alistair Tewksbury's sister
Communal Association	Fictional business owners' secret anti-union group founded 1910. There actually were groups like this in many US cities.
Commissioner Pembroke	59, Minnesota Corrections Commissioner
Corinne Nesheim	21, Lola's best friend, Portland Youth Council Organizer, works at Midwest Candy
Dale Amsel	23, Minneapolis, Dallas & Houston Mainline gandy dancer
Daniel Anker	17, Teen Council member, beloved Nines group leader, aspiring sculptor
Darius Anker	(died 1963 at 30) Daniel's deceased father, was math professor
Darlene Hillilä	(died 1970 at 15) Tommy Hillilä's deceased sister, was budding artist
Dawn Bopp	24, Paul dances with her at Boogie Barn, switchboard operator
Debbie Ahlberg	19, Karen's older sister, runs Workers' Market corner store buying co-op
Della Toro	13, helps Laura repaint mural
Denise Ahlberg	21, Karen's oldest sister, receptionist at mental health clinic
Dennis Brekke	(died 1972 at 19) One of six Creekers killed in 'Nam in same week

Dewey Kaas	37, switch engine engineer in Camden Rail Yard
Dexter Mahmoud	10, helped Laura repaint mural
Diane Ward	37, Diane Ward & The Creektones, jazz singer/pianist, married to Carleton, Charlie and Louie's Mom
Dina Eldin	48, Lebanese baker of baklava, seamstress, Peoples' Union leader
Douglas Viklund	(died 1972 at 20) One of six Creekers killed in 'Nam in same week
"Dozer" (Gary) Walden	19, Teen Council, Paul's friend since kindergarten
Dr. Bucek	38, Free Clinic "galnecologist"
Drummond Duncan	52, president of Foundation for Trade Unions, union buster
Duane Pukari (alias for Steve Hastings-Dankworth)	24, hoodlum paid to attack Creekers by Communal Association, Great-grandnephew of Archibald Hastings-Dankworth
Dudley Courtenay	66, Hennepin County attorney
Earl Smith	40, prison guard, active in Creekers' Neighborhood Association
Edward Mäkinen (Deadwood)	42, Paul's father, truck mechanic
Elijah Streeter	59, *LIFE* photographer
Elmer McGill	38, gandy dancer, anti-union, secretly paid to spy for Communal Association

Ellen Lund	11, Bobby's sister
Elżbieta Witkowski	38, KTCA-TV camerawoman, reporter
Emily Walden	23, Dozer's older sister
Eugene Drass	60, stock clerk at Workers' Market
Eva Korhonen	11, Bonnie's sister
Evelyn Hakkala	37, Susie's mom, Ma's friend, community leader
Finley Campbell, Judge	56, Billings, Montana Federal Judge who helps resolve Karen's legal problem
Fiona Flynn	40, Ruthie's ma, Peoples' Union leader
Frances Hahn	47, Harold's wife, Paul's second HandiVan employee
Frank Ahlberg	45, Karen's father, switch engine driver at Camden Rail Yard
Florence Corwin (Florie)	62, Fred's wife, surgeon
Floyd Ose, Alderman	39, strike negotiator
Fred Corwin	(died 1972 at 62) beloved Parks & Recreation commissioner
Gannon Woodruff, Judge	40, judge in first libel lawsuit against Gremling, cut jury award in half because of Gremling's threats, became Creekers' ally
Georgia Giordano	32, reporter-photographer for the *Gazette*, Susie's mentor, Co-Executive Editor at *People's Free Press* along with Susie and Tom

Giles Knight	52, encourages son Theodore to molest women, Karen sues son for libel
Gloria Michaels	54, Iversen family's home aide
Gordon Walden, Lieutenant (Gordy)	45, Dozer and Jeannette's dad, married to Rose, Police Lieutenant, supports Shingle Creek community
Grant Bailey	81, strike negotiator, CEO of B&D Manufacturing Partners, owns rebar factory
Gregory Overgaard	20, Karen's boyfriend at the University of Minnesota
Greta Björk	11, Kurt's sister
Gwen McCoy	24, Bernie Olson's wife, nurse at hospital downtown
Haarald Korhonen	39, Willi's son
Hank Hallbauer	35, Camden Yard Assistant Boss, coordinator for *Free Press* newsroom work crew
Harley Blecher	43, Li'l Mikey's dad, Stationary Engineer at General Grain, strike leader
Harold Hahn (Harry)	48, park maintenance man, major rebellion supporter, work crew coordinator for mental health clinic and Workers' Market
Harrison Barrow	36, reporter for *Hennepin Afro-American*
Hazel Corwin-Pokorny	32, lawyer, Fred's daughter, runs for county attorney
Helen Magelby	20, witness in Karen's slander suit vs Theodore Knight

Herbert Anderson	43, Dorothy Korhonen's husband, Billy, Wally, and Mamie's father, Peoples' Union leader, kite enthusiast
Hoops Halvorsen (Rosie)	15, Portland Park teen leader, T.K.'s girlfriend, basketball team captain, carpenter, shelf maker
Increase Fitch	77, CEO of Amalgamated Foods Midwest, strike negotiator
Irene Korhonen	34, Sam's wife, Willi's daughter-in-law, Bonnie's ma, community leader
Jack Langacker	24, Brenda Olson's boyfriend, gandy dancer at Camden Yard
Janet Hakkala	13, Susie's sister
Jared Huber	59, security guard at bug spray factory
Jason Kristiansen	24, second-year law student, volunteer intern with Russ
Jeanette Walden	9, Dozer's sister, especially close to Jeffie
Jeffie Gulbrandsen	9, especially close to Jeanette
Jerome Accardo (Jerry)	30, Associated Press reporter
J. H. Kingsbury	88, CEO of Lakes State Fertilizer & Seed Company, strike negotiator
Jim Crow	157, the infamous racist villain born after the Civil War
Jill Frisk	19, Teen Council founder, Ma's daughter, successful singer, Joe's girlfriend, lives in San Francisco

Joni Ahlberg	43, Karen's mother, married to Frank
Joanna Pajari	27, Weber Park librarian, Shingle Creek's official archivist and researcher
Joe Stern	26, the first Park Director, helped teens found Teen Council, moved to San Francisco, Jill's boyfriend
Joshua Williams	40, Ruka's dad, US Labor Department Statistician
Joyce Trockenmann	16, Nancy and Walt's sister, took a bullet for Mabel Anker
Judith Flink	34, first counselor hired by the Teen Council, Russ's wife
Jyri Tuomi	34, Community Affairs and Heritage Coordinator at L&M Federal Credit Union
Karen Ahlberg (Rennie)	16, Paul's girlfriend, Assistant Park Director
Keanna Edwards	18, Paul dances with her at Boogie Barn, golden voice gets her a job as announcer on KPFP, community's bootleg radio station
Kevin Walsh	(died 1972 at 19) One of six Creekers killed in 'Nam in same week
K. H. McGuire	37, *People's Free Press* Editorial writer
Kimmie Hakkala	7, Susie's sister, twin to Tracey
Kurt Björk	9, son of gandy dancer, Clarence, especially close to Tess
Larry Scarpa	31, blacklisted professor, teaches labor history to Teen Council

Laura Thomá	19, Paul's friend since kindergarten, Dozer's girlfirend, muralist
Leonard Clausen	46, supermarket warehouse worker, son Timothy killed in 'Nam
Lester Jeppesen, Judge	52, supports the Creekers
Liam O'Farrell	67, Teamsters Union leader in 1934 Minneapolis Teamsters' Strike, Nora's husband, Todd Flynn's great-uncle
Linda Frisk	16, Jill's sister, three years younger, Ma's daughter, Teen Council member
Lola (Karola) Lillegard	21, Paul dances with at Boogie Barn, veterinary assistant, Portland Park Teen and Youth Council Organizer
Lois Gustaffson	28, Brucie's mom
Lonnie Jacobsen	36, South Minneapolis corrupt cop
Lori McGinnis	23, Paul dances with at Boogie Barn, hotel maid, becomes mill trainee at General Grain
Louie Armstrong Ward	5, Carleton and Diane's son
Louise Doscher	19, witness in Rennie's slander suit vs. Theodore Knight
Lowell Krüger	49, scab brakeman, cabinet maker hired by Creekers
Lydia Rivers	27, Black CPA Carleton hired for General Grain account, advises Teen Council
Lucas Gulbrandsen (Luke)	43, Roy and Jeffie's dad, roofing factory worker

Lucy Dahl	52, new teacher for The Nines
Luther Godwin, Judge	56, Minneapolis Federal Judge who helps resolve Karen's legal problem
Lyle Sund	43, scab railroad engineer, heating systems designer, hired by Creekers
Mabel Anker	36, Daniel's mother, Ma's friend, pie maker
Marcello Fontana	62, roofing factory worker
Marek Witkowski	44, gandy dancer at Northeast Lowry Yard, Peoples' Union leader
Margaret Björk	33, Clarence's wife, Peggy, Greta, and Kurt's mom
Maria Rach	17, Paul dances with at Boogie Barn, looks like Rennie but with green eyes
Mark Mäkinen	(died 1967 at age 19) Paul's brother, killed in 'Nam
Mamie Anderson	9, Billy's sister, Willi's granddaughter, Bonnie's cousin and closest friend
Marmaduke Percy	(died 1911) owned large flour mill in North East Minneapolis
Marshall Aronowitz	28, *Art News* reporter
Marvin Ericson, Doctor	66, helped organize emergency first aid during general strike demonstrations
Maurice Feldschuh	29, *Free Press* Business reporter hired from Milwaukee newspaper

Mehitabel Elak	74, Paul and Jill's third-grade teacher, longtime problem for Shingle Creek community, *elak* in Swedish: mean, bad, evil
Melvin Meilander	60, CEO of Johnson-Meilander Trucking, strike negotiator
Merrill Sasso	21, Lola's Friend, school secretary, Portland Youth Council organizer
Mike Blecher (L'il Mikey)	19, Paul's friend since kindergarten, Teen Council
Mildread Mäkinen	40, Paul's mother
Moe Lehtonen	19, Beth Olson's boyfriend, college student, truck driver
Mollie Whupple	38, Parks superintendent's secretary
Monica Korhonen	6, Bonnie's sister
Montgomery Q. Palmer	43, COO and chairman of the Board at Atlantic & Pacific Trust Bank, strike negotiator
Monya Pedersen	78, widow, Andreas Bidstrup's girlfriend
Nancy Trockenmann	20, Paul's first girlfriend, Communal Association spy
Ndidi Williams	42, Ruka's mom, co-owner Midwest Candy Corporation
Nelson Nesheim	40, Portland neighborhood activist, gandy dancer at City Line Yard
Nora O'Farrell	68, activist, Liam's wife, Todd's aunt

Norma Lund	34, Bobby's mother
Norman deLuca	45, mill hand on General Grain leadership team
Obadiah King (Obie)	65, gandy dancer, strike leader, Clarence's friend, escaped from chain gang as a youth
Oliver Latvala	34, South Minneapolis corrupt cop
Othel Broadwater	55, pastor of Jericho Baptist Church
Pam Hakkala	17, Susie's sister
Paul Mäkinen (Paavali)	19, Teen Councilman, Director at Shingle Creek Park
Paz Evans	33, Portland Park conga drummer, jazz band leader
Peggy Björk	12, Kurt's sister, Clarence's daughter
Peri Korhonen	14, Bonnie's sister
Perrine Fournier	34, Agency France-Press Reporter
Pete Hakkala	38, Susie's dad, press operator for *People's Free Press*
Philip Rasmussen	38, telephone lineman
Poppy Fields	12, cousin Theodore Knight raped
Randy Olafsson	29, St. Paul, Salt Lake, and San Diego Railway gandy dancer
Ray Iversen	(died 1970 at 33) gandy dancer killed in Camden Rail Yard accident

Rennie Ahlberg (Karen)	16, Paul's girlfriend, Assistant Park Director at Shingle Creek Park
Richard Prichard	33, Park Director at Portland Park, appointed new director at Shingle Creek, Tewksbury's wealthy grandson
Roger Tornquist	15, troubled teen Paul helped, budding baker.
Roland Kraus (Rollie)	24, second-year law student, volunteer intern with Russ
Ron Svoboda	64, active in Neighborhood Association
Ronan Flynn	19, Ruthie's big brother, bookkeeper at Red Crow and then Workers' Market
Rose Walden	45, Dozer's Mom, married to Lieutenant Gorden Walden
Roy Gulbrandsen	(died 1972 at 19) One of six Creekers killed in 'Nam in same week, Jeffie's brother
Ruby Ominira	41, Black counselor at Shingle Creek Mental Health Clinic
Rudolph Rinder	48, Republican state representative, strike negotiator
Ruka Williams	16, Linda Frisk's friend, Teen Council
Russ Linwood-Flink	35, Judith's husband, runs Shingle Creek Law Clinic
Ruthie Flynn	9, Todd and Ronan's sister, class leader
Salvatore Mondadori	(died 1972 at 39) Northeast Lowry Yard car inspector

Samantha Gladstone	37, Corey Atkinson's legal associate in Montana, helps with Karen's legal problem
Sampaa (Sam) Korhonen	36, Willi's son, Bonnie's dad, Irene's husband
Sandi Mäkinen	22, Paul's sister
Sarah Nesheim	38, Portland Park Neighborhood Association, Peoples' Union leader
Scott Ahlberg (Scooter)	22, Karen's older brother, engaged to Paul's sister Sandi, locksmith
Senator Erik Kallio	52, Minnesota senator, strike negotiator
Senator Johnson	39, Minnesota senator who investigates Paul
Senator Johnsrud	52, Minnesota senator, strike negotiator
Senator Butch Larsen	76, president of Minnesota Senate, Republican
Sheila Tornquist	11, Roger's sister, delivers *People's Free Press*, adopted by Korhonens
Sherry Anselm	13, organizes picketing of Northeast draft board
Shirley Frisk (Ma)	38, Jill and Linda's mother, Paul's mother-figure, Neighborhood Association leader
Sidney Felsing	54, *People's Free Press* reporter
Steve Rosenquist	44, gandy dancer for Minneapolis, Dallas & Houston Mainline, strike leader

Susie Hakkala	15, Teen Council member, interns at daily newspaper, becomes Co-Executive Editor at *People's Free Press* with Georgia and Tom
Sylvia Hansen	25, third-year law student, volunteer intern with Russ
Terrence Berg	(died 1972 at 18) One of six Creekers killed in 'Nam in same week
Terri Tornquist	9, Roger's sister, adopted by Korhonens
Tess Iversen	9, daughter of gandy dancer killed at work, ardent strike advocate, class leader
Theodore Knight	20, football player Karen sued for libel
Timothée Thomá	45, Laura's dad, cabinet maker
Timothy Clausen	(died 1972 at 20) One of six Creekers killed in 'Nam in same week
T.K. Bello	15, Portland Park teen leader, Hoops's boyfriend, she calls him "Teak"
Tom Hayes	56, Co-Executive Editor at *People's Free Press* with Susie and Georgia
Tommy Hillilä	11, sister Darlene killed herself after Duane Pukari got her drunk and pregnant, she was Tommy's rock
Todd Flynn	17, Ruthie's big brother, founder of pirate community radio station KPFP
T.S. Colding	51, South Minneapolis corrupt police lieutenant
Vanessa Korhonen	12, Bonnie's sister

Victor Niemi, Judge	71, judge for Iversen and Gustaffson vs Minnesota Consolidated Railroad
Victoria Knight	12, cousin Theodore Knight raped
Vincent Wójcik	36, Northeast Lowry Neighborhood Association, strike leader
Virgil Vihainen	86, leader of opposition at Portland Park, on Communal Association payroll
Walter Trockenmann (Walt)	11, Nancy's abused, shy younger brother has been taken in by Clarence and Margaret Björk
Warden Van Alst	44, Stillwater Prison warden
Willi Korhonen	62, railroad engineer at Camden Rail Yard, Bonnie, Mamie, and Billy's grandpa, community leader and strike negotiator
Woodrow (Woody) Dahl	54, Lucy Dahl's husband, owns Dahl's Superette

www.ingramcontent.com/pod-product-compliance
Lightning Source LLC
LaVergne TN
LVHW091615070526
838199LV00044B/810